## APACHE PRIZE

"Rebecca," he said huskily. "There's no need to be afraid of me." At his touch, she drew her breath in sharply, but forced herself to lie still.

Her eyes darkened with emotion as he pulled her to him. She could almost feel herself melting beneath his burning gaze. As her body brushed against his, she felt a shock to her senses. And as his arms tightened about her, holding her more securely beneath him, her heart began to beat wildly.

"No, Lone Wolf," she gasped, squirming, pushing at him, trying to free herself from his grip. "No, Lone Wolf, stop it!"

"Be still, Rebecca," he said harshly.

She quivered and thrashed beneath him, trying to escape from the exquisite pleasure of his intimate caresses. But he was too strong, holding her down firmly as he continued to explore her with searing lips and sensuous hands.

She was his prize to take as he pleased—and it pleased him to have her willing and wild with passion beneath him . . .

SAVAGE FLAME

D1115605

# SAVAGE FLAME
## BETTY BROOKS

**ZEBRA BOOKS**
**KENSINGTON PUBLISHING CORP.**

ZEBRA BOOKS

are published by

Kensington Publishing Corp.
475 Park Avenue South
New York, NY 10016

First printing: March 1987

Printed in the United States of America

*Dedicated to James*
*My husband, my lover, my friend*

# Chapter One

March 1876
Apache Country
New Mexico Territory

The late morning sun hung hot and heavy in the eastern sky, and the wind that blew dusty fingers across Rebecca's face was sullen, chafing, not even strong enough to stir the brown curls that peeked from beneath her small blue riding hat. She brushed her fingers through her loosened hair, pushed the hat farther back on her head, shifted on her sidesaddle, and threw a sidelong glance at the man riding beside her. Pete hadn't wanted to ride as far as she had insisted they go, but he never had been able to say no to her.

No, it was Robert who did so well at gainsaying her. And it had been that same implacability of her brother's that had kept her stranded in the north for so long.

She was home now, though, and had been for six months. And even now she couldn't get enough of this country. Throwing back her head, she breathed in a deep dusty lungful of air.

They were riding along a dry wash now, and the sand muffled the thud of the horses' hooves as they went. Occasionally they passed a cottonwood along the banks, stubby and spindly from lack of water, with twisting, turning branches reaching toward the barren sky.

Some people found the terrain ugly and harsh. Rebecca found it beautiful — with its bleached tans, red clay, dotted here and there with barrel cactus and cat-claw bushes, and its purpled thrust of peaks in the distance.

"Isn't it a marvelous day, Pete?" she asked, throwing him a smile that paled the sun in comparison.

"You ain't gonna think it's so marv'lous if we run into Injuns, Miss Rebecca," Pete said broodingly, spitting a stream of tobacco at the ground, his grizzled face settled into the perpetually worried look she had come to expect from him.

"Stuff and nonsense." She tossed her head, flinging her ribbons back over her shoulder. "You know there hasn't been an Indian attack around here since Cochise signed the peace treaty in seventy-two."

"I reckon a peace treaty don't mean a danged thing with Cochise two years in the ground," Pete stated grimly. "I hear tell the Chiricahuas are gettin' restless on the reservation. Hear they think they're gettin' a raw deal."

"Ps-shaw," she said. "I'm sure Thomas Jeffords has everything under control. After all, didn't the government give him the authority to handle the Chiricahuas as he sees fit?" She stuffed a loosened curl beneath her hat. "And, since he was responsible for Cochise signing

8

the treaty in the first place, the Indians will have to listen to him."

"There could be plenty reason for them not to listen. Seems they think the army ain't livin' up to the promises that were made. And they're blamin' Jeffords."

"But he didn't have anything to do with the army's promises, did he? Besides, he's the one that got the Indians out from under military rule in the first place. Plus getting them guns and ammunition to hunt with."

"That's right."

"Then I'm sure they'll trust him."

"Don't count on it." Pete spat another stream of tobacco onto the sand, which quickly sucked it up, leaving nothing but a brown stain to mark the spot. "He can't keep an eye on all of them all the time. Nope, there hasn't been a raid in a while, but that don't mean it won't happen again, little missy."

*Little missy.* Her forehead furrowed as she stared ahead, her eyes focusing dimly on another time.

*Little missy.* She had cringed under the bed for such a long time, hiding, her little fingernails biting into her five-year-old knees. And finally Pete had been there. *"Come on out, little missy. You can come out now."*

*"Where's Momma, Pete? What happened to Momma?"*

Blinking suddenly, she forcefully pulled her mind away from the past and all its terror, from paint-slashed faces and hag-ridden dreams.

It did no good to remember.

"Pete . . ." She drew the bay to a halt. "I think we should turn back now. Robert will be wondering about us."

His gray eyes piercing beneath his bushy eyebrows,

Pete searched every inch of her pale, drawn face. "I didn't mean to scare you, Miss Rebecca. You just have to be more careful out here in the west than you were back in Pittsburgh. If you plan on seein' tomorrow, that is. But you're right, let's get on back."

And then they began to retrace their steps.

It had been eleven years since she had cowered under the bed, and today it seemed hard to credit tales of marauding Indians. Or desperadoes. At least not in the restful setting the ranch had become.

"Everything is so peaceful here," she said almost wistfully. "Even the few Indians I've seen have been friendly."

"I guess you'd act mighty friendly too, if you was in their village, surrounded by nothin' but Injuns."

"I guess so." Tired of talking of Indians, she scanned the countryside, content to remain silent and simply watch the land go by. The horses stirred up little pools of dust as they rode, and a lizard flicked onto a stone, then lay still, a delicately etched curve of sandy gray, a miniature sculpture perfectly still except for the tiny pulsing of the throat against the hot stone.

Pete turned in his saddle, squinting over his shoulder. "Miss Rebecca, we got company. And whoever it is, sure ain't on a Sunday picnic. They're riding hellbent for leather." He slid his rifle from the scabbard and jerked on his reins. His horse stumbled in the sand, and the old man bit out a sharp curse. Then the roan regained its footing. Pete spat, "Looks like Apaches, Miss Rebecca. *Ride for your life!*" and he smacked her horse on the rump.

Heart pounding, she bent low over the bay, damning the sidesaddle her brother had insisted she use, and

10

rode as she had never ridden before, her hat flying behind her in the wind.

The clatter of the unshod Indian ponies on the hard desert floor almost deafened her as she whipped at the bay, urging him to greater speed. Then a shot rang out and another. Chancing a quick look back, she saw Pete following closely behind her. Although he had obviously hit one Apache, the rest were steadily gaining on them.

A shiver of apprehension went through her as one Indian suddenly shot ahead of the others. He was so close now that she could make out the blue paint streaked across his cheeks in the shape of lightning bolts.

It all seemed oddly unreal — even hallucinatory — yet it was agonizingly real. They were still three miles from the ranch, and, although the report of the gunfire would carry a great distance in the desert air, they were still too far away to count on help from that quarter.

Gunroar.

Stinking reek of power fumes from Pete's rifle.

Thundering hooves.

These had become the sum total of her world.

She whipped madly at the bay, grinding supplicating prayer through her clenched teeth. Please, God!

Then three braves topped a rise thirty yards in front of her, cutting her off from the ranch. Wrenching on the reins, she steered the bay sharply to the east.

Another shot sounded, then a hoarse yell. She jerked her head around one more . . . and saw Pete's riderless horse.

The stirrups slapping against the roan's side as it slowed into the waiting hands of the half-naked

11

Apaches told a chilling tale. Her pounding heart gave a leap of fear.

Pete was down.

She was alone.

And the three savages chasing her were nearer still.

Gritting a hoarse command at her mount, she used her rawhide quirt, but the bay was already giving it all he could. And the Apaches were right behind her, drawing closer until suddenly their ponies were running alongside her, keeping pace with her bay.

A movement at the corner of her eyes alerted her and she turned to see an Apache pull ahead of her, his lank black hair flying in the wind. Then, his dark copper arm was reaching for the reins, and she slashed at him, using her quirt. The Indian yelped and bit off an unrecognizable Indian word.

While her eyes were fixed on his angry face, another Indian grabbed at the reins and pulled hard. Her horse faltered, immediately slackening his speed.

"Run, Diablo, run!" she screamed at the bay, using the quirt again.

It was no use. The Apache pulled harder on the reins, drawing even nearer to her.

"Get away from me!" She slapped at him with the rawhide quirt. "Leave me alone!"

To no avail. Despite her efforts, Diablo's reins were caught and held. Amid the dust and confusion, she was dragged from the horse and pulled to the ground. She landed with a hard thump that knocked the breath from her.

She lay there, struggling for air, choking in the flying dust. When she could breathe again, an Apache warrior, clothed only in a breechcloth and the long Apache boots that pulled up over the knees for protection against cactus, stood over her.

Fear immobilized her. Real fear as her situation suddenly dawned on her. She had heard too many tales of what the Apaches did to their victims, knew that many settlers would rather kill their women and children before allowing them to be taken by the Indians. Feeling a helpless sob rise in her throat, she bit her lip to hold it back, refusing to let him see just how terrified she really was.

Hoofbeats announced the arrival of the rest of the war party. From the lance of one, a warrior whose face was grotesquely streaked with green, hung a bloody scalp.

Pete's scalp.

She shuddered as the full recognition of the pelt of long, straight gray hair hit her.

Another Apache displayed Pete's Colt revolver and cartridge belt while yet another held his rifle. They had lost no time in plundering Pete's dead body.

Rebecca's captor, a thickset Indian with lanky, shoulder-length hair spoke gutturally to one of the braves who then wheeled his pony away. In moments, the brave was back, leading Rebecca's mount. Her captor reached down and, grabbing a handful of Rebecca's hair, tugged hard at it, grunting and nodding toward the bay. Obviously he wanted her to mount.

Her heart pounded loudly in her ears as she looked in anguish in the direction of the ranch, but there was nothing to see except the lonely, empty desert.

Becoming impatient with her, the Indian gave another savage yank to her long, brown hair and she rose unsteadily to her feet, fearing he would pull it out if he yanked again. Her trembling legs just managed to keep her upright, and she gripped the pommel to steady herself.

The Apaches watched impatiently as Rebecca mounted the trembling bay, then with her captor holding Diablo's reins, they rode away.

Rebecca watched her captors carefully, hoping for a moment to present itself when escape might be possible. But with her reins in the hands of the Indians, it was a futile hope.

They led her past Pete's bloodied and twisted body. When she saw the Apache lance protruding from his back, she averted her eyes, sickened, chilled, and fighting for composure. It was hard to believe that Pete was dead, and her eyes filled with tears as she remembered his many kindnesses to his employer's tenderfoot sister.

She blinked rapidly, refusing to allow the Apaches to see her moment of weakness. She had heard somewhere that the Indians despised weakness and admired courage. She tried not to think about what was going to happen to her now. For her own sanity, she knew she couldn't dwell upon it, but the fear hung there, the unknown horror of what waited for her.

She considered trying to jump down from the bay and making a run for it—force them to kill her—at least then her death would be quick. But as quickly as the thought came, she put it aside. There would be no escape from them, and, no matter what, she wanted to live. At least while she was alive, there was still hope.

Dead, there would be nothing.

Her eyes went to the Indian leading her horse. He wore a headband across his forehead, and his appearance was dirty and unkempt. The smell of unwashed bodies hung heavy around her, and she wrinkled her nose in distaste. As if he felt her stare, the Apache turned in the saddle and grinned maliciously at her. His gaze roved over her, seeming to strip her naked, and she gave an inward shudder. But, unwilling to let him see her fear, she kept her blue eyes hard and contemptuous as they held his flat black stare.

Seeming to tire of the game, her captor faced forward again and broke into a fast trot, and it was all Rebecca could do to retain her seat.

They traveled for hours, heading toward the distant range of mountains. The Apaches seemed to feel the need of putting as much distance as possible between the ranch country and them before night. No time was taken for resting, and Rebecca swayed in the saddle as the strain from the long ride began to tell on her muscles.

The afternoon sun hung low in the sky, which meant she had been on horseback all day, and she shivered despite the heat, wondering just how far they had come.

Raising her arm, she wiped the perspiration from her face. She was so hot and thirsty and she knew from the prickling of her skin that she was getting sunburned. Her short, blue riding jacket with its long riding skirt seemed to smother her, and in her flight she had lost the small blue hat. Damp tendrils of hair curled wetly around her face, and she longed for a drink of water to wet her parched mouth and throat.

The riding was becoming more difficult now as they encountered rough, broken canyon country, dotted here and there with mescal, prickly pears, and an occasional bush. Now the riders were forced to go single file as the trail narrowed. Rebecca's knuckles were white as she gripped the saddlehorn tightly. The closer they came to the mountains, the more desperate she became.

She knew if she was going to escape at all, it would have to be soon. But for the life of her, she could not figure out just how she was going to manage it.

As the Apaches in front neared the base of a cliff, they stopped, dismounted, and picketed the horses where tufts of desert grass would be available to them. Rebecca sat silently while her captor dismounted, wondering what was expected of her. She didn't have long to wait. The Apache who had captured her spoke to his companions, then strode to her.

Glaring up at her, he said something in his language, but she couldn't understand and shook her head wearily. Angered, he reached up and pulled her roughly from the saddle, throwing her violently to the ground. She felt a raw pain in her arms and legs as the gravel and dirt dug into her sunburned flesh. The blood was pounding in her ears and her heart beat wildly as the Apache stood over her, grinning.

He looked around at his companions, then with a laugh reached for her. His fetid breath was foul, causing her to gag as he leaned closer. With an evil grin, he put one hand behind her head, his fingers grasping her hair to hold her still, and, hooking the fingers of the other hand between her breasts and the fabric covering them, yanked violently, ripping the material to the waist and exposing her creamy white breasts to his lustful gaze.

Her blood froze in her veins, and she tried to

swallow the anguished sounds that rose in her throat. Her eyes filled with moisture for a moment, but she was determined not to give in to her panic. Whatever happened, she wouldn't allow them to see her fear. At that moment, her gaze fell upon Pete's grizzled scalp hanging from a lance, and, remembering how he had died, her courage returned, her blue eyes blazing with hatred.

"Get your hands off me, you filthy savage," she said, twisting aside and lashing out at him as she tried to pull the edges of her torn jacket together.

Her anger seemed to amuse him. Laughing, he knocked her hands aside and twisted her breast cruelly. Despite herself, she couldn't control the moan that escaped her lips. She was barely aware of the other braves standing by, laughing and shouting encouragement to her tormentor.

Suddenly the adrenalin was flowing fast in her veins as Rebecca's survival instinct erupted. The Apaches had killed Pete, an old man who had harmed no one, but at least he had taken one with him. If she was to be brutalized, and possibly raped, at least she would give a good accounting of herself.

Renewing her struggles, she beat at the Apache with her fists and legs, connecting with his nose and the side of his head. He grunted in pain and fell back. Then, at the hoots and catcalls of his fellow comrades, he closed in again, throwing himself at her, aiming blows at her face and body. She managed to deflect the worst with her arms, but one blow, delivered with his open palm, landed across her face.

Through the ringing in her ears, she fought to stay conscious and was vaguely aware of a warm trickle running from her nose. Shaking her head to clear it, she lashed out with her feet, connecting with his midsection, and something that felt soft beneath her toe. Immediately, he let her go and fell back, clutching his groin with both hands.

Suddenly a hush fell over the crowd as a steel knife blade flashed in the sunlight. She stared at it, cold fear racing down her spine as she waited for it to fall. Then, miraculously he stopped, his hand halting in midair, as he turned to watch five Indian riders approach. She had been so terrified that she had been unaware of their arrival.

Rebecca went limp as her captor glared his hatred at her that promised retribution later, then put his knife away, and turned to face the newcomers.

Feeling incapable of further movement, she lay in the dirt, prostrated by heat, fear and exhaustion, and her overpowering thirst. For a moment, her eyes blurred and she blinked, trying to bring them into focus. She was vaguely aware that a brief discussion was going on. The Indians seemed to know each other.

As they talked, her attention was drawn to one brave who was riding a piebald pony. He seemed to be the leader of the new arrivals. For an Apache, he was extremely handsome, standing out over all the others. Even seated on the pony he looked taller than the rest, his bearing proudly erect. He was shirtless, wearing only buckskin breeches. A bear claw necklace hung around his neck, emphasizing his dark, bronze muscled chest. His face seemed to be sculpted, his features were so well defined, and his shoulder-length hair, drawn back from his forehead, was held in place by a headband. His gaze moved from her captor to her

18

lying in the dirt, taking in her wildly disordered hair, her torn clothing that she was trying so hard to hold together. She shrank back at the harshness she saw reflected there. She gave a slight shiver, wondering who he was.

Lone Wolf stared at the girl lying in the dirt, ripped blouse showing her creamy white flesh, blood trickling from her nose, and his eyes darkened with anger. He turned on her captor, speaking in the language of the Chiricahua. "What does this mean, Black Bear? Why have you taken a captive? Why does Running Elk have a fresh scalp hanging from his lance?"

Black Bear stared at Lone Wolf, his black eyes insolent. "We have been raiding, Lone Wolf. We take white captive, white man's weapons."

"You have done wrong, Black Bear. Since Cochise signed the peace treaty, we have been at peace with the white eyes. Cochise gave his word there would be no more raids by the Chiricahuas."

"Cochise is dead, Lone Wolf. He is no longer chief of the Chiricahua tribe. His son Nachise is chief now."

"Then you were told by Nachise to do this thing? To attack and kill the whites? It is at Nachise's command that you take captives? That you steal and take scalps?"

Lone Wolf knew Black Bear would not dare lie about it. He also knew that Nachise was an advocate of peace. He would never condone what Black Bear had done.

"Nachise is an old woman," Black Bear said sullenly. "He stay on reservation. Give up Apache way." He struck a fist across his chest and said belligerently.

"Black Bear follows Geronimo! Geronimo strong warrior, raid when he want to." Then he deliberately turned his back on Lone Wolf to signify the end of the discussion.

"Black Bear," Lone Wolf called sharply. "Release the white girl!"

Black Bear turned back to Lone Wolf, his expression sullen. His eyes warred with Lone Wolf's for a moment, then he said. "No! The white girl belongs to Black Bear. Black Bear capture. Is law of the Apache!"

"Then fight for her," Lone Wolf demanded, evoking an even older law.

For a moment Black Bear seemed to hesitate although it was clear to all that he had been challenged. He knew of Lone Wolf's propensity for winning fights, and, even though he was a strong man and had counted many coups, he was not a stupid man. Lone Wolf was a subchief of the Chiricahuas and as such had a large following. If he fought Lone Wolf, whether he defeated him or not, he would make some bad enemies.

"Our mothers are sisters, both from the house of Cochise," he said gruffly. "Would you have me bring grief to my mother over a skinny white girl?"

"It is not my decision," Lone Wolf said. "The choice is yours. We do not have to fight. Just give her to me, and I will return her to her people."

Black Bear threw a look at his white captive. Although he had called her skinny, it was not so. Even though her skin was sunburned and a smear of blood marred her face, she still showed great beauty. He looked at her consideringly, remembering the fat wife, She-Who-Walks-Like-A-Duck, that resided in his lodge, then he looked back at Lone Wolf. He didn't want to fight, yet he was unwilling to release the white captive.

"No!" said Black Bear harshly, pulling his knife from beneath his belt and holding it in readiness. "We will fight!"

"Then let it begin," Lone Wolf said, dismounting from his piebald pony and pulling his own knife from its sheath.

Slowly he closed in on Black Bear, his eyes glittering savagely. This fight had been a long time coming, but he had always known that one day Black Bear would leave him no choice.

Circling warily, Black Bear held his knife in readiness. Suddenly he leaped, his knife slashing down in a glinting arc, but Lone Wolf, anticipating the move, had already leaped aside and was coming in low and fast. His knife slashed at Black Bear's belly beneath the right ribs and made contact. A bright stream of blood welled from the cut.

Black Bear gave a coughing grunt and fell back a step, then brought the blade up in a vicious underswing. Lone Wolf twisted fluidly, and the knife grazed past his shoulder. Enraged, Black Bear spun around and kicked Lone Wolf's wrist, causing the other's knife to go spinning away. Then, grinning savagely, he raised his knife and closed in for the kill.

The Apaches were silent, their faces impassive, as they watched the battle. With Lone Wolf disarmed, Black Bear seemed certain of victory. But as they watched, Lone Wolf stepped boldly to Black Bear and circled warily, keeping out of range of the other's deadly blade. Suddenly, his hand darted out and captured Black Bear's wrist.

Sweat broke out on Lone Wolf's forehead as he held the knife hand off for a moment, then sank his fist into the pit of Black Bear's stomach. Black Bear's hands dropped to his belly and the knife clattered to the ground where Lone Wolf kicked it away. Deliberately, Lone Wolf drew back a fist and slugged his opponent in the throat.

Immediately, Black Bear's knees buckled and he slid slowly to the ground. Lone Wolf picked up the knife and went to stand over Black Bear, his face blazing with anger.

Black Bear lay on the ground, his breath wheezing harshly through his tortured throat, his eyes blazing with hatred as he waited for the death blow.

"Kill me," he said harshly when Lone Wolf made no move toward him.

"No," said Lone Wolf contemptuously, shaking his head.

"You would dare shame me?" Black Bear snarled.

"Better that than bring sorrow to my mother's house," Lone Wolf said, turning away from him and picking up his own knife.

Striding to the piebald pony standing nearby, he removed a waterbag made from animal intestines from his saddle and came to stand above Rebecca. With his eyes glittering strangely, he offered the bag to her.

She took it from him and drank greedily, allowing the tepid liquid to flow freely around her thickened tongue.

"Easy," he cautioned in perfectly good English. "Just a little now to quench your thirst and you can have more later."

Reluctantly, she allowed him to take the waterbag back. Her blue eyes were wary as she watched the Apache standing over her. Confused, her gaze moved to the beaten Apache now getting to his feet, then returned to the brave who had bested him, noticing for the first time that his eyes were gray. The fact barely registered as Diablo was brought to the victor, and he motioned to her to mount.

Still dazed from the blows she had suffered, she attempted to get to her feet, trying all the time to hold her blouse together. Her knees buckled at the first attempt and she fell back on the ground, painfully scraping her elbow.

"My name is Lone Wolf," the Indian said. "I have fought Black Bear and won you from him. Now you must get up and mount your horse. Then we will go."

Rebecca stared wearily at the Apache. So that was what it was all about! They were fighting for ownership of her! Groggily, she pushed herself to her knees and, using her hands for balance, managed to rise shakily to her feet.

For a moment, she swayed, grasping the pommel to steady herself. Then, putting one foot into the stirrup, she somehow mounted Diablo.

"What do they call you?" Lone Wolf asked, his gray eyes inscrutable as they held hers.

Her heart leaped with hope. Maybe they would trade her to the army. "Rebecc—" Her throat was raspy, and she swallowed hard, then tried again. She wanted to make sure they had it right, just in case she was being held for ransom.

"Rebecca Shaw," she said, the words coming in a rush. "And I live on a ranch just east of Silver City with

23

my brother Robert—Robert Shaw."

Lone Wolf grunted, took Diablo's reins, and mounted his pony. That seemed to be the end of the questions. Her eyes moved over the band of Apaches and came to rest on her former captor. She sensed the malevolence in his gaze just before they moved away and shivered with apprehension. Apparently he wasn't going with them, yet she sensed she hadn't seen the last of him.

She wondered what it all meant. Where was Lone Wolf taking her? And why had he fought for possession of her? She felt helpless not knowing their language. Then she sagged in the saddle. What difference did it really make? After all, she was still a captive of the Apaches even though it was a different band that held her now. All the same she couldn't still her sense of relief that they were leaving her tormentor behind.

# Chapter Two

Rebecca slumped wearily in the saddle. Her leg and back muscles, unaccustomed to the long hours on horseback, ached with strain. She could not even attempt to estimate the distance they had traveled, but they seemed to have been riding for days since her capture early that morning. She wondered if she would ever be allowed to rest. Apparently the Apaches could go on tirelessly forever. Unlike her, they seemed to need no rest.

A shudder rippled through her frame as she remembered what happened the last time they had stopped. With one hand she clutched the torn edges of her blouse together while the other gripped the saddlehorn tightly. She still felt dazed, hardly able to believe this nightmare was actually happening to her.

Would the Apaches rape her when they stopped for the night?

The thought drove the dazed look from her eyes and they became hard and determined.

No! She refused to allow it to happen.

When the other Indian had attacked her, she had

fought — and she would again. She would never give in to them. She began to look for landmarks, determining that somehow, some way, she would escape, and, when she did, she must be able to find her way back home.

There was that lone cottonwood tree with the barrel cactus to one side . . . Her blue eyes widened in surprise and she straightened in the saddle. Hadn't they already covered this ground once before? Suddenly everything seemed to be familiar! Were they going in circles? Weren't the mountains getting more distant instead of closer?

Her eyes narrowed, more alert now as she studied her surroundings and realized that indeed they were. Instead of being in front of them, the mountains were now behind.

Rebecca's eyes went to Lone Wolf riding just ahead of her, his bronzed body gleaming beneath the late afternoon sun. She wondered how it was that he spoke such good English.

From his speech, he appeared to be an educated man, which led to many questions. She had heard that sometimes the reservation agent took a shine to a particular Indian child and sent him to school. Was that how it was with Lone Wolf? If so, then perhaps some of the white man's ways had rubbed off on him. Perhaps he could be persuaded to return her to Robert.

As if aware of her interest, Lone Wolf pulled his mount up until Diablo was even with the piebald pony and offered her the waterbag. She saw his eyes go to the torn blouse exposing the soft flesh, then return to her face.

She blushed at the blaze of passion reflected in his eyes, then suddenly she was angry. How dare he look at her like that! Her blue eyes sparkled furiously and she was tempted to scorn the water he offered, but her overpowering thirst overcame her pride. Haughtily, she took the waterskin from him, lifted it to her parched lips, and swallowed the lukewarm liquid greedily.

"Put this on," he said, handing her a buckskin shirt as she returned the waterbag.

"Thank you," she said stiffly, swallowing hard in her surprise.

She pulled off the jacket and tried to keep as much of her flesh hidden as possible as she donned the garment. Then pulling her long, brown hair from beneath the shirt, she glanced quickly at him and asked, "What will you do with me?"

"I'm returning you to your people," he said, his face impassive.

Rebecca's blue eyes widened. Had she heard him right? "You're taking me back?" she whispered huskily.

"Yes," he said in a gruff voice. "Black Bear went against the wishes of his people when he took you captive. To make things right, you must be returned to your family."

To make things right. The words echoed in Rebecca's ears. But he couldn't make things right! He couldn't bring Pete back.

"Just like that?" she demanded, suddenly very angry, her weariness disappearing. "You'll put things right, just like that?" Her blue eyes flashed and her hands clutched the pommel tightly, her knuckles showing white. "How can you put things right? My God! What about Pete?"

"Who is Pete?" he asked, his eyes flickering with surprise. He had been unprepared for her rage.

"Just the harmless old man whose scalp is hanging from an Apache lance right now!" she snapped. "How will you put that right?"

"I'm sorry," he said, eyeing her calmly, "but no one can bring back the dead."

"Well, sorry isn't enough," she said grimly. She was so distraught that she was unaware of speaking unwisely. "When I get home and tell everyone what happened, the army will step in and put a stop to all this killing. Before they're finished, you'll all be put where you belong, and there won't be an Apache left off the reservation."

Lone Wolf stared at her impassively for a moment, seeming to weigh her words, then, obviously coming to a decision, he reined his mount around and pulled alongside a young brave.

Even though she was still angry, Rebecca sat a little straighter in the saddle, knowing that she was going home. Then she felt sadness stealing over her as she remembered Pete. She would never forgive the Apaches for killing him. And to think that she had been finding excuses for them just before they attacked and killed Pete. She should have known better and listened to someone who had spent all his life in this part of the world. Maybe, if she had believed such a thing could happen, they would already have been at the ranch before the Apaches attacked them.

But in her inexperience of the west, she had been falsely secure in the knowledge that the Indians were under control. She had been here for only six months, having spent her growing-up years with her Aunt Bess. Her mother had been killed in an Indian raid when she was five and her father had felt that she needed a woman to look after her.

Rebecca knew little about Indians, only what she had heard, but she knew that the Apache tribe was made up of smaller bands: the Kiowa-Apache, the Chiricahua, the Lipan-Apache, the Jicarilla, the Western Apache, and the Mescalero. The bands were made up of groups that shared hunting grounds and cooperated in war and religious ceremonies. And she knew that, since the death of Cochise, there were rumors of unrest among the Chiricahuas.

She watched Lone Wolf as he spoke with the brave in a deep, guttural tongue, becoming uneasy at the looks she was now receiving. Where before the Indians had paid her no attention, now they seemed to be deeply interested in her.

Suddenly, the brave pointed a finger. As one, the Apaches turned to watch what looked like small clouds drifting slowly toward the sky. As another cloud lifted, Rebecca realized that it was smoke.

As one, the band of Indians reined their mounts around, riding off in the direction from which they had just come. Rebecca watched in confusion as Lone Wolf pulled their mounts around to follow.

"What's happening?" she asked, her heart beginning to pound with dread. "Where are they going?" As he ignored her, putting a toe to his pony, she shouted, "Lone Wolf, I demand that you tell me what's happening."

But Lone Wolf didn't speak, and suddenly Rebecca found it was all she could do to hang onto her seat.

Hours later, Rebecca swayed in the saddle as Diablo plodded along the narrow trail that led to the high mesa. Night had long since fallen, but still they rode on into the darkness. Her head drooped forward, her long, brown hair swaying in rhythm with the walking horse, hiding her face from her captors.

Suddenly, Diablo stopped, and she lifted her head to find they had come to a clearing in which stood some sort of dome-shaped dwellings. Although it was night, the area was well lit for a campfire burned brightly in front of each one of the frail hovels. The huts seemed to be made of stick and brush, put together with dabs of mud and well suited to the nomadic life of the Apaches. From somewhere in Rebecca's memory came the word "wickiup," and this must be the Apache village, the rancheria.

One wickiup, larger than the rest, which she suspected housed the chief of the tribe, was placed toward the center, with the others surrounding it in no particular pattern as far as Rebecca could see.

From these rounded brush huts, several Indians materialized, their attention focusing immediately on Rebecca. Some of the men were dressed in buckskin and breechcloths while others were attired in white man's clothing.

Most of the women wore their black hair twisted into coils at the nape of their neck, shapeless buckskin tops that hung past their hips, and buckskin skirts that came to midcalf. The rest of their legs were modestly covered by the distinctive high moccasins that pulled above their knees.

One brave vaulted from his pony and went to join a small Apache woman who waited in front of one of the huts for him. Not more than five feet tall, she was slender with lustrous black hair, her eyes dark and luminous. She had strong-boned features but there was a softness about her that lent a beauty to her face that was uncommon in Apache women. Her smile was shy as she spoke softly to the approaching brave.

Lone Wolf dismounted and pulled her roughly from the saddle. Her aching muscles were unprepared and she sank to the ground, pain stabbing through her back and thighs.

Ignoring her, Lone Wolf walked to stand beside the beautiful Apache woman and the brave. He spoke for a moment, drawing their attention to Rebecca still crumpled on the ground. Then, leaving the couple staring at her, he went into the largest wickiup.

Rebecca sat in the dirt, wondering wearily what was expected of her. She didn't have long to wait. A crowd of women and children began to gather around her, and she shrank back in alarm at the hostility reflected in their faces. Hands reached for her, striking, pinching, pulling at her arms, shoving her back and forth.

She tried to stop them but to no avail. There were too many. A woman grabbed a handful of Rebecca's long, brown hair and gave a sharp tug. Rebecca compressed her lips tightly, refusing to cry out as she called upon an inner strength, a fierce pride for help. Ignoring the pain, she stoically bore the taunts and blows.

Suddenly a harsh voice was heard, and reluctantly the crowd gave way, allowing the brave with the beautiful Apache maiden to approach her. Rebecca lay numb, her bruised body aching as she waited for her fate.

The small woman bent over her, speaking in a soft voice and Rebecca saw the kindness reflected in her large ebony eyes. Helping Rebecca to her feet, the woman motioned to her to follow and led the way to a nearby hut.

Rebecca limped slowly to the entrance and stood hesitantly for a moment, glancing back at the hostile crowd with grim faces. Then, deciding that whatever lay inside couldn't be much worse than what the others had in mind, she entered the hut.

Smiling shyly, the woman gave Rebecca a folded buckskin bundle, indicating she was to open it. On looking inside, Rebecca found a skirt and top such as was worn by the Apache women.

"Thank you," Rebecca said gratefully, wasting no time in stripping off the torn blouse from her body. The woman brought her a container of water and a small calico cloth, which Rebecca accepted gratefully.

The woman watched curiously as Rebecca removed the rest of her clothing, giggling as she saw the pantalets the white girl was wearing. Rebecca managed a weak smile, guessing the undergarments would look funny to the Indians.

Wincing from the pain, Rebecca removed the dirt and sweat from her bruised and battered body. She found two long scratches down her right breast, caused, she was sure, by Black Bear's nails when he had ripped her clothing.

She shuddered at the memory. Thank God Lone Wolf had come along when he had! Then as she remembered where she was, she wondered if she was any better off than before. True, so far, Lone Wolf hadn't treated her harshly, but she was still a captive, and it was obvious that the Apaches felt hatred for her.

When she finished her bath and dressing herself, the woman gestured to the mat nearby, and Rebecca, needing no further urging, sank wearily to the floor.

She lay there for a moment, listening to the drums that had begun beating outside the hut. Her head throbbed with pain and she closed her eyes wearily, deciding that whatever was to happen would, whether she was awake or asleep.

She realized, if there was any hope of escape, she would need every bit of strength she could muster. And to keep up her strength, she needed food and rest. She didn't have the food, so she must make do with resting.

Rebecca awoke slowly, aware that something was wrong. Her pillow seemed to have disappeared, and her bed was unusually hard. She was stiff, sore, and thoroughly chilled. She opened her eyes and memory flooded back. She was at the Apache village, dawn was breaking, chasing the shadows from the wickiup, and the Apache woman was nowhere to be seen.

But she was not alone!

Occupying the other mat was Lone Wolf, his eyes closed, his face looking strangely vulnerable in repose as his chest rose and fell with his even breathing.

Rebecca felt a stirring of panic with the realization that she had spent the night alone with a savage Apache Indian. She looked wildly around the hut, becoming suddenly aware of the silence outside.

Her heart suddenly leaped with hope. Now was the time! Now, while the Apaches slept, she could make her escape. As soon as the thought entered her head, she dashed to the entrance and peeked out, discovering at once that she had waited too long. The women were already busy at their work in front of the other wickiups, some cooking the morning meal and others grinding dried corn into a fine powder with bowls and pestles.

Sighing with disappointment, Rebecca sat down on the mat again and looked around the wickiup. Various leather bags and pouches hung from the ceiling, and resting beside a fire were several bowls and pots. She recognized the braided leather straps hanging near the entrance as the bridle used on the Indian ponies, and nearby was a pile of furs. Her eyes returned to the man lying on the other mat and she was startled to find him awake and watching her.

"Good morning," he greeted softly, his eyes roving over her flushed face. "Did you sleep well?"

"Yes, thank you," she said stiffly, her eyes wary.

He smiled at her. "It is dawn. We must eat as we have much to do this day. Today, Little Turtle will bring the morning meal, but after this you must manage to cook by yourself. Little Turtle can be depended upon to teach you all you must know."

"But Lone Wolf, why is it necessary for Little Turtle to teach me the ways of the Apache? You said you would take me home." When he didn't answer she asked hopefully. "Are we going tomorrow?"

"No," he replied, his smile disappearing. "Your people have made it impossible for me to return you to them. By your own words, you have condemned yourself to live among us. You will have to stay here with my people."

"But they don't want me here," she said angrily. "Look!" She pulled the sleeve of her blouse up, showing him the bruises on her arm. "Just look what they did to me. I tell you they don't want me here! Lone Wolf, you must take me home."

"No."

"But what will become of me?" she asked.

"You will become my wife." His eyes avoided hers as he sat up, picked up one of his moccasins, and pulled it on.

"Your wife!" she gasped. "You must be crazy! I won't marry you!"

"But you will." He picked up the other moccasin, ignoring her indignation at the casual way he had informed her of their plans for her. "As you said, my people will not accept you. And to make matters worse, Black Bear has returned with the tale of your capture and the death of one of our braves."

Rebecca felt chilled at the reminder of the brave that Pete had killed. Would she be blamed for the death of the Apache?

"Black Bear wants revenge and is stirring up the people against you." He took her chin, raising her face to his. "Think on this, Rebecca—if you are to live, then we must marry."

"But why can't you just take me home?" she said, her blue eyes pleading with his.

Lone Wolf sighed deeply, impatient with her questions. "There has been trouble, Rebecca. And not only of Black Bear's making. A small band of Chiricahuas are known to have killed the white men who thought to make a profit by selling them whiskey. The white eyes are angry and the army has been called in to track down all Chiricahuas and either kill them or bring them to the reservation. It would be worth my life to be seen with you near the white man's town."

"Then give me my horse, Lone Wolf, and let me go

35

alone."

"No." The words grated harshly on her ears. "You would never make it. You would die and the Chiricahuas would be blamed for yet another death." His eyes held hers for a long, penetrating moment. "There is no other way, Rebecca. Black Bear wants you, but, if you were returned to him, you would not live long for he treats his captives cruelly. If you are to live, then you have no choice. You must become my wife."

"But—"

"I do not like your way of arguing with me, Rebecca," he said angrily. "It is not the way of the Apache to allow his woman to argue."

"But I'm not your—"

"No more," he commanded harshly. "Soon Little Turtle will come to show you your duties. You must learn the Apache ways." He smoothed her tangled hair with a gentle hand. "And you will be taken to the river to bathe."

"Lone Wolf," she called frantically as he started to leave. "I can't go out there among those—" She bit back the word "savages." "uh—among your people. You saw how much they hate me."

"Yes. They despise you," he agreed. "But they also know you are under my protection for they have been told we are to marry. They will not harm you." He touched her bruised cheek and she winced at the pain. "I am sorry about this, little one, but I will see that it does not happen again. Soon, when the children have started, my people will come to accept you."

"When the children—" Her eyes widened in horror, and her voice failed her. She raised a hand to protest, but he was already rising from the mat, and, before she found her voice, he had left the wickiup.

Lone Wolf stepped from the wickiup, his thoughts on his beautiful captive. He hoped she would have no trouble accepting the life she must now lead among the Apaches. Despite himself, he couldn't feel sorrow that he had been unable to return her to her family.

He had been attracted to her since his eyes first fell upon her, and, although he knew that her life among the Apaches would be harder than what she was accustomed to, he felt that she had the resilience to survive.

He hurried through the village, intent on reaching the verdant green forest a few yards away. He was so intent on his thoughts he failed to see Brave Eagle stepping from his wickiup until they collided.

"You are in a great hurry, Lone Wolf," Brave Eagle said.

"I have much to do, old friend," Lone Wolf replied, clapping Brave Eagle on the shoulder with one hand. They had been friends since they were boys, each knowing he could always trust the other.

"I am surprised you are not already building the honeymoon shelter. I expected you to be eager for the faster you complete it, the sooner you can be married. If it were me, nothing could keep me from the task until it was completed."

"Not even Little Turtle?"

"I see your point," said Brave Eagle with a grin. "So you kept the white girl with you last night. How did she take the news she was to become your wife?"

"She will come around," Lone Wolf said gruffly.

At his words, Brave Eagle looked grim. "She has an objection to the marriage?" At the other's nod, he

37

continued. "That is not good, Lone Wolf. Does she know that she must agree to the marriage or it cannot take place?"

"Have no fear. She will agree," Lone Wolf said, but something in his voice told Brave Eagle that he wasn't as certain as he sounded.

"Perhaps it would have been wiser to return the white girl to her family instead of bringing her here."

"No," Lone Wolf said. "You know that was impossible. Her words would only have added strength to the trouble Geronimo is already making for the Chiricahuas. For the sake of our people, I could not risk her return."

Brave Eagle nodded in agreement, his dark eyes on Lone Wolf's troubled face. "Black Bear has returned to the village. He speaks at length of the bravery of Slow Otter, who died in the raid when the girl was taken. He tells of the cowardice of the white eyes who are responsible for the death of so many of our people. I hear Slow Otter's wife has gone to Chief Tall Feathers, demanding retribution for her husband—the life of the girl in exchange for Slow Otter's."

"I expected as much," said Lone Wolf, "but there is no need to worry. The girl will marry me."

"Let us hope so," Brave Eagle said. Suddenly he slapped Lone Wolf on the back and grinned. "Enough of this morbid talk. It will be as you say and you must be off to build the honeymoon bower. See that it is well hidden with enough provisions to last until it is time to return to everyday life. Then you will be guaranteed of your bride's full attention."

"I do not need you to tell me what I must do," Lone Wolf said with a wide grin. "I know how to build a

38

honeymoon bower. I suggest you come watch me for soon it will be your turn. One thing does worry me though."

Instantly Brave Eagle's smile vanished. "What is that, old friend?"

"The honeymoon bower should be festooned with flowers. Where do I find flowers at this time of the year?"

"I'm sure you will manage somehow," Brave Eagle replied. "Come, I will walk through the camp with you. Maybe I will even see Little Turtle on the way."

"No. You won't see her. She is with Rebecca." His gray eyes were penetrating as he studied his friend. "Why do you continue this way, old friend? Why do you not speak to her father? Then you would not have to walk through the village, hoping to catch a glimpse of her. If you keep delaying, she may grow tired and accept another. Lately, I have seen Swift Arrow with her. I do not think he will be as slow to declare himself."

Brave Eagle's face darkened, his mouth tightened, and his eyes grew stormy at the mention of Swift Arrow. He was nobody's fool, and he too, had seen the way the other brave casually appeared whenever Little Turtle was around.

"She knows my feelings," Brave Eagle said harshly.

"Perhaps," Lone Wolf replied, "but a maiden likes to be told she is loved. If you are interested, you will find her later at the river, but you must be sure and wait until they are finished bathing. I have no liking for the thought of you watching Rebecca at her bath." He grinned to take the sting from the warning. "Come along, old friend. I have much to do."

They walked in companionable silence to the edge of

the encampment where they stopped abruptly as Black Bear and two companions stepped from the woods and blocked their path.

"I demand you give the white captive to me," Black Bear said, his voice menacing.

Lone Wolf's big body tensed. "I fought for her and won," Lone Wolf reminded him. "She is no longer yours."

"You claimed you would return her to her people," Black Bear snarled. "You have not done this so I demand her return."

Lone Wolf faced his enemy, his gray eyes glittering. "No. She belongs to me. I have decided she will be my wife."

"You would take this white eyes for a wife?" Black Bear was taken aback momentarily. His eyes studied his cousin curiously. "She is not of our people," he spat contemptuously. "She is only a slave."

"Nevertheless, she will be my wife," Lone Wolf said grimly.

"I do not believe you," Black Bear said. "The white slave will not marry you willingly." Suddenly a light appeared in his eyes. He hit his chest with his fist. "It was I, Black Bear, who captured her. If she wishes to be a wife, then I will wed her."

"I'm afraid not," Lone Wolf said abruptly. "You have one wife already, Black Bear. She would not take it kindly if you brought another to share the wickiup, especially if the second wife is a white slave."

Black Bear's eyes flashed with fury. He looked around at the warriors who had begun to grin. "I am head of my household," he grated harshly. "It is not for She-Who-Walks-Like-A-Duck to complain."

"Nevertheless, the white girl is mine. The ceremony will be held this very night."

"Does she agree to this?" Black Bear asked, his voice clearly disbelieving. "You cannot force her to marry. It is our law that she must agree to the marriage."

"She agrees."

"You lie!" the squat Apache snarled, his fists clenching tightly in his rage. He seemed ready to launch himself at his cousin, but the memory of his recent defeat caused him to stay his violence. "Let her speak the words from her own mouth. Let her tell the council that she agrees to this marriage."

Black Bear thought he was being clever, Lone Wolf decided. His cousin knew Rebecca was frightened of them, and he felt she would not agree to the match.

And he might be right.

Somehow, some way, Rebecca must be convinced it would be in her best interest to agree to a marriage between them. Lone Wolf knew he would have to return to the hut and find some way to convince her.

"Then call the council together," Lone Wolf said. "I will go for her and bring her before them."

Black Bear's eyes glinted with malice as he smiled at his gray-eyed cousin. "The council will be called, but you will not speak with her first." He looked at the two men with him for confirmation. "He must not be allowed to sway the white girl. Is this not so?"

They nodded in agreement and Lone Wolf accepted his defeat. All he could do now was hope Rebecca would give the right answer when asked about the marriage.

His eyes narrowed. If there was only some way that he could warn her. If she gave the wrong answer, then

41

she would certainly be returned to Black Bear to use as he pleased. And he refused even to consider such a fate for such a delicate creature. She wouldn't last more than six months in Black Bear's wickiup.

Lone Wolf watched Black Bear and his two companions leave, knowing it wouldn't take long to call the council together, then he turned to Brave Eagle who was waiting by his side.

"She must be warned."

"I fear that is impossible." Brave Eagle's eyes were sympathetic as he watched his friend. "You know the white girl does not speak the language of the Chiricahua. And no one can speak her language except Chief Tall Feathers and you, Lone Wolf. If you are not allowed to approach her, how is it possible to warn her?"

"I don't know, but we must find a way. It would be unthinkable to let Black Bear have her."

"I see she has already found a place in your heart."

Lone Wolf did not reply, but the look he exchanged with Brave Eagle spoke volumes. He knew his boyhood friend would do whatever he could to convince the white captive she must agree to become his wife.

Rebecca and Little Turtle were returning from the river when they saw Brave Eagle approaching. A shy smile lit Little Turtle's face and she stopped abruptly to wait for the young brave to join them. They talked quietly for a moment, and Rebecca began to feel uneasy as she saw Little Turtle cast several worried glances toward her. She felt certain whatever they were discussing concerned her. The two spoke for a moment longer, then Brave Eagle favored the Apache woman with a smile and went on his way.

Little Turtle spared one more glance for the brave, then, her dark eyes showing her anxiety, grabbed Rebecca's arm, pulling her quickly in the direction of the wickiup.

Something was definitely wrong.

Rebecca's pulse leaped wildly and her heart began to race.

As they neared the hut, Rebecca heard the sound of muted voices. A group of Apaches emerged from the chief's wickiup a little farther away, catching and holding her attention.

Little Turtle cast a frantic look at the men, her grip on Rebecca's arm tightened as she pulled her quickly inside.

Rebecca felt an immense dread.

Something was happening; something that boded ill for her. She had recognized the squat, thickset figure of Black Bear among the group of Apaches. Her heart began to pound wildly. Lone Wolf had said no harm would come to her, but where was he now?

Little Turtle squatted on the ground near the fire and pulled Rebecca down beside her. Her eyes were grim as she picked up a stick, motioning for Rebecca to watch. Then, with the white girl watching, she began to draw in the dirt.

She drew an animal that resembled a bear, and alongside it she drew the figure of a girl. She pointed to Rebecca, then the girl. Rebecca nodded her head to show she understood. The girl was Rebecca. Then, Little Turtle pointed to the bear and, using the stick, she began to beat the drawing of the girl. Rebecca

43

blanched, understanding the motions. Black Bear was going to beat her!

Panic-stricken, she started to rise searching for a place to hide, but Little Turtle grabbed her arm and pulled her back down.

After making sure Rebecca was still watching, Little Turtle drew a picture of another animal. This one resembled a dog, then she looked up at Rebecca to make sure she understood. Her ebony eyes took on a look of urgency at Rebecca's obvious puzzlement. She studied Rebecca, then her drawing, and added more lines out around the dog's body. It must be fur. She watched as Little Turtle added a bushy tail.

Wolf!

That was it! It was Lone Wolf! Rebecca nodded to show her understanding, and Little Turtle's eyes lit up. Then Little Turtle pointed to the wolf and, using her hands, made pouncing motions on the bear.

Rebecca frowned, her blue eyes narrowed on the drawing. Lone Wolf was going to pounce on Black Bear? Was Little Turtle trying to say that Lone Wolf would save her from Black Bear? She watched as Little Turtle drew another picture. It was a wickiup. Then she pointed to the picture of Rebecca and the one of Lone Wolf.

Before Rebecca could figure out what Little Turtle was so desperately trying to tell her, two braves entered the hut and, grasping her arms, pulled her upright and dragged her toward the entrance. She threw a panic-stricken glance back at Little Turtle who was still kneeling on the ground with her drawing stick.

As Rebecca was taken forcibly away, she looked back and saw Little Turtle take the stick and point to the hut, willing Rebecca to understand her meaning, but Rebecca was terrified, and her wits had completely deserted her.

She was taken to the larger wickiup from which the men had emerged a short time ago and her heart pounded loudly in her chest as she took note of her surroundings. Several men were seated around a fire. To the side stood Black Bear and Lone Wolf.

Her pulse was racing madly, and her spirits sank even lower as she saw the compassion in Lone Wolf's eyes. Her blue eyes widened in fear, her heart beat so fast she could hear its thumping in her ears.

At a nod from one of the men, undoubtedly Chief Tall Feathers, Rebecca was pulled forward to face him. Although quaking inwardly, she threw off the hands of the two braves and straightened her shoulders, determined to keep her fear from them whatever should befall her.

To Rebecca's amazement, the chief spoke in English. "You have been brought here, white girl, to give your answer to a marriage between you and Lone Wolf. Is it your wish to become his wife?"

Startled, Rebecca looked at Lone Wolf, catching a warning in his gray eyes. He seemed to be telling her to consider her answer very carefully. But was that what it was all about? Did she really have a choice in the marriage after all? Her eyes widened indignantly as she stared at him.

Well, she wouldn't!

If she really had a choice in the matter, then they could forget it. She wasn't going to marry anyone. And especially not a savage Indian.

Her eyes were still rebellious as they fell on Black

Bear waiting silently at Lone Wolf's side. As her eyes met the squat Apache's, she caught a glimmer of triumph in his that terrified her.

Suddenly she was desperate to know what he had to do with all this.

Little Turtle had been afraid for her. She had drawn pictures in the dirt, hoping to make Rebecca understand. What had the Indian girl tried so frantically to tell her before the men came for her?

It was obvious she had known where Rebecca was being taken and was frightened for her. Little Turtle had seemed to think Black Bear was going to hurt her in some way. She had indicated Lone Wolf would save her from him. But would he be allowed to help her if she refused him? Would she be turned over to Black Bear?

"I am waiting, white girl," said Chief Tall Feathers. "What is your answer?"

Rebecca looked at Lone Wolf again. His face was expressionless, but his bronzed frame seemed to be tense while he waited for her answer. Her troubled gaze fell on Black Bear, and there was no mistaking the triumph flaring in his flat black eyes.

She made her decision.

"Yes," she whispered, swallowing thickly and lowering her eyes. "I will become Lone Wolf's wife."

As Chief Tall Feathers spoke in the Chiricahua language, giving her decision, Black Bear stared savagely at her. His voice was harsh, angry as he spoke to Chief Tall Feathers. He was obviously protesting the decision. The chief silenced him with a harsh command.

Rebecca glanced at Lone Wolf through her lashes,

willing him to give her some kind of reassurance, but he was either unaware or uncaring of her feelings. He spoke for a moment to Chief Tall Feathers, then, without even looking in her direction, turned and left the hut.

She stayed for a moment longer, but, when no one paid her any mind, she left the wickiup and returned to Lone Wolf's hut. She felt appalled at what she had committed herself to. But, she consoled herself, it really didn't matter. She had only agreed on the wedding to save herself from a worse fate, and, after all, Robert and the soldiers would come for her before the ceremony could possibly take place.

Robert was sure to have discovered her missing early yesterday when she and Pete failed to return from their ride. Pete's body was sure to have been discovered, and a full-scale search for her launched immediately.

Yes. They would come for her soon.

All she had to do was wait.

## Chapter Three

Throughout the day, Little Turtle stayed with her, showing Rebecca how to pulverize dried strips of meat with a stone maul, then mix it with dried berries and fat to make a nutritious food that Rebecca recognized as pemmican, which could be stored away for months on end in the rawhide cases the Indians called parfleches.

When they had finished the pemmican, the small Indian woman helped her to prepare a meal. She showed her how to form a tripod by binding poles together at one end with rawhide. Then, taking a large piece of skin, which Rebecca learned later was the lining of a buffalo's stomach, they bound the ends to the poles to create a type of pot, which they filled with water. Then chunks of meat and dried vegetables were added, and, after dropping heated stones the size of Rebecca's fist into the pot, they left it to cook.

Rebecca was tired by the time they were finished, but Little Turtle refused to let her rest. She took Rebecca to the river again and, despite her protests that she had already had one bath today, pushed her firmly into the cold water, scrubbed her hair and body with a root from the yucca plant, then rinsed Rebecca thoroughly.

"I don't know what all the fuss is about," Rebecca grumbled, shivering as she draped a blanket around her shoulders.

Little Turtle spoke reprovingly to her as she gathered up the soiled clothing Rebecca had been wearing. Then she motioned to Rebecca to follow her back to the wickiup.

Inside the hut Little Turtle pointed to the mat. Rebecca sat down. Then, the Indian woman brushed the white girl's long, golden brown hair with a porcupine quill brush till it was shining.

Rebecca sat huddled in the warmth of the blanket. It felt strange allowing the other girl to administer to her this way and she was surprised the Apache woman should want to. She had understood that Indian women were given few comforts. Why then did Little Turtle insist on helping her?

Little Turtle finished Rebecca's hair, then picked up a bag nearby and removed some leaves with a minty fragrance. She handed them to Rebecca, motioning to her to rub them on her body. Finding no reason to refuse, Rebecca complied with her wishes. Then, Little Turtle gave her a soft, doeskin dress decorated with colored beads to wear.

As Rebecca pulled the dress over her head, she heard the beat of drums and her heart gave a lurch.

Slipping her arms through, she hurriedly pulled the dress down and smoothed it over her breast, her waist, her hips.

Something was going on, some kind of Indian

celebration.

Her eyes widened in sudden comprehension. The wedding ceremony! But it wouldn't happen that fast. There had to be preparations made; preparations that would allow enough time for Robert to come.

Suddenly, Rebecca became aware of a figure standing in the entrance to the wickiup and lifted her eyes. It was Lone Wolf. He was dressed in beaded buckskin too.

"My people wait," he said simply.

She stared at him, her blue eyes wide with apprehension.

*Robert, where are you? You must hurry or it will be too late.*

Lone Wolf entered the wickiup, took her hand. "Come," he commanded. "It is time."

She resisted, tugging at her hand, but his grip only tightened. "Lone . . . Lone Wolf." Her voice quivered, her eyes stricken. "I . . . I've ch—changed my mind. I . . . can't do it."

His gray eyes darkened with anger, his lips narrowed into a thin line. "You have no choice. Did you not understand that you would be given to Black Bear if the wedding does not take place?"

"But does the ceremony have to take place tonight? Couldn't we wait a few days until I get used to the idea?"

"No," his eyes softened. "You will not be safe from Black Bear until you are mine." He pulled her firmly toward the entrance. "Stop resisting, Rebecca. It is necessary my people believe you are a willing bride."

Her blue eyes warred with his as she stood her ground. It wasn't fair, she thought. She had been so certain Robert would arrive in time with the soldiers.

She just couldn't go through with it.

"Would you rather be given to Black Bear?" he asked harshly. "Shall I tell you what you can expect at his hands?"

She shivered, accepting defeat. At least Lone Wolf seemed to have some compassion for her. He took her arm and led her from the hut to where the rest of the Apaches waited.

She sat stiffly through the ceremony and the feast that followed the marriage rites, hardly aware of what was taking place. Just waiting for it to end. Then it was over and Lone Wolf was pulling her to her feet.

Rebecca's stomach knotted with tension as she and Lone Wolf mounted the horses that were brought to them, then he was leading her away from the crowd of Apaches.

Through a daze, she caught a glimpse of Black Bear's thunderous face as they left the village behind them. But she felt too numb to let it bother her.

She had married Lone Wolf, a savage.

True, it was only to save herself, but the deed was done, and now she would have to live with the consequences of her act.

They rode for a while, then Lone Wolf pulled up and dismounted. He lifted Rebecca from her horse and carried her into the honeymoon bower hidden in the dense forest. Her hands and feet felt icy and she held herself stiffly erect until he placed her on a mat.

"Rebecca," he said huskily, coming down beside her and looking deep into her eyes. "There's no need to be afraid of me. I won't hurt you." His hand was gentle as he brushed a silky lock of hair back from her face. At his touch, she drew her breath in sharply but forced herself to lie still.

Her eyes appeared wounded as she watched him and he felt a pain somewhere deep inside. If only he'd had more time, he thought. If only he'd been allowed to court her first, then maybe he could have won her over. But not this way. Never this way. She might never forgive him for what he had to do to her.

"Don't think about it, just rest," he told her quietly. "I will bring you something to eat, for you ate nothing at the feast."

"I'm not hungry," she whispered. Then, afraid he would get the idea she was in a hurry to go to bed, she said quickly, "Maybe I could eat just a little bit after all."

Solemnly, he nodded, bringing her a piece of pemmican and seating himself on the woven mat beside her. Nervously, she shifted her body, edging a little farther away from him. Taking a bite, she chewed slowly, but, when she tried to swallow, she began to choke.

Lone Wolf quickly reached for the waterbag, offering it to her. Her blue eyes evaded his as she took a hasty swallow to clear her throat before returning it to him. His gray eyes disturbed her as they gazed intently at her, doing strange things to her pulse. Feeling breathless, she lifted the pemmican to her mouth again. Her eyes widened in surprise as Lone Wolf took the patty from her and laid it aside.

Her breath caught in her throat and her eyes darkened with emotion as he pulled her to him. She could almost feel herself melting beneath his burning gaze. As her body brushed against his, she felt a shock to her senses. And as his arms tightened around her, holding her securely to him, her heart began to beat wildly.

His long bronze fingers lifted to stroke her hair and her face, causing unfamiliar sensations to race through her body. Then his fingers were tracing her lips lightly, exploringly, and she felt a strange yearning for his mouth to possess hers.

Slowly, as if aware of her thoughts, his mouth lowered gently against hers, molding itself to her li̶ His tongue found its way inside her mouth, draw͟ gasp from her, sending her mind reeling at th͟ pected pleasure.

When his hand caressed her breast, she stiffened i̶ shock, grasping his wrist to stop further exploration. Lifting his head, he gazed intently into her eyes for a moment, then lowered his mouth to kiss her eyelids, her nose, the side of her face.

Then his lips were on her mouth again, moving over hers, and she trembled against him, lost to everything but his love-making. She was unaware that he had unfastened her dress until she felt his lips against her breast. By then it was too late. As he took one rosy nipple into his mouth and laved it with his tongue, white-hot flashes of passion seared through her, and she cried out in longing and arched involuntarily against him.

Groaning, he clutched her tightly to him, holding her still and breathing deeply for a moment, then he began administering to her other breast, showing the same loving attention to it that he had given to the first one. Soon, Rebecca was moaning with pleasure and her own hands lifted to caress Lone Wolf's back, feeling the hard muscles beneath her hands.

Lone Wolf lifted his head and kissed Rebecca's

mouth once more, then he removed her clothing and his own and, before she was aware of what was happening, he had rejoined her on the mat.

"No, please," she gasped, feeling his naked body against hers. But Lone Wolf paid no attention, covering her mouth with his own again. Soon, his mouth moved back to her breast, scorching her with its heat as his lips nursed the swollen, throbbing nipple.

When he had her just as wild as before, she felt his lips moving down, down over her body, stopping to dip his tongue into her navel and she gasped with pleasure, her body squirming beneath him. As his lips searched lower, she came to her senses.

"No, Lone Wolf," she gasped, squirming, pushing at him, trying to free herself from his grip. "No, Lone Wolf, stop it!"

"Be still, Rebecca," Lone Wolf said huskily, his lips finding the warm mound between her thighs. She quivered and thrashed beneath him, trying to escape from his touch. But he was too strong, holding her hips firmly as his tongue entered her wet moistness, stroking gently against her sensitive feminine core.

"No, Lone Wolf." Her shocked voice barely penetrated his concentration as he continued to stroke her gently until Rebecca forgot her indignation and an inferno began to ignite deep within her body. Her whole being quivered with emotion and she heard a curious keening sound coming from deep within as she climbed higher, higher, then seemed to explode in a million fragments as she was brought to completion. Rebecca collapsed in wonder, spasms shaking her whole body as she lay there too stunned to move.

Lone Wolf kissed her softly, then looked into her

eyes, and she smiled shyly at him. She still couldn't believe what had happened to her, but she could see the pleasure he felt at having caused it.

"Is it always that way?" she asked softly.

"Not always," he said. "But with the right people it can be."

He kissed her again, then lay back on the mat and gathered her close into his arms. His manhood throbbed against her as she rested against him, making her blush wildly. He smiled, then placed his lips against hers. She sighed, returning his kiss with fervor, her tongue meeting his, dueling silently. As his hands began to roam again, she felt the quickening of her body. Her nipples swelled eagerly as he cupped her breasts in his palms, then to her astonishment, he was moving over her, covering her body with his. His thighs parted her own and she felt the heat of his manhood pressing against her. For a moment she resisted, but his mouth left hers, his tongue tracing the contours of her earlobe and she gasped in pleasure, her attention diverted.

She felt a momentary pain as he entered her body and gave a surprised gasp that ended abruptly with his searing kiss. For a moment he was still, then he moved, slowly at first, then faster and faster, introducing her to a world of passion that she had never imagined, even in her wildest dreams.

Her body was his, fed by the fires of passion that he was creating. Higher and higher they went as he led her along unexplored pathways. His thrusts became faster and faster, deeper and deeper while her passion slowly built into an all-consuming desire. Finally her body was lifting, meeting each thrust of his, with one of her own until at last they catapulted through eternity together, ripples of ecstasy shuddering through them as they lay entwined, experiencing the joy of their mutual release.

Rebecca woke to bright sunlight. At first she felt disoriented, her eyes traveling around the hut. Then as memory returned, she tried to sit up. It was then she discovered she was held firmly in Lone Wolf's arms. Her eyes lifted to find his on her, and she blushed furiously at the look of passion she saw reflected there.

His smile was slow and sensual as he lowered his mouth to capture hers. She lay quietly beneath his touch, filled with self-loathing as she remembered what had happened last night. How could her body have betrayed her in such a way? My God! The man was an Apache Indian!

As Lone Wolf began to caress her, her eyes filled with tears. What good would it do to object now? The deed had been accomplished. As her tears brimmed over and ran down her cheeks, Lone Wolf suddenly lifted his head and looked at her questioningly. At the sight of her tears, his gray eyes hardened and he moved away from her.

"There's no need to cry," he said harshly. "All you had to do was say 'no.'"

"I said 'no' last night," she reminded him. "And little good it did me."

"That was different," he told her, sitting up on the mat. "I told you the marriage had to be consummated." It was funny, but his voice sounded strangely hurt. "Anyway, you weren't saying 'no' in the end. In fact, you seemed to enjoy it!"

"Damn you!" She rolled away from him and, reaching for her doeskin dress, jerked it over her head. Pulling on her moccasins, she rose to leave the hut.

"Where are you going?" he asked harshly.

"I need a little privacy," she said, her eyes flashing with anger. She waited but, when he said nothing, she left the hut.

A few minutes later, she was ready to return when it dawned on her that she was quite alone.

Cautiously, she looked around to make sure that Lone Wolf was nowhere nearby. She saw nothing and smiled grimly. After one night of love-making, he thought she was his. Well, soon he would know he hadn't won after all.

She began to run.

She had only gone a few hundred yards when she heard him behind her.

Run! Run! screamed a voice inside her head.

Instinct alone directed her steps as she ran, crashing through the underbrush, unheeding of the noise she was making. Her breath came in short gasps, her heart pounded loudly in her ears as she ran on.

It was no use.

He caught her easily, and she sensed his anger as he turned her in his arms. Without a word, he picked her up and carried her swiftly back to the hut, laying her on the mat.

Her chest rose and fell as she tried to still her wildly beating heart. She closed her eyes against the anger in his, unaware of what he was doing until it was too late and she had been divested of her clothing again.

"No," she begged, pushing at his hands.

"Yes," he told her, capturing both her hands in one of his and pulling them above her head. Then his body was on hers, his thighs nudging hers open. His mouth lowered to hers, capturing it, molding it to his.

"Please," she whispered, trying to shove him away, trying to ignore the passion that he was kindling deep within her body.

She felt his hand come between her thighs, his finger slipped into her warmth, evoking a thousand pleasures in her body. Soon she was straining against him, gasping as he entered her body, then made love to her with exquisite thoroughness until Rebecca was mindless with desire, begging him for release.


Rebecca stirred, felt Lone Wolf's arms tighten about her, and became stilled. She felt embarrassed at the response he was able to evoke from her, even against her will. Her eyes lifted to find him gazing intently at her.

His lips twitched slightly as if he were aware of her embarrassment and amused by it.

"Are you hungry?" he asked softly, picking up a long, brown curl and twisting it lightly between his fingers.

"A little," she admitted, lowering her lashes to shield her eyes.

"For food?"

She nodded, blushing wildly in spite of herself. His voice was husky, seducing her senses, doing mad things to her pulse and heartbeat.

"Then I suppose we'll have to get up and feed you!" His voice was dry, and he didn't move a muscle.

"I suppose."

"You know, we could just stay right here. I have some more pemmican. There's no need for us to leave this pallet at all."

The hope in his voice was her undoing. A giggle escaped her lips. He was insatiable. Reaching up, she tugged playfully at his long, black hair.

"Ouch," he said, returning the compliment. Then, as if drawn by the sparkle in her eyes, his lips lowered and he kissed her softly.

She returned the kiss fervently. As her senses began to swim, she pulled away. Several questions were nagging at her, and he seemed inclined to humor her.

"Why do you have gray eyes, Lone Wolf? I thought all Indians had dark eyes."

"They do." he said, amusement lurking in his eyes. "But I suppose, like me, some ancestor of mine found a beautiful white girl and made passionate love to her." He kissed her on the end of her nose. "Shall I demonstrate?"

"I think you're just trying to get out of feeding me!" she joked. "Don't tell me you're a lazy Indian!"

"Now you know my secret," he laughed. "I only married you so I wouldn't have to do my own cooking."

The mention of marriage sobered Rebecca and she looked at him curiously. "Why did you marry me, Lone Wolf?"

"I'm surprised you didn't ask me that before we married," he countered lightly.

"I did," she reminded him. "You said it was to save me from Black Bear, but I'm wondering why you cared."

"Let's just say you're too beautiful to be left to his tender mercies."

Tender mercies. White men's words. She looked at him curiously. Lone Wolf seemed to know a lot about the white man's world. And he spoke excellent English as well.

"You speak English as well as I do, Lone Wolf. Where did you learn it?"

A shutter seemed to come down behind his gray eyes. "Oh, I went to the white man's school when I lived on the reservation," he answered carelessly. "And that's enough questions today. Now come on, lazybones. It's time to get up. His eyes suddenly darkened, and his voice was husky. "Unless you have something else in mind?"

She laughed. He certainly *was* insatiable. "I think we'd better find something to eat," she suggested.

"Would you like to swim first?" he asked, rising and pulling her to her feet.

"I'd love it," she said, finding the idea of swimming with Lone Wolf very appealing.

He led her through the forest, helping her over fallen trees and stumps that threatened to trip her. Soon, she heard the sound of rushing water, and suddenly they emerged from the dense forest into a glade dappled with sunlight. And in the midst of the glade was the source of the running water: an enchanted waterfall cascading into a natural pool where the clear waters reflected the sky.

He draped his arm across her shoulders and pulled her close against his side. "What do you think of it?" he asked with a smile.

"I love it," she breathed softly. "It looks like something from a fairy tale."

"Yes," he laughed, his eyes dancing. "I must admit, I

thought of the brothers Grimm when I first saw it myself."

"The brothers Grimm?" She turned puzzled eyes on him. "I didn't know they taught fairy tales in the reservation schools."

His eyes became hooded. "I learned many things in school, but let's not speak of them now. This is our honeymoon."

"Yes, it is," she said, lowering her eyes shyly. "And you brought me here for a swim." She raised suddenly trembling fingers to her doeskin blouse, lifting it slightly to reveal a patch of pale skin.

"So I did," he said, his eyes seeming to find her exposed skin fascinating. Sensing her hesitation, his glittering eyes met hers, softening as they watched a blush well into her cheeks. "Do you need any help with that?" he asked in a teasing voice.

"I can manage," she said, her blush deepening, her eyes evading his. "Will you turn your back while I get in the water?"

"No."

Her startled eyes flew to his. "Lone Wolf—"

"You must learn not to be shy with me, Rebecca," he said softly, touching her cheek gently. "You have a beautiful body and it's natural that I would want to admire it."

Put that way, she offered no more resistance. But despite herself, when she had shed the last of her clothing, she dove hurriedly into the water, allowing him only a glimpse of high, firm breasts and well-rounded hips as she plunged into the cold stream.

She surfaced, gasping. "It's like ice," she said, wiping away the water dripping down her face. Then she felt his naked body brush hers, and she was captured and held close against his hard, male body. The sensation sent her senses reeling, and her stomach contracted sharply.

She wrapped her arms around his neck, turning her face up to his, and suddenly she wasn't cold anymore. The raw hunger reflected in his eyes had lit a passionate flame deep within her body.

She whispered his name, her lips reaching for his. Then with a husky groan of passion, he was bending toward her, his lips pressing hers with an agony of need.

He lifted her into his arms and, with his mouth devouring hers, carried her to the bank of the creek, laying her down gently on the grass. His lips pressed eager kisses on her neck, her shoulders, her breasts, then moved back to devour her mouth greedily.

As his hands caressed her, a devastating hunger overpowered her until she was pulling at him, trying to draw him into herself, arching her body against him as her senses clamored for relief.

She slid her arms down the tensed muscles of his back, and he shuddered, his tongue entering the sweet moistness of her mouth. She gave a moan of pleasured torment, her nails raking his back, and his love-making became savage and wild.

Animal sounds of pleasure broke from her throat, and her body bucked beneath him. As though unable to endure any more, he parted her thighs with his, then plunged wildly into the core of her being. In and out he thrust, deeper and deeper until she thought she would faint from the pleasure. She withheld nothing from him, bringing her body up to meet his, reveling in his savagery until finally they both reached completion and lay spent and exhausted in each other's arms, too tired to move.

That night, Rebecca sat in the circle of Lone Wolf's arms outside the honeymoon bower. A light wind brought the fresh scent of the pine trees, teasing her nostrils with its fragrance. The campfire had burned low and the full moon rode high in the sky, casting its pale glow on the two lovers.

"Tell me about yourself, Little Blue Eyes," Lone Wolf said, his eyes gentle on hers.

"What should I tell you?" she asked, her eyes smiling up into his.

"Have you always lived near Silver City?"

"No. Although I was born there, I was sent to live with my aunt in Pittsburgh when my mother—died." The hesitation was slight, but he picked up on it immediately.

"What happened to your mother?"

"She was—killed." Her voice was suddenly tense, willing him not to persist.

"By whom?"

"The Indians killed her," she said in a cold, little voice. She made to draw away from him but found herself held firmly to his side.

"And do you blame all the Indian People for this thing that happened to your mother?" he asked calmly. Put that way, it sounded ridiculous and childish.

"Well—"

"Do you?"

"I guess I did," she said in a small voice. "I guess I thought Indians were all alike."

"The only good Indian is a dead Indian," he quoted

savagely.

"Lone Wolf," her voice was hesitant. "I guess I didn't understand—"

"And do you pretend to understand now?" His voice was wry, his gray eyes skeptical as they lingered on her face, studying her expression.

"Well, more than I did—I guess."

"No, I think not yet," he said slowly. "But you will understand, Little Blue Eyes, I will make you understand." He pulled her head against his shoulder, fixed his gaze on the fire, and began to speak.

"Not so very long ago, the great buffalo roamed the prairies," he said. "The Indians depended greatly upon this beast, for every part of the buffalo serves a useful purpose to the Indians' way of life. Then the white men came, slaughtering the buffalo in great numbers, taking the hides, and leaving the rest of the buffalo to rot upon the ground."

Rebecca listened to the mesmerizing sound of his voice. She was faintly aware of the forest sounds—the crickets chirping, hoot owls hooting—but nothing seemed real except Lone Wolf's voice and the deep sadness she heard there.

"The buffalo became scarce, and it was hard for the People for we not only use the meat for our food, we use the buffalo hide for clothing to keep us warm through the cold winters," he said. "And we make pouches and blankets and so many other things that are necessary to the survival of the Indian People."

"But can't some of these things be bought?"

"What would we use for money?" he asked. "The Indians' only means for obtaining goods was through trading buffalo hides. The numbers of the great beasts are so few now the People have had to leave their regular hunting grounds to follow the animals that are left." His voice became bitter and harsh. "But no matter where the People went, the white men followed, pushing them farther and farther away from their homes until, finally, the white men grew so greedy they decreed that all the Indian People should be herded together onto a reservation."

Rebecca lowered her head in shame. For the first time she began to see the cruelty of the white man and to feel the frustration of the Indians as the peace treaties were made, and then broken, over and over again by the white men greedy for land that belonged, rightfully, to the Indians.

For the first time in her life, she began to really understand just what the Indians faced in order to survive. And with the understanding came a kind of acceptance for her fate.

When they made love that night, it was with a furious desperation. She had found something in Lone Wolf's arms that she had never even dreamed existed, and she wished she could stop time right where it was. Something had happened to change her, and now, somehow, the thought of rescue by the soldiers had become a threat instead of a hope.

For ten more days Lone Wolf and Rebecca remained in the honeymoon bower secluded from the world outside. They laughed and loved, then loved again. And she felt such happiness with Lone Wolf that it made her afraid for the future.

One night, lying in his arms, replete from his lovemaking, she voiced her fears.

"I wish we didn't have to go back to the village."

"We cannot stay in the honeymoon bower forever," he chided, kissing the end of her nose. "Although I must admit the idea sounds appealing."

"It's not funny," she said. "The people of the village resent me. What if something happened to you? What would become of me?" She drew herself into a sitting position as the thought suddenly alarmed her. "Lone Wolf, what *would* become of me?"

"Nothing is going to happen to me," he said, drawing her firmly back to him on the pallet.

"But if it did? Then what? Would I be returned to my people?"

"The Apaches are your People now, Rebecca. You would remain here with them." His voice was gruff, impatient. "Now, enough of this kind of talk. Come here and let me love you."

She forced herself to relax, curling against his big body like a kitten. She wanted nothing to spoil the few days remaining to them.

Soon Lone Wolf's roaming hands sent every other thought from her mind except the pleasure he was bringing her. He had learned her body well and soon had her moaning and writhing beneath him, mindless with passion, until finally he entered her, riding above her until both were consumed by the flames of their desire.

Rebecca opened her eyes. Today was the last day of their honeymoon. Tonight they would return to his wickiup in the village. A feeling of regret swept over her that their time alone should come to an end.

Her eyes swept over Lone Wolf's naked form lying

next to her, his bronzed body turned toward her. As she watched him, a feeling of desire coursed through her body, and she smiled. She had called him insatiable, but what was she?

*Insatiable!*

She smiled wryly at the thought. She had gone way past the point of blushing at the way she reacted to his touch on her body.

*He sets me on fire with just a look from those burning eyes.*

She watched him from under lowered lashes, willing him to open his eyes, but he continued to sleep, his breathing deep and even, as though he were utterly exhausted.

She frowned, her lips pouting. Was he going to sleep all day? As though restless, he stirred slightly, turning over to lie on his back, and she grinned, her eyes lighting up wickedly.

Bending over, her lips touched his chest softly. For a moment there was a slight hesitation to his breathing, then it became even again.

She moved her mouth over his chest, her tongue making damp streaks as she made her way to one flat male nipple. As her mouth closed over it, he moved slightly and she suppressed a smile, biting down gently.

Encouraged, she moved to the other nipple, laved it with her tongue, then moved slowly down to his navel. As her tongue dipped into the indentation, his stomach muscles tightened, and he caught his breath swiftly.

Smiling, she looked up, but his eyes were still closed, his breathing deep and even.

*All right*, she thought. *So you're a deep sleeper.* With her mouth open she began trailing soft kisses across his stomach, down to his thighs, touching the soft flesh between his legs.

Suddenly, with an oath, Lone Wolf catapulted upright, dragging her over him. His eyes were burning coals of desire, consuming her in their passion as she lay above him, her hair fanned out across his chest. One hand circled the back of her head, forcing it down until her mouth was hard against his while the other hand roamed her body, teasing and pulling at her already taut nipples. His tongue searched out the inner warmth of her mouth, tasting the sweetness he found within.

A groan escaped his lips and tingles raced up her spine as she felt his manhood stirring beneath her. Suddenly, an imp of mischief possessed her and she lifted her lower body, penetrating herself on his shaft, then began to move slowly against him.

His breath drew in sharply, his eyes glazed with passion as she began a rocking motion against him. Suddenly, unable to stand any more, he shifted her until she was beneath him. Then he began to plunge wildly into her body, faster and faster carrying her up to some far distant peak with him until they were falling down the other side, completely satiated.

## Chapter Four

Silent as a ghost, hidden by the tall pine trees in the forest that bordered the river, the squat, thickset Indian was almost invisible and was not noticed by the women bathing in the river.

The creatures of the forest were silent, and that would have alerted the Indian maiden if the silence had not been covered by the laughter and splashing water. The pale-skinned girl with long, gently waving brown hair was too new to the ways of the forest to notice anything amiss.

The watcher's eyes sparkled with lust as he gazed at the women cavorting in the water heedless of the danger lurking in the woods. But it was to the pale-skinned girl that his onyx eyes kept returning. Her high breasts, firm and full, riveted his gaze. The gently rounded hips made him lick his lips in anticipation.

He looked his fill a moment longer, then faded silently into the concealing forest.

"Are you ready to go, Rebecca?" Little Turtle asked, twisting her long black hair and squeezing the water from it.

"No, not just yet," Rebecca said. "I'm going to swim for a little while." She smiled at Little Turtle. She had been here six weeks now and in that time had grown close to the small Apache woman. "I'm so glad I can converse with you now. It gave me such a lonely feeling when I first came and had to use sign language all the time."

"Lone Wolf has done well in teaching you our language," Little Turtle said.

"You'll have to admit you did your part as well," Rebecca laughed. "You refused to acknowledge me at all unless I spoke to you in your language."

"I'm sorry," Little Turtle said. "I know it was hard for you, but Lone Wolf said it was the only way to make you learn."

"Well, I guess he was proved right, for, if you're thirsty and the only way you can get a drink is to learn the word for water, you learn it."

Little Turtle smiled, watching her pale-skinned friend rinse out her hair. "I think I'll go on ahead, but you stay and enjoy your swim. I must see Many Moons. She has promised me some red beads to finish the shirt I am making for Brave Eagle from the buckskin he gave me."

"You're making Brave Eagle a shirt?" Rebecca asked.

"Yes, but don't tell him," Little Turtle said shyly. "It is meant to be a surprise."

"Are you going to marry him?" Rebecca asked curiously.

"If he asks me," the small Apache woman said. She sighed, and her lustrous ebony eyes were wistful. "I hope he does soon, or I will have to take Swift Arrow for a husband."

"Swift Arrow!" Rebecca said, her eyes widening in surprise. "But why Swift Arrow? Everyone in the village knows you love Brave Eagle."

"That is so, but my father, Crooked Lance, grows tired of waiting. He says that I must marry soon or I shall be too old to bear children."

Rebecca laughed outright. "Little Turtle, you're still a young woman, hardly old enough to marry yet. And I think it's horrible that your father would actually try to force you to marry someone you do not love."

"That is what you did," Little Turtle reminded Rebecca. "And you have grown to love Lone Wolf."

"But that's different!" Rebecca said, blushing furiously. How had Little Turtle guessed her secret? Was she that transparent?

"How is it different?" Little Turtle asked calmly.

"Well, Lone Wolf is kind."

"And is not Swift Arrow kind as well?"

"Well, I guess so," Rebecca admitted reluctantly. "But—" She stopped and stared in consternation at Little Turtle. "You sound like you wouldn't mind if your father made you marry Swift Arrow!"

"Oh, I would mind," the little woman said with a shrug. "My heart belongs to Brave Eagle, but, if I cannot have him, then I must wed with Swift Arrow." She finished wringing her hair and said, "I have lingered at my bath long enough. Now I must dress and go for the beads. Many Moons will be waiting for me."

With a nod, Rebecca watched her leave, amazed at the Apache woman's calm acceptance of her fate. Well, she shrugged, if it didn't bother her friend, then she must accept it as well.

71

Smiling, she dove into the crystal-clear water, surfacing in the middle of the river. Laughing with delight, she tossed the streaming brown hair back from her face, then, using slow strokes, began to swim the distance back to the shore.

Dressing hurriedly, she shivered, for the April breeze was cool against her wet skin. Then she twisted her hair, fastened it into a coil at the nape of her neck, and gathered up the basket she had brought with her. She started back to the village, detouring through the forest where she knew she would find some prairie turnips and wild onions.

A movement at the corner of her eye caught her attention and she turned to watch a scissor-tail flycatcher.

Although she had seen quite a few of the graceful birds in the month she had lived with the Indians, she still found herself stopping to watch the swiftly darting bird, its silver, salmon pink, and black feathers brilliant in the late afternoon sunlight that filtered through the pine trees growing in abundance in the dense forest.

A smile lifted the corners of her lips faintly as she watched it climb an invisible peak, its long, straight tail scissoring out in its flight to capture an insect before it was gone.

Feeling at peace with her world, she pulled another bunch of wild onions, adding them to the growing stack of vegetables in her basket, then continued along the path that led to the Indian village.

Wildflowers grew in abundance along the pathway. There were wild violets, buttercups, black-eyed Susans, and many other flowers she couldn't even put a name to.

She plucked a yellow buttercup and twirled it beneath her nose, remembering how, when they were young, Robert would mash the flower against her nose, leaving behind the buttery residue.

Robert.

She frowned as the thought of her brother intruded.

She had grown used to sleeping in the arms of Lone Wolf, and no longer was the hope of rescue by her brother, Robert, and the soldiers foremost in her thoughts. In fact, she had begun to accept the Indian way of life and Lone Wolf, her Apache husband.

Robert would be appalled if he were to see her now, dressed as she was, with her hair twisted into coils and held in place at the nape of her neck by a stick pin fashioned from a bone.

Rebecca found the shapeless buckskin tops and skirts extremely comfortable, and they took far less care than her cumbersome skirts and petticoats had. And the long hip-length moccasins kept the mosquitoes and bushes from her legs. She found them much more practical than the high-buttoned shoes to which she had been accustomed.

She was even beginning to be as house proud as any of the other Indian wives, taking pleasure in keeping the wickiup clean and the parfleches, hung in abundance around the wickiup, stuffed with pemmican and other provisions so they would be ready if the tribe had to move at a moment's notice.

Rebecca took pride in supplying the best vegetables available for her husband's meals, like the prairie turnips that grew in such abundance it was the Indians' most widely used plant food. It grew to as much as four times the size of a hen's egg, and could be eaten raw or used in soups and stews or sliced and sun-dried for storage.

Rebecca had found Little Turtle to be a storehouse of knowledge about a vast array of useful plants, from which dyes, medicines, and even leaves for smoking were made.

All in all, the Indian way of life had become very appealing to Rebecca.

Her pulses quickened as her thoughts turned to Lone Wolf. She knew wild onions were a favorite of his, and they would go well with the fresh meat he would bring back from his hunting trip. She had not the slightest doubt in her mind of his hunt being a success.

A bright, red feather caught her attention. She picked it up and, with a smile, stuck it jauntily in her hair. Then, as she spotted another batch of wild onions, she put her basket down while she gathered more to add to the other vegetables she had found. The stooping action caused a stray lock of hair to fall in her eyes and she pushed it back from her face.

Suddenly, she became aware of the cessation of sound.

The forest was silent.

She straightened slowly, aware that she was no longer alone. As though aware he had been discovered, a figure stepped from behind a tree and blocked Rebecca's path. Her heart leaped with fear.

Black Bear.

Rebecca's fingers clenched on the wild onions tightly and mashed them to a pulp that dribbled through her fingers. For the past month she had managed to stay clear of him and had come to feel there was no need to fear him any longer. She had obviously been mistaken. Now they were alone, and she could see by the look in his eyes he was after revenge.

"What do you want?" she asked in the Chiricahua language.

"What is mine," he said, grinning at her, lust and triumph gleaming in his black eyes.

"Let me pass," she demanded. She was determined to show no fear but couldn't keep herself from edging farther away from him. "Lone Wolf is waiting for me."

"Lone Wolf is still on the hunt," he told her, his onyx eyes gleaming with satisfaction. He moved nearer, his stance menacing. "There is no one to stop me. No one to hear if you choose to scream."

Before she fully realized his intention, before she could even draw a breath, he lunged for her, one powerful hand reaching out and covering her mouth to muffle her scream.

Rebecca kicked wildly at him and connected with his shin. He grunted in pain but didn't loosen his grip. He drew her hard against his solidly muscled body, rendering her struggles ineffectual. Although she could barely breathe, she sank sharp teeth into Black Bear's hand, feeling immense satisfaction as he grunted in pain and tried to shake her loose.

She hung on grimly, refusing to let go, tasting the warm copper flavor of blood in her mouth.

Suddenly, with an oath, he released her, throwing her to the ground like so much garbage. She felt dizzy with relief and got to all fours, knowing she must run while she could. But before she had time to run, a sharp blow landed on the side of her head and the ground came up and smacked her in the face.

While dizziness assailed her, Black Bear fell on top of her and pinned her to the ground. He gripped her tightly, his fingers cruel, while he stuffed a dirty rag into her mouth.

She grabbed a handful of hair and yanked hard. He laughed cruelly, then put a hand around her neck, and squeezed. Her head began to spin, spots floated in front of her eyes, her muscles loosened, her hand dropped to the ground as consciousness began to slip away, and she sank into a gray mist.

Her last thought was a silent prayer. *Oh God, don't let this happen! Please let this be a nightmare!*

She returned to consciousness all too soon. Her eyes fluttered open to the thrum of hoofbeats, and she got a glimpse of an upside-down world. She lay face down, across Black Bear's horse.

The steady rhythm of the horse beneath her made her temples throb, and she groaned. Her wrists, having been tied with a leather thong, were sore and reddened and dangled below her head on one side of the horse with her legs on the other.

The steady warmth that came from her left side told her that she was not alone on the horse. Her throat felt sore where Black Bear had squeezed it but at least the filthy rag he had stuffed in her mouth was gone.

When they finally stopped at a clearing in the dense forest, Black Bear pulled her from the horse and Rebecca crumpled face down on the soft earth, the pine needles fragrant as they stirred beneath her, biting into her face and bare arms.

Her blood pounded loudly and desperately in her

ears above the sound of her madly beating heart as the squat Apache stood over her for a moment, gazing in satisfaction at his prize. Then with a grunt, he followed her to the ground and pinned her beneath him with his powerful body.

Rebecca shuddered, turning her head away from his lustful gaze and disgusting breath.

"You thought you were too good for such as me," he grunted in the Chiricahua language.

The words chilled Rebecca, and she nearly wished she hadn't worked so hard at learning to communicate with the Apaches. But then, maybe it would help her. Perhaps she could reason with him.

"You are making a big mistake," she said, forcing the words through clenched teeth. "I am Lone Wolf's wife, and he will never stand for this. He's already bested you once, and, if you take what is his, Lone Wolf will hunt you down and kill you." If possible, his eyes grew even meaner at the mention of Lone Wolf. She tried another tack. "You will be disgraced among your people when they find out what you've done. There is no way you can win."

"Lone Wolf will never know what I have done. Nor will my people, Rebecca Shaw," Black Bear grinned. "Everyone at the village knows you have been an unwilling wife. When you do not return, they will think you have escaped and returned to your people. They will say Lone Wolf was foolish to trust his pale-skinned wife."

"Not when they find my body."

"They will not find your body," he growled, his eyes taking on a cunning look. "I have found a cave near here that no one knows about. When I am finished with your body, I will kill you. Then I will hide your body there." As he spoke, he tugged at her skirt, working it up her legs slowly.

*This can't be happening,* she thought. *It's only a dream. A nightmare. Soon, I'll wake up in Lone Wolf's arms . . .*

A smile tugged at the corners of Lone Wolf's mouth as he placed the hide-wrapped venison near the tripod cooking pot. Rebecca would be happy with the meat he had brought her. His stomach growled at the prospect of supper for he had eaten nothing but a strip of pemmican all day; on an empty stomach he would be faster afoot should it become necessary.

From across the village, he saw Brave Eagle entering the hut of Crooked Lance, Little Turtle's father, with a portion of his kill for the day.

His smile widened, his gray eyes alight with humor. There was sure to be another wedding in the village before too long. At least there would be one if Brave Eagle could ever work up enough nerve to offer for Little Turtle. It never ceased to amaze him that a brave so bold and fearless in battle as Brave Eagle could be so shy around a timid little maiden such as Little Turtle. Now Rebecca, she wasn't timid at all, he thought.

Rebecca.

The idea of her was suddenly an ache in his gut, an ache that would have to wait until tonight or else his pale-skinned wife would be shocked.

His black brows pulled together in a frown. It was strange that she hadn't appeared yet; usually she watched for him, but perhaps she was inside. He visualized her lying naked on buckskin robes on the floor of the wickiup and smiled.

"Rebecca," he called softly as he entered the wickiup. No one answered. His gray eyes sharpened as he looked around the empty wickiup. Where was Rebecca? His eyes were puzzled. He left the hut, scanning the village with his searching gaze.

A faint twinge of alarm coursed through him, but he forced it down. Maybe she had gone to visit with Little Turtle and lost track of the time.

He left the wickiup, striding swiftly across the village until he came to the hut that housed Crooked Lance and his family.

"Well, Lone Wolf," Brave Eagle said, exiting from the hut. "What are you doing here? I thought you would be well occupied with your wife."

"And so I would be if she had been there, Brave Eagle," Lone Wolf told his friend. "I thought to find her with Little Turtle. Is she not inside?"

"No," Brave Eagle said, looking curiously at his friend. "Little Turtle is inside but Rebecca is not with her. If you like, I'll ask her if she has seen your wife." At Lone Wolf's nod, he entered the wickiup again, returning a moment later with Little Turtle.

"Brave Eagle said Rebecca is missing," Little Turtle said. Her dark lustrous eyes were worried as they watched Lone Wolf. "We went bathing earlier today, but I had to leave. I had—things to do, and you had told me there was no need to watch her anymore so I did not stay. I have not seen her since that time."

"When was this?" Against his will, Lone Wolf's fear began to grow inside of him, a fear he was unwilling to admit—even to himself. But, despite his efforts, it began to surface. Had he been wrong to trust her after all? Did she still want to escape?

"I left Rebecca when the sun was high in the sky," Little Turtle admitted. "She said she would only be a little while longer. She should have returned long ago."

"Where would she be if not with you?" Lone Wolf asked. "Has she made other friends in the village?"

"No. Maybe, though, she has become lost," Little Turtle suggested with a frown.

"Lost?" His voice was grim, his gray eyes disbelieving. "It would be hard to become lost on the way back from the river. Rebecca has made a habit of bathing in the river daily, so she is well used to the trail. No, I don't believe she would get lost."

"Then what does it mean? Surely you do not think she has run away and returned to her people?"

"No!" he said harshly. "She wouldn't do that!" There was no way he could accept that she had left him voluntarily. Not with the memory of Rebecca lying naked beneath him, moaning with the pleasure that he alone could bring her.

"Don't worry, Lone Wolf," Brave Eagle said. "We will call the braves together and help you search. We will find Rebecca before any harm can come to her."

"No," Lone Wolf said. "I will handle it. There is no need to let the village know she is missing. There is enough ill feeling against her already." He frowned. "Time enough to call out the braves after I have searched the area thoroughly."

Brave Eagle nodded his understanding. "You are probably right," he said. He nodded toward Slow Otter's widow, coming from the river with her water gourd. She was edging stealthily toward them, and she seemed very intent on hearing their conversation.

Lone Wolf threw an angry glare at her as he left to search the river area for his missing wife.

The villagers had been slow to accept his wife, and, if Slow Otter's widow found out Rebecca was missing, she would do her best to make the People believe the pale-skinned girl had run away.

The sun had disappeared from the horizon, the afterglow of orange and red was quickly fading, and the blackness of night would soon be upon him. In the growing dusk, Lone Wolf nearly missed the basket that sat upright in the underbrush. Almost as though it had been placed carefully there by loving hands.

He stooped down and picked it up, noting it had been filled to capacity with wild onions and turnips. He had no trouble identifying the basket as Rebecca's, woven patiently by her own hands while he sat in the evening and watched. If something had happened to her, surely the vegetables would have been scattered, the basket overturned.

A feeling of dread came over him, and his gray eyes darkened with pain. His fingers clenched on the basket as he faced the possibility that she had left him. Either her brother had found her alone in the forest and taken her away or she had gone alone. Pain stabbed through him and he felt an aching loneliness.

No!

He refused to let her go.

His mouth tightened grimly, his gray eyes were cold. Rebecca belonged to him, and no matter how far she traveled—no matter where she went—some way he would find her.

And when he did . . .

* * *

Rebecca twisted frantically, trying to shake Black
Bear loose as he pulled her skirt higher, exposing her
thighs to his lustful gaze. Sh_____ feel
_____With
_____rd at
_____sen a
_____astily.

She gasped as his hands moved across the soft
mound between her legs, bucking frantically beneath
him, trying to throw him off. But her movements only
served to enflame him further.

He pushed her blouse up, exposing the creamy white
flesh to his lustful gaze. Then his head lowered toward
the high, firm breasts.

Horrified, disgusted at the thought of him suckling
at her breast, she grappled with his head, got a handful
of coarse black hair and, with her bound hands,
yanked hard.

His head came up and he glared his hatred at her.
Then, slowly, grinning savagely, he cuffed her on the
side of the head. With her ears still ringing, she felt his
turgid member pressing against her thigh. At the same
time, she felt something sharp pressing against her
side.

It was his knife!

If she could manage to get it—if she could pull it
from the sheath, she might be able to . . .

She jerked again at her wrists, moving the rawhide
in zigzagging motions and feeling it loosen a little
more. Elation and disgust filled her at the same time.
As the rawhide fell free, his wet, moist mouth found
her nipple, biting down hard.

She ignored the pain he was inflicting as her hand went unerringly to the knife handle. Grasping it firmly, she pulled it from its sheath and stabbed wildly at him.

The knife plunged into the man's shoulder, and he cried out and rolled to one side, his fingers reaching for the wound.

Quickly, she scrambled to her feet, the bloody knife in her hand. She looked at it numbly, casting one desperate look at her tormentor who was staring dumbly at his wounded shoulder. Knowing she had only seconds before he recovered his wits, she darted away through the forest of pine trees.

The last sight she had of him, he was still kneeling on the ground trying to staunch the flow of blood on his shoulder with the same dirty rag he had stuffed in her mouth.

She realized she had gained little time when only seconds later she heard the thunder of his pursuing footsteps, but the darkness was in her favor.

She ran mindlessly through the forest, clutching the bloody knife in her hand, deflecting the backlashing branches with her upraised elbows, and soon the throb of her heart covered Black Bear's pursuit.

Slashing branches.

Moccasins pounding on the forest floor.

Thundering heartbeats, throbbing temples, breath coming in short, painful gasps—these things now filled her world as she raced headlong through the forest.

She tripped over a log, lost her grip on the knife, and fell sprawling to her knees. Losing precious time, she scrambled frantically through the dirt and pine needles, searching for the knife.

She heard him crashing through the underbrush,

closer now. Despite his wound, he was gaining on her.

No time to find the knife!

Run! Run! Get away while you can!

In an instant she was up again, dashing away from the horror chasing her. Her eyes wide and terrified, she kept looking over her shoulder.

How close was he now?

Too close.

She stumbled on.

Then, during one of her backward glances, she thudded against a yielding wall of solid flesh.

Her blue eyes filled with horror, and she croaked out a guttural scream. It was cut short by a hand clamped over her mouth, and once again she began to struggle desperately.

How did Black Bear manage to get in front of her?

Her flailing feet connected with a shin and her captor bit out a curse, his hands tightening on her, digging into her soft flesh.

"Be still, Rebecca," a deep male voice ordered harshly.

Lone Wolf? Thank God! The fight drained out of her, and she sagged limply against his hard, muscular body.

Slowly, he removed his hand from her mouth.

"So, Little Blue Eyes, you would run from me after all." Lone Wolf's steely tone sent shivers coursing through her body.

She drew herself proudly erect. "You're jumping to the wrong conclusions," she said. Her blue eyes flashed defiantly. "I was running from Black Bear. He took me from the village this afternoon, and I've just now managed to escape."

Lone Wolf's gaze swept over her disheveled form. "You do not look the worse for it," he said, his voice velvet against steel. "Slightly mussed from your flight through the forest perhaps, but other than that, I'd say you look remarkably well."

"That's because Black Bear got the worst of it," she muttered, lowering her eyes to hide her pain. After all they had shared together, Lone Wolf didn't believe her, and she refused to beg his indulgence. "Whatever you may believe, he *was* chasing me."

He looked in the direction from which she had come, and the quiet forest seemed to give the lie to her words. "Then where is he?" he repeated, his mouth pressed into a thin line. "Has he disappeared into thin air? Or perhaps he is only a figment of your imagination." When she refused to answer, he said. "Do you really expect me to believe Black Bear had you alone in the forest and you escaped him?"

"I don't care what you think!" she snapped, turning away from him. She felt angry at his disbelief, but her feelings of hurt at his mistrust went even deeper, cutting her to the bone. She had thought in the month they had lived together there was more trust than that between them but apparently not where Lone Wolf was concerned.

"Just leave me alone," she said dispiritedly, turning her head away from him.

"I can't leave you alone," he said grimly. "I just wish I could. But before my people, I took you for my wife, and from now on, I am responsible for your actions. It is a husband's responsibility to control his wife by whatever means he can."

His hand gripped her chin, forcing her to look into

his blazing eyes. "And I mean to do just that, Rebecca. And another thing, I've told you before not to argue with me! It's not the Apache way, and I will not permit it." His face was dark with anger as he chastised her.

"I don't care whether you permit it or not," she snapped, refusing to be cowed. "I have a right to defend myself against false accusations."

"You have no rights except those I allow you," he said grimly. "Now, be quiet. I'll stand for no more from you. Now we must return to the village before everyone finds out you are missing. Little Turtle and Brave Eagle are worried about you. I must let them know I have recaptured you."

"Recaptured!" Her blue eyes opened wide, her mouth dropped open. She closed it with a snap. Was that the way he saw it?

Suddenly she slumped wearily as the fight drained out of her. What was the use anyway? He obviously wasn't going to believe her no matter what she said.

## Chapter Five

When they reached the village, it was as if she were arriving again for the first time. The sound of the piebald pony's hoofbeats brought the Indians out of the wickiups in force.

As Lone Wolf pulled the horse up, the villagers surrounded them en masse. Rebecca shivered as hostile faces stared with condemning eyes at her, and she knew, without a doubt, they believed she had tried to escape.

She recognized Slow Otter's widow standing near the wiry figure of Running Elk, her eyes blazing with hatred for Lone Wolf's pale-skinned wife. Shaken, Rebecca turned from the malevolent gaze, hiding her face against Lone Wolf's chest.

"No," he said grimly, his big body held stiffly erect. "Do not hide your face in shame! For whatever you have done, you are still the chosen wife of Lone Wolf. At least you can be proud of that."

That brought her up quick. Why should she hide herself from them? She had done nothing wrong and had no reason to feel shame. Her chin lifted to a defiant angle as she faced the crowd, meeting their eyes with a challenge in hers. She had been kidnapped by one of them through no fault of her own, and she intended to tell anyone who cared enough to ask.

Her cold eyes scanned the villagers, falling on Little Turtle standing near the edge of the crowd. Rebecca flinched, the Apache woman's face was as impassive as the rest.

Chief Tall Feathers emerged from his wickiup, his attention on the horse and his two riders.

"Get down!" Lone Wolf muttered between clenched teeth. "And don't disgrace yourself by falling!"

Rebecca glared at him, then, grabbing a handful of the piebald pony's mane, she slid to the ground. Her legs wobbled unsteadily, but she just managed to save herself from falling by gripping Lone Wolf's buckskin-clad leg.

"So. You have found the girl."

The menace in the voice caused Rebecca to pull herself straighter. She squared her shoulders defiantly and turned to face the speaker.

Her blue eyes were icy, her head lifted proudly, as she met Running Elk's mean, black eyes. She refused to be intimidated by this friend of Black Bear—this savage—who still carried Pete's scalp around on his lance.

Lone Wolf slid from the horse to stand beside her. He put a warning hand on her arm and gripped tightly. "Yes," he said calmly. "Of course I found her."

"Is she harmed in any way?" Chief Tall Feathers asked, his black eyes moving curiously over Rebecca.

"No." Lone Wolf's face showed no emotion.

Rebecca found it impossible not to defend herself.

"Yes, I was hurt," she snapped. "I was knocked out, tied up, and abducted!"

"Be still, woman!" Lone Wolf growled under his breath, his gray eyes glaring fiercely at her.

"No! I won't be still! I was abducted, I tell you! Black Bear found me on the path from the river and took me away!"

Running Elk stepped forward, his dark eyes mocking. "The woman lies! Black Bear could not have done this thing. He has been with me all day. We have just returned from a hunt, and he has not been near the river since sunrise. How could he have taken her?"

"Enough!" Lone Wolf snapped. He took Rebecca's arm in an iron grip and pulled her toward their wickiup. "This concerns only the woman and myself," he told the others. "She is my woman and I will deal with her."

As Lone Wolf pulled her away, Rebecca saw Brave Eagle take the piebald pony and lead him in the direction of the corrals. As Brave Eagle neared Little Turtle, he stopped to speak to her. They spoke earnestly for a moment before he continued on his way with the small Apache woman walking beside him.

Bitterly, feeling as though she had just been abandoned by her last friend, Rebecca entered the wickiup, and Lone Wolf threw her arm away from him as if her touch were distasteful.

"Prepare the food!" he snarled in a curt, biting tone. "I have waited long enough for my meal. You can wait until after I have filled my stomach for your punishment." His face, a hard mask of anger, frightened her, and the tension in the wickiup was so thick it could be cut with a knife. His eyes blazed into hers for a moment longer, then he dropped down onto the buffalo hide on the floor and crossed his arms and legs like some Far Eastern potentate.

She stared at him for a moment, her blue eyes wounded. She had been abused beyond belief today already, she was totally exhausted, and now he meant to humiliate her even further.

She turned on him, fuming, her eyes spitting blue flames. Then, suddenly she exploded. "If I'm to be punished for something I haven't done, then you can either get the meal yourself or go without!" she spat. Her eyes glittered brilliantly with tears of hurt, anger, and frustration, but she faced him defiantly, with tightly clenched fists, her nails digging tightly into her palms.

For a moment she thought her defiance would go unchecked as he stared at her, stupefied. Then, with panther swiftness, he was up, gripping her arms tightly, shaking her furiously until her teeth rattled.

She had had more to bear this day than could be expected of any one woman. Her eyes dulled as dizziness assailed her. Her legs seemed suddenly to be made of jelly. The last thing she saw was Lone Wolf's hard, angry, accusing eyes.

When she regained consciousness, she was lying stretched out on the sleeping mat. Slowly the memory of the day returned, and her eyes filled with tears. She sniffed once, the sound loud in the silence of the wickiup.

"Chiricahua women do not cry."

"I'm not a Chiricahua woman," she said with another

sniff, turning her head to see him sitting on a mat, the flickering firelight casting shadows across his impassive face. "And—and—I wasn't crying either," she denied, her voice quivering.

"Chiricahuas do not lie." The words were spoken almost sadly.

"I didn't lie about being taken away by Black Bear, Lone Wolf," she said, turning her head away from him. "And I refuse to admit to a lie just to satisfy you."

"It does not satisfy me to know you lie to me," he said softly, leaving the mat by the fire to come sit beside her. He gripped her chin firmly, forcing her to look at him. "Rebecca, Slow Otter's wife is demanding you be punished." His face seemed to be finely drawn, and there was something in his gray eyes that she could not define. Surely not sympathy for her plight?

"Have you decided how I'm to be punished?" she asked, swallowing convulsively.

"She demands to see you whipped."

Her face drained of color, and her fists clenched, but she knew it would do no good to protest her innocence. He hadn't believed her innocent before. Why should he now?

She moistened suddenly dry lips. "When?" she whispered.

"As soon as they make ready. But that is not all. Black Bear has demanded you be returned to him. He claims you are not a willing wife."

"Returned to Black Bear!" That snapped her head around. She sat up, gripped his arm tightly, her eyes fearful. "Lone Wolf, you can't let them do that to me! Surely you can stop them! I didn't run away, he abducted me!" She knew she was growing hysterical

91

but the memory of her recent escape was too fresh. "You've got to believe me. You don't know how that man treated me. He would have raped me if I hadn't grabbed his knife and stabbed him with it." She shuddered at the memory.

Suddenly her eyes widened. "I stabbed him!" she whispered shakily. "I stabbed Black Bear!" Her heart began beating fast with hope. She shook Lone Wolf's arm, her eyes appealing to him. "Don't you see, Lone Wolf? I can prove it. He has a wound in his shoulder where I stabbed him!" Her eyes were desperate as she pleaded. "Just go and look. He can't hide something like that."

Lone Wolf's eyes were piercing as he studied her face intently. "Why didn't you mention this before?"

"I forgot!" she said indignantly. The fear had drained away and she was suddenly sure of herself. For a wound such as she had delivered to her captor would be impossible to hide.

"You forgot you stabbed Black Bear with a knife to gain your release?"

"Yes, I did!" Her eyes were flashing angrily now. "Why are you wasting time sitting there? Why don't you go and find Black Bear? Then you'll see I'm telling the truth."

"There is no need."

"You believe me?"

"I did not say that."

"But I don't understand," she said, her face reflecting her confusion.

"There is no need to find Black Bear," he said slowly, "because I already know he has such a wound."

"There!" she said, her blue eyes glittering triumphantly. She tilted her chin at an imperious angle. "Now I expect an apology from you."

"You didn't mention the wound before," he repeated.

"I forgot it," she said, her elation beginning to drain away. Something was wrong. He should have been on his way to find Black Bear at this very moment. "What's the matter? If you've seen the wound already, then why don't you believe me?"

"Black Bear has such a wound but claims it was done when he fell on the knife this morning while crossing the river."

"He's lying!" she burst out. She grabbed his arm again, her fingers gripping him tightly. "Lone Wolf, I promise you, he's the one who's lying. Just ask yourself how I came to know of the wound."

"Running Elk backs him up. He said you knew about it because it happened this morning while you were at the river washing your clothing."

"But they are lying, Lone Wolf. Don't you see? Running Elk is his friend. He's the one who scalped Pete."

"Chiricahuas do not lie, Rebecca, and your friend's death has no bearing on this."

"Chiricahuas do not lie, but I do." She turned away from him bitterly, falling back on the mat to lie curled in a tight ball of pain. Tears coursed down her face, but she brushed at them angrily.

She felt his hand on her shoulder and shrugged it away. "Leave me alone," she said wearily. "At least, until it's time for the whipping to take place."

Expecting him to erupt in anger, she was thus surprised when he stood up from the mat and left her alone in the wickiup.

93

She lay there for a moment, trying to stop the flow of emotion, then finally gave way to her tears. For a long while she lay there, her shoulders heaving with silent sobs, the pain in her breast nearly unbearable at what she thought of as Lone Wolf's betrayal.

At length she closed her eyes tightly in an effort to stop the tears, but still they escaped from beneath her closed lids and coursed hotly down her cheeks as she pondered the hopelessness of her position. Finally, exhaustion took its toll and she fell into a deep, exhausted slumber.

When Lone Wolf entered the wickiup, he found Rebecca fast asleep. She never flickered an eyelash as he sat on the mat beside her. Her face was splotchy from her crying, her eyes reddened and swollen, her hair tousled and tangled, but still the sight of her brought tenderness to his heart. Reaching out, he wiped a tear from her lashes with a fingertip. Then, he picked up a strand of her long, silky brown hair and let it slide through his calloused fingers. It felt like silk against his roughened skin.

Tenderly, his eyes swept over her alluring body, dwelling on her full, rounded hips, small waist, and high, firm breasts. Then his gaze moved upward, coming to rest on her slender white throat. His gaze sharpened to alertness as he studied the welts that were turning a bluish-purple color.

Muttering an oath, he touched the bruises gently with his fingertips, pushing the buckskin aside to view the area more thoroughly.

Rebecca murmured in her sleep, pushing his hand

away as though he had hurt her.

Then he began to go over her body more thoroughly, noting the scratches on her face, arms, and legs that he suspected were made in her flight through the forest. But her wrists were another matter. He picked one up and noted the rough, chafed skin circling both her wrists. His face darkened grimly.

Pulling the doeskin blouse up, he searched the smooth, satiny skin for bruises. Pain speared through him and his face drained of color as he saw the marks around one rosy nipple — teeth marks — human teeth. He knew he hadn't caused the bruise because he was always very careful with her tender skin, but Rebecca hadn't done this to herself either.

A muscle twitched in his jaw, his mouth stretched into a thin line, and his eyes burned with unchecked rage. With narrowed eyes, he searched for further bruises, finding one along her rib cage. Then, he pulled the blouse down gently and left the wickiup.

Lone Wolf's long strides carried him swiftly across the clearing toward Black Bear's wickiup. He was only a few feet away when Running Elk stepped from his cousin's dwelling. Running Elk's hawkish features became suddenly wary, his stance defensive as he saw the thunderous expression on Lone Wolf's face.

"You lied!" Lone Wolf spat, his lip curling contemptuously. He pulled his knife from its sheath. "Defend yourself."

"I had no part in it," Running Elk said defensively, his eyes sliding away from Lone Wolf's. "I was hunting, just as I said."

Lone Wolf's eyes flashed over the cowardly Indian's wiry figure. "If you want to continue to live, then leave the village."

Running Elk need no more encouragement. He left.

Lone Wolf watched him disappear into the forest, then turned to find She-Who-Walks-Like-A-Duck blocking the entrance of the wickiup. The Apache woman's flat, black eyes were hooded under heavy folds of flesh. Her face, as round as her body, was expressionless, but he sensed her nervousness.

"Black Bear is not here," she said, her eyes darting quickly away from him.

"Where is he?"

"Hunting in the forest."

"My cousin does not hunt in the darkness," Lone Wolf snapped. His eyes were cold as they watched her. "You need water, woman. Now is the time to get it."

Shrugging as though to say she had done all that could be expected of her, she went back into the hut. When she returned, she was carrying the water gourd.

Lone Wolf watched her waddle away, then entered the wickiup.

The firelight cast a sinister glow across Black Bear's face as he sat on a mat at the far side of the hut. A poultice of healing leaves was fixed to a small wound high upon his left shoulder. His right hand was hidden beneath his body. He glared at Lone Wolf with hate-filled eyes. "Why are you here?" he snarled.

"You know why I'm here."

"The woman lies!" Black Bear said, his lips peeling back in scorn. "She is trying to protect herself from punishment. She did not expect to be caught when she ran away."

"Where did you get the knife wound?"

"I fell on my knife. Running Elk has already told you this."

Lone Wolf stalked to the mat, gripped a handful of Black Bear's hair and pulled him to his feet with a violent motion. "You dared to lay your hands on my woman," he snarled, yanking hard on the squat Apache's head.

Suddenly, Black Bear drew back his right hand, and Lone Wolf saw the knife, glinting in the firelight. "She is rightfully mine," Black Bear said, his mean eyes glittering with hate. He squared off, flicking a couple of jabs at Lone Wolf, a thin, jeering smile on his lips. "You are not man enough for her," he scorned. "The white woman wanted me." He gave a confident laugh and made a lunge, slashing at Lone Wolf's belly.

Lone Wolf dodged, dancing away. Although rage burned within him, he still had not drawn his knife.

"I rode above her," Black Bear taunted. The man was so full of hatred he didn't see he was in danger of dying. He laughed maliciously. "I had my mouth on her. My body covered her, and she was full of fi—"

That was as far as he got. Lone Wolf had been pushed beyond the limit; he was completely out of control as the pent-up rage suddenly burst.

Leaping forward, Lone Wolf kicked the knife from Black Bear's hand and sent it spinning across the room. Then he struck his cousin a hard blow on the nose, feeling gristle crunch beneath his fist. Black Bear's eyes watered from the pain, and, before he could recover, Lone Wolf wound one hand in the coarse, black hair, and hit the squat Apache in the face again. The blow landed with a heavy thump, and Black Bear went down as if pole-axed.

For a moment, Black Bear lay stunned. Then giving a loud bellow of rage, he sprung to his feet and leaped for Lone Wolf's throat. Lone Wolf grinned savagely, stepped aside, and kicked his cousin in the belly and watched with satisfaction as Black Bear pitched forward, bent with agony.

Lone Wolf stood, with clenched fists, watching the other man flounder onto his hands and knees. He waited, grim and silent, until Black Bear regained his footing, then kicked him savagely in the ribs.

Black Bear's breathing was labored, he was sweating profusely, but he managed to stagger to his feet once again.

Lone Wolf closed in. He struck Black Bear with a thudding impact, knocking him over the fire that burned in the middle of the hut. He landed against the back of the wickiup with a crash and a loud yelp.

Lone Wolf grabbed him up, and hit him in the face with a loud clunk. Then he hit him again, and again, unaware that the other man had lapsed into unconsciousness until he felt a hand on his arm, pulling insistently.

"Come away, old friend," Brave Eagle's voice penetrated through the wall of hatred. "You have punished him enough."

"I should have killed him when we fought before. I was stupid, and she was the one who suffered." His voice was harsh with pain. "He abused her. He—"

"Don't think of it," Brave Eagle said. "He will think twice before he comes near her again."

"If he even speaks to her—I'll kill him!"

"Come away from here with me," Brave Eagle commanded. "His woman will see to him. You must clean yourself up." He smiled grimly. "I think all that blood on you is his."

Lone Wolf spared a glance for his cousin's fat wife. She was bending over a still-unconscious Black Bear. She raised her eyes and met his for a moment. Lone Wolf felt a moment of pity for her. She shrugged and turned back to care for her husband.

Just before dawn, Rebecca's eyelashes fluttered, and she sighed deeply, then opened her eyes. Her head was pillowed against a naked, bronzed chest—Lone Wolf's chest. She smiled, moving back slightly, and groaned. For some reason, her body was stiff and sore. Lone Wolf's arm tightened around her, and she tilted her head back until she could see his face.

His eyes were open, watching her, waiting. She smiled up at him, and his gray eyes reflected something almost like relief. Was something amiss?

"What's wrong?" she whispered.

He didn't answer. His palm cupped her chin, tilting her face up for his kiss. All thought of conversation went out of her head as his mouth closed upon hers. Her body was drawn tightly against him as if he intended to absorb her. At the insistent pressure of his lips, she parted hers, allowing his tongue entrance to the sweetness inside.

His hands searched the curves of her body, touching here, there, until her nipples stood erect on her swollen breasts. Soon, she was moaning with desire as his lips searched out her ear, her eyelids, moving over her face to return to her lips.

Then he was fumbling with her top, pulling away from her for a moment while he pulled it over her head. The skirt went the same way. He returned to her, and she felt his warm, naked body against her own naked flesh.

A thrill coursed through her as his mouth found her breast at the same moment that his hand covered the center of her desire. She shivered with excitement, but something lurked just beyond her reason, demanding to be heard. She ignored it as his mouth suckled her breast, teasing, sending ripples of pleasure coursing throughout her body.

Her hands traveled the hard muscles of his back, then with a groan, she threaded her fingers through his dark hair, clutching him tightly to her breast. She was squirming with the pleasure he was bringing her, twisting and arching against him in her need to have him even nearer.

"Please, Lone Wolf," she begged, her voice sounding strangely hoarse.

At the sound of her voice, his hand tightened on her soft mound. His manhood was pressed against her thigh, and it was hard and throbbing.

He lifted his head, his tongue laving the throbbing nipple, then tracing a burning path up to her shoulder, his teeth nipping gently, then moving on across to the delicate flesh of her throat.

When his lips touched the bruised flesh of her neck, memory flooded back. Her eyes opened wide, and she pushed wildly at his shoulders.

"Get off me!" she spat, her gaze filled with remembered pain. "Don't touch me!"

He closed his eyelids for a moment, shuddered, then

opened them again, his gray eyes smoldering as he stared at her. She wouldn't have been surprised at that moment if he had struck her, but astonishingly he rolled away and reached for his buckskin breeches.

She also reached for her buckskin clothing, wondering at his reaction to her words. Eyeing him warily, she donned her clothing, feeling hurt and confused.

For a moment there, she had forgotten what had taken place yesterday. Black Bear had abducted her and treated her horribly, and no one believed her. She was to be punished for running away.

But when?

Tears of frustration and hurt glittered in her eyes, but she forced them back unwilling that he should see her weakness.

"When is my punishment to take place?" she asked, watching him slide into his breeches and pull them up over his long legs and buttocks. She was determined to show no fear, but as he turned to face her her eyes skittered away from him.

Then, angry at her show of cowardice, she lifted her chin arrogantly, her eyes cold as they met his. She had nothing of which to be ashamed. If the Apaches had made up their mind to punish her, then there was nothing she could do to stop them. Her only hope had been Lone Wolf. She had tried reasoning with him, but it had done no good.

Well, so be it. She would not be cowed.

"When is the whipping to take place?" she asked, her voice quivering despite her efforts.

"Rebecca . . ." His eyes were compassionate. He took her hand, stroking the back gently, but she jerked it away from his touch.

Her eyes glittered. "I want no pity from you," she said grimly. "You control me now, but it won't last. One of these days Robert and the soldiers will find me. If I don't escape first," she muttered.

His gray eyes turned to flint, his mouth tightened into a thin line. He caught her chin tightly in one hand, his gaze boring into hers. "You'll never escape me, Rebecca. Be sure of that! I'll never let you go!"

"You can't be sure of that," she snapped, her eyes blazing with fury. "One day someone will become careless, and then I'll be gone." She knew, even as she uttered the words, she was only making it harder on herself. But his betrayal cut deep, and she was determined that he would not come to learn how much she cared for him. Even now with a whipping awaiting her, it would be like cutting her heart out to leave him.

"I can be sure," he said grimly, his eyes glittering savagely. "Today we leave here. We will travel to a place from which there can be no escape."

"You're taking me away?" she faltered, her eyes suddenly stricken. He was taking her away where she would not even have Little Turtle, who had been such a comfort to her during the bad times this past month.

She put her hand on his arm, swallowing hard. Her blue eyes held his glittering gaze. "Lone Wolf," she said, searching desperately for the words to repair the damage she had done. "I was angry. I didn't mean it. I wouldn't try to escape. Really, I wouldn't." She might as well have been talking to the wall for all the attention he paid to her.

"Pack the food and supplies, Rebecca," he said sternly. "I will come for you at midday."

Rebecca sat on the sleeping mat stunned. She

watched him leave the wickiup. Where was he taking her? He had said it was some place from which there would be no escape. But where could there be such a place? Her mind couldn't even comprehend the horrors that obviously awaited her. And what would happen when they arrived at this place? Would he stay with her, or was she to be left there alone?

She was still staring horrified at the entrance when Little Turtle's figure suddenly filled it. At the look on the face of her friend, Little Turtle knelt beside her and took her in her arms.

"He's taking me away," Rebecca said, her eyes sad and haunted.

"I know," Little Turtle said gently. "But it is for the best. And at least the threat of punishment is over. I was so worried about you." Her eyes were dark and luminous as she held Rebecca against her.

"I'm not going to be whipped?"

"No. Didn't Lone Wolf tell you?"

Rebecca shook her head. "Do you know where he's taking me?"

"No. He didn't tell the council. He just said he was taking you away until you are with child."

"Until I'm what?" Rebecca asked, drawing herself away from the comfort of her friend's arms. Her eyes flashed indignantly.

"With child."

"If that means what I think it means, then he's crazy!" Rebecca snapped. Suddenly the idea of having Lone Wolf's baby sounded appealing, but she refused to let it show. She lowered her eyelids, hiding her expression from Little Turtle.

"Rebecca, you must learn to curb your wayward

103

tongue," Little Turtle said sternly. "You only make it harder on yourself by these outbursts. Lone Wolf is your husband and you must abide by his decisions without ever questioning them. It is the way of the Chiricahua."

"Well, I'm not of the tribe."

"It would be just as well if you were. Then the feeling against you would not be so high."

"I know I am in disgrace again," Rebecca said, her mouth twisting wryly. The hostile faces of the villagers were still fresh in her memory. "But, Little Turtle," she gripped her friend's arm tightly. "I was telling the truth. Black Bear did take me."

Little Turtle's ebony eyes searched Rebecca's face. Then she said slowly. "Black Bear says you are an unwilling wife to Lone Wolf. He is demanding that you be returned to him."

"But that won't happen now," Rebecca said, watching the little Apache woman closely, needing some sign of reassurance.

"No. That is why Lone Wolf is taking you away from the rancheria. He has told Chief Tall Feathers that he will not return with you until you are carrying his child." Her eyes studied Rebecca's face, then she seemed to come to some kind of decision. "Last night there was a fight between Lone Wolf and Black Bear. No one knows what caused it, but Black Bear was badly beaten."

"Lone Wolf fought with Black Bear?" Sudden hope flared in Rebecca's eyes, then quickly dimmed. More than likely, it had nothing to do with her. There had been a natural enmity between the two cousins for years.

"Yes." The small Apache woman rose gracefully from the pallet. "We must waste no more time. Lone Wolf has demanded that you be ready to travel by the time the sun has reached its peak. And there is much to do to make ready. The blankets must be folded, the provisions stored, and you must even take your cooking pot down for it will be needed when you reach your destination. At least Lone Wolf has said there is no need to make firewood, so there must be plenty where you'll be going."

*Or maybe he just doesn't figure I'll need any,"* Rebecca thought crossly, feeling dejected at the thought of losing her only friend. *Maybe he thinks I'll be too busy getting pregnant with his baby to get cool enough to warrant a fire.*

Despite herself, the idea of Lone Wolf's baby brought a flush to her body. His baby. Somehow the thought caused a great satisfaction to steal over her. Just the thought of his child, nestled comfortingly against her breast, made her come to life.

"Well," she said, rising to her feet. "If I must be ready by noon, then I should waste no more time. I am keeping you from your chores, so let's get the packing over with and you can show me how to load it up."

Little Turtle's lips lifted into a smile as she watched the animation in her friend's face. Her lustrous, ebony eyes held a knowledge older than time. "I will miss you, Rebecca," she said softly.

"And I'll miss you," Rebecca answered, throwing her a swift smile as she reached for a parfleche filled with strips of pemmican that hung high on the wall of the wickiup. She frowned, as her fingers barely touched the bottom of the buffalo-hide pouch.

"Why does Lone Wolf hang these things so high?"

105

she grumbled, making a leap for the bag. Her grab was successful and she landed on the floor with it clutched firmly in her fist. Tossing it on the sleeping mat, she eyed the dozen or more parfleches hanging around the top of the wickiup. Her gaze moved over her friend's petite figure.

"You're even shorter than I am," she said, frowning. She watched Little Turtle fold a blanket neatly. "I think Lone Wolf must have hung these bags in the ceiling. Do you think he would mind taking them down when he comes back?"

"No. I think he will not mind," Little Turtle said wryly. "He is a kind husband."

Rebecca grimaced, remembering his unjustified anger with her. "Well, as to that — we'll have to disagree, I'm afraid."

"You must learn to obey him, Rebecca," the little woman said gently. "An Apache brave expects instant obedience in all things. It is his right."

"Hogwash!" Rebecca said rudely.

At Little Turtle's puzzled look, her eyes sparkled with amusement. "Never mind, Little Turtle," she said, her lips quirking in a smile. "It's just a rude expression."

"The washing of pigs is rude?"

Rebecca laughed, the sound ringing out in the wickiup, and it was at that moment that Lone Wolf appeared.

"What is so funny?" he demanded, his gray eyes unfathomable as they gazed searchingly into hers.

Remembering how hateful he had been to her before, her good mood suddenly disappeared as though it had never been. "Never mind," she snapped.

"It's no concern of yours."

"Every breath you take is my concern," he said sharply, her words cutting deep into his body, penetrating to the core of his being. "It will serve you well to remember that."

With the words still ringing in her ears, he turned on his heel and left the wickiup to the women.

# Chapter Six

The water sparkled and shimmered with sunlight, but the man standing on the rock stripping the buckskin breeches from his bronzed body failed to notice. Nor did he notice the buck, standing quiet and still, watching from the verdant green forest a few hundred yards away. His thoughts were turned inward and he cursed himself.

*Dammit! What's the matter with me?* Lone Wolf kicked his breeches aside savagely, taking out his anger with himself on the apparel.

*Why didn't I apologize like I intended? Why didn't I beg her forgiveness instead of snarling like some wild animal?*

He dove into the water and emerged farther out in the river, moving through the stream with the skill of an accomplished swimmer. The water rippled turbulently around his muscular body as he cut through it with powerful strokes. His mouth was drawn into a thin line as he tried to ease his frustration by tiring himself out.

\* \* \*

When Lone Wolf returned, Little Turtle had just left. He took the buckskin bags down from the top of the wickiup and added them to the other supplies stacked in the corner. Then, his gaze fell on the cooking pot, his nostrils twitching at the aromatic aroma coming from within.

"I thought you might be hungry," she said quietly, answering his questioning gaze.

"I am hungry," he said, his eyes softening. "In more ways than one."

Despite herself, she blushed. He smiled, taking note of the color washing over her face. His gray eyes were warm as he sat down and began his meal. She sighed with relief. Perhaps the hostilities were finally over between them. She hated it when he was angry with her.

He sat down near the fire, helping himself to the fresh, venison stew. "Have you eaten?" he asked, spooning another bite into his mouth.

"Yes." She smiled at him. "It's a good thing, too. The way you're putting it away, there won't be anything left when you're finished."

He scraped the bowl with his spoon. "I was hungry. I didn't eat much yesterday." Something in her silence alerted him and he looked up. His eyes grew pained and he swallowed heavily, putting the bowl down.

"I did not mean to speak of it, Little Blue Eyes. I meant to put it behind us."

"Never mind," she said huskily. "It's all right." She felt encouraged that he wanted to make a new beginning and was determined that nothing should get in the way.

"No, it is not all right," Lone Wolf said, rising to take her in his arms. He tilted her chin, forcing her to meet his eyes. "Come with me," he whispered huskily. "I have something to put a smile on your lovely face."

He took her hand, leading her from the wickiup, and her eyes lit up at the sight of Diablo, saddled and obviously waiting for a rider, standing with Lone Wolf's piebald pony beside the packhorse she and Little Turtle had loaded earlier.

"You didn't sell him after all!" she whispered huskily, laying her forehead against Diablo's silky nose. Tears welled up into her eyes, and she blinked them back furiously. She hadn't seen him since she arrived at the Apache village. Many times she had started to ask Lone Wolf what had happened to him but had been afraid of what his answer might be.

"Come, Rebecca," Lone Wolf said firmly, taking her arm. "My people are looking on. This show of emotion is unbecoming to a Chiricahua woman."

She lifted her head, her blue eyes mirroring her delight. She felt no resentment at his words, for, although he admonished her with a frown, his gray eyes were gentle. He seemed to know without being told how much Diablo meant to her.

"Thank you, Lone Wolf," she said softly, running her hand along Diablo's long, smooth neck.

She was certain he almost smiled before he said abruptly, "It is time for us to leave. Get on your horse while I finish loading our supplies."

She nodded, mounted Diablo, settled herself into the saddle, and waited patiently for Lone Wolf to finish.

They traveled for the rest of the day, the April sunlight shining down on them, piercing the late spring foliage, and the fertile green earth. The pungent fragrance of new spring grasses, bursting from the ground, was sweet to her nostrils as the miles sped by.

She felt a sense of freedom she had never had before with her long brown hair blowing wildly in the wind. Her skin had turned to a light, golden brown since she had come to live with the Indians, and she knew it was becoming to her. Quite often she felt Lone Wolf's gaze rest on her.

Darkness had fallen by the time they stopped to make a temporary camp. Dismounting, she began to unload what she would need for the night.

She looked up in surprise when Lone Wolf came to help her, for she had learned the Apaches considered it demeaning for a brave to lower himself to do women's work.

When they had finished unloading the supplies, Lone Wolf said, "I will care for the horses, then gather the wood for a fire while you fetch the water and begin the meal."

She turned a startled look on him. "Gathering wood is women's work," she commented.

"Are you complaining because I do not allow you to do everything?" he asked, one dark brow shooting upward.

"No, of course not!" she said hastily, but her blue eyes showed her puzzlement. "It's just that I know it isn't usually done."

"Outside the village I feel bound by no rules except my own," he said in answer. "But you should keep in mind, Little Blue Eyes, that I have a reason for everything I do."

Now what did he mean by that? Bewildered, she watched him lead the horses away.

Frowning, she decided she would have to puzzle it

out later when she had more time to think. Right now, they needed water.

Picking up the empty water gourd, she followed a path that led to a nearby stream, working her way around fallen rocks worn smooth by the elements and time.

When she reached the stream, she cried out in delight. A small waterfall, formed by multileveled rocks, cascaded into a natural pool at its base. Surrounding the pool, a dazzling growth of verdant green ferns grew in abundance, creating a fairyland effect.

Suddenly, she was overcome by an urge too strong to resist. Divesting herself of her clothing, she dove into the middle of the pool, surfacing a moment later on the other side. She laughed in delight, wiping away the water streaming from her face. She could actually feel herself relaxing, the cares of the past slipping away as she cavorted in the water, unmindful of the passing of time, reluctant to give up the cool luxury of the stream.

Lone Wolf tossed the armload of firewood near the fire he had lit earlier. Then, casting an anxious glance down the path that Rebecca had followed, he began to stack the wood carefully. She would come, he told himself. She hadn't really been gone very long, it just seemed that way. He would only make a fool of himself if he went looking for her.

She hadn't really meant it when she said she would escape the first chance she had. She had only been speaking in anger. He should have told her when he found out she spoke the truth about her abduction. He had returned to the hut with the intention of telling her, but she had become angry with him. And he had decided not to say anything, knowing it was important for her to accept the Apache way of life. She must learn that a husband had no need to explain his actions.

He threw another look down the pathway. What was keeping her? Surely, he had not misjudged the distance to the stream.

He fed another stick to the flames. She would not try to escape him. Not without her horse. But suppose something had happened to her? After all, there were many dangers in the forest. Perhaps someone had come along and surprised her. Perhaps Black Bear had . . .

Rebecca lowered the water gourd, dipping it into the clear water, and filled it completely to the brim. She was completely relaxed from her swim and she hummed softly to herself.

As she straightened up, she felt the strain in her back and grinned ruefully, setting the gourd down while she massaged the tight muscles in her lower back.

She had never done any kind of manual labor until she was stolen from her home. Aunt Bess, with whom she had lived back east in Pittsburgh, had always kept a houseful of servants to do the chores. And even at the ranch there was plenty of help. How the Apache women held up so well was beyond her imagination. For all that, they enjoyed surprisingly good health considering there were no doctors available to them.

A sharp, crackling sound broke the silence, and she turned, her heart beating wildly, to find Lone Wolf coming from the forest. His gray eyes were dark with emotion.

"Where have you been?" he demanded, his voice grating harshly in her ears.

"Right—right here," she stuttered, staring at him warily. She tingled with apprehension.

He reached out, caught her upper arms in his rough grip. "What kind of game are you playing?" he asked, drawing her against the muscular wall of his body. "I have been waiting for my meal."

"I—I only went for a swim," she said apprehensively, trying to collect her scattered wits.

"A swim!" His tightly leashed control snapped. The dammed-up fury broke loose, darkening his eyes, knitting his dark brows together. His fingers dug sharply into her flesh as he held her in an unrelenting grip. His knuckles were white as he shook her savagely. His face was so close to hers, she could feel his breath on her cheeks.

Suddenly, she began to struggle. "Let go of me, you bastard!" she spat just as furious as he was.

"What did you call me?"

The tone of his voice warned her, and for a moment she hesitated, afraid she had gone too far. But, then her chin lifted belligerently. He had no reason to chastise her! She had done nothing wrong!

"I called you a bastard!" she snapped, glaring at him defiantly. "And that's exactly what you are. A bastard!"

She was unprepared for the blow. He slapped her on the cheek with his open palm, snapping her head around. Her breath caught in her throat, and she felt completely stunned. Unbidden tears filled her eyes, and she put a hand to her stinging face.

"Never call me that again!" he threatened, his eyes

black with fury. Then suddenly, he released her, turning on his heels, leaving her standing at the pool.

Rebecca felt chilled as she stood alone where he had left her. Her hand held her stinging cheek where he had delivered the blow. She felt cold, abused, sick at heart, and so very, very much alone.

Feeling a numbness creep in, she picked up the water gourd, then walked up the path to the camp. Lone Wolf leaned against the thick trunk of a pine tree, gazing broodingly into the fire. He ignored her as she went about preparing the meal. It didn't take long, for the Indian diet on the trail consisted mostly of pemmican or jerky and dried vegetables.

By the time she placed the food before him, the fire had burned low. She added another stick of wood to keep the fire burning, and the burned-out logs hissed and flared, sending sparks shooting into the night as the wood broke apart.

She watched the display of fireworks for a moment, then, choosing a spot some distance from Lone Wolf, sat down to eat. Although she was determined not to look at him, she felt Lone Wolf's flinty gaze. She could feel the tension emanating from his large frame and a sudden chill shivered up her spine.

*What does he want from me anyway?*

*Could he be waiting for an apology?*

*Well, he would have a long wait.*

She raised a hand to touch her still-reddened cheek, flicked her eyes quickly in his direction, and wished she hadn't.

His mouth was compressed into a thin, angry line, his eyes hard as he watched her.

The orange moon cast its pale light down on them,

merging with the flickering flames from the small fire, casting shadows across the bronzed planes of his face to make him appear almost satanic.

Nervously, she bit off a piece of venison, chewing it thoroughly before trying to force it past the lump lodged in her throat.

It was long past time for bed, and she knew they needed rest, but still she remained unmoving, delaying the inevitable. As the fire began to diminish again, she added another log, laying it on the smoldering embers, watching the sparks spew as it caught flame.

When Lone Wolf finally moved, she was startled. She eyed him warily as he rose from his cross-legged position. "It is time to sleep," he said, his voice deceptively calm. "We have a long journey ahead of us tomorrow."

She nodded. Although she had been dreading the thought of bed, she knew he was right. Her back and thigh muscles were sore from the unaccustomed ride, and they screamed out for rest.

Her neck began to ache from tension as she moved about the camp, storing the uneaten food. His gaze never wavered from her and her body was stiff with dread, her movements automatic. Although she was desperately tired, she was afraid to go to bed with him. The memory of his harshness at the pool was still too fresh in her memory.

"Have you finished?"

His voice startled her, and she instinctively flinched away from his hand on her elbow. His eyes darkened with fury as she retreated a step.

"What is wrong with you?" he demanded harshly, dropping her arm as if it scorched him.

"No—nothing." Her voice quivered. "You just startled me."

With lips compressed into a thin line, he motioned her toward the buckskin robes he had made ready for them. She wondered if she dared suggest separate sleeping arrangements.

She steeled herself to impassivity, following behind him, stopping beside the makeshift bed while he stripped his buckskin breeches off, then slipped beneath the cover, and turned to watch her, his gaze burning into her as she stood hesitantly watching him.

"Come to bed," he said huskily, his voice purposely seductive, beckoning her.

But she couldn't!

Her feet were frozen to the ground; her fear too great. "Lone—Lone Wolf," she stuttered, wrapping her arms around herself, lowering her eyelids, hiding her expression. He must not see her fear. "I—I'm very tired . . ."

A muscle twitched in his jaw. "Come to bed," he grated harshly, his gray eyes becoming savage.

Knowing she had no other recourse, she turned her back to him, completely hiding her expression, and began to undress. Then, unable to delay longer, she slipped into the bed beside him and lay still, her body quivering, nerves stretched as tautly as bowstrings.

She felt his hand on her breast and gritted her teeth to stop them chattering. If only he wouldn't make love to her now. Not while he was still angry.

And he had no right to his anger!

Suddenly, her sense of injustice that she could be treated so overcame her fear. She glared at him in the darkness as his hands roamed her body. She was

117

determined to maintain complete indifference to his love-making.

But slowly, against her will, her body betrayed her. As one calloused hand cupped her breast, she felt it swelling to his touch. Long fingers searched out her nipple, teasing the sensitive tip until it stood fully erect.

His lips touched her closed eyelids gently and her nose, then continued their searching quest until they found her mouth.

At her continued resistance, his hand cupped her chin, holding her still while he forced her lips apart, probing them with his tongue, causing a sensual warmth that started a languorous yearning deep inside her.

As he lifted his head, she opened her eyes, staring dumbly into his watchful face. Her resistance had been weakened, anger and fear draining away as though it had never existed.

As his head lowered again, she watched, hypnotized by the intent stare in his eyes. Then his mouth was on hers, his hands roaming her body at will, touching, teasing, tantalizing until, with a groan, her arms slid around his neck, urging him closer.

Her fingers tangled in his dark hair, then moved against the back of his head, feeling the tension of the muscles in his nape.

Burying his face in the side of her neck, his mouth sent a trail of fire everywhere it touched. Strong fingers molded her body lovingly until her body was arching into his, pleading without words for the fulfillment that only he could bring.

With their mouths still entwined, he lifted his body,

then fitted it over hers, parting her thighs with his own. She moaned low in her throat as she felt the heat of his throbbing masculinity poised against her.

Then, he thrust, entering her deeply, muffling her gasp of pleasure with a searing kiss. Her senses were reeling as he began to move against her. His thrusts set her body afire, burning with a mindless passion as he took her higher and higher until at last a cry broke from her lips, escaping as she reached ecstatic heights, then plunged over the other side, shuddering rapturously with her release.

As her breathing quieted, she snuggled against his hard, muscled body, content to be lying in his arms. She finally faced the fact that fighting against her love for him was useless. Even though he angered her and at times caused her to be fearful, he was everything she could ever want in a man. There could be no escape for her for she belonged to him totally now, body and soul.

With a shy smile, she raised love-filled eyes to him and flinched, her eyes suddenly stricken. He was watching her, triumph glittering in his cold, gray eyes. His insolent gaze traveled slowly down her naked body, and she felt a chill slide down her spine.

She drew herself away from him as sharp pain slashed through her. It was obvious he had acted with deliberate calculation in arousing her. All the while he had been making love to her, he had felt nothing. He had only set out to prove she was unable to resist him.

Unbearably hurt, she turned over, lying with her back to him, while silent tears slipped slowly down her cheeks. She huddled in a cold ball of misery lying beside the man she loved, loneliness and despair washing over her. She felt abused and humiliated beyond belief, desolated that the man she loved could treat her so unfeelingly. Finally, his even breathing told her he was asleep.

As she lay there, wallowing in her misery, an idea began to take form in her mind. She wiped the remaining tears impatiently from her face as she turned it over and over, considering the possibilities. Instead of feeling sorry for her circumstances, it was time she quit crying and did something about them.

Her Apache husband had made it plain that he did not return her feelings. To him she was only a possession, and people had a habit of becoming bored with their possessions after awhile. He could grow tired of her and take another wife, someone who might take a dislike to her, and then what would be her fate?

If there were to be discord between his two wives, then he might even take it into his head to sell her. At that thought, a feeling of dread came over her.

She refused to let it happen!

Slipping quietly from the buckskin robes, she stood motionless until she was certain her husband was still sound asleep. Then, moving quietly, she donned her clothing, all the while casting anxious glances toward the man who was still sleeping—unaware of her plans.

When she had finished dressing, she took one last, lingering look at Lone Wolf, her Chiricahua husband. A deep sense of loneliness washed over her. She would never see him again, never feel his warm embrace.

Her eyes welled with tears, and she nearly changed her mind. But she blinked them away furiously, remembering his anger, his contempt. Her blue eyes chilled and her mouth compressed grimly. It was foolish to cry over such a man. She must leave him.

She had no choice and she must do it now.

Silently, she crept away to the clearing where the horses were tethered. Diablo snorted as he recognized her, and her heart beat wildly as she scrambled on his back, wishing she had her saddle but knowing she dared not risk trying to saddle him. She started at every sound, expecting discovery at any moment. As silence held, she twined her hand in Diablo's mane and walked him as silently as possible away from the camp.

As soon as she deemed they were far enough away, she dug her heels into Diablo's flanks, urging him into a gallop, feeling the need to put as much distance between Lone Wolf and herself as possible.

The full moon cast its pale glow on the black horse and rider, giving them almost a ghostly appearance as the miles fell away beneath the hooves of the big, black stallion.

She did not allow herself to think as she continued on her way south for she was in territory that she was unfamiliar with, and, not used to riding bareback, she found it was all she could do to stay on Diablo. Because of the darkness, she had to rely totally on him, praying that he would not step in a rabbit hole in their flight homeward.

On and on they rode through the black night, away from Lone Wolf, her Apache husband, her lover, her tormentor.


In the half-gray light that precedes dawn, Lone Wolf woke with a start and his eyes snapped open. Something—some sound—had reached into his dreams, pulling him awake. He turned automatically, reaching for Rebecca and encountering nothing but emptiness.

She was gone.

Instantly alert, he sat up, his brows pulled together in a frown. Where was she? Pulling on his breeches and moccasins, he rose. His narrowed gray eyes were anxious as they probed the surrounding area—trees, bushes—nothing.

*Control yourself. She's only at the pool bathing.*

He strode grimly down the path, his eyes scouring the forest as he went, trying to quell his sense of urgency. A moment later he arrived at the pool. There was no sign of Rebecca.

Alarm clutched at him, sending tiny fingers of chills spreading down his spine. Forcing down his panic, he returned to the camp, his eyes intent on the ground as he searched for signs.

Stopping beside their bed of buffalo skins, he picked out Rebecca's moccasin prints and followed them, his pulses quickening as the tracks led toward the glade where he had picketed the horses overnight. Rebecca's face as he had seen it last—her eyes wide with hurt— rose in his mind. It came as no surprise to find Diablo missing.

She had run away from him.

Cursing, he put Diablo's saddle on the packhorse, and quickly broke camp. The big black stallion's tracks were easy to follow for Rebecca had made no attempt to cover their trail. She seemed to be more concerned with getting a good lead on him and she had accomplished that. The nearest he could figure, she was a good six hours ahead of him.

His eyes were cold, his expression grim as he followed Diablo's tracks. As the sun burst over the horizon, he encountered rocky ground and found himself backtracking. It took over an hour before he was on the trail again, his face even grimmer.

The sun had drifted low in the afternoon sky when he cut the trail of a small band of Crows on the move. As their paths crossed Rebecca's, they turned their mounts to follow. A hard kick of emotion hit him in the stomach but he gave no sign, intent on reading the tracks.

Raw with tension, his eyes began to blaze as he turned his mount to follow the tracks of the Indians and his wife. He refused to allow himself to dwell on what would happen to Rebecca before he could reach her.

# Chapter Seven

The morning sun burst over the horizon, touching the tops of the pine trees with a bright burst of color. Its rays barely penetrated the darkness hovering beneath the branches of a giant willow tree where the black stallion waited patiently for its rider to dismount.

Heaving a tired sigh, Rebecca slid off Diablo beside a creek that was little more than a trickle and allowed him to drink his fill. She bent over and splashed water on her face, then slumped dispiritedly on a bed of fern beneath the shimmering gray-green canopy of the willow growing near the stream.

Dropping her head wearily, she wrapped her arms around bent knees. She had been so certain she knew where she was, but she had been wrong for she had become hopelessly lost.

She had traveled around in circles without knowing it until the plains gave way to a forest of pine trees again.

Still, she couldn't worry overmuch about it, for her bruised heart carried vividly those last months with Lone Wolf—the way his lips had curled, his eyes raking over her nude form in that insulting way.

She shuddered. Her foolish heart had even dared believe he was coming to care for her, but his actions made her realize just how absurd it had been to build her hopes and dreams around him. Now she only wanted to escape, to go some place where she would never see him again.

Home. Home to Robert — her brother, Robert. He would never allow anyone to treat her as Lone Wolf had.

She lifted her head, her eyes burning with the desire to hurry on, to ride for home as fast as she could. This time, with the sun to guide her, she could find the way.

Then slowly her lashes drifted downward, down over the realization that she couldn't.

Diablo was tired. He had carried her throughout the night and needed time to graze on the new spring grass growing in such abundance beside the swiftly running stream.


She woke with a start, a tingle of fear running down her spine, the fine hairs on the back of her neck standing up. What had awakened her? Something — some sound — had broken into the fabric of her dreams.

Her pulse throbbed, all her senses alert, as her eyes swept the area. Was it possible Lone Wolf had found her already? She was certain he would come looking for her. And if he found her? She didn't even dare think of what might happen if he ever caught up with her.

Her searching gaze found nothing amiss, finally coming to rest on Diablo placidly cropping grass by the stream. He, at least, showed no sign of alarm.

Still, her skin prickled at a rustling in the underbrush, her startled eyes darting quickly, catching a fleeting movement.

"Oh, lord," she whispered, her heart pounding loudly in her chest. Although the sun was shining brightly overhead, the shrubbery was thick and shadowed, and the residue of a dream Rebecca couldn't even remember threw its own darkness across the day. Slowly, she rose to her feet, feeling at a distinct disadvantage from her position on the grassy earth.

Suddenly, a large, furry brown creature ran from the brush, freezing in position momentarily, nose twitching, then dashing quickly away.

Drawing a startled breath, she almost laughed aloud in relief. It was only a harmless marmot, nothing to cause her worry.

Realizing she had taken more time to rest than she had intended, she called quietly to Diablo. He lifted his head to look at her, perked his ears forward, and blew softly through his nose. Then he lowered his head and began chewing at the grass again.

Knowing it was past time to be on their way, she knelt beside the stream, dipping her cupped hands into the clear, sparkling water, and drank deeply. Then, catching sight of her reflection in the water, she studied it intently. Large, blue eyes set in a gold-bronzed face gazed back at her. She had confined her hair into two braids earlier for easier traveling, and in the doeskin dress she would easily pass for one of the women of the Apache tribe. That thought made her pause.

What would Robert say when he saw her? She couldn't even begin to imagine, but her appearance would surely cause him shock. She laughed wryly.

126

After all this time, no matter how she was dressed when she arrived, Robert couldn't help but be shocked.

Dipping her cupped hands in the water again, she splashed it over her face, allowing the cooling liquid to trickle down her neck.

Still dripping, she rose. Now she could be on her way. She turned toward the horse, then stopped in mid-turn, a cry slipping from her lips. An Indian warrior, his face streaked with red war paint, dressed only in a breechclout and moccasins stood before her.

Instinctively, she stepped backward, into a hole that sent her sprawling. Grinning maliciously, he reached for her, but she reacted instantly, regaining her feet in a single movement.

She backed away from him slowly, her arms lifted protectively in front of her. His naked bronze chest glistened with sweat as he approached, his flat black eyes glinted wickedly.

Suddenly, to her horror, she saw a second warrior rise from the brush and join the first.

She retreated slowly, shaking her head back and forth with disbelief. Her face was drained of color, her eyes wide and staring as the Indian warriors stalked her, seeming to take pleasure in her utter helplessness.

*Lone Wolf! Help me!*

She knew the cry was useless. No one could help her now. Lone Wolf was countless miles away, and she had no one but herself to rely on.

She broke into a run, racing through the dense forest. Branches tore at her hair and exposed flesh as she ran, but she ignored them, running, arms pumping, feet flying as fast as they could.

Long, drooping briars tore at her shirt, digging into

her bare arms. She barely felt the pain. She heard a tremendous rustling and crackling behind her, could almost feel their hot breath as she ran, unheeding of the noise she was making, her only thought to get away from them.

Her breath was labored, coming in sharp gasps and she had a pain in her side but her fear drove her. A thicket grew across the pathway ahead. She knew it would slow her down. Her eyes searched frantically for a way out as her mind tried to deal with this new problem.

Go around!

Find another way!

She felt a hand grip her arm, but she tore it loose.

Suddenly, her legs gave way and she tumbled to the forest floor. For a moment she lay there, completely winded, unable to draw a single breath. Then, her tortured lungs began to expand, taking in large gulps of air. She lay flat on the ground, staring up into the murderous face of an Indian warrior.

Slowly, the Indian raised his arm, and her eyes fell on the tomahawk in his hand. His confident leer sent a chill of apprehension through her. Was this the end then? Would Lone Wolf ever know what had become of her?

A curious sense of resignation washed over her, but she fought the feeling. She lashed out with her fists, catching the brave that loomed above her with a hard blow on his legs. The blow proved ineffectual, serving only to make him sink down on her body, pressing the softness of her breasts into her rib cage.

His knees bit into her upper arms, and she swallowed raggedly, a cold sense of dread washing over her as she watched certain death approach. The tomahawk began its downward curve, and she felt a deep sadness wash through her. She would never see Lone Wolf again. The blow landed with a thud and darkness descended.

Rebecca's eyelids fluttered and she stirred as pain intruded on the darkness that held her in its grip. Her head pounded with a thousand war drums, and she closed her eyes tightly, trying to stop the hurt. She tried to lift a hand but found she couldn't.

Her breath caught sharply. What was wrong? Suddenly, she realized that both her hands were bound tightly behind her.

At the realization, memory flooded through her like swiftly flowing water. Cautiously, she opened her eyes. At first, her vision was blurred, and she saw everything through a misty haze.

She blinked rapidly, focusing on the flickering flames of the campfire just a few yards away. Her eyes widened, and fear surged through her. An Indian warrior sat cross-legged beside the fire, his head turned toward the creek where she could hear the sound of splashing water and voices, indicating there were more than just the two braves she had seen.

She tried to still the pain in her head. She had to concentrate. She had to figure out a plan of escape. She was leaning against something hard, something that gouged into her back. A tree. Her arms were stretched around it and bound together at the wrists behind the tree. She flexed her wrists, pulling against the rawhide bonds, and her arms scraped painfully against the bark.

As if some sound had alerted him, the brave stiff-ened. Quickly, she dropped her head, letting it loll against her chest. She felt the Indian's stare burning into her and knew that any moment he would get up from his position beside the fire and come to torment her.

Bitter tears stung her eyelids, but she refused to let them fall. She realized now that she had been a fool to leave Lone Wolf. She wondered what he had done when he had discovered her missing. How did he feel? Did he even care? Would he search for her, or just forget about her?

Lone Wolf worked his way quietly through the trees growing on the banks of the shallow creek, his nar-rowed gaze fixed on the smoke that wisped skyward ahead. Tension coiled tightly inside of him as he inched his way closer, unable to allow himself to even think about what he would find in the camp.

Over the sound of the splashing water he could hear the voices, low and indistinguishable as the men talked among themselves down by the water, hidden from view by a bend in the creek.

He moved stealthily, careful to stay in the shadows, out of the pale light cast by the full moon. He moved around a large boulder and found he could look down into their camp.

His lips tightened grimly, his eyes slight with a blazing need for vengeance. For there, tied to a tree about twenty feet from the fire, was Rebecca, her head lolling to one side, her chin resting on her chest as though she were unconscious. His stomach tied itself into knots as hatred flared anew. He would kill them all for daring to harm her.

Lone Wolf's gray eyes slitted narrowly on the lone brave left as guard. Although the small band of Crow Indians were obviously on the warpath, they weren't expecting any trouble. His lips stretched into a tight grin but there was no humor in it. They might not be expecting trouble, but they were sure as hell going to get it. But first, he had to get Rebecca free. He couldn't risk her getting killed.

As silent as a shadow, he crept through the underbrush until he knelt behind the tree where Rebecca was tied. Pulling his knife, he sawed at her bonds, willing her to be silent if she was conscious.

She started slightly at his touch and her breathing changed slightly. She lifted her head and slowly turned it in his direction.

Her eyes met his and they leaped with joy. The hard lines of his face softened and he crossed his lips with a commanding finger. She nodded, indicating she understood the need for silence.

As the leather bonds at her wrists parted, freeing her hands, the warrior beside the fire lifted his head. His eyes met Rebecca's and he stood and came toward her, grinning savagely.

He had nearly reached her when Lone Wolf rose from behind the tree and threw his knife; it flew through the air, and, as it penetrated deeply into the yielding flesh of his chest, the brave grunted, crumpling like a rag doll in the dust.

Lone Wolf moved swiftly, afraid that the brave's companions might have been alerted by some small sound. Bending over the fallen Crow warrior, he jerked his knife from the man's chest, wiping it down his breeches before returning to Rebecca.

"How many?" he whispered, his mouth against her ear.

She understood instantly and shook her head. She didn't know.

He nodded his head in understanding and pushed her into the bushes. His lips came against her ear again. "Horses back down the draw. Go to them, quickly. If I'm not with you by the time you reach them—leave."

She nodded again, her eyes wide with fear. But this time, the fear was for him instead of herself. His eyes blazed into hers for a moment, then something warned him and he turned. A painted warrior was approaching the camp.

"Go!" he commanded sharply, turning away from her. In a single fluid movement, he fitted an arrow to his bow and sighted down the shaft. The only sound was the hiss of his arrow as it left the bow.

Rebecca heard the arrow strike the brave with a thud and the man died with a surprised expression on his paint-streaked face.

Fitting another arrow to his bow, Lone Wolf moved toward the stream, and, with one last look, Rebecca moved swiftly in the direction Lone Wolf had indicated.

She reached the horses, but there was no sign of Lone Wolf. Although he had told her to leave if he wasn't there, she couldn't bring herself to mount. What had happened? Had they killed him? In that case, she would do well to leave so he wouldn't have given his life in vain. But suppose he was only injured?

She was still wavering with indecision when Lone Wolf appeared from the bushes.

"Why are you still here?" he growled. "I told you to leave."

"I couldn't," she whispered.

Expecting to be chastised, she found herself drawn against Lone Wolf's chest.

His grip was inflexible, his arms tight around her. A tremor shook his large frame as he held her tightly against his chest.

"Are you badly hurt?" he asked, his fingers probing the bruised and bloodied area where the flat side of the tomahawk had landed.

"I don't think so," she said. "I was knocked unconscious and my head hurts but otherwise, I'm all right." Her eyes were anxious. "Shouldn't we leave?"

"There is no need to hurry now," he said grimly. "I found all of them and they won't be bothering anyone again."

She shuddered and felt his arms tighten around her.

"You should not have run away," he growled huskily, his breath fanning her cheek. "I thought I had lost you, Little Blue Eyes."

She felt the fear draining away as he held her in his arms. She gave a long, shuddery sigh. There was nothing more to dread now. Lone Wolf had found her. She looked into his eyes and a wild elation filled her. She had thought she would never see him again, but he had found her and she could even admit to herself that, even if she hadn't needed rescuing, she would still have been shamelessly glad to see him.

"Why did you run from me?" he asked.

She stiffened. Why did he have to remind her? "I had to," she muttered. "I couldn't stay with a man who would treat me as you did."

"What happened between us is as much your making as mine. An Apache woman would never humiliate her man by calling him names," he grated, his lips tightening.

"Perhaps not," she said stiffly. "But I'm not Apache. Nor will I ever be."

"But you are, my Little Blue Eyes. As my wife, you already are."

"I will not be any man's possession."

"In your world, would it not be the same? I have heard it said a woman has no rights in the white man's world? Is this not true then?"

"At least I would have had the choice of whether or not to marry. You gave me no choice in the matter," she said bitterly.

"That is not true," he said harshly. "You were given a choice. Now I want to hear no more of this. It is useless to rail against fate. And it was surely fate that brought you to me."

"Fate, my foot. Black Bear brought me to you. And I'm beginning to think you are no better then he!"

Lone Wolf's face was savage. "Be careful," he advised grimly, his fingers digging unmercifully into her shoulders. "Be very careful that I don't take you at your word and give you back to him, Little Blue Eyes."

Though her face paled, her chin rose defiantly. The endearment, coupled with the threat, sent a stab of pain through her heart. How could he even suggest such a thing after what she had been through? She stared over Lone Wolf's shoulders into the sumac beyond, unaware of the fleeting look of regret that appeared in his gray eyes.

Suddenly remembering her attempt to escape him and its disastrous results, he hardened his expression against her. She must learn to obey him without question.

He lifted her onto the piebald pony's back and took the reins of both the piebald and the packhorse in one hand. Then they began retracing their steps toward the camp where the Indians had picketed the horses.

Her fingers clutched the piebald pony's mane tightly and her eyes flashed indignantly. She was having trouble understanding him. He had gone to a lot of trouble and put his life in danger to save her from the warriors. Why? What did he want from her? She was thankful that he had saved her, but she could still hardly believe he would threaten to give her to Black Bear if she displeased him.

She refused to admit, even to herself, how deeply that had hurt.

He would probably do it too!

*Yes, Lone Wolf, my husband, my Lord. Whenever you wish, my body is yours.* Her lips twisted wryly, her eyes growing cold as she silently addressed his back.

*Whatever you desire shall be yours, Master. Shall I climb off the piebald and spread myself on the forest floor for your pleasure?*

A hysterical giggle suddenly escaped at the mental picture she was creating, breaking the silence that surrounded them.

He twisted around, his eyes sweeping over her, causing a guilty flush to spread up her neck, over her cheeks, and suddenly, suspicion darkened his eyes.

"What's so funny?" he snapped.

"Uh—nothing," she squeaked.

"Then perhaps you would do well to save your energies for the long ride ahead!"

She clamped her lips together in a tight line, staring balefully at him, but held her silence. She didn't think he would find her thoughts the least bit amusing. But somehow, she felt it was either laugh or cry at the situation she found herself in, and she had decided she had done enough of the latter.

# Chapter Eight

When they reached the horses, she slid off the piebald pony and went to Diablo, examining him quickly for injuries. She found none.

Lone Wolf handed her a strip of dried venison and Rebecca, knowing she must eat to keep up her strength, forced the meat down.

Lone Wolf ate a piece, then without a word put Diablo's bridle on, and transferred the saddle from the packhorse to Diablo. Then, still in total silence, they continued their journey single file.

After a while Rebecca found the silence unbearable, and, determined to break it, she urged Diablo forward until she was riding next to Lone Wolf.

"How far is it?" she asked, glancing at him from beneath lowered lashes.

For a moment, she thought he wasn't going to answer. When he did, his voice was abrupt. "We should be there by dark."

"Dark?" She was startled. Her puzzled eyes raked the forest of pines, looking for some sign of their destination. "Are you sure?" She turned questioning eyes on him. "I rode Diablo all night long and then the — Indians captured me and . . ."

"They took you closer to our destination."

"Oh." Her eyes filled with sudden shame. "Lone Wolf," she said. "I haven't thanked you for rescuing me."

His gray eyes met hers and she felt relief flow through her as the anger drained away from him. His eyes softened and the tension left his body.

"We won't speak of what is past," he commanded firmly. "A new day has dawned. Perhaps we will both profit from our mistakes."

"*Our* mistakes?" she asked quietly, her puzzled eyes meeting his. She was surprised at his words. She realized she had made a mistake in running away from him, but what was his mistake? "Did you make a mistake too, Lone Wolf?"

"Yes." His spoke abruptly, refusing to elaborate.

A gust of wind whipped through his black hair as she watched, blowing it across his bronzed cheek. She wanted to reach out and smooth it away.

She puzzled over his words. What had been his mistake? Was it because he had married her? Perhaps he regretted interfering with Black Bear. After all, he had threatened to return her to him.

She shuddered.

She would kill herself before submitting to that animal. A sudden thought occurred to her. If he wanted to be rid of her, then perhaps he would take her home.

"I don't suppose you would consider taking me home to Robert?" she asked hesitantly.

"You are home, Rebecca," he said. His eyes were cold again, all the warmth draining away. "You are my wife, and your place is with me, not with your brother. No matter what happens in the future, nothing can change that."

"Don't you even care if I'm not happy with you?"

"What is happiness?" he asked harshly. "In time, you will learn to be content."

Hurt, she turned away from him. For a time they had shared something special together, but somehow — some way — it had disappeared.

When did it start to fall apart, she wondered, searching her memory. Was it when he refused to believe she had been abducted? Why had it been so hard for him to believe her? Would he be willing to listen now? She had to try. Anything was better than going on this way.

"Lone Wolf —"

"Enough!" he said sharply, turning blazing eyes on her. "You persist in arguing with me, and I won't have it!"

"Well, I was just —"

"Leave it!" he snapped. "I want to hear no more of your useless chattering."

Tightening her lips resentfully, she pulled Diablo up, waiting until Lone Wolf and the piebald pony were in the lead again, then she followed along behind him.

It was late afternoon when the forest began to give way to high plateau country that stretched in all directions across a broken, rolling landscape rising with abrupt, sandstone mesas.

Finally, Lone Wolf led her into what looked like a box canyon with brush-covered slopes and high canyon walls.

He pulled to a stop at the base of a great cliff,

139

waiting for her to draw abreast of him. He sat motion-less for a moment, his narrowed eyes intent on her drooping form.

"We are here," he said quietly. "Soon you can rest."

She gave a relieved sigh, straightened in the saddle, and looked around her. Her eyes flickered uncertainly. There was nothing there except a few large rocks that had fallen from the great cliff face.

"Here?" she asked. "But there's nothing here."

"Look closer," he commanded, pointing to the rock face of the cliff.

She narrowed her eyes against the sun, searching the cliff for something—anything. Finally, she saw it.

What resembled rooms and towers bound together in a single mass of sandstone was built into a huge recess in the vertical cliff a hundred feet or so from the mesa top. It lay quiet and protected under the cap rock in a natural cavern that elements and time had carved into the face of the cliff. Small windows stared vacantly across the valley, and empty doorways seemed waiting to be filled. It appeared to be the ruins of some ancient civilization that had been abandoned long ago.

The wind sighed through the tops of the pine trees, pushing its way between the canyon walls, and the droning of bees could be heard among the wildflowers. The muted babble of water from a nearby creek merely emphasized the silence surrounding the empty dwell-ings.

"What is it?" she asked, her voice barely above a whisper.

"It is the city of the ancient ones, the Basket Makers."

"It looks abandoned."

"It is."

"Why did the people, the ancient ones, leave?"

"No one knows."

She stared fascinated at the ruins, finding it hard to believe that people had really lived there. But she had to admit it would be inaccessible to the enemy, for the only way to reach it would be with a ladder. Suddenly a chill of apprehension went through her, and she turned reluctant eyes on Lone Wolf.

"You aren't expecting me to live up there with you?" she asked fearfully.

"Yes."

Her heart gave a sudden lurch of panic. "You've got to be crazy!" Her chin snapped up, and she eyed him belligerently.

His lips curled in a lazy smile that normally would have sent her pulse leaping but at the moment she felt only fear.

"No, not crazy," he said. "Just determined. No one will disturb us there."

"How can you know that? If you know about this place, then so could others."

"Yes, they know, but they do not come here."

A tingle of apprehension was added to her fear at his words. She had a feeling there was some reason the Indians deliberately avoided the place; just as she fully intended to.

She wasn't going up there, but, if she refused, he would only insist. She decided to appeal to his logic. "There's no way we can reach it," she said. "I—I think we'll have to forget about it."

"Don't worry," he said lightly. His gray eyes lit with humor. "There's a ladder hidden nearby."

"Well, you use it then!" she snapped, her panic-stricken eyes gazing up at the cliff dwellings high above the earth. "I'm not an eagle and I won't climb up there!" Her heart began to pound with dread as Lone Wolf laughed outright.

"You won't fall," he teased. "I'll stay right behind you." He dismounted and came to her side, putting his hands on her waist to help her dismount.

"No! No, Lone Wolf!" Despite herself, her voice rose with hysteria. She clung tightly to the saddlehorn, digging her feet into the stirrups. "I mean it! I couldn't climb up there! I'm afraid of heights. There's no way I can do it!"

His eyes narrowed, and he stood motionless, realizing finally that she wasn't being coy. She was really frightened. "Don't worry," he said softly, soothingly. "Everything's all right. Just calm yourself."

She relaxed slightly, allowing him to lift her down. She put her arms around his neck and clung tightly to him, her eyes meeting his anxiously. "You won't make me go up there?"

His eyes held regret. "I have no choice, Rebecca. That will be our home for a while. But there's no need for you to worry. The ledge upon which the city rests is much larger than it looks from here. You will feel differently once you're there, and you need never go near the edge."

"I won't go!" she snapped, pulling away from him.

His hand fastened tightly around her wrist, and, despite her protests, he pulled her to a crack in the mammoth rock about two feet across. Reaching inside, he pulled out a ladder made from weathered poles that had been carefully hidden from view. He placed it against the cliff face and pulled Rebecca to him.

She struggled furiously, trying to pull away. "Stop it, Rebecca," he said firmly.

"No," she snapped. Her panic warred with the fury surging through her. He was an unfeeling brute to discount her fears so lightly. "I'm not going up there. You can't make me." She struck out at him, striking his face with her balled-up fist.

"I told you, an Apache woman does not tell her husband no!" he ground out harshly.

With a determined motion, he wrapped one arm around her waist, ignoring the blows from her fists. Grabbing the ladder with his other hand, he began to climb.

"Lone Wolf, no!" Her voice was shrill with panic.

"Hold onto me!" he growled.

"Lone Wolf, please, don't do this," she begged, her heart beating wildly in her breast. "I told you I can't stand heights." One hand clutched wildly at him, grabbing a handful of hair, while the other pulled at the hand around her waist.

"Be still, woman!" he hissed, impaling her with his furious glare. "Do you want me to drop you?"

Rebecca froze instantly, closing her eyes and squeezing them tightly shut, afraid to even breathe for fear he would lose his grip and she would fall.

It seemed an eternity before Lone Wolf stopped climbing.

"Are—are we there?" she asked fearfully, her teeth chattering. She was afraid to open her eyes.

"No. There's another ladder at this level," he said in a slightly softened voice. "But be calm. It will soon be over."

Another ladder! How far up was it? Despite her

143

intentions to keep perfectly still, she shuddered involuntarily. She was unaware when Lone Wolf stopped climbing, but when he laid her down on solid earth and began to pull away from her, her arms went around his neck and tightened convulsively.

"Don't leave me," she said, forcing the words through gritted teeth, her eyes still closed tightly.

"I must," he said gently, smoothing back her hair. "But only to bring up the supplies. There's no need for you to worry. You're safe now." When she didn't respond, he gripped her chin firmly in one hand. "Open your eyes, Rebecca," he commanded firmly. Hesitantly, she obeyed, opening her eyes to find him smiling at her.

"That wasn't so bad, was it?" his voice asked gently.

Her eyes darted quickly from one side to the other afraid of what she would find, and she discovered Lone Wolf had deposited her near a crumbling adobe wall. From her position on the rock floor, the proportions were so vast that she was nowhere near the edge. A large spruce tree grew in front of the dwellings, as did several juniper and pinõn pines. At the sign of such lush vegetation, her fear began to evaporate as though it had never been, her color returning to her face.

"What has made you so afraid of heights?" He spoke hesitantly as though he was afraid the question would bring back the fear.

She couldn't look at him, feeling suddenly ashamed of the fuss she had raised. She knew her fear was out of proportion — although the city was built high off the valley floor — but she didn't know how to deal with it.

"Don't you want to talk about it?"

"Not really," she said. "But I guess I'll have to. It was

a stupid accident when I was small—only three or four years old. I—wandered too near a cliff and fell off. I guess it's a good thing there was a deep river below. Robert was with me and went for our father. I was swept down the river, more dead than alive when they found me."

"Poor little girl," he whispered. "It's a wonder you're not afraid of water. You swim quite well."

"Yes. I was afraid for a while. I couldn't seem to forget the way the water closed over my head, filling my ears and nose and mouth, and the pressure—" She sighed. "Living near the river, I finally got over that fear. It's just the other thing—my fear of heights—that I can't seem to get rid of."

"Well, don't worry. You're perfectly safe here," he said, smoothing back her tousled hair, frowning as he felt the sizable bump on her head where the Crow warrior had struck her. "Have you got a headache?" he asked.

"Yes. But I don't think there's any real harm done."

"Nevertheless, I'm sorry I had to be so rough with you down below. You'd already been through enough in the last few days without my adding to it."

"You really mean that, don't you?" she asked in surprise.

"Of course, or I wouldn't have said it." He smiled at her. "Are you going to explore your new home?"

He took her hand, pulling her upright, and she became interested in her surroundings. She was suddenly anxious to explore.

She was in what looked like a courtyard surrounded by the dwellings. Some of the buildings were as much as three stories high, made from shaped and mortared sandstone, and most of the dwellings seemed to be in surprisingly good condition.

"Will you be all right until I return?" Lone Wolf asked.

"You won't be long?" Although her fear had gone, the question held a note of anxiety.

"No, I won't be long," he assured her softly. Then he rose to his feet and, in a few strides, disappeared over the edge of the cliff.

Rebecca walked slowly, careful not to look in the direction Lone Wolf had taken, but she felt a deep curiosity about the people who had lived there so long ago.

The ancient ones. The Basket Makers, Lone Wolf had called them. She wondered what had caused them to leave the place? The sturdy trees and large plants suggested a plentiful water supply. But then, she mused, a dwelling such as this one suggested that a large number of people had lived here: possibly even as many as a hundred. Maybe there had not been enough water for a community that large.

Growing curious, she walked to the nearest wall and peeked through a window. The room was small, about eight by five feet in size, suggesting it had been used for housing only one or two people, and probably its primary use was as a bedroom or as a work area in unpleasant weather. The ceilings were low, having been made of brush and sticks, and plastered with mud, held up by wooden beams. The walls were covered with a heavy layer of soot where fires had burned to keep the inhabitants warm, and the doorways of the rooms all seemed to face out on the canyon.

Rebecca turned her attention to the other side of the

courtyard where part of a balcony was still in place, extending completely across the back wall of the courtyard. From where she stood it was nearly sixty feet to the back wall, and probably at least two hundred feet across. The immense size was overwhelming.

She saw a ladder protruding from a hole in the courtyard floor and went to investigate. It proved to be a round, circular room set low in the ground, measuring about twelve feet across.

"What have you found?" Lone Wolf's voice at her elbow startled her.

"Look at this," she said, her blue eyes flashing with excitement. "They apparently had to dig down in the rock to build this room, and it even has a fireplace."

"That is a ventilator shaft," he laughed. "And the room is a kiva."

"A kiva? What was it used for?"

"It was used for ceremonial purposes or as a social gathering place. Sometimes, even, the men would use it for a work place. Do you want to see inside it?"

"Yes," she answered promptly. Then, hesitantly, she asked. "You will go with me, won't you?"

He laughed. "Yes, I will be right behind you." His voice was amused.

"If you don't mind, I think I'd prefer you go first."

He grinned, then gripped the ladder, and lowered his large frame into the darkness below. She waited only a moment before she followed. When she reached the bottom, it took a moment for her eyes to adjust to the dim light.

Her gaze swept around the circular enclosure, taking note of the stone benches running around the sides of the room. Stone pillars supported the roof. There was the ventilator shaft and a couple of holes in the floor.

She looked curiously at them, wondering what they were for. As if sensing her curiosity, Lone Wolf pointed to the holes in the floor. "The larger hole is for a fire and the smaller one represents the opening through which mankind emerged onto the face of the earth," he said.

She looked at the small hole again and felt a sudden awareness of the differences in their cultures. The light spilling from the hole in the ceiling fell across Lone Wolf's face, accentuating the planes and curves of his features, and the passion that suddenly flared in his narrowed eyes.

Her heart stopped as she stared back at him, then began to beat wildly. Her face was soft and hesitant, showing a trace of fear of the stranger who stood beside her.

"It's getting late," she muttered, trying to disguise the throbbing hunger of her body. "Did you bring us some food?"

"Yes," he said, looking down at her in the semidarkness. He seemed mesmerized by her lips, and his head lowered slowly until she could feel his breath on her forehead.

She stopped breathing altogether. As she felt his hand at her waist, hers went to his muscular chest and rested there on his warm flesh while she waited for his lips. She heard a soft sigh, a touch as fleeting as a butterfly's wings, then found herself released.

She felt bereft. As she stared at him in confusion, a cold chill touched her and she shivered.

"Are you cold?" he asked.

"A little," she said.

"Then let's go back up."

She climbed the ladder, then waited until he was standing beside her.

"What shall I cook for our meal?" she asked, looking up at him.

"I killed a rabbit," he said, stretching his arms above his head lazily.

"When did you have time to do that?" she asked, unable to keep her eyes off the lean, hard-muscled length of his body.

"I was gone longer than you realized." His smile was wry. "You were so taken with the ruins that you didn't even miss me, did you?"

Not miss him? No chance of that! If he but knew how she felt! Her hungry eyes followed him as he picked up a bundle of firewood he had obviously gathered, and bent over to lay a fire. Then they strayed over his lean hips, long, powerful legs, and even down to his moccasined feet. Conflicting emotions tore at her self-control.

What did he want of her? Was it only her body he wanted, or could there be just a little bit of feeling for her in his heart? Finally, she managed to tear her eyes away from him.

While he busied himself with the fire, she set up the tripod of poles, attached the buffalo pouch to form her cooking pot and added water. She saw Lone Wolf had already put several stones into the fire to heat so that left her free to add rabbit, wild onions, and turnips to her cooking pot. Then she dropped the heated rocks into the pot until the water was boiling.

Soon, the aroma of fresh rabbit stew filled the air,

and Lone Wolf was dipping a buffalo horn spoon into the pot, filling an earthenware bowl, and offering it to her. She accepted the bowl of piping-hot stew and ate silently, smiling at him as he helped himself and began his own meal. He seemed different here, more relaxed somehow.

"What do you think could have happened to the People who lived here, Lone Wolf?" she asked suddenly.

"It could have been a drought or maybe even the plague," he said, finishing his meal and wiping his hands down his breeches. "Even the old ones of our village cannot say what really happened."

"Why does no one ever come here?" she asked, suddenly remembering his words.

His eyes darkened, grew watchful. "Sometimes, when the wind is blowing hard, it makes a moaning sound like a lost soul in torment. The Apaches believe it to be the spirits of the dead."

She shivered slightly, moving closer to him. "But you don't believe it?"

"No," he said. "It is only the wind. And the wind cannot harm you. You must remember that if the wind blows when I am gone."

"You're going away?" she asked, her eyes widened in fear. Surely he wouldn't leave her alone here!

"Sometimes I will have to hunt for meat or go for fresh water. I cannot be here every moment."

"Then let me go with you!"

"No," he said firmly. "You will stay here."

"For how long?"

"Until you are carrying my child," he said, staring arrogantly into her turbulent blue eyes.

150

Her fear vanished, overcome with anger as she stared back at him. And she had actually begun to hope he would come to care for her!

She glared at him, her blue eyes sparkling furiously. Then standing up, she flounced away, coming to an abrupt halt as a thought suddenly struck her.

"What if it doesn't happen?" she asked, turning back to him. "After all, some women never have babies."

"It will happen," he said firmly. "Until it does, we will wait."

# Chapter Nine

*We will wait.*

Lone Wolf squatted on the ground, his arrogant words echoing in his mind. His passion-filled eyes followed Rebecca as she moved away from him. He wanted nothing more than to throw her to the ground and make mad love to her, but he knew he must go carefully.

She was a fighter, there was no doubt of that, and he had no intention of breaking her spirit. His thoughts dwelt on last night with regret. There was no way he wanted to repeat that experience. She had responded passionately to his love-making, and afterward cuddled against him so trustingly, but—fool that he was—his pride had made him act in such a way that she had tried to escape him.

A flicker of pain crossed his features before he schooled it to its usual impassivity.

*Damn my pride!* he thought. For that was all it had been. His male ego just hadn't been able to deal with his wife not wanting his love-making, and he had been determined to show her she couldn't resist him. But at what price? If her body was all he wanted there would be no problem, but somehow, somewhere along the way, his pale-skinned wife had stolen his heart.


*We will wait.*

Her eyes flashed with indignation and she gave an angry yank to the buffalo robe she was spreading on the floor. Her lips lifted in a wry smile as she thought of her arrogant, Apache husband.

"Nothing to it!" she muttered, frowning, reaching for the bright blanket to spread over the hide bed. "We'll just wait until you're pregnant, he says!"

"Did you say something?"

Startled, she looked up to see Lone Wolf edging his large body through the doorway of the small room that measured only eight by five feet.

"Uh — I was just wondering if there's enough room in here for you?" she said, lowering her lashes evasively. "The People who lived here must have been awfully small. Do you think we should look for a larger room?"

"All the rooms are small," he said. "I don't think the ancient ones were much taller than you are." His gaze swept over her diminutive form, lingering for a moment on the braids that fell against her high, firm breasts.

He knelt on the bed, reached out, picked up one of the plaits, and unbraided it. Then he unbraided the other one, and soon her hair was lying in gentle waves, falling past her shoulders. With his eyes holding hers, he removed his buckskin breeches and settled down on the robe.

"We will sleep here," he said, his voice slightly husky.

Rebecca's heartbeat quickened and she could hardly breathe as she watched Lone Wolf, stretched out on the buffalo hide, completely unself-conscious of his glorious, naked masculinity.

She thought of her attempt at escape and her face paled, her eyes filling with sudden pain. Why had she thought she could leave him? Without Lone Wolf, life would be empty and meaningless. But at least now she had a second chance. And somehow, she would use everything in her power to make him fall in love with her.

They were alone here in this place, with no interference from anyone, and she would use the time well. She would show him what a good wife she could be. She would learn to curb her temper and practice being sweet and gentle instead.

*How about obedience, Rebecca?*

She frowned. Obedience seemed to be high on his list of what made a good Apache wife, so — yes, she would even be that too!

Even though she believed a woman's place was beside her man and not ten paces behind, if he wanted her behind him, then that was where she would go. But first, she would apologize for her attempt at escape.

"Lone Wolf —"

"Come here, Rebecca."

His slow husky drawl brought goose bumps on her arms, and her stomach muscles contracted, quivering.

"Come to bed."

Suddenly, his words and husky tone of voice brought back memories of last night — the insulting way he had looked at her after they made love, and she eyed him nervously, her eyes darkening with sudden emotion that he misinterpreted.

"There's no need to look that way!" he said harshly, his eyes flickering with something almost like pain. "I'm not going to hurt you!"

Silently, she turned away from him, blinking back the tears that filled her eyes at his sudden harshness. Then, swallowing around a lump in her throat, she pulled her blouse over her head, folded it, and laid it carefully aside.

She was aware of his eyes on her as she bent to remove her knee-high moccasins, then slipped out of her one remaining garment — her skirt.

He watched as she laid the skirt with her blouse, then reached out, capturing her wrist, tugging, and causing her to lose her balance. She fell against his chest and found herself immediately bound by the arm that locked her in place.

She lay in the circle of his arms, tense and silent, held intimately against his warm, naked body. She was far from comfortable but she dared not move for fear of angering him again.

"Relax, Little Blue Eyes," he said, his voice grating softly as he broke the silence. His breath felt warm against the side of her face, stirring the silky tendrils of hair around her ears. "I'm not asking anything from you except a little human comfort."

Slowly, she relaxed her tensed body, but she couldn't sleep. She lay for what seemed like hours, her traitorous body longing for the naked flesh pressed against her own, wondering at his sudden lack of desire. Had he grown tired of her already? After so short a time? The thought was unbearable. Finally, too weary to even think anymore, her eyes closed and she slept.

Lone Wolf lay still, his face grim, his eyes stricken, until finally she relaxed against him in sleep. He cursed himself for a fool. He had done more damage last night than he had realized. It would take time and patience to heal the wounds he had given her. It would be hard to control his passion, but, if it won him her love, then it would be worth all the suffering he would feel. He stared bitterly into the darkness, until finally the ordeal he had been through—losing her and trailing her—took its toll, and he relaxed in sleep, savoring the warmth of her body held tightly against his.

She stretched, yawned, then opened her eyes. Slowly, she let them move around the unfamiliar room. Where was she? She searched her memory for clues but the answers eluded her. She was lying naked on a buffalo hide, covered with a blanket, and she was cold and alone.

Shivering, she pulled the blanket higher under her chin.

"So you're finally awake."

Startled, she turned her head to see Lone Wolf's large frame filling the doorway.

"Why is it so cold?"

He laughed, his eyes taking in her scowl. "It's cooler this high in the mountains. You didn't feel it yesterday because the sun had already warmed the stones. Don't worry, soon it will be warm again."

"Meanwhile, I freeze!" she grumbled, shivering again.

"Put your clothing on," he said. "Then come by the fire. I already have a warm meal prepared. That should help warm you up."

At his words she gave a guilty flush. Well, so much for her effort to show him she could be the perfect wife. She had learned during the time she had been at the village that it was considered beneath a brave's dignity to do what was designated as woman's work, and preparing the meals most definitely fell in that category.

"I'm sorry I overslept," she said, hastily sitting up and reaching for her doeskin top. The action caused the blanket to fall away from her naked breasts, and she shivered as cold air hit her body causing the nipples to stand out in taut peaks.

He drew in his breath sharply, quickly averting his gaze from the sight of her naked form, determinedly damping down the flames coursing through his body.

Unaware of his problem, she pulled the blouse over her head, lifting her long brown hair at the nape of her neck and shaking it free. "I must have been overtired," she said. "It won't happen again."

Sweeping the blanket back, she rose from the buffalo robes, stepped into her skirt, then pulled her moccasins on. By the time she finished, her teeth were chattering.

At the sound of her teeth clicking together, he looked quickly at her, his eyes narrowed on her slender form and frowned. "Wrap the blanket around you until you warm up," he said. "I didn't think it was that cold, but I guess you need more heat than I do. Come to the fire."

He took her hand, led her to the courtyard, and seated her beside the fire away from the chill breeze. "Is that better?" he asked.

She nodded, accepting the warm earthenware bowl he offered, wrapping her hands around it. Steam rose from the contents, which proved to be corn meal mush with several plump, juicy berries mixed in.

"Blackberries!" she exclaimed, her eyes lighting up. "Where on earth did you find them?"

"There's a spring a little farther down that way." He nodded toward the box end of the canyon. "I found blackberries, and wild mint growing there. There were plum bushes too, but the plums are still a little green."

"Do you mean it's up here with us? On this ledge we're sitting on now?"

He laughed at her surprise. "Yes," he agreed. "On this ledge we're sitting on now."

"Will you show me?" she asked eagerly.

"You must eat first," he commanded. "Then I'll take you there."

She didn't have to be coaxed. Hungrily, she spooned the honey-sweetened mush and berries into her mouth, savoring each and every bite.

"My Aunt Bess had a blackberry patch," she said, swallowing another berry. "When they turned ripe each year, she made the most delicious blackberry cobblers ever imaginable."

He smiled at her, watching her animated expression. "She's the aunt who lives back east?"

He remembered! For some reason, she was pleased that he had. "Yes," she said, using her fingers to pick a big juicy berry from the mixture and pop it into her mouth. "She's my father's sister."

"Don't pick your berries from your food, Rebecca," he reprimanded. "Eat it all."

"Yes, sir!" she answered tartly, her eyes alight with mischief as she grinned at him. She saluted smartly, then dipped her spoon into the bowl again.

His eyes glinted with humor. "The cold climate seems to agree with you."

"Hunh uhh," she denied, shaking her head. "It's the blackberries."

"The blackberries?" He was puzzled. "What do the blackberries have to do with it?"

"They bring back memories. Aunt Bess used to tell me not to pick the berries from my mush."

"Ahhh—yes," he said, nodding his head slowly. "Now I remind you of Aunt Bess. I wonder—do you think this aunt would approve of me?"

She threw back her head and laughed at the idea of Lone Wolf with Aunt Bess. Her aunt would take one look at him, dressed in nothing but buckskin breeches and moccasins, with his hunting knife at his side, and faint dead away.

"I see she wouldn't," he remarked. His voice was light but there was something curious in his eyes—something almost like regret.

Lone Wolf finished his bowl of mush, then reached for the cooking pot for a refill. Her eyes fell on the cooking vessel for the first time and they grew wide with delight.

"Where did you get that?" she asked, leaning closer for a better look.

The earthenware vessel was decorated with a black-on-white geometric design, and, although blackened by the flames from countless cooking fires, the pot still retained some of its original beauty.

"I found it in a room near the back." Lone Wolf said. "There are many others there as well. Do you like it?"

"Oh, it's just beautiful," she enthused, her eyes sparkling with delight. "You said there were more?"

159

"Yes," he said indulgently. "And baskets as well. I'll show you later. But first, finish your meal. Then we'll go to the spring."

Soon, he was leading her along the tan limestone cliffs to the head of the canyon. Far below, she could see the canyon floor and she marveled that nature had actually provided water so close to the city of the ancient ones. She remarked on this to Lone Wolf and he laughed, saying it was the other way around. The water was there first, leading to the building of the city.

As they drew closer to the source of water, the scrubby oak trees growing beside the trail soon gave way to tall, sturdy trees, and a wide variety of lush vegetation growing in abundance indicated a plentiful water supply.

Then they were there. Beneath a cliff overhang a thin sheet of water fell from the cliff, splashing gently onto the protruding ledge below. And behind the waterfall was an open cavern containing the spring. Her nostrils twitched, as the cool, damp breeze carried the fragrance of fresh mint on the air. As they drew nearer, a small green frog leaped with a splash into the spring.

"I can't believe this!" she exclaimed, turning to Lone Wolf. "How could a spring be halfway up a cliff?"

He grinned, pointing to the moisture seeping from the rocks. "The cliffs are made of sandstone," he explained. "Beneath the sandstone, there is a layer of hard rock through which the moisture cannot penetrate. When the water reaches that point, it emerges in the form of a seep, or spring, such as this one."

She looked at him through lowered lashes. He seemed to be surprisingly knowledgeable about such things. Did they teach him all that at the reservation school? "Where did you learn about such things, Lone Wolf?" she asked suddenly.

"The Indian People are not stupid, Rebecca," he said abruptly.

"I didn't mean to imply they were," she said, quickly putting a hand on his arm. She had unwittingly caused him to withdraw from her, and she attempted to rectify her mistake.

"I was just surprised at the amount of knowledge you possess." She smiled, sliding her hand down his arm until she found his hand. "Now, show me where you found the blackberries," she commanded.

He led her to one side of the spring where she saw the blackberry bushes, loaded with large, juicy berries. "Why there's enough here to make a dozen blackberry cobblers," she said. "Now if I only had some flour and lard . . ."

"Even then it would do you no good," he said with a grin.

"Why?" She turned puzzled eyes to him.

"You have no oven."

"Oh." That thought had not occurred to her. "Well, fresh blackberries will have to do." She picked a handful and popped them into her mouth one at a time. As she swallowed the last berry, she lifted mournful blue eyes to him.

"Now what?" he sighed.

"Well . . ." she hedged. "I was just thinking . . ."

"Go ahead. You may as well tell me. What were you thinking?"

"Well—blackberries taste better with cream."

"Eat your blackberries," he commanded, his gray eyes glinting with humor. "We do not have cream, nor will we be having it anytime in the near future. Cream is a luxury you will have to do without." Suddenly, the humor vanished, and his eyes darkened with emotion. "Do you really mind so much, Little Blue Eyes?"

"About not having cream to go with my blackberries?" she asked. "Of course not! I was just teasing! Blackberries are good by themselves."

"I wasn't speaking of just blackberries and cream," he said softly.

"Then what?"

"I was thinking of all the other things you've left behind."

"Are you offering me a choice, Lone Wolf?" she asked, holding her breath.

For a moment he was silent, but she could feel the tautness of his body as his intent gray eyes searched hers. "No," he finally said. "I can't offer you a choice, Rebecca. Despite what either of us wants, you must stay here."

"Then there's no need to discuss it!" she said stiffly, feeling unaccountably hurt. Was he regretting the actions that caused her to be with him? She knew he had desired her in the beginning, but maybe he had already grown tired of her. After all, he had felt no desire to make love to her last night. He had even admitted all he wanted was human contact, and, if a warm body in his bed was all he wanted, then any female would do. Suddenly she lost her desire for the blackberries.

"I'm ready to go back," she said shortly.

His gray eyes were penetrating as he studied her pale face and turbulent eyes. Then he said. "If you think you will be all right on the way back, I will stay here and bathe."

She shrugged, lowering her eyelids to hide her pain. He couldn't wait to be away from her. "All right," she said. "It's only a short distance there." Then she spun on her heel and without a backward glance moved down the path leading back to the cliff dwellings.

When she reached the dwellings, she sat down beside the dwindling fire, placed another stick of wood on it, and watched the sparks spit and sizzle. Misery consumed her, just as the flames consumed the wood. Her heart was heavy, and a deep sense of loneliness welled from within her being. As always, when she was at her lowest point, her thoughts turned to home and her brother, Robert, who loved her.

"Oh, Robert," she whispered. "Is it so impossible for him to love me? Am I just chasing rainbows to think I can make him care?" She drew her knees up and rested her head against them.

"Will I ever see you again, Robert?" she whispered huskily, giving a deep, shivery sigh.

"No!" The words were snapped harshly from behind her. "You'll never see him again! Must I keep reminding you that you are mine now?"

Lone Wolf grabbed her arm angrily and jerked her to her feet. His eyes were blazing furiously as they stared into hers. "I have tried to make allowances for you, but my patience is coming to an end! I demand that you stop this sentimental dreaming right now and accept your fate!" He gave her a hard shake to punctuate his words.

A fire began to burn deep within her body, and, as he gave her another shake, it erupted violently. "Damn you! Take your hands off me!" She threw up her arms, catching him by surprise, knocking his away.

Immediately, he seized her again. His fingers dug into her arms cruelly, and she winced. Her pained expression went unnoticed as he shook her again. "I have had enough of your disobedience, Rebecca. I have tried to allow you time to adjust to your fate, but I see my consideration for your feelings has done no good. Well, so be it! I am tired of waiting. Tonight, you resume your duties as my wife."

"Consideration?" she spat. "You call yourself considerate? You kidnapped me! You stole me away from my home!" Suddenly her eyes narrowed and she drawled insultingly. "But then, what else could I expect? You're nothing but a savage Indian!"

In the silence that ensued, she began to feel she had finally pushed him too far. She was afraid of the wild darkness in his eyes and his fingers were white, digging into her upper arms, threatening to break her bones.

Suddenly, as if her touch disgusted him, he flung her away from him, spun on his heels, and strode away toward the ledge. He gripped the ladder with one hand, then disappeared over the ledge.

She watched in disbelief, her anger draining away. He was leaving her!

"No," she whispered. "Don't leave me." But she knew he couldn't hear. And even if he had, it would have done no good. She had finally driven him too far. He had finished with her, and she didn't really blame him. After all, she had accused him of things he hadn't done. Then, as if that wasn't enough, she had called him a savage.

White-faced, she stared across the valley. He had left her alone, and, with her fear of heights, there was no way she could even attempt the climb down into the valley floor alone. She gave an uncontrollable shiver, and the tight rein she had held on her fears gave way. The tears she had managed to keep at bay welled up and fell silently down her face.

When Lone Wolf returned, he saw her at once. She was kneeling beside the fire, feeding another stick of wood to the flames. Her long, brown hair was spread out on the blanket wrapped around her slender form. He frowned at the blanket, clutched tightly in her fingers. Was she really that cold?

"Rebecca," he said softly, dropping the doe he had killed on the ground.

Startled, she looked up, rising fearfully at the same time. "Lone Wolf!" Tears welled into her eyes. "You've come back!"

His dark brows drew together in a frown. "Of course I've come back," he said. "Did you think I wouldn't?"

"I didn't know," she said, throwing herself into his arms. Her head was tight against his bare chest, her voice muffled as she said. "I was afraid you wouldn't."

"Not return?" His hands went to her waist, forcing her away a little. Then he lifted her head until blue eyes met gray. His breath caught as he gazed down at her.

"Did you really think I would not return for you?" he asked hoarsely. "Do you not know yet that you can never escape me? I would follow you to the ends of the earth, Little Blue Eyes."

Suddenly she wasn't cold anymore. The raw hunger in his eyes lit a flame inside her that began to burn with a fiery intensity. She whispered his name with unbearable yearning, her arms clutching his waist tightly, convulsively.

He gave a husky groan, bending toward her, his arms pressing her body to his in an agony of need and wanting.

"Hold me tight, Lone Wolf," she said, her voice shaking. "Hold me tight and don't ever let me go."

"I will," he groaned huskily, his eyes wild with passion. "I'll never let you go. Remember that always, sweet one. I'll never let you go."

Then he lifted her into his arms, devouring her mouth with his kiss. The deer lay forgotten as he carried her to their bed, laying her gently down on the buckskin robes. His mouth pressed heated kisses all over her face, her eyelids, her neck, returning to devour her mouth again, never drawing completely away from her as he divested them of their clothing.

Soon they were lying together, his naked flesh pressed against her slender body. His chest pressed tight against her soft breasts.

"I was afraid I would never be able to hold you like this again," he said fiercely, a shudder racking his powerful body.

She shivered with joy, sliding her hands around his neck and burying her fingers in his dark hair. Her hunger for him was so devastating she wanted to bury herself with his body.

"Love me, Lone Wolf," she begged, intense longing in her eyes. "Please."

Her words were his undoing. He groaned, seizing

166

her head between his large hands, pressing his lips to hers feverishly. His tongue darted in and out of her mouth, then across her lips. His hot breath seared her senses as his mouth moved across her face, down her throat, stopping to caress the throbbing pulse beating at her neck.

His mouth moved past her collarbone, brushing against the swell of her breast before it captured one taut nipple. As his mouth fastened on the throbbing peak, his hand moved down her silken skin, stroking her stomach, moving along her inner thighs, until finally it came to rest upon the center of her desire.

Her senses were swirling madly as he tormented her with his fiery caresses. She responded to him with a vibrant passion that was overwhelming her senses. She immersed herself in the sensual pleasure that swept away every thought in her mind except for him and her passion.

She could feel his throbbing masculinity and shifted beneath him, almost crazy with longing. Engulfed by searing passion, her body arched upward igniting his smoldering frame.

As he entered her, she groaned, surrendering to the overpowering sensations that filled her being. As though aware of her high level of arousal, Lone Wolf began to move inside her, slowly at first, then increasing his pace and force until they were both consumed by a furnace of passion. They reached their peak simultaneously, clinging together as they rode out stormy waves of passion.

Afterward, he rolled onto his side, exhausted, and held her perspiration-dampened form tightly clasped against him until her trembling stilled.

She snuggled peacefully into his arms, resting her cheek against his shoulder. She knew with a certainty that this deep fulfilling hunger would always be a part of her. She realized as well that no one would ever be able to fill it but Lone Wolf.

Closing her eyes, she gave a contented sigh. This was the man who held her heart in his grasp. She would love him always, and, wherever he was, there would be her home for without him there was nothing. On this last thought she fell asleep, content in the arms of her Apache husband.

He lay beside her silently, unable to sleep. He listened to Rebecca's slow, even breathing, thankful that she slept. He felt a deep regret at his anger with her earlier in the day. Why couldn't he learn to be patient with her? He wanted her to be content with him, hoped that one day she might even come to accept him as her husband. But still, she had wanted to return to her brother.

His arms tightened around her and she murmured his name in her sleep. He smiled in satisfaction. At least it was his name that she spoke. If he practiced patience with her, then perhaps, one day, she might even come to love him.

Bending his head, he placed a featherlight kiss on her love-swollen lips. His eyes roamed possessively over her face, her breasts where the cover had fallen aside.

She was his.

Before he found her, he had had no one. But despite that, he had never known the meaning of loneliness until he had woken up and found her missing. He

168

relived in his mind those hours of agony before he had finally found her. Never again, he promised himself. He could not bear the thought of losing her. If that should ever happen, life would not be worth living.

# Chapter Ten

"Look what I found!"

At the sound of Lone Wolf's voice calling to her across the cavern, Rebecca looked up. She arched her back, stretching tired, aching muscles, turning her head at the same time to locate Lone Wolf.

She smiled, her eyes admiring his masculine form as she watched him approach, wondering what he had discovered.

"Just what we needed. Would you not agree?" he asked, holding out a cradle made from the tightly woven leaves of a yucca plant.

She blushed, her thick eyelashes sweeping down to hide the confusion in her eyes. "Not yet, I'm afraid," she said, keeping her voice deliberately light. He had unknowingly touched a sore spot. He seemed to be counting heavily on her ability to have a child, but suppose she proved to be barren? Would he still want her? She scraped the powdered meat she had been pulverizing on a flat stone into a pile, sifting her fingers through it to make sure it was fine enough.

"Are you, little one?" His voice was so gentle that her eyes lifted again, and she couldn't help wondering at the tenderness reflected in his gaze. "Are you afraid to have my baby in this wilderness where one of your doctors could not reach you?"

"No. Of course not," she whispered, losing herself in the gray depths. For a moment their eyes held, then she looked away, returning her attention to the pulverized meat. "Anyway, it doesn't matter one way or another," she said, struggling to sound casual. "I'm *not* expecting your baby."

"No matter," he said quietly, his eyes never leaving her, and ripples of desire coursed through her body. He smiled at her. "We will wait."

She felt suddenly dismayed at his words. "You keep saying that!" she snapped irritably. Her blue eyes were pained as they met his fleetingly then slid away.

"Why does it disturb you so?" he asked, laying the cradle aside and kneeling beside her. He pulled her into his arms, tilting her chin firmly, forcing her to look at him.

"Lone Wolf, what if I can't have children?" The agony in her voice was reflected in her eyes.

"What is this?" he asked quietly, his eyes darkening. "Is there some reason for you to believe such a thing?"

"No! Of course not!" she said, hurrying to reassure him. "It's just that you seem so sure I'll get pregnant. That's why you left your People and brought me here. But I'm so afraid that it won't happen and you'll be disappointed in me."

"Never that, Little Blue Eyes," he said tenderly, drawing her into his arms. "No matter what happens, I could never be disappointed in you."

Her eyes were tremulous as she gazed into his, and the slumbrous passion she saw reflected in the depths of his gray eyes ignited a flame deep within her. Suddenly, she laughed, chiding herself mentally. Every time he came near her she melted like candlewax.

"Why do you laugh?" he asked, his dark brows drawing into a frown.

"I wasn't laughing at *you*," she said quickly. "I was laughing at *me*." At his questioning gaze she shrugged. "It's a private joke, my friend."

"Friend?"

"Lover, then."

"That is better," he said although he couldn't help wishing she had said "husband." No matter. Before they left the city of the ancient ones she would concede that they were truly married. His gaze roved hungrily over her slender form, the swell of her breasts, her narrow waist. "Never would I accept just being your friend." His voice sent shivers racing up and down her spine.

Chiding herself for her weakness, she laughed, backing away from the passion she saw in his eyes. "We have work to do, remember? And I have to finish making the pemmican."

He looked down at the meat on the flat stone. "You have already made the meat small enough," he decided.

"Well — maybe," she agreed, sifting her fingers through it again. "But I've still to pound the berries to mix with it." She wrinkled her nose at him, her eyes suddenly lighting up with mirth. "Why don't you go back to your digging, and see if you can find something useful?"

"Like the cradle?" he asked drily.

"Well, maybe," she said defensively. Her eyes darkened. "We might even find we have need for it someday."

The corners of his mouth lifted in a wry smile. Picking up a strand of silky brown hair, he gave it a gentle tug. "All right, my sweet little captive. I will go and dig through some more of the rubble and see what treasures I can find."

Giving her a look that spoke volumes, leaving her in no doubt about what he would rather be doing, he returned to the crumbling back wall of the courtyard and renewed his search. Soon, from beneath the rubble he unearthed a pottery cup complete with handle.

"How do you like this?" he called across to her, holding the cup aloft so she could see it.

"Lone Wolf, it's beautiful!" she exclaimed, getting to her feet, and hurrying over to examine his find. It was decorated around the edges with the same geometric design of black on white that had been on the cooking vessel he had found earlier, and halfway down the cup a bird had been painted with a remarkable sense of design and balance.

Excited over his find, knowing an archeologist back east who would gladly trade places with her, she began digging where he had left off. Soon they unearthed several bowls, two more cups, a large jar with a small neck, and a curious double mug that was joined together at the handles.

"What do you think this could have been used for?" she asked, picking up the double mug and calling Lone Wolf's attention to it.

173

He took it from her hand, his eyes intent on the black-on-white geometric pattern they had encountered in most of the other pottery they had found.

She watched him study the object, unconsciously holding her breath as she waited for him to speak. He turned the mug over once, studied the bottom intently, then glanced at her. Her blue eyes widened in anticipation.

"Well?" she whispered, her voice low and hushed, wondering what monumental discovery was at hand.

"Well . . ." He stopped, his eyes going from the mug to her face. "I would say—from the looks of this—"

"Yes?" She could barely contain her excitement while she waited for the verdict.

He smiled. "I would say it was most likely a mug for lovers."

"Really!" she asked in an awe-struck voice. She took the mug carefully, almost reverently, from him.

*A mug for lovers.*

She turned it over carefully, intent on seeing the evidence for herself.

Her eyes flashed to his, then back to the bottom of the mug. There were no markings on the bottom. In fact, there was nothing there but smooth white pottery.

Her brows drew together in a frown, her eyes narrowed intently as she searched, wondering what she had missed. "How can you tell it's meant for lovers?" she asked, casting a puzzled look at him. "I don't see anything."

"Of course not," he said, his eyes lit with amusement. "There is nothing for you to see. But since you found it, and we will be the ones to use it, then it must have

174

been intended for us."

She stared at him, her gaze still uncomprehending.

"Are we not lovers?"

Her mouth dropped open as his meaning became clear. He had actually been teasing her! For some reason, a warm feeling spread throughout her body, and she laughed in exultation.

His gray eyes held a curious tenderness as they dwelt on her animated face, and his usually expressionless features seeemed softer than normal.

He took her arm. "I think that is enough digging for today," he said when she looked at him questioningly. "We have other work that must be done." He grinned wickedly at her. "And you must not be tired when we go to bed."

"No headaches?"

His eyes sparkled with humor. "If one should develop, be sure and let me know because I have a cure for headaches."

"You have headache powders?" she asked.

"No, Little Blue Eyes," he said drily. "But I have a better cure than headache powders."

"What is it?" she asked, her eyes suddenly suspicious as she remembered his teasing.

"A small amount of the water taken from a walnut tree," he said. "The walnut trees are plentiful here, and, taken at intervals, the water will cure even the most violent headache."

"Truthfully?"

"Cross my heart," he said, grinning as he made the sign across his naked bronze chest. "It is an old Indian recipe that has been passed down from the ancient ones. And it is guaranteed to work."

She stared up at him, totally confused. He was an enigma that she was having trouble understanding. One moment he was coming up with an old Indian recipe for headaches, and the next moment he was using the words for honesty that she had learned as a child. She couldn't help wishing he weren't so reticent, almost secretive even, when it came to speaking of his childhood. It was as though there were something in his past he was hiding from her.

She shrugged mentally, refusing to dwell on the puzzle. She liked him in this teasing mood and she would do nothing to disturb it. His recent anger was still too fresh in her memory.

"Do you have other remedies too?" she asked, gazing up at him with twinkling eyes. "I'd better know what it's safe for me to come down with."

"I have more remedies than you can find sicknesses," he boasted. "For was not my mother a medicine woman?"

"She is?" She had missed his use of the past tense, and in her excitement she failed to notice the shadow passing over his face. "Lone Wolf! You never told me that! I'd love to meet your mother."

"That would be impossible I'm afraid. My mother has entered the spirit world." His voice held almost unbearable sadness.

Entered the spirit world? Did that mean she was dead? *Of course, stupid!* Immediately she was contrite. "I'm very sorry," she said quietly, laying her hand on his arm and squeezing gently.

As though unable to bear her sympathy, he bent over

and picked up a bowl they had found. Then, straightening up, he called her attention to it, trying to distract her, but she barely looked at it.

He had never mentioned his mother before except to say she and Black Bear's mother were sisters who were both from the house of Cochise, and she was intensely curious about her. She felt if he would just open up to her it could lead to a much better understanding between them, and so, she refused to give up the subject so easily.

"Were you very young?" she asked hesitantly, afraid it was painful for him to speak of his mother. "When your mother—passed on into the—spirit world?"

"I was eight summers," he said, his voice abrupt. And although his face was expressionless, she saw the pain in his eyes.

"If—if you'd rather not speak of it—" She tightened her grip on his arm, silently offering comfort.

"I wouldn't."

"Oh." Feeling unaccountably hurt, she turned away, but he grasped her arm tightly.

"Rebecca," he said slowly. "There are things of which I find it very hard to speak . . ." He stopped, searching for the right words. "My father was—"

"No." She put a finger against his lips, silencing him. "Don't speak of it if it bothers you. I should never have been so inquisitive. Please accept my apology. After all, your past is none of my affair."

One hand clasped her tightly around her waist, pulling her against him. The other hand raked her curling mass of light brown hair, holding her still while he studied her face with a curious expression. "You are not angry with me?"

"Of course not," she said, a smile lighting her eyes. "How could I possibly be angry with you over something like that?"

Putting her arms around his waist, she laid her head against his chest, inhaling his clean masculine scent. His arms tightened about her, and for a moment they stood there, each drawing comfort from the other. Then with a deep sigh he put her aside.

"This is not getting the work done," he said regretfully. "I must go hunting again for fresh meat, and you have much dried venison to store for the winter."

"Yes," she sighed, allowing him to see her reluctance to be left alone. "But we *could* eat dried venison for our evening meal, and you could hunt tomorrow," she added coaxingly. "And anyway, I've used nearly all the parfleches for the pemmican. By the time I finish this batch, there will be nothing left in which to store any more."

"Then that is even more reason for me to leave, my sweet wife. When I return, I will bring some of the yucca plant. You can strip the fibers from the leaves, and use them for sewing hides I have prepared to make parfleches."

She knew he was right. They must prepare the food while it was there, but still she remained unmoving, watching him hungrily, feeling a slow stirring of excitement begin deep within her being. She wished the hunting trip were already over and night had come so they could return to their bed.

"Do not look at me in such a way," he groaned, pulling her back into his arms, tilting her face and pressing kisses on her eyelids. "I do not want to leave you, but I must go hunting."

"I know," she said huskily, clasping her hands behind his neck and stretching until she could reach his mouth. She could feel his body stirring to life against her and was delighted she could affect him in such a way.

"I know," she whispered again, her lips moving softly against his.

There was only a slight hesitation before she brushed his mouth with a featherlight kiss. Then her mouth moved over his copper face, his jaw line until she reached his ear. She blew softly into his ear and felt him shiver.

"What are you doing to me?" he groaned.

"What does it look like?" she asked huskily, drawing back slightly to examine his features. His face was flushed and his breathing had become ragged, and the pained expression in his eyes was somehow encouraging. Her gaze focused hungrily on his mouth again.

She pressed her lips softly against his, then deliberately hardened the kiss, feeling an immediate reaction in the lower part of his body. Emboldened, the tip of her tongue came out, tracing the outline of his mouth, then dipping quickly inside.

He groaned loudly, then unable to stand the temptation any longer, he swung her up into his arms. "You little witch," he whispered huskily. "What are you trying to do to me?" He kissed her, pressing hot, feverish kisses all over her face.

Eagerly, she searched for his mouth, but as though he were bent on punishing her he turned his head away, evading her lips. Tendrils of silky hair teased her jawline as he blew in her ears, bent on tormenting her just as she had tormented him until finally the waiting was at an end and his mouth was crushing her lips against her teeth.

As his tongue invaded the sweetness of her mouth, she sucked in her breath sharply. Then her tongue touched the tip of his, engaging in an erotic dance, and she moaned low in her throat.

She felt a sensation, almost of floating, as he carried her. Then he was lowering her to the pallet, his calloused hand sliding beneath the doeskin blouse, touching and caressing the fullness of her breasts, molding and shaping them with his rough hand until the nipples were taut, hard, and aching.

Impatiently, Lone Wolf shifted her, pulling the blouse over her head and throwing it aside. Almost immediately her skirt went the same way, and, when he returned to her, she felt his naked flesh against hers.

His lips found her breast, and he drew one of the taut buttons into his mouth, laving its tip with his tongue while his calloused fingers worked its magic on the other breast.

His other hand slid slowly down her body sending a tidal wave of desire racing through her. Her pulses were going wild, and her breathing sounded harsh in the silence as his hand reached the center of her desire.

She drew her breath in sharply as one finger plunged into her moistness, joined a moment later by another, stroking, and probing the hotness between her legs, making her quiver for relief.

Unable to control herself, Rebecca's hips began to

move suggestively as the ache in her body grew, becoming almost unbearable.

Then, his mouth was following the same path his hand had taken, blazing a trail down her stomach, nipping, and biting at the sensitive flesh as he worked his way down, lower and lower until, finally, he reached the soft mound between her thighs.

She stiffened, gasping in shock, her eyes opening wide as she suddenly realized his intentions.

"No, Lone Wolf," she whispered, pushing at him desperately. "Please don't."

Frantically she tried to close her legs against him for although he had made love to her this way before, it still seemed unnatural to her.

Lone Wolf ignored her protestations, both hands coming down to hold her thighs apart, and, as his tongue probed the moistness within, she shuddered, goose bumps prickling her flesh. She grabbed his head with both hands, twined her fingers through his thick, black hair, and tried to shove him away.

His lips tightened on the sensitive button, making her forget all her intentions to resist. She writhed beneath the pressure of his lips. The goose bumps had been replaced by a slow burning fire, and the flames were being fed by the delicious stroking motions he was making with his tongue.

Her resistance completely evaporated. Her thighs parted, allowing him more room, and she moaned, pressing against him as she surrendered to the ecstasy he was creating, urging him on. As the tension of desire continued to grow, he increased the pressure, driving her into a frenzy. She cried out, nearly senseless with pleasure.

And as she reached her peak, the final explosion came, splintering her emotions, scattering them throughout the universe, and she heard someone wailing in the distance, realizing a moment later that it was she, crying out her release in a convulsive climax of rhapsody.

As her shudders of ecstasy ceased and the muscles of her legs relaxed, she grew still. Then, Lone Wolf moved up her body, and she felt his weight heavy upon her.

Involuntarily, she wrapped her arms around his narrow waist, holding him close against her. As she felt his hardness throbbing against her, she realized suddenly that he had received no satisfaction while she lay satiated beneath him.

"Lone Wolf," she groaned. "I'm sorry—"

"Hush," he whispered, his lips brushing hers softly. Then his mouth captured hers, and he entered her, thrusting deeply within, riding high above her, burying himself in the moist, warm folds of her femininity.

Instinctively, her body took command, and she raised her hips, arching against him to meet his masculine thrusts, feeling an ache that must be assuaged as the tension began to build again deep within her body.

He drove into her body, over and over, harder and wilder, and she slammed forward against him, until finally, together, they reached their release, shuddering with ecstasy until she lay slack in his arms.

\* \* \*

"Lone Wolf." Rebecca tickled his nose with a strand of long brown hair, grinning when she saw his nose twitch as though trying to dislodge a fly. Amused, she brushed the hair across his nose again. This time, he didn't move a muscle.

Disappointed, she leaned closer, her eyes fastened on his nose, and slowly dragged the hair across again. But, still, there was no reaction. She frowned, moving back slightly and found herself staring into his amused gray eyes.

"You're awake."

"Yes," he said, trying to stifle a grin. "I sleep light, Rebecca. I knew exactly when you woke up."

"Then why did you pretend to sleep?"

"I was hoping you would use the same tactics to wake me as you did in the honeymoon bower," he said, and his voice spoke of his disappointment.

A blush crept up her cheeks, spreading across her face. "Shame on you for speaking of such things," she chided.

"Shame on you for doing such things," he countered with a grin.

"You didn't seem to mind," she said.

"You're right, I didn't. Perhaps if I closed my eyes again and pretended to sleep . . .?" His voice trailed away hopefully.

"Not this time," she said calmly, refusing to be embarrassed by his teasing. "If my memory serves me right, you claimed you had to go hunting. And, although I would much rather lie abed, I must finish making the pemmican."

He sighed, gathering up a silky length of brown hair

183

and letting it slide through his fingers. "Yes," he said, his voice showing his reluctance. "My mind tells me there is much work to be done, but I would far rather stay here and make love to you."

"That doesn't put food on the table," she pointed out to him. "Not that we have a table anyway," she grumbled lightly.

Something undefinable flickered in his gray eyes. "What need have we for such white man's luxuries," he said in a gruff voice.

"No need at all," she assured him, touching his face lightly, caressingly. "We have everything we need right here."

"Do you really mean that?" he asked, bending his face to hers, his narrowed eyes intent, for her answer was very important to him.

"Yes. I—"

The rest of her words were lost in his kiss. The kiss was so full of sweet longing that, by the time it ended, she had completely forgotten she had been about to confess her love for him.


Rebecca rubbed the root of the yucca plant over her hair, then laid it aside while she worked up a lather with her fingers. Using scrubbing motions, she worked until her scalp and hair were clean. Then, stepping from the cavern, she stood beneath the water that fell from the cliff overhang, drawing in a sharp breath as the cold water hit her naked body. Shivering, she rinsed her hair thoroughly.

When she had finished, she stepped back, away from

the fall of water, squeezed the excess water from her hair and snatched up the blanket, wrapping it around her slender form.

She shivered again as a gust of wind caught the edge of the blanket, flattening it against her body, sending icy fingers along her spine.

Then, using part of the blanket, she dried her hair quickly, for, although it was the latter part of June, the air still felt cold when the wind blew.

Picking up the clean doeskin shirt she had laid on a nearby rock, she stepped into it, then donned its matching top. Although the clothing helped chase the chill away, she was still shivering as she pulled on her moccasins. Then, picking up the water container she had already filled from the spring, she hurried down the path toward the dwellings.

Suddenly, a sense of apprehension filled her; the hairs at the back of her neck prickled with awareness, and she stopped abruptly. Her eyes scoured the bushes beside the trail ahead for some kind of danger, but she saw nothing unusual.

The wind gusted again and blew the loose dirt, spraying her with particles of dust and debris. Her eyes stung. She blinked rapidly at the sudden pain, and moisture filled her eyes to rid them of the offending grit. As though from a great distance she heard a sound that she had heard only once before. It began as a soft sigh and rose in volume until it sounded uncannily like the wailing of a multitude of spirits.

It was the wind blowing through the caverns.

She shivered. Despite the fact that she knew what it was, it still sent a chill racing up her spine. If she had

185

not already experienced it when Lone Wolf had been with her, she knew she would have been completely terrified.

She blinked her eyes again and felt some of the grit come out. Her vision cleared a little, but the moisture and dirt in her eyes caused a serious distortion in her world—a world suddenly gone mad with confusion.

"What the hell!"

She whirled around, her long, brown hair flying wildly in the wind. Dropping her container, she was barely aware of the water splashing her moccasins and skirt. Her eyes widened in shock, her pulses leaping wildly, and she stared at the buckskin-clad figure confronting her.

Fear raced up her spine. Although he was distorted by dust and tears, she could still see that he was a big man. She blinked rapidly, trying to clear her vision, her heartbeat drummed loudly in her ears. Another gust of wind hit. At the same time the moaning began again—louder this time. As the wail rose in tempo, it sounded as though the gates of hell had opened and unleashed thousands of tormented souls from the bowels of the earth.

"What in hell is that?" said a harsh male voice.

When he spoke, she recognized the words as English. She rubbed her eyes, finally succeeding in ridding them of the grit and dirt. Then she stared in astonishment at the grizzled old-timer confronting her.

Although he was a big man, he was slightly stooped. His battered coonskin cap dipped low over a beetled brow, and his faded-blue eyes held a hint of humor.

The old man looked about a hundred years old, with

deep lines arching from the flare of his nostrils and disappearing into the wealth of his snow-white walrus mustache. His chin was bearded, echoing the color and fullness of his mustache, just as the fabric of his weathered face mirrored the buckskin of his clothes. In the crook of one arm, he carried a flintlock rifle.

"How did you get here?" she whispered, her blue eyes wide with shock.

"Easy enough," he growled. "I just clumb down a tree back a ways." His faded-blue gaze was unwavering as he took in the wet buckskin clinging to her slender body. Beneath the clinging leather, her curves were unmistakable. "What I'm a wonderin' is what you're doin here? And what the hell was that godawful noise."

"I — it was the wind blowing through the caverns," she said, wondering if he presented a danger to her. "And I live here."

"I kinda figured it was the wind after I got studyin' about it," he said, nodding his head. "But when I first heared it, I weren't too sure. Reckon it could make most folks a mite uneasy." He leveled his gaze on her. "You live here alone?"

She studied him intently, wondering how far she could trust him. Even if he meant her no harm, if she told him she lived with Lone Wolf, would she be endangering her husband? "Why do you ask?" she hedged. "And just who are you?"

"Folks call me Buck," he said, spitting a stream of tobacco on the ground. He studied her with shrewd eyes. "I'm what's known around these parts as a mountain man. Don't much like folks. Specially un-friendly folks." He looked around, studying the trail leading to the cliff dwellings. "Now, the way I see it, if a feller was to be up in them rocks ahead, with his rifle sighted on me, I wouldn't take too kindly to it."

She remained silent, watching him with wary eyes.

"You appear to me to be a right nice little lady. More'n likely a mite scared. Don't reckon as how I blame you though. A gal caught in these parts alone don't always fare so good. Now I'll make you a little deal. If'n you was to tell me the truth, then I just might lay aside this rifle here." He patted the flintlock.

Could she trust him? Her eyes searched his faded-blue gaze and she saw something there that made her believe she could.

"Yes, I'm alone at the moment," she said. "My husband went hunting."

"Then you live here?"

"Yes."

"This husband a your'n. He an Injun?"

She hesitated, wondering how to answer him.

"Yep." He nodded his grizzled head. "I reckon he is." He spat again. "Guess it don't matter none to me. I ain't got nothin' against Injuns. Fact is, I got me a Injun wife waitin' in my cabin in the Rocky Mountains." His faded blue eyes studied her intently. "This Injun. He holdin' you prisoner?"

"No!" she said sharply. "He's my husband. I'm here because I want to be."

"Well, just thought I'd make sure. I couldn't rightly go away and leave a white woman a prisoner. I don't like mixin' in other people's business, but a case like that, reckon I'd naturally have to."

She smiled at him, finding a liking for the old man.

188

"You said you climbed down from the top?"

"Yep. Just happened to be standin' up on top and the sun was shinin' on some peculiar-lookin' rocks across the valley yonder."

"There's some more of the cliff dwellings across here. You must have seen them."

"Reckon that's what it was. And seein' as how I'm just naturally the curious type, and not in any particular kind of hurry, I decided to take a closer look. Happened to find that tree over yonder." He gestured at a spruce tree growing near the area of the spring.

She looked at the top of the tree and for the first time noticed it grew to a height of a couple of feet above the top of the cliff.

"You climbed down that? It doesn't look strong enough at the top."

"It is." He picked up the water container. "I'll get you some more," he offered. "Seein' as how I caused you to spill it."

"There's no need in that," she protested.

"Don't mind," he said, ignoring her protests. "And seein' as how I'm all ready down here, I'd like to have a look-see around." His eyes met hers. "If'n you don't mind, that is."

"No. I don't mind at all," she replied with a smile. "In fact, my husband shouldn't be back for a—" Suddenly she broke off, wondering if she was making a mistake.

"Don't worry none," he said gruffly. "You got nothin' to fear from me."

Somehow, she found herself believing him. "Would you like to stay and have something to eat?" she asked eagerly.

"Wouldn't want to put you out none." He eyed her keenly.

"It wouldn't." She smiled at him. "Please do. My husband will be gone most of the day."

"If it won't get you in any trouble with your man, I'd be much obliged."

"It won't," she assured him, determining not to tell Lone Wolf about it. She was eager to speak the English language with someone for, although Lone Wolf could speak it well, he insisted on using the language of the Chiricahua People.

With Buck carrying the water and following behind, they returned to the cliff dwellings. She had left a pot of stew cooking near the fire and she answered his questions about the city of the ancient ones as best she could. When the old man rose to leave, she found herself wishing she could invite him to stay the night.

"You got folks, girl?"

Rebecca hesitated a moment. "No," she said. "No one but my husband."

His faded-blue eyes were wise. "I don't go round tellin' folk's secrets," he said sagely. "If'n you want word carried you're alive, then I reckon I'd see your folks found out."

"No," she said, shaking her head. "There's no one I want notified."

"Uh huh. I reckon that's best. If'n you did have folks, it wouldn't make 'em feel any better knowin' you was livin' with an Injun. The way most white folks look at it, they'd rather see their womenfolk dead."

Rebecca shivered. Would Robert feel that way? Would he really rather see her dead than know she was living with an Apache Indian?

"Didn't mean to upset you none," Buck said. "Just wanted you to know. You seem like a contented little lady. If your man's good to you, you'd prob'ly be better off with him."

As he moved to take his leave, she stopped him. "Buck . . . I do have a brother. Would you mind not mentioning that you've seen me to anyone?"

"Figgered as much. And you can count on it." He picked up his flintlock rifle. "Reckon I'd better git movin'. Prairie Flower's been awaitin' too long already." His mouth split into a wide grin, showing tobacco-stained teeth. "Reckon she'll be right glad to see me." He waved his hand and moved down the trail to the spring. Suddenly he turned back. "Maybe you better not mention I was here."

She nodded. "I know," she said. "Be careful on your journey home."

She watched until he was out of sight, then, remembering she hadn't even brushed her hair since washing it, she went to remedy the matter.

Coiling her hair at the nape of her neck, she fastened it with porcupine quills. Then she began her preparations for the evening meal for Buck had made short work of the stew she had made.


She kept thinking of what Buck had said. Until then, it had never occurred to her that some people would feel she should have killed herself before submitting to the touch of an Apache.

It was then she realized just how much she had

changed. Ever since she discovered her love for Lone Wolf, she hadn't thought of him as an Indian. He was just the man she loved—her husband. But she knew Buck was right. If she returned to the white man's world, she would be condemned for loving him for the white man's world was filled with prejudices.

She looked out across the valley, saw the shadows on the opposite canyon wall and suddenly frowned. Lone Wolf was later than usual. Her gaze became anxious. Wondering what was keeping him and moving as close to the cliff edge as she could, she searched the forest of pines but saw no movement.

Chiding herself for her fears, for Lone Wolf could surely take care of himself, she moved the cooking pot a little farther back to allow for slower cooking. Lone Wolf would want to clean up before eating when he returned.

When an hour had passed and Lone Wolf still hadn't returned, she became even more anxious that something had happened to him. What if Black Bear had been waiting for him and had attacked him? What if he had even—No. She stilled her overactive imagination.

Nothing had happened. He just had to travel farther than usual to find game. Yes. That was it. He had been hunting here for months now. Of course the game was getting scarce. Soon, his head would appear over the ledge, and—

Suddenly, she could bear it no longer. Suppose he had fallen from the ladder while climbing the cliff. Cold sweat broke out on her at the thought of Lone Wolf lying helpless below.

Perhaps he had broken a leg or was even lying dead.

She couldn't bear it. Her heart began to drum loudly in her ears as she moved closer to the edge of the cliff. She must make sure he wasn't down there. And that meant overcoming her fear of heights.

Although panic-stricken, her feet carried her forward. Her blue eyes were fastened on the verdant green forest stretching out in the valley below but she could still see no sign of movement. It was as though she were all alone here, perched in an eagle's eyrie high above the earth.

She was perspiring freely now, but fear for Lone Wolf was greater than her fear of heights. Dropping down on her hands and knees, she crawled the last ten feet, then stretched out on her stomach as she peered over the edge, searching for some sign of her Apache husband.

## Chapter Eleven

The late afternoon breeze blew tendrils of black hair across Lone Wolf's lower jaw, teasing at the quiver of arrows hanging from one shoulder, lifting the feathers on the fat turkey hanging from his back by a leather thong. The headband fastened around his forehead kept the silky strands from his eyes, and that was good because right now he had great need of them.

He was being followed.

He had known he was being trailed for a couple of hours now. He could actually feel his shadow's eyes but he gave no indication of this. He had curbed the impulse to look back, knowing if he did he would see nothing for whoever was following knew what he was about and gave no sign.

His nostrils twitched, inhaling the clean fragrance of pine, the tangy scent of moist earth. The cool breeze bore no indication of his shadow upon it, but still Lone Wolf knew he was there.

He had left Rebecca early that morning and was anxious to return but dared not. It could be Black Bear who followed him, and his cousin's lust for Rebecca was great. Lone Wolf wasn't sure Black Bear's fear of the spirits he believed dwelled in the city of their ancestors would keep Black Bear from trying to take her if he found her alone.

Lone Wolf knew he must take care to lead his shadow away from the cliff dwellings where Rebecca waited. Then he must lose him.

He shifted the wild turkey to a better position, positioned his quiver of arrows where he could draw one at a moment's notice, and, gripping his bow lightly in the other hand, stepped up his pace, following a well-traveled deer track deeper into the forest.

He ran swiftly, putting a distance of miles behind him as he raced through the pine trees and quaking aspens. He breathed evenly as he ran, showing no signs of growing tired, for as a child he had trained as a long-distance runner, traversing four-mile courses through rough country, carrying a mouthful of water all the way without swallowing it or spitting it out.

As part of his training, he had been made to stay awake for long periods of time to learn how to deal with exhaustion, and now he could cover seventy miles a day on foot in the most forbidding terrain.

Farther and farther he ran, carefully laying a trail away from his beloved until he finally decided he was far enough. As he came across a stream, he entered it, wading through knee-deep water, making only a light swishing sound as he followed it downstream for several miles. He covered his trail carefully as he left the concealing water, knowing it would at least slow his tracker down.

Soon he encountered rocky ground and jumped

from stone to stone, taking care not to mar the surfaces as he went. Keeping a watchful eye to the rear, he made his way silently through the shrubs and rocks. Then, keeping low, he climbed a large boulder where he had a vantage point and anchoring his moccasined foot in a small crevasse, searched the area he had just vacated with narrowed eyes. Nothing moved; even the forest creatures were silent. He settled down to wait; an hour later he was still waiting.

Good.

He had lost him.

Retracing his steps, his heart beat swiftly with anticipation as he drew nearer the city of the ancient ones. He was eager to see Rebecca again. She would be pleased with his kill for it wasn't often that he bagged a turkey, and it would make a nice change from venison.

They had been at the cliff dwellings for a month now and she seemed to have adjusted well to her new life. As for him, he had never been happier. His love for her deepened, and with each passing day he hoped and prayed one day she would come to care for him.

A movement at the corner of his vision caught his eyes, and as he turned, he was already fitting an arrow to the bowstring. His relief was great as his eyes fell on the tall, slender form stepping from behind a concealing shrub at the edge of the forest.

It was Brave Eagle.

"So it was you," he said with a smile. "Why did you not show yourself?"

"I wondered if I could take you by surprise," Brave Eagle said, grinning widely as he clapped his friend on the shoulder.

"You never could before," Lone Wolf pointed out. "Why should it be different now?"

"I know, but thoughts of your bride could make you careless, and there is need for you to be wary."

Lone Wolf paid no attention to the teasing reference to Rebecca, going straight to the words which had caught his attention.

"Why is there need for me to be cautious?" he asked, his dark brows drawn together, his eyes narrowed on Brave Eagle. For some reason, visions of Black Bear attacking Rebecca filled his mind.

"I'm afraid I am the bearer of sad news, Lone Wolf." The words were spoken solemnly, and Lone Wolf's frown deepened.

"What is this news, Brave Eagle?"

"The bluecoats came to the village and searched it. They brought the disease they call smallpox with them, and now many of our people are sick."

Lone Wolf's eyes became grim. He knew how deadly small pox was to the Indian People, who possessed no natural resistance to it. When contracted, the disease wreaked a dreadful toll, often wiping out whole villages. "How many are sick?" he asked harshly.

"At least half of our people are infected already. Chief Tall Feathers has left with the families who are not infected. The others will follow later — if they survive."

"Little Turtle?"

"She is one of the lucky ones."

"Why did the cavalry go to the village?"

"They were searching for your wife. Many angry words were spoken, but the soldiers were few, and we

197

were many. It is good that it was so, or there would have been bloodshed. The bluecoats said we must return to the reservation to live."

Lone Wolf frowned. He had been expecting something like this ever since Black Bear had stolen Rebecca and killed her companion.

"They told us we must give up our hunting grounds and join Nachise on the reservation," Brave Eagle continued. "They claim the government will provide us with food and clothing."

"And what was Chief Tall Feathers' answer?" Lone Wolf asked grimly.

"Tall Feathers became angry and told them we had heard the flour and grain they provided was not fit to eat and the meat was rotten. They claimed they knew nothing of this and repeated their words of warning. If we did not go to the reservation, they would return and kill us."

Lone Wolf eyed his friend sadly. He had always known this day would come. The white men would never be able to live side by side with the Indians. They would never let it rest until they had herded all of the Indian People together on their *reservations*.

"Was anyone hurt?" he asked.

"No," Brave Eagle said. "But there is more news. You will be glad to hear it." He grinned widely, clapping his friend on the shoulder. "Yellow Hair was slain in the valley of the Greasy Grass."

Lone Wolf's expression lightened. "Custer was killed?"

Brave Eagle nodded. "Our Sioux brothers, along with the Cheyennes and Arapahoes, killed Yellow Hair and all his men. It was a great victory for our People."

"Yes," Lone Wolf agreed. So General George Armstrong Custer was finally dead. At last, the glory-seeking, merciless Indian fighter who was intent on personal glory had been defeated. Many hearts would be gladdened at the news, for he had been responsible for the deaths of countless men, women, and children.

"The soldiers will not take his death lightly," Lone Wolf warned. "They will want revenge. Our People will not be safe if they return to the village. I must return to help defend the rancheria against the bluecoats."

"You cannot help them. You would only risk death yourself and it would serve no purpose. The People who left with Chief Tall Feathers will be safe. If the bluecoats return, even they would not make war on the sick."

"I hope that is true," Lone Wolf said.

"There is more," Brave Eagle said. "Nachise has said Washington is dissolving the Chiricahua reservation, and sending our People to San Carlos in Arizona. We must leave our homes — find new ones. The bluecoats have been ordered by Washington to hunt down all of the Chiricahua people left off the reservation and kill them. Nachise is worried, my friend. He said peaceful and hostile bands will be treated alike and we must either return to the reservation or flee for our lives."

"Chief Tall Feathers has always spoken out for peace between our People and the white eyes," Lone Wolf replied, his gray eyes hard.

"That seems to be of no importance to the white men," Brave Eagle said. "Nachise met with Victorio, chief of the Mimbres Apaches. Victorio is worried. He has heard rumors that his people will also be moved from the reservation to San Carlos. He is well known for his peaceful ways but, if the bluecoats try to move him, he will lead the Mimbres against them."

"What does Geronimo say to this?"

"Geronimo has gathered his family and followers and left the reservation. He has gone to Mexico where the government cannot reach him." Brave Eagle's expression was grave as he watched Lone Wolf absorb the news.

"Chief Tall Feathers sent me to tell you where you could find us when you are ready to leave this place. I am to join the tribe where the waters come together. He believes the soldiers will not find us there."

"I regret my people have had to leave their homes," Lone Wolf said.

"You are not to blame," consoled Brave Eagle.

"It is because they were searching for my wife they found the rancheria, and so I must take the blame."

"The fault is Black Bear's," said Brave Eagle. "It was he who took her captive." He gave Lone Wolf a long, searching look. "Perhaps it would be better if you returned her to her people."

"I cannot," Lone Wolf said harshly. "Rebecca is my wife!"

Brave Eagle nodded. His ebony eyes studied his friend's face. "Then, you must keep her here," he said. "But do not let her leave the place of the ancient ones. Black Bear has left the village, and I fear he is searching for you."

Lone Wolf's eyes darkened. "I will handle Black Bear," he growled. "Rebecca will not leave the dwelling and Black Bear is afraid of the spirits. He will not be able to reach her and that is well for, if he ever touches her again, I will kill him."

Brave Eagle studied Lone Wolf's fierce expression, then changed the topic of conversation to a less disturbing one. "How is your wife adjusting to her new home?" he asked.

Lone Wolf's expression lightened considerably. "Better than I had expected."

"She is not yet with child?" Brave Eagle asked.

"No. And it seems to bother her. But there is time yet. I am in no hurry to leave. The game is plentiful here, as is the water. The ancient ones chose well when they built their city here."

"If I lived here with Little Turtle as my wife, I am sure I would feel the same about leaving."

Lone Wolf nodded. "Have you offered for Little Turtle yet?"

Brave Eagle flushed, his brows drawing into an angry scowl. "No," he said abruptly.

"What is wrong, my friend?"

"Swift Arrow spends much time with her."

"And Little Turtle smiles too much at him?" Lone Wolf questioned.

When Brave Eagle's scowl deepened, Lone Wolf knew he had guessed right. His friend was suffering from the pangs of unrequited love. He could sympathize with Brave Eagle for had he not gone through the same thing with Rebecca? Had his need for her not become obsessive and irrational?

"If you do not wish to lose her to Swift Arrow, you must act without delay," Lone Wolf told his friend.

"Her father will not wait forever."

"I know," Brave Eagle snapped gruffly. "My mind tells me this is so, but—when it comes to approaching him . . ." his voice trailed away.

"Be brave, Brave Eagle," Lone Wolf said, curbing the impulse to laugh at his friend. He knew from experience how hard it was to tell the woman you loved how you felt about her. For he had still not told Rebecca of his great love for her. But, surely, she had to know without his telling her. His actions had given him away, time and time again, and even now, his heart beat faster knowing he would soon be with her again.

Brave Eagle caught the swift look Lone Wolf threw toward the cliff several hundred yards in the distance. "You are anxious to be with your bride," he said. "I will not keep you longer."

"Come and eat with us, old friend," Lone Wolf said. "You must rest the night as well, for you have a long journey ahead of you."

"Yes," Brave Eagle said grimly. "And I must hurry for Swift Arrow wastes no time. Do not worry about me for I have dried venison."

Lone Wolf did not press him for suddenly Brave Eagle seemed very anxious to be away. Perhaps Little Turtle's father would receive a visit soon. From the look on Brave Eagle's face he would nearly bet on it.

"I have one word of advice, my friend," Brave Eagle said. "You must not let Rebecca leave the city of the ancient ones, for the bluecoats are moving in this direction. If she is found, you will lose her." With these sage words of advice, Brave Eagle took his leave.

Lone Wolf stared after his friend for a moment,

then, leaving the concealing forest behind, he hurried to the base of the cliff and began his climb up the pole ladder.

A heavy feeling of foreboding was upon him. Suppose Rebecca was still bent on escaping him and had found enough courage to climb down from the cliff dwellings after all. Brave Eagle said the soldiers were headed this way, and, although he was sure the white men knew nothing of this ancient city, if Rebecca saw them coming from a distance and managed the climb down to the valley floor . . .

It did not bear thinking about!

He knew he had hurt her by keeping her from her brother, but she wasn't the only one hurting. He had been tormented for some time by the absence of one particular confession.

She had never admitted her love for him.

Did that mean it did not exist? He could hardly bear such a thought. Rebecca had so much love to give a man and he wanted it all. Just being with her brought a contentment beyond compare. She was intellectually stimulating and when they made love his passions were met with a fervency equaling his own.

He began to climb faster, sighing with relief as he neared the top. Soon, he would see her. As his head reached the ledge, he gave one last pull on the ladder. Then he was there.

He stopped, startled, as his eyes fell on Rebecca lying on her stomach on the protruding ledge at the far side of the cavern. She was perspiring freely, her face colorless, her hands clenching tightly on the ledge, her eyes so intent on searching the wooded area below that she had missed him climbing the ladder.

Although he was careful not to make a sound, something must have warned her because she turned her head suddenly and jerked convulsively, her blue eyes widening in surprise as she saw him.

"Don't move!" he ordered sharply, moving slowly toward her. When he was close enough, he grasped both ankles in a tight grip and pulled her toward him. When he had her away from the ledge, he snatched her upright, clutching her tightly against his chest.

"I told you to keep away from the ledge," he grated harshly, "Can't I trust you at all?"

Tears gathered in her eyes, falling silently down her face. She knuckled them furiously away. "I was worried about you," she snapped. "You're late!"

"Late?" He arched a dark brow. "I didn't know I was expected to return at a certain time."

"I—It's only c—common courtesy to let me know if you're going to be this late getting home," she stammered, flushing. "The meal is ruined and . . ."

He stared at her, his jaw dropping in complete surprise. He snapped it shut. "You sound like a nagging wife," he teased, grinning widely.

"Well—I—" Her flush deepened, and she lowered her eyelids. She burrowed her head into his chest, muffling her voice. "I was worried about you."

"Were you really?" His eyes gentled, and he tilted her chin, forcing her to look at him. "Were you really worried about me, Little Blue Eyes?"

"Of course."

"Why?"

"Well—well—how would I get down from here if

204

something happened to you?"

His eyes darkened. He released her and moved away to the courtyard. His muscles rippled beneath his bronzed body as he removed the turkey from his back, then laid his bow and quiver of arrows aside. She shivered from the sheer pleasure of watching him.

She crossed the courtyard to stand beside him, her eyes dwelling on his expressionless face. Her eyes clouded over. She had liked his teasing mood. What had caused it to disappear? She wondered what would have happened if she had told him of her love.

As if sensing her eyes on him he looked up, catching her unaware. Flushing guiltily at being caught staring at him, she quickly averted her gaze, missing altogether the accusation in the turbulent gray depths of his eyes.

"What did you do today?" he asked, his tone deceptively mild as he plucked the feathers from the turkey.

"Do? Why—n—nothing," she stuttered, flushing guiltily. She wondered if he had found some sign of her visitor.

She sat down on the courtyard wall, picking up the unfinished basket she had been patiently weaving from the fibers of a yucca plant. Her fingers fumbled as she felt his gaze on her.

Unable to bear his scrutiny in silence, she looked up and smiled tentatively at him. "Is something wrong, Lone Wolf?" she asked.

"That's what I'm wondering," he said, his voice smooth as silk, his eyes never leaving her. "You're acting very strange today—almost guilty. It makes me wonder why. Do you no longer worry about being left here alone while I'm gone?" The words had a curious intonation.

"Not as much as I did in the beginning," she said. She threw a quick glance at him. "But today was an exception. I really thought something had happened to you. Usually it doesn't bother me though. After all, we've been here two months now, and I've had time to become accustomed to it." She threw him a quick glance, then her eyes skittered quickly away. Although his voice hadn't given any indication, his eyes were stormy, his body tense. Something wasn't right. Perhaps it would be better to risk his rage and tell him about the mountain man's visit.

"Lone Wolf—"

He interrupted her. "The heights no longer terrify you?"

"No. Not the heights." She sighed in relief. So that's what this was all about! He was only worried about her fear of heights. She hastened to reassure him. "In fact, I've grown so used to living up here with the eagles, when it's time to leave, I'll probably be able to climb down on my own." She knew she was exaggerating, but if it would take away his black mood then she would worry about the consequences later.

It didn't work.

His scowl deepened. "You would not try to leave this place alone, would you, Rebecca?" he asked in a voice as hard as tempered steel. "If that's what's in your mind, then you would do well to forget it. It would serve no purpose, even if you reached the valley. I've taken the horses to a pasture several miles away and you would never find them."

206

She stared at him, her blue eyes fringed with dark lashes wide with apprehension. His expression had turned forbidding, as cold and harsh as the winter, and deep within the depths of his gray eyes something flickered—something undefinable, something that told her she must proceed with care, and she felt hurt beyond belief.

Rebecca looked at him with wounded eyes. After all their time together, he *still* didn't trust her! Against her will, tears welled into her eyes.

With a muttered oath, Lone Wolf turned away as though unable to bear the sight of her. Then without another word, he strode down the pathway leading to the spring.

She stared after him for a moment, unable to believe he had just left her. Why couldn't he tell her what was wrong? Why was he so angry with her? Didn't he even want to try to clear the air between them?

He had been acting strange ever since he had returned from the hunt. He was such a complex character and so bewildering. Everytime she thought she had him figured out, something would happen to prove her wrong. Would there ever come a time when she would completely know him?

As the tears she had been fighting spilled over, sliding down her face, her mouth tightened, and she brushed angrily at them. She refused to cry over him! She had done nothing wrong, except maybe to worry over him, she decided, and, if he thought she was going to fall all over herself just to get him out of his bad mood, then he had another think coming!

* * *

Lone Wolf stood beneath the waterfall, allowing the cooling liquid to wash over his body. As his body cooled, so did his temper and by the time he had finished bathing, he was cursing himself for being every kind of fool.

Remembering the tears he had brought to Rebecca's eyes, he felt ashamed. How could he have reacted in such a way? She said she was watching for him so why had he jumped to the conclusion right away that she was lying?

It must have been the talk he had had with Brave Eagle. He was greatly concerned about what he had been told. From the sound of it, he suspected an all-out war was going to break out between the white men and his People. If that happened, no one would be safe. Not even Rebecca. He knew he couldn't keep her here indefinitely. They would have to leave some time and rejoin his People, and, if the soldiers attacked their village . . . In the heat of battle, the soldiers didn't always look to see who they were killing. They swept through the villages slaughtering anyone who got in the way. Women, children, old People — it made no difference to them. Rebecca would not be safe in the village, but how could he bear to take her to her home?

No. The thought was unbearable. He must think of a way to keep her safe with him. His eyes darkened. Suppose the soldiers came near enough so Rebecca could reach them? He didn't like to think of that. He hoped she no longer wanted to be rescued.

Of course, he could be wrong about what was troubling her. But then, even though he had been delayed on his hunt, he had been much longer a few times before, and he did not find her hanging over the cliff searching for him then. In fact, she had always made it a habit to stay well away from the cliff.

He forced the thoughts from his mind, determined as he donned his breeches and moccasins to return to her and get an explanation. This time, he would keep his mind open for he knew in his heart she would be able to explain her actions to his satisfaction.

On his return trip he saw something sparkling beside the trail and stooped to examine the object. It turned out to be only a stone. The sun glinting off the quartz had been responsible for the sparkle.

His gray eyes narrowed thoughtfully as he studied the rock. Maybe Rebecca would like it made into a necklace. A small smile tugged at his lips. Yes, that's what he would do. He would make her a necklace as a peace offering.

As he reached to pick up the stone, his eyes sharpened, narrowing intently on the unmistakable print of a boot in the sand. The print had been made recently, and it wasn't Rebecca's. It was too large and, although she still had her boots, she no longer wore them, preferring the comfort of the softer moccasins.

Someone else had been here.

His gray eyes began to glitter strangely as he remembered how Rebecca had acted. He examined the ground closely, finding tobacco stains marring the ground near the boot prints. And something else— something he had hoped desperately not to find.

Her moccasin prints!

She had stood near the visitor!

His expression was thunderous as he straightened up. So—he had been right all along. She had lied—if only by omission.

Who had been here? One of the soldiers? Her brother? If so, then why had he not taken her with him? Could it have been because they were expecting him, Lone Wolf, back and feared they would not have time to get away?

Perhaps they were only waiting for him to go hunting again before Robert returned for Rebecca.

If Robert planned to take her away, then he would have a fight on his hands. He would not allow anyone—even her brother—to take Rebecca from him.

His features became even grimmer as he followed the two sets of prints back to the ruins. Whoever it was, she had actually taken him to their home.

When he reached the ruins, he stood silently in the shadows, unnoticed by his wife as she moved fluidly about the courtyard, preparing their evening meal. His thoughts were full of turmoil, his thunderous expression becoming even blacker as he watched her.

He would keep her with him, by God! Even if it meant never leaving her side. No one would take what belonged to him!


She straightened up from testing the meat and vegetables, deciding they had cooked long enough. Now where was her husband? She looked down the path he had taken, her eyes widening in surprise as she saw him in the shadows, watching her in silence.

"The meal is prepared," she called to him.

The only indication he gave that he had heard was to come nearer. His steps as he approached were deliberate, almost stalking, and she noticed his body was stiff with barely controlled anger.

So—he was still angry with her.

Ignoring his black expression, she dished out meat and vegetables and handed him the filled bowl, then filling her own. He was standing so close that she could smell the leather from his buckskin breeches. Unwilling to let his mood spoil her supper, she carried her bowl to the wall of the courtyard farthest away from him and sat down to eat her stew.

As she scooped a spoonful into her mouth, she glanced over and saw him watching her. His steely gray eyes seemed to bore into her, mesmerizing, making it impossible for her to look away. As she watched, she could actually feel the tension emanating from him as his anger grew by leaps and bounds.

Becoming completely unnerved, she finally looked away, chewing her meat carefully, then trying to force it down. The silence was becoming unbearable and suddenly she began to grow angry.

*This is ridiculous!* she decided. *If he wants a fight, then he'll get one!*

Lifting her eyes to meet his, she placed her bowl on the wall. Then, standing up, she smoothed down her doeskin skirt, carefully gathered her courage, and moved to stand directly in front of him.

"All right," she snapped, crossing her arms over her breasts, and holding him with suddenly blazing eyes. "I've had enough. Out with it!"

His gray eyes flickered with something like surprise

211

as he stared up at her belligerent form.

"Don't pretend to be surprised," she said in a curt, biting tone. "You've been itching for a fight ever since you got back from your hunt, and by God! now you're going to get it!"

"And do you think you have a chance of winning such a fight?" His voice was silk on velvet and a trace of amusement flickered in his eyes.

"Maybe not! But I'm getting tired of you watching me all the time with that hateful look on your face. If you have something to say, then say it!"

"I thought maybe *you* had something you wanted to tell me!"

"Now what is *that* supposed to mean?"

"I am sure, if you put your mind to it, you can come up with an answer."

"You and your innuendoes!" she snapped. Her eyes were spitting blue flames at him, her expression furious. "Why don't you just say what's on your mind, and stop all this pussyfooting around."

He stared at her, his lips twitching suddenly. "Have I been — pussyfooting around?"

She nodded her head.

"Perhaps you're right," he said. "But I must say, you surprise me."

"I can see that. But I'm still in the dark. What are you angry with me about?"

"Answer a question for me first. Who was here today?"

Whatever she had expected, it hadn't been that. Her anger drained away, her face flushed with guilt. How did he know? Her eyes skittered away from his.

"Well, I'm waiting for your answer!" he grated harshly, standing up to tower over her. "Or does it take a while to think one up—to protect your precious Robert!"

"Robert?" Her eyes snapped back to his as her wits completely scattered.

"Yes, Robert! You thought to deceive me, didn't you? What happened? Was there not enough time to steal you away from me before I returned?"

"Steal me!" she gasped, her expression wavering between anger and disbelief. "Steal me! You call my brother coming to my rescue, stealing me?" Her mouth tightened angrily, and the little amount of control she had maintained broke loose.

"Damn you! You kidnap me, carry me away to some godforsaken place in the wilderness and subject me to your sexual urges. You hold me prisoner and then dare to accuse my brother of trying to steal me!"

She was too worked up to realize that, with every word she spoke, Lone Wolf was growing a little paler.

"But what else could I expect from you, you're nothing but a savage? You don't have the least idea how a *civilized* man would act."

"So it is true," he said heavily, his anger suddenly draining away to be replaced by a sadness so great it was terrible to see.

For the first time she became aware of his pale face and a pain stabbed through her breast. Her eyes clouded over with regret. "Lone Wolf," she said, gripping his arm tightly. "I'm sorry. I didn't really mean it. You just made me angry with your suspicions."

"The truth usually comes out in anger, Rebecca," he

213

said in a weary voice, pulling away from her hand as though he found her touch distasteful. When he turned away from her, it seemed so final.

"Lone Wolf, please let me explain," she said. "Robert wasn't here. It was someone else. He was an old mountain man just —" She broke off, for there was no one to hear. Lone Wolf had gone. She had driven him away with her thoughtless words. He had disappeared over the ledge.

Her eyes filled with futile tears as she stared at the empty ledge. Why couldn't she learn to control her wayward tongue? What had happened to her resolution to become the kind of wife Lone Wolf wanted? She wouldn't blame him if he never returned.

With a hopeless sob, she sank down on the courtyard wall, covering her face with her hands.

## Chapter Twelve

The full moon cast its pale glow through the window as Rebecca lay on the buffalo-hide bed. She listened to the soft swish of Lone Wolf's buckskin breeches as he removed them. She had undressed while he was gone and slipped between the covers to await him. Sitting down on the pallet, he pulled his moccasins off and tossed them aside.

She waited until he had slid beneath the blanket, then turned to him, searching for the words that would breach the wall he had raised between them. She couldn't stand his anger again; she had to make him talk to her, make him understand. Putting her arms around his neck, she cuddled close against him.

"Lone Wolf," she whispered, her words slightly muffled as she nuzzled her face against his neck. "I'm sorry. I didn't mean it. When I get angry, I can't seem to control my tongue. Please forgive me."

"Forget it, Rebecca," he said in a weary voice. "It doesn't matter. Go to sleep."

"It doesn't matter?" She drew back, closing her eyes against the pain. She felt torn apart at his words. Did it really not matter to him?

"No," he said harshly. "Now go to sleep." He lay unmoving, his eyes on the ceiling of the small room. When he spoke again, the words seemed to be dragged from him. "You said it was a mountain man. Why was he here?"

"He was just curious." She raised up on one elbow, staring at him through the faint light. Perhaps now, he would be willing to hear her explanation. Her eyelids drifted shut. Please let him listen.

"How did he get here?"

As she explained Buck's descent from the mesa top, her words fell into the distance between them like stepping stones. A path one or the other could cross if the desire was there. Then, Lone Wolf's harsh voice scattered the stones.

"Why didn't you tell me about him?" he grated. "Why did you try to hide it?"

"I didn't hide it. I—I just didn't mention it."

"A lie by omission is no less a lie, Rebecca." His gaze flickered over her face for a moment, then touched his own clenched hands before returning to a study of the ceiling. "Did you use him to send word to your brother?"

Her heart lurched. How could he think she would do such a thing? Didn't he realize how much she wanted to stay with him? Her throat closed over her denial. If he didn't already believe, she had no words to make him believe. So she said nothing at all.

"Rebecca," he growled warningly. "Answer me."

Still she didn't speak.

"Rebecca." His fingers closed over her shoulder, and he shook it softly. "Dammit, tell me."

"No," she snapped, jerking her shoulder away. "I didn't send word to my brother. I wouldn't think of it."

"Yes," he said softly. "You didn't do it because you didn't think of it. I can believe that."

"Of course you'll believe that." She crossed her arms over her chest and made her own study of the ceiling. "You'd believe anything about me but the truth."

He levered himself upright. "The truth being that you *did* send word?"

She hefted herself up next to him. "No. The truth being that I have never lied to you. The truth being that I had a visitor but I sent no word to my brother. The truth being that I didn't send for him because I didn't want to leave you."

"I suppose the mountain man just went on his way and forgot about you?" His voice was sarcastic.

"I suppose he did."

"Do you really expect me to believe that?" he asked incredulously, clearly disbelieving.

"Whether you believe it or not, it's true." She held his gaze steadfastly, her heart damped down as much as possible. Why was he always so willing to believe the worst of her? Of course, she realized now she had been wrong in keeping Buck's visit a secret from him; she realized that now, but it was really a well-intentioned mistake.

"If you're telling me the truth, Rebecca," he growled, "why did you try to hide it from me?"

"Because I knew this would happen," she said. "I *knew* you would react this way."

Swallowing over her anger, swallowing over the ball of hurt in her throat, she touched his face lightly, smoothing his dark hair back from his brow, caressing

217

the angry lines of his face as if she could erase them.

"Lone Wolf, please. Hasn't there been enough fighting between us already?" Her voice was as soft as the touch of her fingers. Love soft. If his ears couldn't hear that love, or his eyes see it, surely there was at least one part of his body that could recognize it. Just one square inch if she could but find it.

He was silent for a moment, his muscles tightening. She could feel him fighting to bring his anger under control. Then suddenly he relaxed, all the tenseness draining from his body, and he gave a heavy sigh.

Wrapping his arms around her, he pulled her close against his hard, masculine chest.

She laid her head against him, her ear above the thumping of his heart.

"I do not want to fight with you," he murmured softly into her hair. "In fact, it is the last thing I have ever wanted to do."

His breath whispered on her forehead, followed closely by the touch of his lips brushing lightly against her skin. He slipped his arm beneath her, drawing her against his hard chest.

She shuddered in relief. Her hand rested on his chest, feeling the steady rise and fall of his breathing. "Love me, Lone Wolf," she whispered, her mouth trembling against his skin.

His lips found hers, his breath flowing warmly, mingling with hers. His hand moved in soft circles against the sensitized flesh of her naked back.

Weaving his fingers into her hair, he deepened his kiss. His tongue circled her mouth slowly, awakening a slow burning flame. Her nostrils registered the clean male fragrance of him, and, beneath the fingers resting

218

on his chest, she could feel the increased tempo of his heartbeat.

His hand moved to the swell of her breast, making slow circles as he teased the tautened peaks. Rebecca's pulse began to beat rapidly as his hand touched her hip and moved over her stomach until it reached the apex of her desire.

As his hand searched out the most intimate part of her body, his tongue speared her mouth, plunging deeply, dueling with hers. His finger entered her moistness, rubbing gently, igniting a fiery passion that flowed outward, creating an incredible sensation that spread out, threatening to consume her entire body.

He pulled his mouth from hers, and she sighed into his parted lips in agony at the separation. Then he slowly moved down her body, leaving small love nibbles as he went, cherishing each little section equally. When he reached her breast, he darted his tongue out to stroke her tautened nipple, to circle the pebbled crest, before he pulled it wetly into his mouth, treasuring it with his teeth.

Her heart pounding erratically, she arched against him, moaning, twining her fingers through his thick hair as she clutched him desperately against her. She could feel his desire, thick and hard against her thigh, and, as his mouth found hers again, the searing passion of his kiss lifted her to dizzying heights.

She reached out and grasped his strength, touching the satiny skin, caressing it gently, reveling in her power. Then suddenly, she sucked in a dizzying gasp of air as he slid his solidness into her softness. Gasping with pleasure, she writhed against him, wild with desire.

His masculinity filled her with the thrust of life itself as he lay deep inside her body. The shadows of her earlier fears had been chased away by the fires he had kindled deep within her being.

He moved slowly against her, his body beaded with sweat as he tried to restrain himself until her desire was as great as his. As he began to move, she shuddered, arching wildly against him, raking his back with her fingernails.

"Now, Lone Wolf," she pleaded.

Then he was plunging wildly, moving against her, faster and faster until with agonizing pleasure, they both reached the pinnacle of desire together.

He lay still for a moment, then Lone Wolf rolled over, easing her gently to his side. He brushed the dampened hair back from her perspiration-streaked face and pulled her head against his chest.

She gave a soft sigh of relief, snuggling against him like a contented kitten. As his arms tightened about her, she turned her face to his chest and kissed him softly. She felt content, for she was where she wanted to be—in his arms. As her eyes closed in sleep, he whispered the words of love that she had longed to hear for so long.

Slowly, Rebecca opened her eyes, her mouth curving enigmatically. Raising her elbows in a bone-lengthening stretch that bared her upper body, she turned to greet Lone Wolf. Only he wasn't there.

She was alone.

He must have risen early. She rose from the buffalo robes and dressed quickly, then stepped out into the gray light of dawn.

She looked at the empty courtyard and a frown creased her forehead. Where was he? Her eyes swept the silent cavern, then fell upon the trail leading to the spring. She felt relief flow through her and smiled. Of course. He must have gone to the spring to bathe.

Her eyes lit with mischief and she headed down the trail. She pictured his surprise when she joined him beneath the waterfall. But when she reached the spring, she stopped abruptly for only silence awaited her. There was no sign of Lone Wolf.

Unbidden tears welled up into her eyes, but she brushed them away impatiently. *Damn him.* And damn herself. Damn the tears that flowed like a mountain spring. Lone Wolf had no right to be angry with her. *She* should be angry with him. And even if he had the right to be angry, tears would still do no good.

Sniffing defiantly, she set about preparing a lonely meal. Finally, her breakfast was ready, and, with a furious glare at the pole ladder resting against the ledge a few hundred yards away, she sat down.

But she had to force herself to eat, force herself to clear up when she was done, even force herself to search for something to do, for something to keep her busy.

Walking to the drying racks where strips of venison were hanging to dry, she turned them over. She tried to keep her mind off Lone Wolf as she worked but found it impossible. No matter how she pushed it away, his face kept rising to her mind.

Her actions were automatic as she stoked the fire. When the smoking process was done, she would store the meat in buffalo-hide pouches and put it with the rest of the supplies.

As the sun rose in the sky, she kept herself busy, with one task leading to another, until finally she picked up her weaving. Before long though, she laid it aside, realizing the work required more concentration than she had to give it. She began to pace back and forth across the courtyard, while Lone Wolf's accusations ran through her mind.

Why was he so willing to believe she would lie to him? Why so unwilling to accept her sincerity? Her love? Of course, she had known he would be angry about Buck's visit, but why should he think she had sent for help? And where was he now? Could Buck have betrayed her and actually sent word to Robert? She rubbed her damp palms uneasily down the side of her deerskin skirt.

If he came for her, she wouldn't go!

She sucked in a heart-wrenching breath. She wouldn't, couldn't leave Lone Wolf. But, she thought, her throat choking, that would be a bit foolish, wouldn't it? Lone Wolf didn't love her. For a while she had hoped he might, had even, for the space of a heartbeat, believed he did. But his lack of trust proved her wrong. After all, hadn't Aunt Bess always said that love and trust walked hand in hand? Without the one, the other had no substance.

So there was no sense in fooling herself any longer. Lone Wolf didn't love her. It was only desire he felt.

She stared into the distance, into the sun-scorched, endless blue of the sky. Why did she stay? Hadn't she even an ounce of pride left? And if she hadn't, what would there be left for her when Lone Wolf had had his fill? Would she be passed around like a tasteless stew, handed from one brave to another?

"No," she spat, clenching her fists as she remembered how she had begged him to make love to her. She tried to push the memories away but they wouldn't let her be; they clamored at her, elbowed her, poked and prodded and punched.

She dropped her head into her hands. "No-o-o," she moaned. He was using her, selfishly taking what she had to offer and giving nothing in return.

She whirled, her hair flying out behind her, and paced to the back of the cavern. Its dimness slipped around her, a shadowy cloak, the coolness caressing her heated skin. Her thoughts were in a turmoil. How could she continue to live with Lone Wolf, knowing he cared so little for her? Then again, how could she face leaving him?

Perhaps he wanted her to go.

No! Her eyelids shut tightly as her mind skittered frantically away from that thought, remembering instead the passion-filled nights they had shared.

But no matter how tightly she squeezed her eyes shut, they proved insufficient barriers to her skittering thoughts, to a puritan side of her personality she hadn't known existed before. Passion, it informed her, didn't necessarily mean love. Besides, it insisted, he only lusts after your body.

Tears filled her eyes, and she knuckled them away, refusing to cry. She pushed the thought from her mind, refusing to allow it room to grow. Feeling the need to keep moving, she gathered up her water jug and left the cavern to take the path that led to the spring. There was no contentment to be had there though, so she returned to the dwelling, still fighting to calm her wayward thoughts.

They refused to be calm.

Why had Lone Wolf gone hunting again? They had plenty of meat. Had he grown tired of her already? Was that why he had left without waking her this morning? Pain radiated through her breast. She was the one who instigated their love-making last night. Perhaps he had left before she woke for fear she would make advances again. Perhaps he had hoped she would be gone when he returned?

Closing her eyes against the pain within her head, within her heart, she crossed her ankles and scissored down onto the floor of the cavern, in a pose that mimicked Lone Wolf as she had seen him so many times before an open fire. Then, she dropped her forehead into her hands.

What if he had hoped she would leave? After all, it was because of her he had left his people.

*Do him a favor, Rebecca*, she told herself. *Leave.*

She sighed. She couldn't leave now. She hadn't finished the shirt she was making for him.

"Fool!" she bit out, lifting her gaze to the rocky wall. "You're just making up excuses!"

Okay. She admitted it. She *was* making excuses. But, if he wanted her to leave, then she would.

First though, she would finish the shirt. As a token. A parting memory.

She stood and, heavy-hearted, took the shirt she had meant to be a surprise from its hiding place.

Using the tough fibers from the yucca plant, she finished seaming up the soft doeskin. Then, with slightly clumsy fingers, she added blue beads for decoration from the small bag Little Turtle had given

224

her and spread it out to look at it.

Despite the fact she had been clumsy working with the unfamiliar items, it was a beautiful shirt and should fit Lone Wolf well.

In their bedroom, she spread the shirt carefully across the buffalo robes. He couldn't fail to see it there. Nor fail to accept it. When winter set in, perhaps he would even appreciate its warmth.

Afterward, she crossed the courtyard, stopping by the kiva where their goods were stored. Then, gripping the pole ladder, she lowered herself through the hole, squinting slightly as her eyes adjusted to the sudden darkness. The air was stale, musty, but it was cool and had proved to be the perfect place to store their supplies.

As her gaze touched each of the buffalo-hide storage bags she had filled with dried meats and fruits and vegetables, a feeling of pride rose within her. She had accomplished a lot in the two months she and Lone Wolf had been here.

Even up here, halfway to the heavens, she had managed to collect and dry several different kinds of fruits and vegetables.

The variety of stalks and roots she had put up was even greater than the fruits and vegetables. Some of these, such as the wild turnips, had been gathered in the valley below and carried up by Lone Wolf. At least, she told herself, Lone Wolf would have plenty of food for the coming winter.

Selecting two parfleches filled with pemmican, she located an empty water skin, knowing she must be well supplied with food and water, remembering well her last attempt at escape. She dared not take much for

Lone Wolf had said the horses were several miles away and she knew she mustn't load herself down. She refused to even consider what would happen should she not be able to find Diablo.

Finally, she turned. Now she must face the cliff.

Slinging the two buffalo-hide bags across her shoulders, she secured them around her body, then moved closer to the edge. As she stared fearfully out over the valley, her mouth dried, and she wiped away a sheen of perspiration from her forehead.

It was a long way down to the valley floor.

She breathed in a raspy chestful of air, then let it out, steeled herself, and gripped the pole ladder tightly with both hands. Her knuckles whitened, and the wind felt cold in her lungs, clammy against her damp flesh.

Closing her eyes, she searched for the first rung with her moccasined foot. When her foot connected with the pole step, she tested it, found it firm, then lowered herself to the next step.

*Open your eyes, fool!*

She opened her large blue eyes and focused them on a fluffy white cloud floating lazily in the clear, blue sky. She tried to concentrate on it while she searched with her foot for the next rung in the ladder.

As she found another step, she faltered.

*Don't look down!*

Her hands were slick with perspiration, and she gripped one of the long poles tightly with one hand, while she wiped the other down her doeskin skirt. Then she repeated the process with the other hand. As soon as her hands were dry she began her descent again.

She was halfway down when she froze — and hung there — a quivering lump of flesh clinging to a few

226

insubstantial twigs.

Lone Wolf watched a squirrel dart out from the underbrush, halt, cock his head quizzically, then scamper up a pine tree.

It wasn't the first sign of life Lone Wolf had seen this morning, but neither was it the one for which he waited—waited, yet hoped his wait was in vain.

He had sat beneath the concealing branches of this pine tree all morning. Now, he watched for Rebecca to try to leave the cliff dwellings, even while he prayed she wouldn't.

Then all hope died in him. She was there on the ledge. And even from where he sat, even though the distance between them was so great, he could still sense her terror.

Though his face was impassive, his fear for her froze him as immobile as a freshly startled deer. Not a whisper of air stirred in his nostrils.

For a moment, as her slim body poised at the top of the ladder, he felt as if his heart might burst inside him. *For God's sake, Rebecca*, the refrain pounded in his brain. *Stay there. Don't—for God's sake—don't try to come down.*

Time ceased to exist for him. Each second, each step she took, measured an eternity. Each moment stretched itself a hundredfold.

As she descended, light slithered across her silky hair, bronzing it to burnished gold.

Still, his heart almost refused to believe his own lying eyes. God, how he had prayed she would prove his fears wrong.

Still silent, still barely breathing, he watched every faltering step she took, each one stabbing into the dream that refused to die.

She was his. Only his, and no other's. It was written in the stars, etched into his heart, burned into his brain. He would not, could not let her go.

When she halted, midway down the ladder, and stayed there, he waited.

And waited.

Then he was up, fluidly jack-knifing himself upright, cursing, running toward the cliff, moving against what seemed incredible resistance, fear a hundred-weight in his chest, his gait slow, too damned slow, the underbrush grabbing at him, yanking handfuls of his trousers, slowing him down, holding him back.

God, would he ever reach her?

He knew from the part inside of him that shared her every breath that she was overcome by terror and had frozen on the ladder. He had to reach her before that terror became so great that she fainted.

When he was still a distance away, he jumped for the ladder and scrambled up it, two steps at a time.

Sweat rolled off his face, into his eyes, and he shook it away. He couldn't slow down. Even should his heart burst inside of him, he couldn't stop — couldn't lose control. He didn't dare. He had to stay calm for Rebecca.

*Hold on, Rebecca. I'm coming, Little Blue Eyes.*

Then he was there and she was in his arms. He clung weakly to a pole with one hand and stroked her hair with the other, his heart still laboring. By no means were they out of danger, but at least now they were together. And he would take her to safety.

"Rebecca," he whispered, looking with concern at her beloved features. Her face was damp with perspiration, her blue eyes blank and unfocused. He had to get her off this ladder. Carefully, he pried her fingers loose from around the pole. She shuddered convulsively, fresh beads of sweat dotting her hairline.

He twisted his arm around her waist and, drawing on his last reserves of strength — reserves he hadn't even known existed — he carried her to the top. On the ledge, he swung her fully into his arms, then laid her down in the courtyard, holding her tenderly against him until she moved slightly. Then, she shuddered, and gasped, taking in large gulps of air.

"It's all right, Little Blue Eyes," he murmured, and, if she had looked into his eyes, she would have seen a reflection of his pain, of his love. "Everything's all right. You're safe now," he soothed.

"I was so scared," she whispered, her arms clenched tightly around his waist. "Lone Wolf, I couldn't move."

"I know," he said sadly, stroking her hair gently. "I know, love. But there's no need to worry now. You're safe here with me."

He held her tightly against him. He stared unseeingly over the top of her head into the valley and relived over and over again the horror of seeing her, frozen on the ladder, unable to move at all.

What if she had fallen? Had died in the falling? Shadows crept across his gray eyes at the thought of losing her so irrevocably.

Even letting her return to her brother would be preferable to that. At least then, he would know she was alive and breathing and that, someday, they might even meet again. Though at the moment the idea seemed far-fetched, still the thought of one day passing her on the only street in Silver City teased at him.

The muscles in his jaw tautened as he thrust the notion away. If Rebecca returned to the white man's world, he knew he would never see her again. He would never breathe in her fresh scent again. He would never know the joy of their love-entangled limbs. And she had become as necessary to him as the air itself. He couldn't give her up.

"Lone Wolf," she whispered, her blue eyes lifting to meet his turbulent gaze. "Are you terribly angry?"

He brushed a kiss across her forehead. "I am trying not to be, but I find it very hard. Your foolish actions could have killed you."

She buried her face in the hollow of his neck. "I know."

"Then, why, Rebecca? Why did you do it?"

Her answer was muffled. He had to strain to hear it. "You left without waking me up."

He pulled her away from him and studied her trembling face, his brow knitting. "You tried to run away because I left?"

She nodded, her eyes downcast. Then, with a weak smile, she lifted them. "Have you eaten today?" she asked.

"No."

"Then I'll fix you something," she said, trying to rise.

"No," he said, holding her steadfast. "I'm not hungry."

"But you need to eat," she insisted, wiggling out of his arms. "It won't take me long." When she tried to rise, though, her legs wobbled beneath her.

"Sit still, Rebecca," Lone Wolf said sharply, settling

her back down. Then he stood. "If it will make you feel better, I'll prepare the meal."

"But—you mustn't."

One dark eyebrow floated upward. "And why is that?" Lone Wolf asked.

"Well—" Rebecca toyed with the edge of her skirt— "you know." She swallowed and stared up at him. "It's woman's work."

His chuckle was humorless. Now, when she was finally beginning to adapt to the Apache way, he wasn't sure he wanted her to. "I think I can make one meal," he said, "without becoming less of a man."

"But—it's not the first time!"

"Still, I doubt my manhood's in danger." His voice was hard, cold almost. Then, softer, warmer, he asked. "Would you like to lie down?"

She shuddered and wrapped herself in her own arms. "I don't want to be alone," she told him.

"You're cold, aren't you? I'll get you a blanket."

In their bedroom, he knelt to remove the blanket, and, as he did, his eyes fell on the doeskin shirt, decorated with blue beads and spread out to catch his attention. His breath caught sharply.

He touched the shirt almost reverently. When had Rebecca made it? And more to the point, why?

Returning to her, he wrapped the blanket around her shoulders and tucked the ends carefully beneath her chin. "Thank you for the shirt," he said quietly.

"You liked it?"

He nodded. "It's very beautiful. More beautiful than any I've ever seen." His eyes studied her intently. "Why did you make it?"

"Because winter can be cold."

Yes, he thought, as he stoked up the fire, his eyes returning to her repeatedly. Winter can be very cold. Bitter even.

And, as much as he tried to hide from it, he had a strange feeling his coldest, bitterest winters were yet to come.

# Chapter Thirteen

The afternoon sun was warm, even under the cliff overhang where Rebecca stood, picking plums. The birds sang among the trees at the head of the narrow canyon, and her gaze roamed the trees occasionally, catching a flash of color as one flitted through the branches. She dawdled, listening to their cheerful melody, then plucked a fat, red plum, checked it thoroughly to make sure it was free of worms, then dropped it into the basket.

She gave a long sigh. At the rate she was working, it would take a while to fill the basket, but she didn't care. Plum picking was only an excuse to get away from Lone Wolf's overwhelming presence anyway.

Three days had passed since her attempt at escape, and during that time he had not left the cliff dwellings. She could tell by his temper he was growing tired of the inactivity.

How long would it take before he felt he could trust her again, she wondered. She scuffed her moccasined foot in the buffalo grass, watching it bend and flow, bend and flow, as if her fate hung on the flexibility of the spiny strands.

Obviously, she had done a great deal of damage with her aborted escape attempt. And not just to their relationship. After freezing on the ladder, she found herself terrified to even think of going near it again.

And now Lone Wolf refused to leave her alone!

She perched on a large rock, resting her basket beside her. She knew he didn't trust her now. His eyes followed her everywhere she went. Of course, she didn't really blame him. But by not hunting for fresh game, they were depleting their winter supplies.

She realized now she had been a fool to try and leave, but, for some reason, she seemed to have no control over her emotions of late. She didn't wonder that Lone Wolf was impatient with her; she was impatient with herself. She had even begun to wonder if something might be physically wrong with her.

A rustle sounded to one side of her, startling her, and she twisted toward it, her heart beating madly, knocking her plum basket to the ground to lie unnoticed in the leaves near the base of the rock.

Her blue eyes narrowed intently as she searched for the source of her uneasiness, but she saw nothing out of the ordinary. The sun cast a golden light over the bushes and trees at the head of the box canyon, making everything appear innocent and peaceful.

Her eyes traveled farther, lowering to the top of one pine tree growing on the valley far below. Because the canyon floor was higher at this point and because the tree itself was so tall, the top reached a height of only a few feet from the ledge on which she stood.

While she watched, the treetop moved, its branches quivering and her pulse leaped with fear.

234

Had Buck returned? Was he climbing the tree this minute?

No, no. She rubbed her fingertips against her creased forehead. It couldn't be Buck. He had come down from the mesa top, not the valley floor.

Could it be Black Bear? First, she shuddered at the thought, then forced herself to consider it.

The treetop was spindly and didn't *seem* strong enough to hold a man's weight, especially a man as heavy as Black Bear. Still, there was always the chance.

But, if it was Black Bear, she would deal with him. She refused to be caught off guard for a third time.

She looked around for something to defend herself with. All she could find was a rock about the size of her fist. She picked it up and hefted its weight. It would do nicely, especially if she caught him by surprise and conked him on the head with it.

In her determination to catch her enemy off guard, she forgot her fear of heights enough to move closer to the ledge and lean over, bracing her fingertips on the edge for balance.


Lone Wolf sat on the courtyard wall, whittling impatiently at a piece of aspen. Rebecca had been gone for over an hour and he was worried. He slanted a narrowed glance down the trail leading to the spring.

She had told him she was going to pick plums. How long could it take to fill a basket when every bush was laden?

He had not protested because he had a need to be alone with his thoughts, away from her disturbing presence. Besides, since she would have to pass him to use the ladder, he felt it would be safe to let her go.

He stood up, stretching tense muscles, and casting another look down the path. He was annoyed at himself that he couldn't control his emotions where she was concerned. And he knew he couldn't stay here in safety much longer and let his People do all the fighting. His mind had been in a turmoil since Brave Eagle's visit. He knew the time had come when they must go, and yet he worried for Rebecca's safety. She was not among them willingly. She had been taken captive. He couldn't put her life in danger. But neither could they continue to stay here and leave the fighting to others. He was sure the braves were readying their war gear and he should be there with them.

Moving to the fire, he hunkered down beside it and stirred it to life with a stick. Then he added another limb. Rebecca would need a blaze to cook their meal when she returned from the spring.

If she returned!

*Damn!* He pushed himself upright. The waiting was getting to him.

He looked down the trail again, found it still empty, and scowled. His patience had long since gone, and, if she didn't return soon, she would find him in a foul temper.

Crossing to the courtyard wall, he sat down on it. A scuffling noise caught his attention and his gray eyes narrowed on a collared lizard darting away to the farthest reaches of the dwellings, its bright green color brilliant even under the shade of the cliff overhang.

Again, his eyes narrowed on the trail.

*Empty.*

His scowl grew blacker.

He looked out across the valley, his slitted eyes scanning the distance for any kind of movement. Perhaps the old-timer had already sent help for her. The only thing he saw was a turkey vulture riding the air currents above the canyon's floor.

His gaze moved back to the trail.

*Dammit! Where was she?*

Unable to stand it any longer, he rose from the courtyard wall. His big body was tense as he strode down the path to the spring.

*Slow down. Don't let her see your concern.*

His legs seemed to have a mind of their own as they carried him swiftly down the path. As he rounded a curve, he stopped short. She was near the edge of the ledge, studying the top of a tall pine tree intently.

*Dammit!*

*She wouldn't try to climb down. Not that way. She couldn't be so stupid.*

He approached her cautiously.

"Rebecca."

Despite his soft voice, she jumped, her eyes flashing quickly to him.

"Lone Wolf," she said, a trifle breathlessly. "You startled me."

"Come back to the camp," he ordered, clasping her hand in an iron grip and pulling her away from the ledge.

"But I haven't finished gathering the plums."

"Forget the plums!"

"Is something wrong?" Her puzzled eyes searched his thunderous expression.

"No," he said, but voice was grim, and he began dragging her toward the camp.

"Wait. My basket."

Grimly, he pulled her with him as he returned for the half-filled plum basket. He didn't relinquish his tight hold on her as he stooped to pick it up, then headed for the camp again at a fast pace.

"Lone Wolf," she said, her breath quickening as she ran to keep up with him. "Why are we in such a hurry?"

"It's past time for you to start the evening meal," he snarled, tightening his grip on her hand.

"Past time for—but it's only the middle of the afternoon," she protested. "There's plenty of time."

"I'm hungry now!" he snapped.

"Well, I'm not!"

She dug in her heels. She was tired of his moods. Tired of his dragging her along with him like so much baggage. Her chin lifted defiantly as she faced him.

"What's the matter with you?" she demanded. "You've been this way since—since . . ." her voice trailed away.

"Go on!" he snarled. "You might as well say it! Since you tried to run away." His eyes were dark with fury. "Well, what would you have me do? I don't dare let you out of my sight for fear you will try to leave and kill yourself doing it!"

"Would it matter so much to you if I did manage to kill myself?" she yelled, her fury at his treatment overcoming her good sense.

He stared at her silently for a moment, then with a frustrated oath he yanked her to him, picked her up, and tossed her over his shoulder.

"Let me down! You—you—Neanderthal!" she screeched, wriggling her legs against his restrictive grasp and flailing his back with her fists.

He lifted a hand and brought it down with a resounding whack. Smack on the softness of her rear end.

"Aa-ah! Wha— You—you heathen!"

She struggled wildly, pounding her fists against the small of his back. Her long brown hair flew wildly about her face and down to his knees.

He delivered another blow, harder this time, and she yelped and tried to buck herself loose to throw herself from his shoulder. She would rather land on the rocky ground like a sackful of grain than be carted on his shoulder like one.

"Let me go!" she screamed, twisting and clutching wildly at him, trying to get a grip on his hair. "Let me go!"

His hand came down again, delivering a bruising blow, and her eyes flooded. Flooded and overflowed. Damn him!

She gulped down a rising sob, and raised her fist again. She would show him she wasn't some weak little ninnie who would put up with this indignity. She would show him.

She sniffed, her puny fist raised to strike, and waited for his next blow to fall. *Then,* she would attack like a banshee.

Nothing happened. Only the jolt of her stomach against his shoulder as his long strides carried them forward. What was he doing? Was he through thrashing her?

Well, she wasn't done. She—

She twisted, almost contorting her upper body in order to see over his shoulder.

His hand was poised over her rump. Positioned and ready.

She let out a long futile breath and relaxed, allowing herself to dangle loosely again. She wasn't surrendering, exactly. She was merely making an advisable retreat. Until conditions were more favorable.

Once they reached the cliff dwellings, Lone Wolf didn't stop until he reached their sleeping room. Then he pitched her onto the buffalo hides and she landed with a resounding thud.

She lay there, her heart still racing, and eyed him speculatively. What did he intend to do with her?

As he leaned over her, she tried to scoot away, but he caught her and held her.

One of his hands cupped her chin, tipping her head so he could see her face. His fingers explored her delicate features, which were barely discernible in the dim light. His eyes glittered strangely.

"Let us not speak of what has happened," he said in a quietly controlled voice. "I want to hold you in my arms for one more night. I want to make love to you madly for soon there will be no more time."

"What do you mean?" she whispered, her fear showing in her voice.

"I have decided that tomorrow we will leave this place," he grated roughly. "Tomorrow, we will begin the journey back to your home."

Still she refused to understand. "Why?"

"I have decided to return you to your brother."

Her head jerked away from his fingers, her breathing blocked somewhere in the region of her heart. For a minute, she couldn't speak. Words refused to come.

"Return me?" she choked. "To Robert?" Her voice

was barely above a whisper, a quiver away from a sob.

"Yes," he ground out savagely.

"No-o-o." It was little more than a sigh. Not much more than a bitten-off objection. He was sending her away. He had tired of her, just as she had feared. Please, God, give her strength. Don't let her break down completely. Don't let her beg. But she *was* begging. "Please don't do this," she whispered. "I don't want to go."

His heart leaped with happiness, then, remembering the danger, he said, "I must take you home. I have no other choice."

"But why?" Her eyes were moist as they pleaded silently with him. "Why must you? We were going to stay here until I was—w—with child," she stuttered. "That's what you said."

"I know," he said, tracing her cheekbone with his thumb, and at his gentle tone a tear leaked from the corner of her eye. He brushed it away with a gentle finger. "But things have changed. General Custer has been killed, and—"

"General Custer was killed?"

"Yes. Along with all his men. The white men will be seeking revenge. I'm afraid you'll be hurt, perhaps even killed. That's why I'm taking you home. You will be safe there."

"But—but—" She wondered why she was arguing with him. Wasn't this what she had longed for? Suddenly a thought intruded. "You could be killed," she whispered.

"Yes," he agreed. "But if I am slain, others will take my place. I fear the white men will never rest as long as one Indian remains free. It will come to a point when all the Indian nations will rise up against the white men, and then there will be a war."

"Lone Wolf," she said, clutching at him. "Come with me. We can live at the ranch. I'll explain to Robert how you saved me. He—he'll understand."

"No," he said gently. "I cannot desert my People when I am needed."

She turned her face away from him, hiding her pain.

"I never meant to hurt you, Little Blue Eyes," he murmured. "I only meant to—." He broke off abruptly, groaning low in his throat and turning her face to his.

As his lips brushed hers, she slid her arms around his neck. How can I bear to be apart from him? she thought.

Their clothing became an irritating barrier between them and he pulled away long enough to remove it. His burning gaze never left her, roaming over her pink-tipped breasts down past her narrow waist until they reached the downy triangular patch of curling hair. Then he came to her again.

Her lips opened beneath his, and she darted her tongue into his mouth, into the moist cavern that tasted so uniquely of Lone Wolf. He shuddered, and it traveled through her body with the impact of summer lightning, leaving behind heat and moistness.

His arms tightened around her, uncaring of his roughness as he tried to defy the limitations of the flesh and absorb her into his body, trying to satisfy the raging fire that consumed him. She could hardly draw a breath but she didn't complain.

Winding her fingers through his hair, she held him closer, deepening the kiss, trying to draw him into her body as they kissed passionately.

He moaned low in his throat, and, as she felt his manhood grow against her body, a fire began to burn deep within. She wanted him. God! how she wanted him.

Was there no pride left in her at all? He was going to return her to her brother like so much tarnished goods, but that made no difference to her feelings for him at all. She couldn't force him to love her, and she was unable to control her desire for him.

They made love wildly, their parting uppermost in both their minds, and, when they lay sated, he held her fiercely against him as though he would never let her go.

The next morning, they went wordlessly about their packing. She took dried strips of venison from the drying racks and filled the parfleches until they were almost bursting.

Rebecca picked up the curious double mug and handled it tenderly for a moment, turning it this way and that as she studied it. Then, wanting something tangible to take along with her memories, she quietly slipped it into a container of its own. She would take the double mug with her as a reminder of the happiness she had shared with her Apache husband in this city of the ancient ones. When he had gone and she was left alone, she could take it out and set it beside her bed. It would always be a reminder of her love.

Finally, there was nothing left to be packed, and, with a heavy heart, she waited for Lone Wolf to carry all of the supplies down. When he returned, she put her arms around his neck and closed her eyes, knowing

243

he would see her safely to the valley floor.

They reached their destination all too soon and mounted the horses and went on their way. As they moved into the forest, she couldn't help one backward look at the place where she had been so happy: the city of the cliff dwellers, the place she had come to call home.

They rode in silence for the rest of the day, stopping for only short periods to rest a while and eat a sketchy lunch. The July sun hung hot and heavy above them as they mounted the horses again. Rebecca found the heat more unbearable with each passing hour as they moved to a lower elevation. Her body felt hot and sticky and perspiration dripped between her shoulder blades.

The sun had disappeared, and the shadows were lengthening when Lone Wolf finally called a halt. Rebecca dismounted, sinking gratefully to the grassy earth. Her legs were tired from the unaccustomed riding, and she sat there for a moment, regaining her equilibrium while Lone Wolf ground-tied the horses in a grassy glade nearby, then disappeared into the dense forest.

She began preparations for the evening meal. By the time she had finished, Lone Wolf had returned. They ate in silence, each occupied with his or her own thoughts.

Darkness had closed in about them by the time they had finished. Using the subdued light provided by the campfire, Rebecca stored the uneaten food, then spread the buffalo hide upon the grassy earth.

She added a blanket to protect them against the chill of the night, then turned to Lone Wolf, who was sitting just outside the circle of firelight. He seemed to be just

"Are you having trouble sleeping too?" she asked.

"The fire was going out," he said harshly.

"Come back to bed," she said, taking his hand. "I want to lie in your arms again."

His eyes softened as he looked at her. He took her hand and they returned to the buckskin robes.

Rebecca woke before dawn to a gray and misty morning. She lay quietly for a moment, feeling a heavy sense of foreboding. She raised herself to her elbows and watched her husband while he slept. Her husband. Her mind teased with the words.

He *was* her husband.

Even though they had been married in an Apache ceremony, she felt married to him in every sense of the word. A pain stabbed though her at the thought of never seeing him again. Suddenly, it was more than she could bear, and tears welled into her eyes. She would give anything—do anything—if she could only stay with him. But she couldn't. It had been his decision. Not hers.

Determined not to spoil their last day together, she blinked rapidly, forcing the tears back. With glimmering eyes, she leaned over, blowing softly into his ear.

Suddenly his eyes popped open, gazing into hers.

"I thought you were asleep," she said.

"I sleep light," he reminded her. He lifted a gentle hand and stroked her golden brown hair, enjoying the smooth silky texture of it. He felt hollow inside.

She watched him through narrowed eyes, her thick lashes hiding her expression, searching his impenetrable gaze for something she needed desperately to see.

247

But she found nothing in the gray depths to ease her mind. She wanted to beg him to keep her with him, to never let her go, but she knew it would do no good. He would refuse. This man who was her husband had changed. He had become a total stranger.

"I guess we'd better go," she said, her voice reflecting the sadness in her eyes.

"Rebecca." The words were spoken hesitantly.

"Yes?" Her voice was ragged, her eyes meeting his. Her lips were parted slightly, tempting.

"I—nothing," he said, his voice rasping harshly.

He sat up and pulled his breeches on. Then he went to build the fire.

The final day had begun.

She rose and they moved about, preparing and eating their meal. They remained silent, each thinking deeply, as they completed the necessary work, and soon they were on their way.

The hours passed and a slight breeze began to rise, a cluster of rain clouds gathering as the horses' hooves ate away the miles. At length, they were traveling over country she was beginning to recognize.

All too soon, they left the forest behind, and were traveling through arid desert country. The bleached tans of the earth were familiar, as were the barrel cactus, and cat-claw bushes. Every now and then they passed a lone cottonwood tree with twisting, gnarled branches.

Deep misery filled her. It was all so familiar.

She was keenly aware of Lone Wolf as she rode beside him. She closed her eyes against the pain of leaving him. The taste of his kiss still lingered on her lips. She fought against the memories, willing herself to forget.

The air had turned sultry, the sky darker as the clouds became heavier. The slight breeze had turned into a wind, that blew and whipped Rebecca's hair, pulling it loose from the bone stickpin to fly wildly around her face. She scarcely noticed.

By late afternoon, streaks of lightning could be seen reaching for the ground, and the heavy rumble of thunder meant that rain was not far behind.

As the elements raged around her, the intensity of the storm in her heart was increasing, for, with every moment that passed, she was brought closer to the time when Lone Wolf would leave her.

She thought again of begging him to let her stay with him. One look at his grim face changed her mind. It would be useless. She might as well remain silent and keep what little pride she had left. He already knew it was not her wish to leave.

All too soon their journey ended.

They were there.

On the hill above the ranch.

She tried to keep her face expressionless as Lone Wolf pulled the piebald pony up. She was determined he wouldn't know about the pain in the region of her heart.

The wind blew a thick strand of hair across her eyes, and she brushed it back with a trembling hand. His dark eyes focused on her pale face as her gaze searched his face for some sign—any sign—that he wanted to keep her with him, but his expression was inscrutable.

She looked away from him to hide the pain in her eyes. In the valley directly below the sun was still shining, and she could see the red barn and the horse corrals. A little farther distant was the house where she was born, gleaming white in the afternoon sun.

"Your ordeal is over, Little Blue Eyes," Lone Wolf said, his voice rasping harshly. "Your brother is waiting below." His mouth was tight, his shoulders stiff and rigid.

She turned to face him, forcing her gaze to meet his one last time. "I think it's best if we say our farewells here. It wouldn't be wise if Robert or any of the ranch hands saw you."

Lone Wolf's eyes glittered strangely, his mouth tightening in a grim line, but he remained silent.

As she stared at him, tears filled her eyes, welled over, and slid down her cheeks. He reached an arm out and seized her fiercely, holding her tightly, possessively. She closed her eyes, burying her face against his shoulder, clinging tightly to him.

"Oh, God!" he groaned, breathing in the fresh scent of her hair. Agony twisted his features as he held her. "How can I let you go?"

Her heart gave a sudden leap of hope. "Don't," she begged, pulling away to look at him. "Take me with you."

For a moment, their eyes met. "I can't, Rebecca." His voice was hoarse with anguish, and the words seemed torn from him.

A shot rang out and she flinched. The alarm had been given.

She pulled away from him. Logic told her to go, but logic had nothing to do with the emotional pain she felt. "You must go," she said raggedly. "They won't give me time to explain. They'll kill you." Her anguished eyes held his. "Lone Wolf," she said desperately. "Don't leave me here. Please. Come back for me. I'll meet you anywhere you say. Anytime you want."

"I will," he promised, unable to bear the look in her eyes. "I'll return as soon as it's safe." But he knew it was a useless promise. She would never be safe with the Apaches.

A shout sounded in the distance and she spared a glance for below. They were coming. She had to leave. She must delay them until he could make his escape.

"I must go," she said, her voice trembling.

His face was grim, his eyes wild as they held hers. "Go!" he grated harshly. "What are you waiting for?"

She jerked on Diablo's reins, looking away quickly so Lone Wolf wouldn't see the fresh tears that flowed. She held her chin at a defiant angle and rode down toward the ranch.

# Chapter Fourteen

Thunder split the heavens, and lightning streaked the sky. Then the clouds opened up, sending down sheets of rain, blurring Lone Wolf's vision of Rebecca, and the men riding to meet her.

*He had to let her go*. The muscles in his jaw tightened as he steeled himself against the pain. Nothing would be gained by giving in to it now.

As the storm broke in full force, rain fell in slanted sheets and he lowered his head to the elements raging around him while a battle just as fierce raged within.

The reality of leaving Rebecca was worse than he had dreamed possible, and, even though it could mean his death, everything within him urged that he go after her—take her back to the city of the ancient ones.

But he couldn't. His People needed him. Custer's death would bring reprisals. There would be repeats of the Sand Creek and Washita River massacres. Countless women and children would be slain by the cavalry and his beloved must not be one of the numbers. He would rather lose her than risk her safety.

A shot rang out.

He reined the piebald pony around. He had to go. Fresh agony seared through him, but he dug his heels into the animal's flanks. If he were to die, he would have lost her for nothing. He rode away from his pursuers, completely oblivious to the water streaming down his face and neck. How could he even contemplate life without her?

Yet he must. Somehow.

A strange numbness crept through him. Forcing all thoughts of Rebecca from his mind, he nudged the piebald pony into a gallop, then held the ground-eating pace as he began his long trek back to his people.

As he followed the path homeward, the storm passed and the sky lightened. Soon the sun burst through the clouds, but the warmth didn't touch him. He stopped for only short periods of time to rest his horse for he was still too numb to feel the weariness of his body.

The sun went down, and twilight descended but still he did not stop. He rode on as if he were soulless, unaware of the rider who came across his tracks, then began to trail him, keeping far enough back to remain unnoticed.

When the darkness was complete, Lone Wolf finally pulled the pony up and made camp, forcing food down his tight throat. Then he rolled himself in a blanket, hoping sleep would come quickly and erase his thoughts.

Black Bear waited patiently on the outskirts of the camp, hidden by the night. He waited for the moment when his enemy would relax his guard and sleep. At

253

that moment he would be ready, ready to wreak the vengeance that burned within him. A grim smile touched his lips. He had waited long for this moment. Soon, his cousin would be dead. He waited and waited. Then, drawing his knife, he moved soundlessly, his eyes intent on the blanket-wrapped figure near the coals.

"I can scarcely believe they let you go unharmed. Are you really all right, Becky?"

Clad in a flannel wrapper and fresh from a hot bath, Rebecca stood before her brother's anxious searching eyes and recalled with a cringe the look in his eyes an hour earlier.

"Get her out of those heathenish clothes," he had told the housekeeper. There had been curiosity in Juanita's furtive glances as she led Rebecca away. It wasn't difficult to imagine the direction of the other woman's thoughts, and, if Juanita as almost part of the family could view her so strangely, how would her brother's friends behave?

Probably much the same as Robert was acting right now. Guarded. Almost wary. As if his sister were a complete stranger.

Rebecca moved to her dressing table and picked up her ivory-backed brush. In the reflection of the mirror, her gaze flickered over the familiar setting. Robert had changed nothing while she was gone. Then her eyes returned to meet those of her brother's, the same blue as her own. Only something had been added to Robert's. Something undefinable.

She knew she must have seemed alien to him before in her doeskin skirt and top, with moccasins covering her feet and legs. Even now, with the doeskins replaced by the wrapper, she hardly looked the same person she had been. Her once much-pampered lily-white skin was brown from long hours in the sun, her brown hair streaked with gold.

Not only her appearance had changed though. There was more to her now, more to what made her Rebecca. The part that made her "Little Blue Eyes" had been added. Irrevocably. Robert couldn't see that of course. He could only see the outside changes. The unimportant ones. And he was still waiting for her answer.

She returned the brush to the table and turned to face him. "I'm certain I'm all right."

"Did they hurt you?" His voice was harsh with restrained anger as his eyes searched over her for injuries.

"No." She paused slightly. "At least — not the way you mean. Not physically," she said.

His eyelids closed in relief. Then they flickered open, and, as though uneasy in her presence, he shoved his hands deep into his pockets, walked to the window, and gazed outside.

Lightning flashed, followed by a clap of thunder. "The storm's getting bad," he said. "I'm glad you're not still out in it. You'd be soaked to the skin."

Rebecca crossed to stand beside Robert. A frown creased her forehead as she looked anxiously out the window. Lone Wolf was out there, alone in the storm, and it was miles to any kind of shelter. If only — But no — She squared her shoulders resolutely — Lone Wolf was gone, and wishing would not bring him back. She was lucky they hadn't killed him.

Robert continued to stare out the window, as though facing the storm outside was preferable to facing the sister who was now so foreign to him.

He cleared this throat and said gruffly, "Becky, I just want you to know I made every effort — did everything I could think of."

His voice was a hum in the background, disturbing her thoughts of Lone Wolf, and she was vaguely aware that he was apologizing for something. When he stopped talking, she looked at him, politely raising an eyebrow.

Something flickered deep within his blue eyes, and suddenly he exploded. "Dammit, Becky! I've hoped and prayed for this day — dreamed of having you home again —" His eyes were anguished as they met hers. "I promised Father I would take care of you, Becky. And now I can't even talk to you!"

"I know what you're trying to say, Robert," she said, forcing her thoughts away from her husband. She put a comforting hand on his arm, squeezing it gently. "You don't have to tell me you searched for me. I know you did. But the Indians who captured me took great pains to hide the trail well."

"We never stopped looking," he said. "It took us six weeks to do it, but we finally found the village where they took you. But as you already know, we were too late. You had already been moved."

Her blue eyes narrowed, and she frowned as his words penetrated her worry over Lone Wolf. "You went to the rancheria?"

"Yes. Lieutenant Young and a handful of men from the fort went with me. We would never have even known you were there—Those Indians are a close-mouthed bunch—if a squaw hadn't been waiting just outside the village. She obviously didn't want the others to know she had spoken to us. She told us you had been there, but some Indian called Lone Wolf had left with you a few days before. Would you believe she actually wanted money for the information?" He hesitated again, his eyes sliding away from hers. "She said you—you—" He swallowed. "She said you had married the Indian."

"Yes," she said quietly, wondering if he expected her to feel shame for her marriage. If he did, it was just too bad. She felt no dishonor in her marriage to Lone Wolf. "Yes," she repeated, her blue eyes locked on his. "Lone Wolf married me."

"Lone Wolf?"

"My husband," she said, her gaze intent on him, waiting for his reaction.

"Not your husband, Becky," he said, his eyes darkening, his face grim. "A marriage performed by those damned heathens is not legal."

"I looked on him as my husband, Robert," she said, her eyes meeting his steadily. "And I fell in love with him."

"No," he said harshly, refusing to believe her. "It was just your mind's way of dealing with the horror you were living."

"No," she denied quickly, refusing to deny her love even to make Robert feel better. "I love him!"

257

As though struck by something in her voice, his eyes narrowed thoughtfully. "Who brought you home, Becky?"

"Lone Wolf."

"The savage who kidnapped—" As her chin lifted stubbornly, he caught himself up. "The Indian who married you?"

"Yes."

"Hell!" His fist slammed into his palm. "If I had suspected it was him, I would never have let him leave." His blue gaze was accusing. "You told me he was a friend who had helped you. I thought you meant he helped you to escape from the savage who held you!"

"I know." There was calm acceptance in her voice. "That's the reason I didn't tell you before."

"I don't see how you can just stand there looking so calm when the savage who killed and scalped Pete, who never harmed anyone, is riding casually away from here scot-free. Not to mention your own captivity and rape," he said sarcastically. "Or doesn't that matter to you any more?"

As her face slowly drained of color, he was immediately contrite. He took her hand in his and squeezed it gently.

"I'm sorry," he said. "That was damned callous of me. "I didn't mean to remind you what had happened to Pete. I know you cared for him a lot. And as for the other matter—the other thing—well, it was certainly no fault of yours it happened. But if I ever get my hands on that damn savage who did this to you—" He didn't finish the sentence, but then, he didn't have to. His meaning was clear.

"I accepted months ago what happened to Pete," she said, hoping she could make him understand. "But Lone Wolf had nothing to do with his death. I'm afraid you still don't understand the part he played in this whole thing." As he moved to protest, she held up a silencing hand.

"Robert, I'm going to tell you once, and then I don't want to speak of it again." Her voice wobbled dangerously, a lump rising in her throat, as she whispered huskily. "Not ever."

Her blue eyes were beseeching. "Could I please have something to drink before I begin, and—" she laughed disparagingly at her sudden weakness. "I think I need to sit down for a moment. My legs feel kind of wobbly."

She moved to the bed and sank down on it. "I'm sorry to be such a baby," she said.

"If you would rather wait until you're rested before we talk, then . . ." His voice trailed away.

"No," she said, fighting the temptation to put it off. "I need to tell you now. I want to get it told now. I don't think I could bear to speak of it later."

"I'm not sure exactly where to begin," she said, leaning back on the bed, and closing her eyes. "So much has happened since that day Pete and I went riding—I guess the first thing is to tell you that Lone Wolf didn't kidnap me and kill Pete."

"He didn't?" His voice was clearly disbelieving.

"No, he didn't. But it was an Indian of the same tribe."

"A Chiricahua Apache?"

"Yes. Anyway, Black Bear and several of his friends kidnapped me and one of them killed and scalped

259

Pete." She shuddered, remembering the scalp hanging from the lance. "It was horrible, and I was terrified, but no one else was to blame. Chief Tall Feathers and the others of the village didn't know what Black Bear and his friends were doing."

"If this Black Bear stole you, then how did you wind up with the other Indian?"

"Lone Wolf came along and won me from Black Bear."

"They gambled with you for a stake?"

"No, Robert," she laughed shakily. "They fought for me. It was a fight to the death, where only the winner survives, but, when Lone Wolf won, he refused to kill Black Bear because he was his cousin."

She had hoped the explanations would make Robert feel better, but he was scowling deeply.

"What happened then?" he asked.

"Well, Lone Wolf started to bring me home but found out there had been two white men killed by some of his people, and he decided it would be too dangerous for them to bring me back. He took me to their village instead." She paused for a moment, the memory of the hostile faces that had greeted her in the village fresh in her mind.

"Go on," he said gruffly, his eyes on her drawn face. "Tell it all."

"When we arrived at the village, the Indians were hostile to me. Pete had killed one of the braves who'd been in the raid, and his widow wanted me killed." She shuddered, remembering.

"Did they hurt you?"

"They pinched me and pulled my hair, and I think

260

they would have done more if Lone Wolf hadn't claimed me. I think he was still meaning, at that point, to bring me back here when it was safe. And then, Black Bear returned. He began stirring up trouble as soon as he arrived. He claimed Lone Wolf should have returned me to the ranch, and, since he hadn't, Black Bear was demanding that I be returned to him." Her eyes pleaded with her brother. "Can't you see? The only way Lone Wolf could protect me from the others was to marry me!"

She wasn't really surprised at Robert's snort of disbelief, for hadn't she reacted in much the same way at the time?

"He did, Robert," she protested. "I would have been returned to Black Bear if he hadn't married me, and, if that had happened, then you can be sure that I wouldn't be sitting here telling you all about it, for he would have used me cruelly."

"Did he—did he—" He couldn't seem to find the words to ask but she knew what he wanted to know.

"Yes, he did," she said calmly, refusing to show shame. "He had no choice but to consummate the marriage. I wouldn't have been safe until he did." She could tell by his look that he didn't believe it had really been necessary. "I believed him, Robert. And if you had been there and seen the way those people looked at me, then you would too."

Still he did not answer, even refusing to meet her eyes. She studied his face, noticing the gauntness of his cheeks, and he badly needed a haircut. It was very unlike her usually tidy brother.

"You've lost weight while I was gone," she commented.

"Didn't have any appetite," he said, his voice grating harshly, his blue eyes staring at some distant point beyond her left shoulder.

"And your hair isn't so brown as before. You've grayed around the temples."

"Worry over you," he sighed, his gaze coming back to meet hers. "Why are we talking about me?" he asked, his voice exasperated, his eyes pained. "The grief and pain I endured from your loss was nothing to what I knew you must be suffering." He slammed a fist in his palm again.

"Dammit! I told Father I would take care of you. On his deathbed, I swore it!"

"You couldn't help what happened to me, Robert," she consoled him. "Now, please. If you don't mind, I would like to rest. Suddenly, I'm feeling quite exhausted."

"Of course," he said quickly. "I shouldn't have been so thoughtless. Of course you must rest."

As she rose from the bed, intending to see him to the door, he stopped her.

"Becky, just one more thing."

Something in the tone of his voice warned her. She stiffened, asked cautiously. "Yes?"

"Where did he take you?"

"I'm sorry but I can't tell you, Robert." He might go there again. She couldn't let anyone know where she had been all this time! No one knew about the cliff dwellings but the Indians, and Buck of course, and it must stay that way.

"You'll have to tell us sooner or later, Becky."

"Us?"

"Major Canton will be wanting to question you. He will probably want you to go over some maps with him to give them some idea of the trails the Indians use. I'll have to send a messenger off right away to let them know you're home. Those damned savages have too many hideouts already, and we need to know as many of them as we can."

When she spoke, Rebecca's tone was steely. "I will not tell anyone where Lone Wolf took me. And I won't answer any questions from the Cavalry. So you can forget sending for them."

He started to argue but, as his blue eyes scanned her exhausted face, decided to let it wait. "You're tired, Becky," he said. "We'll talk later. Lie down and get some rest now." His eyes, which had been soft with concern, hardened to chips of ice at a sudden thought. "Maybe it's not too late to catch that damned Indian."

Rebecca stiffened, her lips tightening, but she knew from the tone of his voice he was barely holding his temper in check so she refused to comment. His eyes traveled over her slender, wrapper-clad figure, then slid away as though the sight of her was distasteful to him.

"Does the sight of me offend you, Robert?" she asked through tightly clenched teeth.

"Why, no, Becky," he protested, his anger draining away as he turned startled eyes on her. "It's just — just —" his voice trailed away as he continued to stare at her.

Suddenly he exploded. "Yes, dammit! It does! You looked like an Apache squaw when you arrived, dressed in those animal skins! And the way you're

263

acting now—refusing to help us catch the savages who did this to you—"

"I'm sorry you found my appearance offensive," she said. "But I'm afraid I find those clothes much more comfortable than my cumbersome gowns, petticoats, corsets, and pantalettes."

"Becky," he said, his voice shocked, his eyes filled with consternation. "Have you no sense of decency left to speak of such things?"

"What things?" she asked, her surprise genuine. What had she said that was so shocking?

"Women's underthings!" he snapped, looking utterly appalled, his eyes refusing to meet hers again.

"Oh." She had actually forgotten for a while the many restrictions the white man's world placed on such things. Her lips twitched. What her brother would make of her swimming stark naked didn't even bear thinking about.

"I must speak to the men. We'll talk more later," Robert said, hurrying toward the door, obviously eager to escape from her presence.

She watched him leave, then sank back on the bed, her eyes tracing the familiar patterns on the ceiling. Well, she was home again. Back where she could be contained within four walls, hidden away from the sunlight and fresh air. She lifted her hands and stared at them, brown and calloused from hard work. Soon, they would be pampered and white again, and she would feel absolutely useless. She didn't belong here anymore.

Lifting herself to her elbows, she looked around the room that had been hers since she was a child. Her mother had made the simple patchwork quilt that covered the four-poster bed dominating the room. With his own two hands her father had lovingly carved the bedside table. The straight armoire that held her gowns had been her grandmother's, as had the large wing chair that stood by the window. A pair of small, rag throw rugs, braided by a twelve-year old Rebecca, were the only coverings on an otherwise bare wood floor.

These possessions that were so necessary in the white man's world were all so familiar and yet, somehow, alien as well.

"Mees Becky?" The voice was hesitant, unsure, coming from the doorway behind her.

"What is it, Juanita," she asked, turning to see the plump Mexican woman who had worked at the Shaw ranch for several years.

The woman stood hesitantly just inside the door, and Rebecca wondered if Juanita felt she would be contaminated if she got too close to her. If Juanita and Robert acted this way, what then would be her neighbor's reactions?

She remembered a woman from her childhood who had been taken by the Indians. On her return, the townspeople had acted as though the woman had leprosy. She had been shunned, as had the half-breed child Rebecca had seen clinging to his mother's skirts. The woman had had a sense of sadness about her that had always stuck in Rebecca's mind even though she had only been a child. Was this to be her lot, then?

"Senor Robert, he say to me, Juanita, go see if Mees Becky, she is hungry." The plump woman smiled hesitantly. "I come," she said simply.

Rebecca smiled gently. "Thank you, Juanita, but I'm not hungry."

As the small Mexican woman turned to go, Rebecca stopped her. "Juanita —" she paused, unsure of herself. "Juanita —" she repeated. "It's — it's so good to see you." The tight reins she had held on her feelings since Lone Wolf had told her of his decision to return her to her brother gave way, and her eyes filled with tears.

When Juanita saw Rebecca's distress, the hesitation disappeared and the older woman rushed to her, clasping her against an ample bosom. *"Pobricita,"* she murmured, soothingly. "It is over now, and you are safe at home."

When Rebecca had cried her last tear, the Mexican woman dried her eyes, then, with a sympathetic pat on her mistress's hand, left the room.

As the door closed behind her, and her footsteps receded down the hallway, Rebecca lay on the bed, listening to the rain beating on the roof outside, hoping Lone Wolf had found some sort of shelter for the night.

Lone Wolf lay motionless in the bedroll. Although his breathing was even and his eyes closed, he had been unable to sleep, for thoughts of Rebecca filled his mind. He knew that he had done the only thing he could by taking her back to the ranch. So many times on the journey to her home, he had wanted to confess his love for her, but fear of rejection had held him back.

Suddenly, he heard the soft swish of a moccasin near his bedroll and his eyes flew open. Before he could

266

react, Black Bear was on him. Black Bear had surprise as his ally and, as his knife began its downward course, Lone Wolf's gaze caught the flicker of the blade in the firelight.

*I'm going to die, I'll never see her again.*

Then the knife ripped into him, sending a pain like he had never before even dreamed of even in his worst nightmares ripping through him, gouging into his body. Then the knife was withdrawn, but, before he could even move, it was shoved into him again, ripping into his chest, sending white-hot flashes of pain through him.

Even in his agony, he grappled with Black Bear, grabbing at the knife as it made another downward plunge, grasping it with the palm of his hand, feeling the blade cut into his flesh.

Black Bear grunted, wresting the knife from him. Lone Wolf grasped his own knife, and as Black Bear began another downward plunge, his face blazing with hatred, Lone Wolf stabbed out, feeling his cousin's flesh beneath his blade.

As Black Bear's knife penetrated Lone Wolf's chest, sending another pain through him, Black Bear fell forward on his cousin.

Lone Wolf had enough strength left to push the other man off him, then he lay there with pain pulverizing him, feeling his lifeblood leaking, leaking, leaking away. As his strength went, his eyelids became heavy, fluttering shut, and he knew it was too late now. He would never see Rebecca again.

\* \* \*

The next few weeks were the hardest Rebecca could ever remember. Although Robert was losing his uneasiness with her, he seemed reluctant to allow her to accompany him anywhere. She was even beginning to feel like a prisoner in her own home. But above all was her loneliness for Lone Wolf.

She worried about him constantly. Had he found shelter from the storm? Was he now reunited with his people, and what did Little Turtle and Brave Eagle say when he returned alone? Did Black Bear cause him trouble?

If she could have shared her thoughts with someone, maybe it wouldn't have been so hard. But there was no one. Not even Juanita. For although she had unbent a little, there was still a questioning in her eyes that wasn't there before.

Rebecca had been home for two weeks when Robert entered the parlor and found her sitting on the settee working on a sampler.

"Cletus Brown and his wife, Molly, are giving a welcome home party for you, Becky. He rode over this morning to invite us."

"And what did you tell them?" she asked, raising her eyes to him and laying her needlework aside.

"Naturally I accepted," he said. His blue eyes seemed to find something interesting about her gray merino gown as they refused to meet hers. "There was nothing else I could do. These people are our friends. They would have looked on it as an insult if I had refused them. After all, they are throwing the party for you. All your friends will be there."

"I am beginning to wonder if I have any friends now,"

she said quietly. "No one has called on me since I've been home. I didn't suggest you should have refused the invitation, but I am surprised you accepted. You seem to be ashamed of me since I came home. Would you rather they had killed me, Robert?"

"No, Becky," he said, his eyes flying to hers. "It's just that—" He stopped, seeming at a loss, unable to find the words to explain.

"Just what, Robert?" Her chin lifted with determination as her eyes held his steadily. The time had come for them to talk about his feelings for her. "Is it because Lone Wolf took me for his wife?"

"Yes, dammit!" he exploded, unable to contain his anger any longer. "It's because I can't stand the thought of some damned redskin's hands on my sister!"

Rebecca flinched. Well, she had asked for it, and she had certainly got it. "I'm afraid I can't change what happened, Robert," she said, her eyes meeting his steadily. "And no matter how you hate the thought, it *did* happen. If that makes me unacceptable in your eyes, then I'm sorry. But the deed is done, and nothing I can do will change what's happened, so you're just going to have to accept it."

"That I'll never do!" he said savagely. "The army has cracked down on the red devils, and, even if he managed to escape, it will do no good. He will eventually be caught. He can't run forever, and, when I get my hands on that damned Indian—"

"What do you mean by that?" she asked quickly, her heart suddenly pounding with dread.

"The army has a wanted poster out on that Indian. They'll get him sooner or later, if they haven't done it

269

already!"

As her face blanched, his eyes softened. "Don't take on so, Becky. He deserves everything he gets. And he'll get plenty when they find him. I'll personally put the rope around his neck and watch him hang."

"Then you'll be hanging the father of my baby," she said.

A silence spun out between them. Then his anguished, "Oh God!" tore at her. He looked shattered. He walked to the window and stared outside.

"Are you sure?" he asked, his voice muffled.

"Yes," she said. "I'm sure."

"Oh, Becky." His voice was anguished as he turned back to her. "What are we going to do?"

"I don't know what you're going to do, Robert, but I'm going to have a child."


"Land's sake, Becky. I think I would have killed myself before I let one of those savages touch me!" Mary Beth Williams' strident voice rang out, causing a hush to fall over the room. Her bright blue eyes were hard with malice as they swept over Rebecca's trim figure, resting resentfully for a moment on the blue gown she was wearing. The gown was one of many Rebecca had brought west with her less than a year ago and was still very much in fashion.

"You don't know what you would do, Mary Beth," Rebecca said, lifting her head high and staring challengingly at the dark-haired girl. "Not unless it happens to you." She wanted to say so much more, resenting the girl's slur on Lone Wolf, but the knowl-

270

edge that nothing she said would change the other girl's opinion held her tongue. She had quickly interpreted the other girl's envious look at her gown, but, had Mary Beth only known the little value Rebecca placed on such trappings now, she would have been astonished.

Across the room, Rebecca saw Melanie and Susan. She smiled at Melanie, but the blonde pretended not to see. She watched Melanie and Susan exchange glances, then join a circle of their friends nearby. Realizing she had been snubbed, she felt stricken for both girls had always been friendly to her.

Robert, noticing her distress, moved quickly to her side, taking her arm and offering moral support. He squeezed her arm as a gentle reminder that he was with her, and, whatever happened, she could count on him.

"Oh, but I do know what I would do, Becky," Mary Beth said, refusing to let go of the subject. She shuddered delicately. "There is no way I would let one of those savages touch me. I'd kill myself the first chance I got!"

"Then let's hope the Indians never kidnap you, Mary Beth," Robert said, his smile not quite reaching his lips. "For it would be a shame to deprive the world of such beauty as yours."

Mary Beth laughed delightedly. She folded her fan and cracked him sharply on the arm. "You do say the nicest things, Robert," she said. Then her eyes returned to Rebecca. Even with his flattering speech, Robert hadn't managed to distract Mary Beth from her purpose. She was out for blood.

"Come meet Lieutenant Young, Becky," Robert said

271

before Mary Beth could renew her attack.

As he led her toward a young man with blond hair, she could feel Mary Beth's malicious eyes following her across the room.

"Damned witch!" Robert muttered between tight lips.

"Now, Robert," she chided. "Mary Beth is our friend and neighbor. We mustn't be rude to her."

He threw her a speaking glance but refrained from an answer as they neared the blond young man. "Lieutenant Young. I would like you to meet my sister, Rebecca," Robert said.

"It's a pleasure to finally make your acquaintance, Miss Shaw," Lieutenant Young said, his admiring eyes sweeping her slender form. As his gaze returned to hers, she gave a mental sigh of relief. Apparently the lieutenant was able to accept her with no problems. He showed none of the uneasiness—even aversion sometimes—that the others displayed. "You look none the worse for your ordeal, Miss Shaw. I'm very happy to see you looking so well."

"Thank you," she said quietly, taking an instant liking to the man. "Robert told me you helped in the search for me. I would like to thank you for your efforts on my behalf."

"I am just sorry we were never able to find you," he said quietly. "We never stopped looking and your brother never gave up hope. But you seemed to have disappeared off the face of the earth." His dark eyes told her he was sincere.

"Yes, I know," she said. Afraid he would question her whereabouts, she quickly changed the subject. "Robert tells me you came here from the Seventh Regiment," she said. "Do you find our climate very different?"

"It's much the same," he said. " A little more arid."

"And how do you like Major Canton?" she asked, naming the fort commander.

"I find him capable," he replied. "A little more reserved than General Custer, my former commander." His eyes darkened. "I was lucky, being transferred when I was."

"Lucky? How so?" she questioned, raising her eyebrows.

"If I hadn't been transferred, I would probably have been killed along with General Custer."

Rebecca lowered her eyes. With everything that had happened, she had forgotten about Custer, who was indirectly responsible for her return.

"I suppose you didn't know of it. He was killed at the Little Big Horn River last month, along with a third of the Seventh Regiment," Lieutenant Young said.

"How terrible!" she murmured, pretending surprise. Rebecca had no intention of admitting prior knowledge. That could cause the fort commander to wonder what else she knew. She meant to do everything in her power to protect Lone Wolf.

"Yes, it was," he agreed. "Over two hundred men died that day. I'm surprised your brother never told you about it."

"No, he didn't tell me," she said. "Will this affect the way the army deals with the Apaches?"

"I'm sure of it," he said. "They need to be taught a lesson. The massacre at the Little Big Horn just taught us there is no way you can be lenient with Indians. I wasn't a bit surprised when the major ordered us to attack Chief Tall Feathers' village." His eyes flitted away. "Although I didn't agree with everything that took place there."

"Attacked Chief Tall Feathers' village!"

"Yes, Miss Shaw. He intended to teach them a lesson they would never forget, and I guess he did!"

She blanched. "What happened?"

"They were all wiped out," he said quietly. "Killed! Every last man, woman, and child."

Killed! Everyone in the village killed — Little Turtle . . . Brave Eagle . . . Suddenly, she stopped breathing. Lone Wolf had gone back there. Lone Wolf was dead! Suddenly, the shock was too much to bear. The room whirled around her and she pitched forward and fell to the floor in a dead faint.

## Chapter Fifteen

"It's the best thing all the way around, Becky," Robert said, pacing back and forth across her bedroom. He stopped to look at her as she lay in bed, his eyes dwelling on the white lawn nightgown trimmed with point lace at the throat and sleeves. He seemed unaware of his gaze as he continued. "You won't be able to hide your condition very much longer, and I don't want you to have to endure the scorn of our friends."

"They're not my friends if they would scorn me so easily, Robert," she said, eyeing him coldly. She wished Robert would just go away and leave her with her pain. "I don't like repeating myself but I have done nothing of which to be ashamed. I never dreamed I would be held to blame for my captivity. I wish I had never returned. I didn't want to. I even put aside my pride and begged Lone Wolf to keep me. If only he had. Perhaps he'd still be alive now."

"Don't say that!" he said gruffly, his eyes meeting hers and then quickly sliding away.

"It's true," she said. "I loved Lone Wolf and I was happy with him. I would have stayed with him gladly if he would've let me. I begged him to come with me, but he refused."

Robert's eyes flared. "Do you think I'd let that savage live here?" he asked. His face was grim as he watched her. "He didn't care about you. He wouldn't have brought you home if he did."

"He cared a little," she whispered, closing her eyes against the pain eating away at her. "He must have."

"I'm sorry, Becky," Robert said gruffly, coming to stand beside the bed. His blue eyes softened, and he took her hand, patting it gently. "Can't you see I'm only thinking of you?" he asked. "You know Aunt Bess would want you to come to her. She always hated the idea of your returning home to Silver City after what happened to Mother."

"Yes, I know," she sighed. She had never doubted her welcome in her aunt's home for a moment. That wasn't the problem.

Silent seconds skittered away as he waited for her decision. She knew he only wanted what was best for her, but what if Lone Wolf wasn't really dead? After all, he may not have reached the rancheria before it was attacked. If there was the slightest chance he was still alive, there was no way she was going to put that much distance between her love and herself. She would never accept his death without proof.

Never!

But how could she obtain such proof? How could she be sure?

"Robert?"

"Yes?"

"What do you think happened to the bodies?"

"What bodies?"

"You know," she said, her voice strained. Her blue eyes met his and he flinched as he recognized her pain. "The bodies of my friends." She couldn't bear to say her husband because that would be admitting his death. She swallowed thickly. "The — People — the Chiricahuas at Chief Tall Feathers' village," she continued in a raw, husky voice. "Did the soldiers — bury — them?"

"I — I think not, Becky," he said uneasily. A red flush began to creep up his neck and his eyes slid away from hers. He walked to the window, pulled the gauzy curtains aside, and gazed unseeingly outside. He seemed almost shamed by something, or perhaps he was just unable to face the pain he saw in her eyes.

"Then what happened to them?" she grated through tightened lips. She stared at his rigid back as he remained silent. "Robert!" she snapped. "I asked you what happened to them?" She refused to allow him to evade the issue.

"I think — " his voice was low, the words seeming to be forced from him. "I think they just — just let them lie where they fell."

Even though she had expected it, the impact of the words hit her like a fist in the stomach. She drew in an agonized, shuddery breath. Images of bodies — Little Turtle — Brave Eagle — floated through her mind. She refused to let her memory produce the image of an even greater loss. She couldn't — not and keep her sanity intact.

Silent moments skittered away as she stared at her

277

brother's back. She felt such a feeling of outrage and pain at what he had revealed but forced herself to remain outwardly calm.

"I refuse to accept Lone Wolf's death without proof," she said harshly. "And if what you say is true, then the proof is at the rancheria."

"You're mad!" he burst out, appalled, and spun around to face her again.

He stared at her as if she had taken leave of her senses. And perhaps he was right. Perhaps what the cavalry had done had driven her mad.

"You surely aren't suggesting you should go there, are you, Becky? That would be utterly impossible. Why, the attack on the village took place last week. The scavengers would have—"

He stopped as she flinched, her face draining of what little color she had managed to retain.

"I'm sorry, honey," he said, striding to the bed and taking her hand again. He squeezed it gently. "But you must see how impossible it would be to even consider such a thing."

"Just go away, Robert," she said, her voice barely above a whisper. She pulled her hand free and turned her face into the pillow, feeling as if she had been kicked in the stomach. The pillow muffled her voice as she pleaded with him. "Just go away and leave me alone."

"Becky," he said, eyeing her with concern. "You know you're going to have to accept—his death. You're going to have to be strong."

She moved her head slightly so she could look at

him, and his eyes slid away from the condemnation he saw there. She felt betrayed by him. How could he have allowed such a thing to take place? He must have known about it. Was there no humanity in this brother she had thought she knew?

Her expression hardened, her eyes turned cold as she studied this stranger before her. "Why didn't you tell me what the cavalry had done when it happened, Robert?" she asked in an icy voice. "Why did I have to find out from someone else."

"Because I knew how you would feel, Becky, and I wanted to spare you any more pain. You had already been through so much, and I hoped you would never need know about it. I guess I should have made some excuse to keep you away from the party, but I knew that would only cause more speculation, and there's been enough of that already."

Her eyes filled with scorn at his words. Robert seemed to be more concerned about what their neighbors thought of them than about what the cavalry had done to a whole Indian village. His only concern seemed to be that she had discovered what they had done.

She clenched her fists tightly, leaving nail prints in her palms, and welcomed the resulting pain. "I would think the slaughter of innocent women and children would concern you more than what your neighbors might say, Robert," she said, her voice cold and condemning. "But no matter what you say, you can't make me believe Lone Wolf is dead. I'll never believe it until I have proof."

"Damn it!" He swore at her inflexibility. "You can be so stubborn sometimes, Becky. I don't say that Major Canton was right in what he did, but the deed is done and it does no good to pretend that it never happened. I realize it's hard for you to accept, but you'll eventually have to. That damned Indian is dead, and, even though I had no hand in it personally, I can't help but be glad of it!"

"No," she spat, her eyes blazing into his. "Stop saying that! If he was dead, I would feel it. I know he's not! He's out there somewhere, maybe hurt, even needing me. But he's not dead!" Suddenly she broke out in wild sobs, and Robert knelt beside the bed, taking her into his arms, holding her tightly until her crying dwindled down to an occasional hiccup.

She pulled away from him, her moisture-filled eyes steady on his. "He is not dead, Robert," she said in a determined voice. "I know he's not! He's not dead! And somehow, wherever he is, I know I'll find him!"

"Stop it right now!" he demanded, unable to deal with her refusal to accept Lone Wolf's death. "You don't really believe what you're saying. You're just fooling yourself. He's dead, and you must accept it."

"No," she said, her voice rising. "He's not dead! And I *will* find him! Wherever he is, I *will* find him!"

Rebecca waited that night until the house grew quiet and she knew everyone was asleep. Then, unable to lie still any longer, she threw back the covers and rose quietly from the bed.

She pulled her white lawn nightgown over her head and tossed it carelessly aside, uncaring as it fell to the floor in a crumpled heap. The moonlight streaming through the opened window cast its pale glow over her naked body as she strode swiftly to the wardrobe and removed her riding habit.

She dressed in the darkness, then picked up her boots. Tiptoeing across the room, she listened for a moment before opening the door, then crept to the kitchen, pausing occasionally to listen, knowing if she was heard she would be stopped.

When she reached the kitchen, she eased the door shut. In an economy of movement, she lit a lamp, filled a canteen with water, slung the straps across her shoulder, wrapped a loaf of bread in a cloth, and put out the lamp, leaving the kitchen in darkness again. Then, she let herself silently out of the house.

She sat on the steps long enough to put her boots on, totally unaware of the warm breeze that blew across her face. Then, she made her way across the moonlit yard, being careful to keep to the shadows in case one of the hands should happen to be awake.

As she entered the barn, Diablo snorted softly, recognizing his mistress immediately even in the dim light of the building. She spoke quietly to him, sliding her hand down his long, smooth neck, and, with the same quick movements she had used before, slipped a bridle over his head and saddled him, taking care not to make any more noise than was necessary.

Then, filling a tow sack with oats, she tied it on the saddle, knowing they would be riding hard, and there would be no time to stop to graze the horse. They would have to share her canteen of water.

A few minutes later, she was riding Diablo across the moonlit plains. The black stallion and his rider rode long into the night without stopping. They rode into the wind, her long brown hair streaming out behind her, her slim figure hugging the stallion.

Somewhere in the distance, the high-pitched, drawn-out lonely wail of the coyote sounded, but it went unnoticed by the rider, and the only sign the horse made was a twitch of the ears.

As she rode through the rough, broken, canyon country, the mescal and prickly pears went unnoticed, except where needed for an occasional guide to keep her on her path. Her knuckles were white where they gripped the reins, and her face was expressionless as she approached the base of the cliff where Black Bear had attacked her.

When dawn streaked the sky, painting it with hues of apricot and red, she stopped for a short rest, feeding and watering Diablo sparingly but taking nothing for herself. Then, they continued on their journey. Rebecca refused to allow herself to contemplate what she would find when she finally reached her destination. She only knew an all-consuming desire to get there.

She saw the buzzards long before she saw the rancheria. They circled overhead, occasionally dipping low, then dropping out of sight completely as they landed. A few moments later they would fly up to begin their never-ending circle all over again.

She shuddered, her skin suddenly cold. The sight was unnerving. As she watched, reality took over, and numbness set in. She had refused to believe, but the sight of the scavenger birds was too much to bear. An occasional gust of wind brought the scent of death to her nostrils. Still, she never faltered. She urged Diablo forward along the narrow trail that led to the high mesa.

When she finally saw the village, she stared, stricken. All that was left of the dome-shaped dwellings were a few fire-blackened remains of the wickiups where a proud race of people had once lived.

Dazed, Rebecca pulled Diablo up, staring blindly at the unrecognizable charred remains. Nearby, a buzzard pecked at some unidentifiable object, and she swallowed the bile that rose at the sight. Grimly, her eyes searched for something, anything, to give her hope, but she knew it was no use for she was in the middle of death and destruction. The stench of blood and roasted flesh still lingered in the air even though it had been a week since the attack. A few bodies littered the ground, horribly mutilated, but most were gone. Obviously, what the soldiers had left, the jackals had taken.

As she made her way through the body-strewn village to where Lone Wolf's wickiup had stood, a gruesome spectacle awaited her. She saw a severed head hanging from a lodgepole. The eye sockets were empty, picked clean by the buzzards, and the ears had been cut off by the soldiers. She recoiled from the sight in shock, circling warily around the severed head.

She didn't want to see any more, but still she went on.

To her right, about six feet away, lay the burned-out remains of the wickiup she had shared with Lone Wolf. Her feet began the long journey there.

A moccasined foot came into view — then another. Just inside the entrance to their wickiup, she found what she was looking for. What was left of a headless body, dressed in buckskin breeches, lay inside. She sank to her knees in agony, picked up the bear claw necklace lying near, and rocked herself back and forth, back and forth.

Robert found her there several hours later. He took one look at Rebecca, still rocking back and forth, then the badly decomposed body inside the wickiup remains. Holding his handkerchief across his nose, he led her away to the far edge of the village. Then he set about the grisly chore of burying the body of the Indian who had come to mean so much to his sister.

He recognized her state of mind and kept Diablo's reins, leading her along like a small child. She spoke not a word all the way back to the ranch.

She rode when he rode, she stopped when he stopped. And if he wanted her to dismount, he had to take her off the horse. She seemed to have retreated into a world to which he could not follow. She was in a state of shock that was almost catatonic, totally unaware of the worried looks her brother cast her throughout the day. When they stopped, she drank when he held the canteen to her lips but refused all food. She was unaware of when they reached the ranch and of the doctor's arrival.

"I don't know, Robert. I just can't say. She's had a great shock. Maybe you should go ahead and send her on to Pittsburgh. Maybe a complete change is what she needs."

She heard the voices as from a distance. *What were they saying? Why didn't they go away?* She turned over, pressing her head into the pillow.

"Told her not . . . but it didn't . . . found her with . . ."

The voices were too loud. She squeezed her eyes shut. For some reason, they hurt.

"I don't know Robert, the baby . . ."

"Baby?" As though the word had opened a door, she turned over and struggled to a sitting position while the astonished men stared at her.

"Why it's your baby we're talking about, Becky," Robert said, kneeling beside the bed. His eyes were damp as he took her hand. "Don't you remember about your baby?" he asked softly.

"Remember?" The words caused a frown to chase across her forehead. Then suddenly it cleared as if by magic. "Yes," she breathed, a tiny smile touching her lips. "My baby. Lone Wolf's ba—" She broke off as her memory surfaced, slamming into her mind like a ton of bricks. Her face drained of color and she shuddered. Her eyes widened with remembered horror.

"Lone Wolf?"

"I buried him, Becky."

"Thank you," she whispered brokenly, tears gathering, welling up, and streaming silently down her cheeks.

Robert reached out and gathered her close against his strong chest. "Cry all you want, love," he said. "Maybe it will help."

No. Nothing would help. Lone Wolf was dead.

"You've got to be strong for the little one."

The little one. Lone Wolf's baby. She pulled herself away from Robert. "Yes." she said, sniffling. "I have to take care of the baby, don't I?"

"Yes, you do, Rebecca," came a gruff voice from the other side of the bed, and she turned to see Doctor Kincaid watching her intensely.

"Is the baby all right?" she asked, turning to see the doctor.

"I don't think you did it much good riding through the countryside like that, but yes, I'd say the child is in good shape."

"My son is in good shape, doctor," she corrected. When he looked puzzled, she said. "The baby's going to be a boy. Lone Wolf wanted a son."

"Well, as to that, I couldn't say," he said. "No way to determine the sex of the child just yet. I would suggest, though, for the sake of both you and the child you should return to your aunt in Pittsburgh."

She lifted her chin. "Because of my neighbors? Let them drive me out?"

"Think about the child, Becky," Robert coaxed. He had found the magic word and he intended to use it. "Do you want your son to endure the cruelty of the people around here?"

"People are the same all over," she countered.

"Maybe so. But Pittsburgh is a long way from New Mexico. No one there will know what happened to you. You could say you're a widow. After all, it's the truth, isn't it?"

Robert's words silenced her. It was the first time he had made any show of accepting her marriage to Lone Wolf, and for that, at least, she was grateful.

"I think Robert's right, Rebecca. There's no need for the baby to bear the stigma of being a half-breed."

"Half-breed," she murmured. "My son will be a half-breed. Half me, and half Lone Wolf! But there's no stigma in that. He'll be the best part of two worlds."

"Not everyone will see it that way," Robert reminded her gently. "And you must do what you can to protect your baby. The Indian—" He paused, then added firmly. "Your husband would want you to do that."

He couldn't have said anything that would have helped more, because she knew he was right. Lone Wolf would want his son protected at all costs. He had wanted this baby, and she would cherish him. If she couldn't have Lone Wolf, at least she would have his baby.

So she would go to Pittsburgh, would go to Aunt Bess.

Aunt Bess had been Rebecca's haven once before and would be again. Suddenly, she was eager to see her aunt, to tell her about the baby.

"How soon can I go?" she asked.

"It would be better if you went right away," he

answered. "While you're still able to travel. Don't you agree, Doctor Kincaid?"

Doctor Kincaid nodded. "The sooner you leave, the better it will be for both of you," he said, patting Rebecca's shoulder.

A week later, Robert saw her off at the train station. She couldn't help but wish he was going with her, and he obviously felt the same for he stayed with her until the last moment. Then, with a long look he leaned over and kissed her on the forehead.

"Take good care of yourself," he whispered.

"All aboard." The conductor's call reminded him he must hurry.

"Tell Aunt Bess hello for me," he said. "And give her this letter." He took a long, white envelope from his breast pocket and handed it to her. "It explains everything so you shouldn't have to answer questions."

She nodded, her throat constricted.

He started to say something else, then apparently changed his mind as the conductor's call rang out again. Waving his hand, he smiled wistfully and left the train.

She looked out the window for one last look at her brother standing in a cloud of steam. Indecision was plain on his face, and she knew he was wondering if he was doing the right thing in sending her away, so she summoned up a smile for him. Immediately, his face cleared, and he smiled at her, making the effort she had put out to ease his mind seem worthwhile.

As the train moved slowly out of the station, she leaned her head back against the seat and sighed. It

The Monongahela, alive with barges and tugboats, came from the south while the Allegheny bore barges carrying freights of crude petroleum from the north.

By day the view spreading in the distance from Elizabeth Roberts' house was cluttered and ugly with jagged stacks and bulky crude sheds, dirtied with the eternal pall of smoke. But at night, it was a different matter, for the darkness covered the prosaic and ugly sights and gave the city and its surroundings a picturesqueness sadly lacking by day.

At night the city gleamed with a thousand points of light which were reflected by the rivers, whose waters glimmered in the faint moonlight.

Rebecca stood at the window, wondering if she could ever become reconciled to living in a place so crude and ugly with its eternal dirt and soot that made life one constant struggle to keep clean. She longed for the clean air of New Mexico with its forest and mountains and clear blue skies, but most of all, even after so many months, she still longed for Lone Wolf, her Apache husband.

"I don't know why you keep refusing all his invitations, Becky," Elizabeth Roberts said. She lifted her blue eyes from the lace she was mending long enough to eye her niece with mild reproval. "After all, it's not as though Jake Logan is a stranger. Why you've known him since you were a little girl, and you'll have to admit you're not getting any younger."

"Forrest needs me, Aunt Bess," Rebecca said, turning from the window, managing to keep her voice level. Her gaze swept impatiently over the diminutive figure of her aunt sitting in the Boston rocker.

Although Elizabeth was a small woman, she was in the peak of health. Being the youngest, and the only one left, of Rebecca's father's three sisters, she had naturally taken charge when her brother needed a haven for his motherless daughter. She was a handsome woman with luxuriant brown hair as yet unmarred by silver streaks, and she dressed with an elegance all her friends envied. Her forty years had treated her kindly, although much of the reason could be accountable to losing her husband, who had proved to be overly fond of spirits and loose women, after only five years of marriage.

Rebecca moved to the large, gilded mirror that hung on the wall opposite the fireplace, and studied her reflection intently for a moment. She could see no sign of the aging process her aunt spoke of. She loved her aunt dearly, but this argument about her refusal to accept social invitations was recurring with more frequency of late. She knew it was partly her fault. She had been showing increasing signs of restlessness lately. After all, she had been a widow for more than a year now, and she was young, healthy, and full of energy. During her months with Lone Wolf, she had become used to hard work and no longer cared for the life of indolence she had always led here with her aunt. It hadn't mattered so much during her months of confinement, but Forrest was six months old now.

"You shouldn't feel the need of staying with the baby constantly," Elizabeth said. "I'm sure you don't mean to, but you're spoiling him terribly. And besides, that's what Robert is paying Nanny for. If your brother were here, he would agree with me. He wouldn't like this obsession you have with the baby."

"I'm not obsessed with Forrest, Aunt Bess!" Rebecca snapped, her blue eyes flashing. "Have you forgotten so soon that I'm a widow?"

Not waiting for an answer, Rebecca moved restlessly around the room amid rustling brocade skirts. She stopped before a small mahogany table and picked up a Viennese enamel snuffbox. She lifted the lid and frowned heavily at it.

"Is there something wrong with that snuffbox?" Elizabeth asked drily.

"No," Rebecca said, her voice slightly muffled, closing the lid with a snap.

"Then would you put it down, dear?" Elizabeth asked, a note of censure in her voice. "It's two hundred years old and you're treating it roughly."

"I'm sorry," Rebecca apologized. She knew the snuffbox was the only thing her aunt had left that had belonged to her grandmother. She set the box gently down on the table and sighed heavily.

Elizabeth watched Rebecca, indecision in her eyes. Then, making up her mind, she put her needlework down. She didn't like meddling in her niece's affairs, but sometimes one had to for a loved one's own good.

Her voice was filled with determination as she spoke. "I don't want to be disrespectful to the memory of your dead husband, Becky, but I suspect you're using him for an excuse, just as you used Forrest. Your husband's been dead for a year now, and it's time you put away your widow's weeds and thought about getting another one."

"I'm afraid I can't get a new husband as easily as I

293

can a new gown," Rebecca said. Her voice was cold, and her eyes equally chilling as she spun from the window to face her aunt. At the hurt look she encountered from Elizabeth, she relented slightly, her eyes softening considerably. She didn't like arguing with her aunt, but she had never known her to be so insensitive before, and she suspected Robert was behind Elizabeth's refusal to drop the subject.

"Have you heard from Robert lately," she asked, changing the subject abruptly.

"Well—as a matter of fact, I did," Elizabeth said, her eyelids lowering evasively. "When the postman delivered your letter a few days ago, there was one for me as well."

"I see," Rebecca watched her aunt's fingers moving with sudden swift motions, in and out of her lace. Yes, she did see. So that's what was at the bottom of all this. Robert thought she needed a husband, and he more than likely had him all picked out.

"And do you think Jake received a letter from Robert as well?"

"What?" Elizabeth lifted puzzled eyes to Rebecca. "Why on earth should Robert be writing to Jake? They aren't really that well acquainted."

"Indeed."

Her aunt looked at her strangely. "Sometimes I don't know what to make of you," she said. "Since you came home, you're so—so—" She stopped as if unable to find the right words to describe her niece.

"Sometimes I don't know what to make of myself," Rebecca said, sighing. She knew her aunt's only motivation was concern for her, and she was suddenly contrite.

"I'm sorry, Aunt Bess," she said. "I don't mean to be so difficult. But you don't seem to understand how much I loved my husband."

"I know, dear," Elizabeth said, her faded blue eyes softening. "And I'm sure it doesn't help matters to know he was killed in that way. I know it must have been completely devastating for you."

"In what way?" Rebecca asked. She didn't want to speak of Lone Wolf's death for it still brought her pain, but she was curious to know exactly what Robert had told her aunt. Elizabeth had never mentioned Lone Wolf to Rebecca in the entire year she had been there. Even when she met her at the train, she had read the letter Robert had sent, then wordlessly gathered her niece into her arms.

"Well, you know," Elizabeth said. "Being scalped by the Indians, and all."

Rebecca stared at her aunt in shock. Then suddenly, her eyes were blazing. "My husband wasn't scalped by the Indians!" she snapped. She couldn't believe Robert had had the gall to tell Aunt Bess such a thing. Robert had insisted on presenting her to Pittsburgh society as a widow, but had it really been necessary to tell Aunt Bess the Indians had killed her husband?

"Wasn't he?" Aunt Bess asked. "Maybe I got it wrong, but I'm sure that's what he said. I have the letter somewhere—in my dresser upstairs—if you would like for me to—No," she said quickly, shaking her head in denial. "I guess you don't want to see it." Her eyes were puzzled as she watched her niece. "But

295

maybe I just got that idea in my head because he was a cavalry officer who fought against the Indians for so many years before they finally killed him."

"The Indians did not kill my husband!" Rebecca said angrily. "Will you stop saying they did?"

"But I said scalped before, Becky. Not killed," Elizabeth said, her eyes clouding over in confusion. "I—oh, can't we talk about something else?"

"I think we'd better."

Elizabeth searched frantically for a safe topic of conversation. "Becky, what about Jake? Will you accept his invitation to the opera?"

"I'm just not ready to go out with anyone yet, Aunt Bess. And I'd appreciate it if you would accept my decision."

"Master Jake Logan!"

They both turned around quickly as the butler announced the very man they were discussing.

"Jake, how good of you to come," Elizabeth said, politely greeting the tall, well-built foppishly dressed man who entered the parlor.

"Elizabeth," he said, bending over her hand. "It's good to see you again. I hope I'm not intruding."

"Of course you're not intruding!" Elizabeth said stoutly, beaming at him. "You know you're welcome here anytime."

"And how are you today, Becky?" he asked, straightening up and turning to regard Rebecca. His sleepy brown gaze moved over her cool, oval face, then barely touched the supple body in the gray mourning dress before moving up to her shining brown hair secured with ivory combs and brass hairpins.

"Just fine, Jake," she said, smiling at him in welcome. Jake was a lawyer, respected and well liked by all. Just five years older than Rebecca, he had been an orphan—raised by his uncle—and had felt an empathy with her motherless state. He had been her protector as a child, replacing her absent brother. He had a droll sense of humor that usually kept her laughing, and they shared many childhood memories between them. She did enjoy Jake's company. She just didn't want him to get any romantic notions in his head, and she felt that accepting his invitations now might put them there.

"I've come with an invitation," he said, taking her hand in his.

"Jake. I couldn't possibly—" she began.

"No," he said, interrupting her. His usually sleepy brown eyes were direct, his chin set with determination. "Don't refuse me until you hear what I've got to say. This isn't an invitation to the opera or to dine out. I ran into Cassie in the park today, and she's having a spur-of-the-moment birthday party for John. She suggested I bring you along." When she started to shake her head in refusal, he protested. "You can't possibly refuse, Becky, or they will certainly be offended."

She thought about that for a moment, her eyes on his strong features. He had a point there. Cassie and John had always been friendly to her, although she couldn't help wondering how they would react if they knew her husband had been an Apache. Still, because of Forrest who would be growing up here, she could certainly use all the friends she could get.

"All right," she said, coming to a quick decision. "I'll

go with you. And you're right as usual. They probably would be offended if I refused."

"Good," he said, smiling softly into her eyes. "Then I'll come for you at eight."

She nodded, watching him leave. She found herself wondering why he had never married, for he was undoubtedly handsome. It was a well-known fact his rich brown hair and sleepy brown eyes had set many a heart in a tailspin. Why, then, was he still single?

"What are you going to wear to the party, dear?" Elizabeth asked, her voice curious.

"I really haven't had much time to think about it, Aunt Bess," she said, her lips quirking in a smile. So Aunt Elizabeth had got her way after all. Rebecca was going out with Jake, even if it was only to a birthday party given by mutual friends.

"What about you new yellow satin?" Aunt Bess seemed a trifle nervous, picking up a marble statue of Venus from a nearby table and examining it thoughtfully.

"No, it's much too bright," Rebecca said, her eyes on her aunt. She had no intention of wearing the bright yellow dress and she was surprised that Elizabeth thought she would. "I told you when you ordered it from the dressmakers that I wouldn't wear it, Aunt Bess. After all, I'm still in mourning."

"Your period of mourning is surely past, Becky," Elizabeth insisted. "And I think the yellow satin will do nicely for this birthday party."

"And I don't!" Rebecca snapped, her blue eyes flashing as she suddenly lost patience. Elizabeth didn't look up, her gaze remained on the statue. Eventually,

Rebecca relented a little. "All right. I'll wear the mauve velvet," she conceded. "But that's as far as I'll go."

She thought her aunt's lips twitched, and something like triumph showed in her eyes as they met Rebecca's for a moment before skittering away.

Rebecca looked suspiciously at her aunt. Well, perhaps she was right. It was time she put her outward mourning aside.

Jake came for her promptly at eight, and the party was already in full swing when they arrived. Rebecca was surprised to see so many people. It looked like the largest party Cassie and John had ever given. The whole house was brightly lit and Japanese lanterns had been strung from tree to tree on the lawns and throughout the garden.

They climbed the wide, carpeted stairs that led to a spacious, beautifully furnished hall. Chandeliers sparkled brilliantly, and urns of fresh flowers adorned the hall.

"Becky. How lovely to see you. And Jake. So good of you both to come," Cassie said, touching her face delicately to Rebecca's, then extending her hand to Jake. Cassie looked elegant in a rose satin gown that set off her pale skin and dark hair.

Jake smiled, bowing low over her hand. "Thank you for inviting us, Cassie. It never ceases to amaze me how you manage to grow lovelier with each passing day."

"Flatterer," Cassie said, fluttering her lashes flirtatiously at Jake. "Just go on in. I think you know most everyone here. Be sure to pick up your dance program, Becky. You'll find them on the rosewood table just inside. I'll be with you in a moment." She turned to greet another couple who had just arrived.

"Quite a turnout for such a hasty party," Jake remarked, laying the side of his hand against his lips to lower the sound. "It tends to make me wonder if she just forgot to invite us until the last minute."

"Shhhh!" she hissed, unwillingly amused. "Someone will hear you."

"But you are inclined to think I'm right?"

Her eyes swept the room, moving past their host and hostess to the countless guests displayed in their finest. The men wore lightweight summer flannels, the girls ruffled satins and dimities. A dance program, held by a gold silk cord, dangled invitingly from each girl's wrist. Rebecca wondered if Jake could be right. Certainly, Annabel's gown was new, the decolletage dipping alarmingly low. And it took the better part of the day to style Cynthia Wallace's hair.

"Yes," she grinned, touching her fan to her lips to hide her mirth. Her blue eyes twinkled up at him over the ivory and lace fan. "Should we be insulted, do you think?"

"Not this time," he said, his sleepy eyes smiling down on her. "In fact, I think I have to thank her."

"How so?" she asked, stopping beside the rosewood table that held the Wedgwood vase filled with flowers, the dance programs, and a pile of dainty gold pencils.

"It brought you out with me," he said, and the teasing quality had left his voice.

300

A blush crept up her neck. "Jake," she said warningly.

"Don't worry," he said softly. "I'm not going to push my luck. I've got plenty of time. Here, let me have that dance program."

"I hadn't really planned on dancing, Jake," she said. "I only picked it up because I knew it would cause comment if I wasn't carrying one."

He laughed. "Come on, give."

She handed him the card, her eyes worried. She didn't want him getting romantic ideas. It would only serve to complicate their relationship. Before she had decided if she should pursue the matter, they were joined by Annabel.

"There you are," she said, looking up at Jake, blinking her impossibly long eyelashes rapidly at him. "I was afraid you wouldn't come on such short notice. Cassie didn't know until we were checking the guest list earlier today that she had forgotten you."

"No harm done," Jake said, returning Rebecca's dance program with an "I told you so" look. "We didn't have anything special planned for tonight anyway."

"Are you going to sign my dance program, Jake?" Annabel asked, spreading her elaborate fan—an eighteenth-century chinoiserie "peep-hole" fan decorated with mother-of-pearl—over her lower face and casting a coquettish look at him.

"Why certainly, Annabel," he responded politely, although obviously startled by her boldness. "I would be happy to." He took the program and the little gold pencil she handed him, and he added his name to the list as the orchestra began to play.

"What luck," Annabel exclaimed, studying her dance card. "This dance belongs to Walter Myers, but I don't see him anywhere, so you can have it."

For a moment Jake looked stunned. He looked helplessly at Rebecca. "Uh—I'm afraid I'm already committed for this dance."

"But you couldn't. You just walked in the door." She looked at him suspiciously. "Whose card did you sign?"

"Becky's," he admitted.

"Oh. Well, that's all right then." She looked at Rebecca appealingly. "You don't mind, do you, Becky?"

A small smile tugged at Rebecca's mouth at Jake's helplessness before the other girl's pursuit. Ignoring the appeal in his eyes, she said. "Of course not, Annabel. You two go on ahead."

Jake sighed unhappily. "Just let me get Becky settled first, Annabel."

"Never mind, Jake," Rebecca assured him. "You go ahead. I'll just wander around for a moment."

"Well, if you're sure," he said doubtfully before leading Annabel onto the floor that had been stripped bare of its carpeting for the party.

Rebecca smiled to reassure him, then, unheedful of the amorous looks she was receiving from several quarters, wandered through the assemblage. She could see at a glance the guests were from the town's most prominent and wealthy families. Silks and satins glittered like stars beneath the brilliant candles placed in lustrous holders and sconces around the room.

When her glance intercepted a stranger approaching, his admiring eyes fixed intently on her, she quickly skittered away, crumpling the dance card tightly in one hand. She searched the packed dance floor for Jake, finally locating him dancing with Annabel, standing a head above most of the other men in attendance. He was graceful and danced well as she had occasion to remember from the past. As he caught sight of her, he stopped short, casting her a quizzical look across the room. She smiled at him, giving him a reassuring nod, then continued to circulate.

"Hello. Please tell me I haven't arrived too late to sign your dance program?"

She turned to find the stranger at her elbow. She knew they hadn't previously met, so she stared at a point behind his ear. "I'm afraid we haven't been properly introduced, sir," she said, her voice stiffly polite.

"That's easy to fix," he said with a grin, turning away from her to hurry away.

A moment later he was back, dragging Cassie along behind him. "All right, love," he told an astounded Cassie. "Introduce us."

"Rebecca Morgan," Cassie laughed. "This is my irrepressible brother, Mark Layton. You may not remember him since he spent most of his growing-up years in boarding school." She cast a mischievous glance at her brother and added, "Father seemed to think the discipline would be good for him."

"Now that you've given me such a glowing recommendation," Mark said, glowering at his sister. "Will you please go away?" He held out his hand to Rebecca. "And will *you* give me the honor of the next

303

dance?"

"I'm afraid this dance is taken," a hard voice said at Rebecca's elbow, and she turned astonished eyes on Jake.

"Well, the next one is mine," Mark said. His eyes appealed to Rebecca. "Please tell me your dance program isn't filled already."

"Uh — I'm afraid I lost it," Rebecca mumbled, squeezing the program tighter, hiding her hand in the folds of her velvet gown.

"Then I'll get you another," Mark said. "And I'll put my name at the top of the list."

When Mark turned away, Jake took her hand, leading her to the dance floor. She wondered at the stormy look in his eyes. Was he angry because Mark was so obviously flirting with her?

She flushed guiltily as he reached for the hand with the crumpled dance card. A smile lit his face as he pried the program from her fingers and put it in his pocket.

"I'll sign the whole thing when we finish this dance," he whispered, taking her hand and whirling her around as the orchestra struck up a waltz.

"What do you hear from Robert these days?" Jake asked, attempting to make light conversation.

"His letters are always rather on the short side," she said. "He doesn't have much to say when he writes."

"Are the Indians still causing a lot of trouble in his area?"

"I don't think there is as much raiding in the Silver City area."

"Isn't Geronimo a threat down around the Mexican

border?"

"So the newspapers say."

"Robert doesn't mention it?" he asked in surprise. "I should have thought he would keep you well informed on such matters."

"No."

"I take it you don't want to discuss Geronimo," he said, his sleepy brown eyes dwelling lazily on her.

"Not really."

"What would you like to talk about?"

She smiled up at him. "Must we talk at all?"

"Are you flirting with me?" he asked in astonishment. He seemed somehow to be pleased at the idea and she hurried to dissuade him of it.

"No!" Quick color stole up her cheeks.

"Oh." He sounded disappointed.

"Well, are you enjoying yourself then?" He swung her around in a swirl of petticoats.

"Actually, I am."

"Good." He smiled down at her. "I had an ulterior motive for inviting you, you know."

"Oh." She smiled archly. "And what was that?"

"I wanted to break the ice. Show you just how much you're missing by staying in all the time." His arm tightened around her waist. "You're much too young and entirely too beautiful to cut yourself off from the world the way you've done in the past." His eyes dwelt on her glowing features. "I can only hope this will be just one of many times we shall enjoy together."

When the dance ended, they drifted toward the refreshment table, and Jake helped himself to a cup of peach brandy for each of them, then moved away from the crowded table before offering her one.

"Thank you, Jake," she said softly, sipping slowly at the drink.

"You're very welcome." His sleepy brown eyes smiled over the rim of the cup at her.

She returned the smile, feeling at peace with the world. Then slowly that feeling disappeared, replaced by a creeping eerie sensation. The hairs on the back of her neck prickled. She felt as though eyes were on her. Disapproving eyes. She frowned, her blue gaze lifting to scan the crowded room.

"Uh, oh."

Jake quickly followed her glance, his eyes taking note of the tall, lean man bearing down on them. It was Mark, coming to claim his dance.

"This air is stifling, Becky," Jake said, turning back to her. "Shall we stroll through the garden for a breath of fresh air?"

"Yes," she agreed quickly, wanting to avoid Mark as much as Jake did. There were enough complications in her life already, without Cassie's brother adding to them.

"Then let's go," he said, grinning down at her. He took her elbow and steered her toward the doors opening on the veranda.

She couldn't help one backward glance as they left the room, for the feeling of being watched was even stronger now. Although she scanned the crowded throng thoroughly, skimming over a disappointed Mark—for he surely wasn't the problem—she saw nothing out of the ordinary, and yet the feeling persisted.

"I believe we've lost him," Jake said, once they were in the garden.

"I guess that really wasn't very polite?" She laughed up at him.

"No, it wasn't, was it?" he said, his sleepy eyes amused. "What I'm wondering is why you were so willing to come with me?"

"Well, it *was* stifling in there," she said, eyeing him with sudden trepidation. She had been so determined to put Cassie's young brother off, that she hadn't stopped to realize the implications Jake might put on it.

The air was warm, and the sky was a vast black arc, sprinkled with starlight that was occasionally obliterated by the flames gushing from some distant furnace.

"The furnaces are beautiful at night, aren't they?" she said softly, her ears attuned to the delicate strains of a waltz that drifted through the open doors.

"Yes," he agreed. "The dark covers the ugliness. I've done a lot of traveling, but I've never seen a more beautiful city than Pittsburgh by night."

"Nor uglier than Pittsburgh by day," she said, thinking of the forests of New Mexico—and Lone Wolf . . . She blinked rapidly, her mind skittering away. "I guess that's the price we have to pay for living in the heart of the soft coal region."

He laughed. "I had occasion to take a visitor from out west to some of the factories and foundries last week. He was interested in investing in iron. He was horrified to see the columns of smoke belching from the tall chimneys. Would you believe he kept a handkerchief over his nose during the whole visit?"

307

She laughed. "Can you really blame him? We were raised here and we know the smoke has some healthful benefits, but I'm sure the poor man must have thought he would get a lung disease." She looked up at him. "Did he invest?"

His eyes glittered. "No. He did not. He couldn't get out of town fast enough."

"Now you should have told him if he didn't want to invest in iron, he could invest in coal or glass. We've plenty of both."

"I tried that. The only thing he was interested in was leaving our fair city as fast as he could." He picked up her hand. "Let's look at Cassie's garden."

She nodded in acquiescence, and they began their tour of the garden.

The sweet fragrance of flowers teased their nostrils. Gladiolas, lilies, phlox, and roses grew in abundance along the paths. The Edwards house was one of Pittsburgh's most fashionable homes, and two gardeners were employed just to keep the gardens.

They stopped beneath the branches of a magnolia tree, and Rebecca took a sip of her brandy punch. The sensation of being watched was still with her, but she put it down to nerves for there was no one around but Jake and herself.

"Would you have believed such a tree could grow here, Jake," she asked. "The size of its flowers in the spring was unbelievable."

"It wouldn't dare not grow and produce after the fuss Cassie made over it."

"What do you mean?"

"I guess you were too young to remember." He

grinned. "You should have seen it."

"What happened?"

"Well, when John proposed to Cassie, she made her acceptance depend on his procuring and successfully planting this tree."

"You're making that up," she accused. "No one would do a thing like that."

"Honest. It's the truth."

"But that doesn't make sense." She looked at the tree again, her eyes puzzled. It looked like an ordinary magnolia tree to her.

"I think it was meant to be a joke in the beginning."

"In the beginning?"

"Yes. She didn't really expect a southern magnolia tree to grow here, I wouldn't think. I don't think she expected it to survive the planting, let alone the cold winter."

"But then, why would she say such a thing?"

"Well, John had been courting her so earnestly for over a year, and her father and mother were pressing her to accept his suit because they were worried she was spending too much time with the gardener's son. So — knowing her parents would be told of her answer when he proposed, she told him she had always wanted to marry a gardener. John promptly laid claim to being the world's greatest gardener. Well, she thought about that for a few minutes, then told him if he could purchase a magnolia tree from Louisiana, and make it grow and flourish, the year it produced flowers, she would marry him."

She chuckled, the humor of the situation growing in her. "I don't believe that! You're making it up1"

"Swear to it," he said, holding up his right hand. "On a stack of Bibles, I'll swear to it."

"Well, for heaven's sake." She stared at the flowering tree again. "Who told you?"

"The whole town was in on it."

"She never told what she'd done!"

"No, I'll give her that. She only wanted her parents to know, but John was so certain he could do it, he went around telling the whole town." He laughed softly. "You should have been here. The whole town was rooting for John. You know how snooty Cassie was a few years back."

She nodded her head. Indeed she did. Cassie had been spoilt terribly by her parents. "But I don't understand," she said. "You're insinuating that Cassie doesn't love John—"

"No. No," he protested, holding up a silencing hand. "That's the funny part. He was so determined to plant this tree and make it thrive so he could marry her that, in the end, it was because of her the tree survived."

"I don't understand."

"Neither did anyone else," he said dryly. "But it's true. John spent all of his spare time watering and nourishing that blamed tree. Sometimes a crowd would gather to watch him protect it from storms. He had rigged a box-like structure with breathing holes to put around it during the worst weather, and everyone would stop by and pass the time of day with him and listen to him talk about what he and Cassie would do after they were married. They teased him a lot but he accepted the good-natured ribbing for what it was.

310

Then one weekend a storm came up unexpectedly. He didn't have the tree covered, and he was in a meeting with the city officials. He happened to look out the window, saw the rain coming down hard, and suddenly rushed out, leaving everyone dumb-struck. When he made it home, he found Cassie out in the garden, soaked to the skin and covered with mud, trying to keep the rain from battering the tree into the ground. When she saw him, she flew into a rage at him for forgetting about it."

She smiled delightedly. "So his persistence paid off. She obviously fell in love with him."

"Yes," he said, his voice suddenly husky, his eyes tender as he stared down at her.

"Jake," she said, casting an uneasy glance around, suddenly aware of the darkness surrounding them. "I hope you're not leading up to something." Without her noticing, they had drifted to the side of the house nearest the library.

"Don't worry," he said. "Like I said before, I'm not going to push my luck. But you'll have to admit it did make a good story."

"It wasn't true?" she asked.

"Of course it was. What I meant was, it seemed like an opportune time for me to tell you about it."

"Oh." She took another sip of her peach brandy, lowering her eyes evasively, unwilling to face what she saw in his gaze.

"Here, let me take that." He reached for the glass at the same time she tried to give it to him, and their hands collided, splashing peach brandy onto his fingers. "Sorry," he said, setting the glass onto a bench and wiping his fingers with a linen handkerchief.

She smiled up at him, just as the library doors were flung open, sending a stream of light flooding the courtyard, light that fell over the two of them standing with heads so close together.

A rustle in the shrubbery nearby caused her to turn her head, and she grasped Jake's arm, her fingers clenching tightly for support. Then her features paled as she saw the ghostly apparition floating just beyond the circle of light.

Only the face could be seen, a hard, unsmiling mask, but she recognized it instantly.

It was Lone Wolf.

Her hand went to her throat. What in God's name was happening? It couldn't be Lone Wolf. He was dead. Dead and buried.

Yet it was. Or rather it had been. For now the face was gone, replaced by a still quivering oleander branch.

Her skin was icy. Her mouth was dry and she swallowed thickly. He was dead but his spirit had come back to haunt her. What else could it be?

Her knees buckled and she swayed. But she would not faint, she swore silently, locking her knees in place and clinging to Jake's supporting arm.

"What's wrong, Becky?" he asked anxiously, putting a steadying arm around her.

Her head lifted, her eyes focused on Jake. "Did you see him?" she choked.

"See who, Becky?" His gaze was puzzled, concerned.

"Lone Wolf," she whispered, her voice shaking, her

body trembling uncontrollably.

"A wolf?"

"Over there, near the bushes."

He looked. "There's nothing there."

There was though. Didn't you see?" Obviously he hadn't, for his forehead was pleated in concern. Suddenly, she felt a need — an overpowering desire — to be alone.

"Are you feeling unwell, Becky," Jake asked gently. "Would you like to go home?"

"Yes, please," she whispered through stiff lips. She leaned against him, drawing from his strength. "Please take me home."

## Chapter Seventeen

"Are you sure you're all right?" Jake asked anxiously, his eyes intent on her pale face as he took her arm and helped her into the carriage.

"Yes," she said shortly, leaning back against the seat. She wished she were alone. She didn't want to talk, didn't want her thoughts disturbed.

As though sensing her mood, Jake didn't press her. He patted her hand and settled back against the seat opposite her.

Her thoughts were in turmoil as she stared out the carriage window into the darkness beyond. What on earth had caused her to think she had seen Lone Wolf? It had seemed so real at the time, and yet she knew it could not possibly be.

She didn't believe in ghosts, and Lone Wolf was dead. It worried her. Was she going to start seeing Lone Wolf everywhere she went? Was that what happened when you were haunted?

Could it have been her imagination? Was her mind

playing tricks on her? Yes, she decided. That was it. It had been nothing but a trick of the light that had caused her to imagine she had seen him.

But if that was so, why then, had she imagined him so angry? Did she feel guilty over what had happened to him? If so, why? She hadn't been responsible for what the cavalry had done.

Or had she?

After all, it was because of her they had attacked Chief Tall Feathers' village. Perhaps she hadn't really come to terms with Lone Wolf's death at all.

"We're here, Becky," Jake said, squeezing her hand gently. She had been so preoccupied with her thoughts of Lone Wolf that she had scarcely noticed the trip home.

She was still absorbed in thought as she descended from the carriage and climbed the wide steps to the house. As they entered the dwelling, Bess came toward them. The smile on her lips wavered, then died, concern replacing the happy expression as she saw her niece's face.

"What happened?" she asked, alarmed.

"Nothing," Jake assured her. "All the excitement just proved to be too much for her."

"Pshaw!" her aunt snorted. "That's hard to believe! Why, Becky thrives on excitement. It's a good thing too, for Forrest keeps her jumping all the time."

As if mention of the baby reminded her of Rebecca's reluctance to accompany Jake, she turned suspicious eyes on her niece. "What is all this nonsense about your getting too much excitement?"

Rebecca forced a smile through stiff lips. "This is ridiculous! Everyone is making such a fuss, and all because I happened to feel a little faint."

"You felt faint?" Bess asked. "Are you coming down with something?" She laid the palm of her hand against Rebecca's forehead. "You don't feel the least bit feverish. In fact, if anything, you feel rather on the cool side."

"I'm all right, Aunt," she said irritably. "I just didn't eat much today."

"Humph! I shouldn't wonder! You don't look after yourself properly. Well, just go get into bed and I'll bring you some nourishing broth."

"She would do better with some good, red meat," Jake put in. "A rare steak, perhaps."

Elizabeth shuddered delicately. "No! Broth's the thing for her." She turned to Jake. "I don't want to rush you Jake, but—"

"Of course," he said swiftly. "You must take care of her. Don't mind me, I'll just let myself out." He turned to Rebecca. "Thank you for coming with me, Becky," he said formally. "And I'm sorry you were taken ill."

"It was kind of you to ask me, Jake," she replied. "I sincerely hope I haven't completely ruined your evening. Perhaps you could return to the party."

"I wouldn't think of it," he said, quickly reassuring her. "I'm afraid I was finding the party a dead bore anyway. Would you mind if I call on you tomorrow?"

"You'll be most welcome, Jake," her aunt answered for her. "I'll see you to the door."

Rebecca's lips stretched into a smile for Jake's benefit, but she was glad to see the last of him. She felt a great need to be alone, but—there was still Aunt Bess to get past.

"Now, come along, Becky," her aunt said, bustling

into the room. "Let's get you into bed."

"I must check on Forrest first, Aunt Bess."

"Forrest is fine," Bess assured her. "I was just up there."

"Nevertheless, I want to see my baby," Rebecca said firmly.

"Well, you go on up then," Elizabeth said, giving in gracefully. "And I'll fix you something to eat."

Knowing there was no use arguing about the food, Rebecca went up the stairs and entered the nursery. She moved to the baby bed where Forrest slept and gazed down on her infant son. He was the image of his father with his coal-black hair and gray eyes, and, since his birth six months before, he had been growing by leaps and bounds. She was always amazed at his sweet temper for he was always smiling and cooing and hardly ever cried. As she watched, his lips twitched in a smile, and her eyes softened. Even in his sleep, Forrest's good nature showed through. Who could possibly ask for a better baby?

Having assured herself that her son hadn't suffered from her being away from him, she retired to her room. She had removed her party attire and was standing before the dressing table fastening the tiny, ivory buttons on her nightgown when her aunt arrived carrying a silver tray containing a cup of tea and a bowl of thin broth.

Rebecca watched her aunt move to the bedside table with the tray. Idly, she picked up her ivory-backed hairbrush and, keeping her back to her aunt, asked in a deceptively light tone. "Aunt Bess, do you believe in ghosts?"

"Ghosts?" asked Bess, setting the tray down and

turning to look at her niece. "What in the world made you ask such a question?"

"Oh, no reason in particular," Rebecca said, twirling the hairbrush idly. "But I really am interested in hearing your answer."

"Well—I never really thought about it much," Bess said. "But I guess I don't. At least," she amended, "if there are such things as spirits floating around, haunting the living, then I've never seen one." She shivered suddenly. "And that's just fine with me." Her eyes were curious as she asked Rebecca. "What made you bring up such a thing? Surely you don't believe in them?"

"No!" Rebecca said sharply. But she knew she had been too emphatic when her aunt's eyes narrowed suddenly. Rebecca didn't want to answer any questions so she plunged nervously into speech. "It's all in the mind. A trick of the imagination. People can't possibly come back from the dead to haunt the living!"

Bess shivered delicately. "Why are we having this conversation anyway? Now, you just forget all this nonsense, and crawl right into that bed and drink your soup and tea."

Although Rebecca didn't feel the least bit hungry, she was more than happy to end the conversation. She got into bed and forced herself to swallow the thin soup, knowing, from past experiences, that her aunt would not leave until she had finished.

As she finished the last drop, she gave a sigh of relief and watched her aunt gather up the dishes and leave the room. Finally, she was alone. Now she could mull over what she had seen earlier.

She had been so sure, when she saw the apparition, that it was her husband. And yet, even without her aunt's assertions, she knew how impossible that was. She didn't believe in ghosts, but what else could it be? Although she had refused to allow her mind to dwell on it, had sealed it far back in the recesses of her mind, the fact remained that she had found her husband's dismembered body in their wickiup.

Sliding out of bed, she went to the closet. Her fingers searched the topmost shelf until they felt the object she was looking for. Careful to grip it firmly, she removed the double mug that she had brought from the cliff dwellings. Her fingers traced the rims lovingly as they had so many countless times before.

*A mug for lovers*, he had said. And that was what she and Lone Wolf had been—lovers. She caressed the cup as tenderly as though it were Lone Wolf himself. Was her mind playing tricks on her? Could it be possible she imagined she saw her husband because she felt she had betrayed his memory by attending the birthday party with Jake?

The answers eluded her. She kissed the mug tenderly, then replaced it carefully on the shelf. It was all she had left of their time together at the cliff dwellings. Except for the baby. Her lips curled in a tiny smile. Yes, she had Forrest, and he would always be a living reminder of his father—Lone Wolf—her Apache husband.

She returned to the bed, but sleep eluded her. Long into the night the image of Lone Wolf's angry face persisted. She tossed and turned in the bed, her body refusing to rest just as her mind refused.

Finally, after long hours, sheer weariness overtook her and her eyes closed as she fell into a restless slumber.

* * *

His hands were everywhere, touching her body, searching. He whispered into her ear, but she couldn't understand what he was saying. Then his lips moved across her mouth, leaving a trail of fire everywhere they touched. She moaned low in her throat, trying to capture the lips that so carefully evaded hers.

She felt her breasts swelling, thrusting into the palm of his hands, begging for his touch. Her nipples were taut, eager for his possession.

She moaned again.

As his mouth touched hers, tenderly at first, then harder, cutting off her breath, her eyes opened wide, staring in shocked silence at the face so close to hers.

It was the ghost of her husband!

Lone Wolf.

He had returned to haunt her again.

Frantically, she pushed against his chest, forcing him away, forcing his body . . .

"What's wrong?" he whispered gruffly. "Don't I have as much finesse as your friend?"

The meaning of his words escaped her. She heard only the sound of his voice, and it sounded surprisingly human.

"Lone Wolf?" she questioned, her voice decidedly shaky, her blue eyes confused.

"Who were you expecting?"

"It can't be you?" she whispered, her blue eyes wide with shock. "It can't possibly be!"

"Why not?"

"You're dead!" Her dazed eyes moved over his body, his face. Everything seemed to be intact.

"Am I really?" he asked, his gaze moving over her

stricken face.

"Aren't you?"

"No, at least I wasn't the last time I had occasion to check."

"You're not?"

"Do I look dead?"

"No."

"Then why do you keep insisting I am?"

"Because I thought you were." She suddenly realized the conversation they were having was totally ridiculous. He wasn't a ghost. He was alive!

She put out a trembling hand, touching the warm flesh of his chest and a wild rush of joy swept through her. She could actually feel the beating of his heart against her fingertips. Tears of happiness welled up into her eyes, running over to slip down her cheeks.

"It was you," she whispered in a shaky voice. "It *was* you! I thought you were dead." She touched his face gently, feeling the warm flesh beneath her palm. "All this time, I thought you were dead." She stared into his eyes. "Where have you been?"

"That's a long story," he said, wiping the tears away with his fingertips. "And I really don't feel like going into it right now. I had making love to you in mind, not talking all night." His hand reached out and drew her unresisting form into his arms. His lips touched the end of her nose, then her eyelids.

"Lone Wolf—" she began, loving the security of his embrace but wanting answers to the questions that filled her mind.

"Shhh," he said, blowing into her ear, sending the wispy tendrils of hair feathering out, causing goose bumps to ripple across her body.

"We will talk later," he said softly, cupping her face tenderly with his hands. "Right now, all I want to do is love you."

His mouth crushed down on hers, and as the familiar flame leaped between them, the past year fell away. His tongue probed her lips, forcing them apart, and she opened to the searching penetration, feeling a hungry wildness in him. His lips hardened, and, despite the consuming intensity of his kiss, it was so full of tenderness she thought she would die from the sweetness of it.

His lips left hers, trailing across her face, lingering on her chin. He opened his mouth, biting softly at the soft flesh, then moved slowly down her neck. One hand moved, touching her breast through the thin fabric of her nightgown exploringly.

"Lone Wolf," she groaned, her eyes squeezed tightly shut. Her body felt on fire as she pressed against him, her senses blazing out of control. "Please, love me."

"Always," he said, lifting his head and gazing at her through the dim light. His voice sounded shaken, but the import of his words escaped her in her eagerness for his caresses. His mouth returned to her lips, taking them with a satisfying swiftness that left her breathless. As his tongue probed for entrance again, she opened her mouth for him eagerly.

His fingers began to unfasten the tiny buttons nestling against her neck. Then, as the nightdress parted, his lips found the hollow in her throat. The contact of his lips against her skin had a sensual impact on her senses. Her mind had ceased to function.

Her nightgown was cast aside, but she remained unaware of how it was removed. Her hands remained

322

locked at the back of his dark head, her mouth clinging to his as though she would never let him go. She had forgotten how it felt to be kissed, and she felt a driving hunger in her that had been long denied. Suddenly, she craved the feel of his naked flesh against hers, and her fingers struggled with the buttons in his shirt, working desperately at them, moaning as they continued to evade her struggles.

With an oath, he shoved her fingers aside, pulling himself away for a moment, then he was back, kneeling above her. His mouth closed over her nipple and she shuddered with pleasure. It had been so long. She had thought she would never feel this way again.

His mouth left her breast, moving lower. His tongue dipped into her navel then continued on its downward course. Her body began to twist and writhe beneath him. Her breath was erratic, her blood pounding loudly in her ears.

When he found the core of her being, she gasped, feeling the heat between her thighs moving up her stomach, burning, tingling, every nerve end sizzling. His tongue dipped into her moistness, insistent, leaving her almost mindless with desire.

"No. Please. I can't stand anymore," she moaned, clutching his hair and tugging frantically at him.

As though he felt the same desperation as she, he shifted until his strength was pressing hard against the delicate core of her being.

Unable to stand the tension, and refusing to be denied a moment longer, she arched her body upwards. He gasped at the movement, then plunged quickly, entering her moistness, burying himself totally in her femininity. Rebecca clutched him to her convulsively, little moans escaping from her throat.

He lay still for a moment, then began a slow movement. As his movements became faster, tension coiled deep inside of her and her body took command. She lifted her hips, meeting his thrusts with a slamming force that shook her. Soon, they were there, crying out their release together, then their bodies went slack and they lay sated, arms wrapped around each other.

They lay quietly together, his arms tight around her, until their breathing became normal again. Then, Rebecca spoke. "How did you find me, Lone Wolf?"

"It wasn't easy," he said. "I went to the ranch and wasted several days there, waiting for you to appear. When you did not, I went to Silver City and asked questions of a friend who has been loyal to me there."

She frowned. "You have a friend who lives in Silver City? You never told me that."

"I'm afraid there's a lot I haven't told you," he said, and, although he spoke lightly, she sensed an underlying note of sadness.

"Anyway," he continued. "I found out you had come to Pittsburgh to live with your Aunt Bess. But what I failed to learn was that Aunt Bess was Elizabeth Roberts. I wasted a lot of time looking for Bess Shaw. I suppose if I hadn't seen you at John's birthday party, I would still be looking."

"I thought you were dead," she said, her voice breaking, her eyes filling with moisture.

"And did it bother you, Little Blue Eyes?"

She turned hurt eyes on him. "Of course it bothered me. You're my husband. But I still don't understand. I saw your body at the rancheria. The head—the necklace . . ." She couldn't go on.

"I never reached the rancheria," he said. "I don't know who you saw, but it wasn't me."

"It wasn't you?"

He shook his head. "No. Black Bear ambushed me the night I left you. He left me for dead."

"But — your — your bear claw necklace . . ." Her eyes widened. "He took it from you," she said. "It was Black Bear I found."

"More than likely."

Remembering why they had parted, she asked. "Is the trouble — the fighting — over?"

"No. I fear it will never be over."

"But you came for me anyway," she said.

"I came," he agreed, kissing her eyelids. "I couldn't stay away. Now be quiet. I want to make love to you again."

"Now?"

"Yes, now!"

"You're in an almighty hurry for someone who's taken a year to come look me up," she said, her voice showing her bitterness.

"I would have come sooner, Little Blue Eyes, but I was unable, for Black Bear wounded me grievously."

"Oh, my love, no, where?"

Her eyes moved to search his body, and she drew in a sharp breath as he pointed to a scar very close to his heart. She kissed it gently, finding another scar with her fingers a little farther down.

"How bad was it?" she asked in a trembling voice.

"Bad enough," he said. "I would more than likely have died, had it not been for Brave Eagle who found me. I lost a lot of blood, and it took me a while to gain

325

enough strength back just to look after myself. Brave Eagle is a good friend. He stayed with me until I was able to take care of myself."

"Then Brave Eagle was not killed either in the slaughter?"

"No. There had been sickness in the rancheria and only half the people were left there, the ones who were unable to travel. The rest were moved to safety by Chief Tall Feathers."

"Little Turtle?"

"She lives."

"Thank God!" Rebecca said, feeling relief that Little Turtle was not among the dead. She felt compassion for the sick who had been unable to travel, but she knew it was the law of the land. Only the fittest could survive.

"Enough of talking," he murmured, nibbling at her neck. "I want to make love to you again."

As he bent to take her lips again, she heard her aunt's voice from the first floor. Then the sound of footsteps ascending the stairs.

"Lone Wolf," she said frantically. "You've got to hide! Aunt Bess is coming."

"Dammit," he bit out. "I've got to get out of here. Hurry and dress, then stall her till I'm gone."

After dropping a hurried kiss on his mouth, Rebecca jumped out of the bed and pulled her nightgown over her head. When she could see again, Lone Wolf was almost dressed and halfway to the window.

"Wait," she called, reaching out for him.

He stopped, turned, then bent to kiss her lingeringly. "Don't worry," he said. "It will be all right."

"You will come back, won't you?" she asked, clutching at him.

326

"Yes, Little Blue Eyes," he said. "I'll return for you."

For you! The words sliced into her! There was something he didn't know! Something she had to tell him! "Lone Wolf," she tugged at his arm. "There's something—"

"Later," he said, placing his fingers against her mouth to shush her.

Outside the door, her aunt called again. Then the doorknob turned, and Lone Wolf moved. By the time her aunt had opened the door, Rebecca was staring at an open—empty—window.

"Becky," Aunt Bess said. "I heard noises up here, so I thought you must still be awake. I guessed you couldn't sleep either, and I decided a cup of hot cocoa would do us both some good."

Rebecca turned to look blankly at the steaming cup her aunt held out to her. "Hot cocoa?" she repeated in a dazed voice.

"Yes, dear," Bess said. When Rebecca didn't respond, she crossed to the bedside table and set down the china cup. "Rebecca, I've been lying in the dark worrying about you, wondering if I should write to Robert and ask him to come to Pittsburgh for a visit."

"Robert? In Pittsburgh?" Rebecca repeated parrotlike. "Yes, that would be very nice."

"Good. I'll do just that then. And right now," Bess said, in a hand-dusting tone of voice. "Now you drink this right down and try to get some sleep, dear. Everything is going to be just fine."

"All right. And thank you, Aunt Bess." Rebecca picked up the cup and sipped obediently at the hot cocoa, her mind turned away from her departing aunt, still locked into the realization that had hit her as soon as Lone Wolf had slipped away.

He was alive. Alive and here in Pittsburgh. He had come for her.

And he knew nothing of their child.

He was standing in the light to illuminate the paper the letters drifting out from their wild

# Chapter Eighteen

Rebecca stood at the window, and watched the sun climb over the rooftops, its rays purpling the grime from the steel mills. It was early, yet she had been awake for hours. Waiting. Impatient for the first time in a year. For the first time since she had rocked herself next to the body she had believed was Lone Wolf's.

She had so many questions to ask him. So many things she hadn't thought of last night until he was gone. But there hadn't been that much time then. Just time enough for love.

If only Aunt Bess hadn't . . . But no, last night was gone.

Still she couldn't help but wish she had had time to tell him about Forrest. Her lips curled in a soft smile as she thought of Lone Wolf's surprise when he came to take her home. And he would be coming for her. She had no doubt of that.

He would be expecting one traveling companion. Instead he would find two. It would be a happy surprise for him. He had wanted a son. Now he had one.

She strode to the dressing table, picked up her brush, and pulled it through her hair. She was very impatient, impatient for Lone Wolf to return, eager to begin her life with him again.

*But what about Nanny?*

The thought of the baby's nurse intruded on her dreams of Lone Wolf, irritating her, and she tugged her brush harshly through a long, brown curl. Nanny slept next door to the baby. It was her habit as well to check on the child several times during the night. Robert had told her Lone Wolf had been a wanted man, with a ransom on his head. Would his supposed death have changed that?

Probably not. At least not if he were known to be still alive. So no one must know. Somehow they would have to steal away, the three of them, and Rebecca knew they would need as much headstart as possible. So how?

Well, no matter. Lone Wolf would have some kind of plan to see them safely away.

An eager smile touched her lips, lighting her eyes. She must be ready when he came. She must pack her portmanteau.

Her portmanteau!

Where was it?

Would she find it in the attic? She started for the door, then stopped. She must curb her eagerness for a while, for that way led to discovery. She could wait a few hours, then she could casually ask James, her aunt's butler, to bring it to her room—

That wouldn't do either. He would wonder why she wanted the traveling bag, and she couldn't tell him. James was too astute by far.

Unable to wait longer, Rebecca dressed quietly and picked up a candle. Then, she moved silently into the hallway, her eyes intent on the door at the end of the corridor that led to the attic.

She crept quietly toward it, pausing occasionally to listen, but the only sounds she heard came from below stairs where the staff was busy preparing breakfast.

If she hurried, she might be able to retrieve the bag and return to her room without being discovered.

Her hand froze on the door when she heard a noise from Nanny's room. She quickly opened the door to the attic and slipped inside, pulling it tightly shut just as Nanny came into the hall.

Breathlessly, she waited until she heard the woman leave the upper hallway, then, holding the candle high, she made her way up the stairway to the attic.

The air was musty, and her feet stirred clouds of dust while she walked. A cobweb caught at her face, and she wiped it away with the back of her hand. The candlelight fell around her like a golden cloak, casting shadows across long forgotten discards: a green stenciled rocker with flaking paint; a tarnished, gilded mirror; a Queen Anne cherrywood highboy; an old dressing table; a large leather-covered trunk. And there, beside the trunk, the portmanteau.

Blowing out a relieved sigh — the whole place seemed more ghostly than she had imagined it would be — she grasped the bag's grimy handle. As she turned to make her way back across the room, her toe stubbed against something solid and she yelped, dropping the bag and candle at the same time. She was in total darkness.

Suddenly, the door at the foot of the stairs was flung open, and a bright beam of light streamed up the stairway.

"Is anyone up there?"

Rebecca recognized Nanny's voice and shrank back into the shadows, trying to still her wildly beating heart. She heard Nanny muttering something about the wee people and the door closed again. She waited a few moments, then picked up the candle and the bag and went down the stairs.

She encountered no one on her return journey, and she breathed a sigh of relief as she closed her bedroom door behind her.

Rebecca used the next three hours to sort through her clothing and pack what she felt would be necessary for the journey. As she reached into the top shelf for her black, kid boots, her hand encountered the double mug they had found at the cliff dwellings. Unable to leave it behind, she pulled it from the shelf and tucked it away inside the bag, nestling it beneath her under-garments.

She had only packed one of her gowns, because she knew Pittsburgh's clothing would be out of place on the prairie. She was sure Lone Wolf would provide her with something to wear as soon as they reached the encampment. Meanwhile, she would need most of the room for the baby's things, but she would wait until later in the day to pack that. First, she must think of an excuse to get rid of Nanny for a few hours.

When she had finished packing to her satisfaction, she hid the bag, then went downstairs where she breakfasted heartily. Then she searched out her aunt, finding her in the blue parlor.

"Good morning, Aunt Bess. Isn't it a beautiful day?"

Elizabeth stabbed the needle into her embroidery

work, pulled the thread through, then looked up from the Boston rocker where she was sitting. "What's left of it," she said dryly. "You slept most of it away."

"It must have been the hot cocoa, Aunt Bess. For after I drank it, I went right off to sleep and slept like a log." Rebecca crossed to the window and pulled the sheer curtain aside. From the window, she had a clear view of the driveway and side garden. That way, if Lone Wolf came, she would be sure to see him. Hopefully, before anyone else did.

"That's too bad, in a way," her aunt said, pushing the thread aside, before inserting the needle in the fabric once again.

"Too bad?" Rebecca half-turned from the window, casting quizzical eyes on her aunt. "How so?"

"We had a surprise caller earlier. I should have liked to have you meet him. He seemed disappointed to miss you as well."

"Oh, yes?" Rebecca's stomach sank inexplicably. It couldn't have been Lone Wolf, of course. He would not have come, *could* not have come in the daylight. "Who was this mysterious caller?"

"Grant Mallory." Elizabeth took another stitch, seemingly intent on her needlework, but a small smile played around her lips.

"Who is Grant Mallory?" Rebecca turned the name over and over in her mind, but it rang no bells. "Have I made his acquaintance, Aunt Bess? The name sounds familiar somehow, and yet I can't place him."

"He's John Mallory's son! You remember John Mallory, don't you?"

"Well—yes. At least . . ." Her brows drew together in a frown as she concentrated, trying to place him. And yet, all the Mallory name brought to mind was a small, dark-haired woman, always dressed in black, even to the petticoats that rustled beneath the silk of her gown. She had the air of someone who had suffered great tragedy in her life. "Was this John Mallory related to Anne Mallory?"

"See. I knew you would remember," her aunt said. "Yes, John was Anne's brother."

Rebecca picked up on the past tense quickly. "He died about three years ago, didn't he? And Anne the year after. Yes, I remember now. But I don't recall a son."

"I don't really suppose you should. He's probably about ten years older than you. And he's been away, in Europe, I think, for quite some time now. But he did make it back for his father's funeral, though he missed Anne's."

Rebecca studied the older woman speculatively. Grant Mallory, it appeared, was only a few years younger than Aunt Bess. Was that why her aunt placed such importance on his visit? Could she be romantically interested in him, wanting perhaps Rebecca's approval? It was possible.

"What makes this man so special, Aunt Bess?"

"Why"—Elizabeth fluttered a slender hand—"he is a very presentable gentleman, Rebecca. Hearts are atwitter all over town because of him. And he is very eligible."

"Oh, I see," Rebecca said, her eyes twinkling. "Very eligible, is he? Well, I'm delighted to hear you have a gentleman caller. And if anything should come of it, I'll be most happy—"

"Me?" Her aunt's shocked exclamation cut her off.

"Who else? Oh no. Not me." She waved her hand at her aunt, admonishingly. "Now, Aunt Bess, I will not have you pushing another one at me. It's enough that you use every opportunity that presents itself to get me and Jake together, but I will not have you encouraging strange men to hang around here."

"Well, I wouldn't exactly call Grant a strange man, dear, and it never hurts anything to have several gentlemen lined up." The lines of her face softened. "And I couldn't help but notice you've laid aside your mourning and put on that pretty, blue pastel gown that becomes you so. I was so hopeful it meant you were ready to go out in company."

"You like the way it looks?" Rebecca twirled around amid a flurry of skirts. "Thank you, ma'am," she said, dropping a curtsy.

"You're in a high old mood, too," Bess remarked drily. "Well, I'm glad to see that."

Suddenly the parlor door burst inward, and Nanny scurried in, clutching Forrest to her ample bosom.

"What's the matter, Nanny?" Rebecca asked quickly, snatching the baby from his nurse. "Has something happened?"

"No, ma'am," Nanny said, curtsying slightly, her red curls bobbing as she did so, then breaking into hurried speech. "And I'll be beggin' your pardon for runnin' into your parlor like that, but it's fair excited I am."

"I can see that, Nanny," Bess said. "Now calm down, child, and tell me what has happened to make you that way."

"Well, it's me mum, ma'am. She's done sent me word that me sister is marryin' tomorrer mornin' and me sister has always planned on havin' me there." Her blue

335

eyes widened defensively as though she would stall any forthcoming objections. " 'Tis the truth, ma'am. As God is me witness. Why, if I don't make it to the weddin', she's goin' to be that put out, she'll never get over it." Her eyes appealed to Bess, then turned to Rebecca hopefully. "It would only be for three days, ma'am. Honestly. Then I'd hurry back here so quick like, you'd hardly even know I was gone!"

"All right, Nanny," Rebecca said, cradling Forrest in her arms. She could hardly believe her luck! Nanny was actually providing the way for her. "You go ahead and take all the time you need. If you hurry with your packing, you could catch the morning coach. I can look after my baby quite well."

Suddenly, Nanny caught the possessive way Rebecca was holding the child and her glance became uneasy. "You'll not be refusin' to let me come back, miss? I wouldn't want to be separated from the little tyke. I've grown that fond of the little one, I have."

"Of course you may come back, Nanny," Bess said. "But you mustn't be gone overlong. My niece has just started coming out in society again and will need you."

"Oh, yes, ma'am," Nanny said, curtsying. Her face was wreathed in smiles. She turned to Rebecca. "I'll take the little one now," she said.

"There's no need, Nanny," Rebecca said, looking down on Forrest. His gray eyes were alight with mischief, his mouth opened to show the two pearly front teeth gleaming whitely in an otherwise toothless mouth. He poked a chubby little finger into his mother's eye, his gaze inquisitive as she blinked rapidly, and she grinned, barely glancing at Nanny before turning her attention back to her son. "You go ahead with your packing, Nanny. I'll keep Forrest here with me."

"Well—if you're sure, ma'am." The uneasiness was back on the Irish girl's face. She looked from the baby to Rebecca, her expression troubled. Nanny came from a poor family and had need of this post. She wondered suddenly if she had made a mistake in mentioning the wedding. Maybe she should have just sent word back that she couldn't make it. But what was done was done. "Well, if there be nothin' else, ma'am, then I guess I'll be goin'."

"Very well, Nanny," Elizabeth said kindly. "And don't worry," she added, as if sensing the Irish's girl's unease. "Your place will still be here when you return. The baby is used to you and I'm sure he would fret if you stayed away too long."

"Oh, thank you, ma'am," the girl said, her natural exuberance returning. "Thank you kindly, ma'am." She bobbed a curtsy, then left the room.

As Nanny left, the butler entered, followed closely by Jake.

After the greetings were over, Jake turned to Rebecca. "How are you feeling?" he asked.

"Marvelous, Jake," Rebecca exclaimed, her blue eyes sparkling. "In fact, I couldn't be better."

His sleepy eyes appraised her. "I must say, you look it. I don't think I've seen that much color in your cheeks since you returned from out west."

"Precisely what I was telling her," Elizabeth put her needlework away and rose from the rocker. "Becky, let me take Forrest and you can show Jake the gardens. The roses are in bloom, and the gardenias never looked better."

"Jake has seen the gardens, Aunt Bess," Rebecca said

dryly. "Haven't you, Jake?"

"Well, I certainly wouldn't be averse to seeing the roses again. Did't you tell me you ordered some rosebushes from England, Bess?" he asked with a lazy smile.

"Yes, I did, Jake," Bess smiled. "And they're doing quite well too, although the bushes were in such sad shape when they arrived, I didn't really expect them to live." She looked at her niece. "Do show him the roses, Becky."

"Then come along, Jake, by all means." She gathered her skirts and spread them wide, curtsying low before him. "Let me show you the gardens."

Jake sauntered to the double doors, threw them open, then allowed her to lead the way through them.

"You shouldn't encourage Aunt Bess," Rebecca admonished as they walked down the flagstones. "You know what she's up to, don't you?"

"Of course I do," he laughed, taking her arm. "It's no big secret that your aunt wants you to remarry."

"And you do nothing to discourage her either," she said, frowning at him.

"Why should I?" His smile widened, and there was a decided glint in his sleepy brown eyes. "I think it's a grand idea myself."

"I wonder if you would think it was such a grand idea if you woke up one morning and found yourself married!" she said.

"Perhaps I wouldn't mind all that much, Becky," he said, his voice soft as velvet. "Indeed. Perhaps it is what I have had in mind all along." He took her hand, his thumb caressing the back of it gently. "You ran away from me once, after we left school. Will you do it

338

again, I wonder?"

She suddenly wished she had never started this conversation. Jake could only be hurt by it, for Lone Wolf held her heart in the palm of his hand. Maybe, if Lone Wolf hadn't returned . . . Perhaps, in a few years she might have . . . but no. Even the thought of someone else touching her as Lone Wolf had was unbearable.

Neither Rebecca nor Jake saw the man who stopped just outside the garden gate. Tall, dark-haired, tanned, he stood immobile, watching the two of them laughing together, his hand on the lifted latch of the wrought-iron gate. As he watched the two of them, a light breeze lifted a golden brown curl from Rebecca's crown and whisked it gently across her face. He saw the man reach out and brush it tenderly aside. Hot-tongued jealousy flowed through him, shocking him with its force. His system charged with violent, possessive emotion. His gray eyes hardened to chips of ice. The latch clicked as he dropped it back into place, obviously changing his mind about entering the garden. He spun around and strode away, his body held stiffly erect.

Rebecca spent the afternoon with her aunt, then when night fell she settled down to wait. She waited long into the night, lying on her bed with the gaslight on, dressed for travel with her bags beside the bed. When several hours passed without a sign of Lone Wolf, she finally decided he wasn't coming. With useless tears of frustration and pain spilling over, she finally turned out the light, undressed in the dark, and crawled beneath the bedcovers.

But she couldn't sleep. Finally, unable to bear the darkness any longer, she rose and selected a book from her bookshelf. Then she returned to bed, trying to lose herself in a fantasy world where love conquered all.

Finally, in the wee hours of the morning she turned off the light and drifted off, still trying to convince herself there was nothing to worry about. Lone Wolf had merely been delayed.

She came awake with a start, then lay muzzily in bed, wondering what had awakened her. Some noise, she thought, something outside the sphere of normal night sounds. Her eyes scanned the shadows of the room, searching—for what?'

At first there was nothing. No movement, nothing tangible. Only a sense of being not alone. Then the curtain stirred, and a tall figure stepped away from the window to stand for a moment, saying nothing at all, just watching her silently.

He had come for her. How could she have thought for a moment that he wouldn't? Her heart began a frantic beat in her chest as her gaze raced over the slender form clad in dark trousers and shirt, and her stomach fluttered as if it were filled with butterflies. She swallowed thickly around the lump in her throat.

"Lone Wolf?" she questioned, her voice cracking.

"Who else would be visiting your bedroom at this time of night, I wonder?" he asked harshly.

She didn't answer but rose from the bed and threw her arms around him. "I had begun to think you weren't coming!"

He held her stiffly for a moment, then drew back, and fixed her with a hard stare. "Was there some reason I shouldn't come?" he asked mockingly.

Her eyes widened. Something was wrong. He seemed different. Almost angry. "Of—of course not," she stammered, pulling back slightly. "I—I" She frowned. What was the matter with her? She had done nothing wrong, and yet he was making her feel almost guilty of something.

"What's the matter?" she demanded.

He grinned, and she felt a chill creep along her spine. He definitely wasn't amused.

"Are you angry with me?" she demanded bluntly.

"Should I be angry, Little Blue Eyes?" he asked, his voice grating harshly against her ears. His gaze held hers, as he tucked a long curl behind her ear, exposing her neck. Then he pushed aside the neckline of her gown and bent his head, letting his mouth caress the smooth skin of her throat. She held herself stiffly erect, her muscles tensed as his teeth teased her flesh. Despite herself, shivers of desire coursed through her, trembling all the way to her nerve ends.

Against her will, her body arched against his, eager for his caress. When he lifted his head, she wrapped her arms around his neck and her hands, tangled in the hair at the back of his head, brought his lips down to meet hers in a hungry kiss that carried all the longing of the year they had been separated in it.

There was a raw urgency in him as his hands moved to caress her body, but, when they encountered the lawn of her nightclothes, he broke the kiss and lifted his head.

"Get rid of that," he growled harshly.

She heard the anger mingled with the throb of desire in his voice and stepped away from him. "Not this way," she whispered, shakily. "I won't let you take me while you're angry."

"Dammit! I said, get rid of it!"

She shook her head. "You'd better go," she said, lowering her head. She wouldn't let him see how much he had hurt her.

Suddenly, before she could react, his hand had gripped the nightdress and ripped it to the waist. Her startled eyes flew to his and she stood motionless, shocked, as the silky garment slithered to the floor.

Silence hung heavy in the room as their eyes remained locked. For some reason, she felt he was nearly as shocked at his action as she was. But what had caused it? She shivered, feeling chilled to the bone.

"I'm sorry," he said harshly. "I had no right to do that. I'll leave." He turned to go.

"No!" she said quickly, moving toward him, clutching his arm desperately. "Don't go!" Her voice was ragged with emotion. She wasn't sure what had happened, but he couldn't leave her. He mustn't. She might never see him again.

His arms reached out and gathered her to him, crushing her tightly against him. Her face rested against his chest, and she could hear his heart pounding loudly beneath her ear.

She pushed his shirt aside and opened her mouth, trailing wet kisses across his chest. He groaned.

Taking the initiative, she unbuttoned his shirt, her mouth fixing on the flat, male nipple. He drew in a sharp breath. Encouraged, she moved to the other one, giving it the same careful attention.

Her heart hammered loudly in her chest as she felt the strength of him rising sharply against her lower body. She drew away, her eyes lifting to meet his. He seemed mesmerized by her gaze as she boldly stripped the shirt from him, then knelt, and attended to his breeches. He sat down on the bed and she pulled off his boots, casting them aside.

At her touch, he lay back on the bed, his eyes never leaving hers. Then she came to him, leaning over, her mouth touching his lightly before trailing streaks of fire across his skin.

She made love to him, caressing his nipples with slow, sensual movements, watching the emotions flicker across his face as she teased and rolled them between her soft fingers.

A groan escaped him as she replaced her fingers with her mouth, and she felt a wild pleasure envelop her, knowing somehow that no other could bring him such pleasure. Emboldened, she released the nipple and moved lower, dipping her tongue into his navel. Her hand moved lower, grasping the proof of his virility. Her fingers closed around the satiny skin, and she became aware of a sensuously musky odor.

Excitement began to build in her as her mouth moved wetly toward him. Did she dare? Her heart was beating erratically in her chest as her lips touched his throbbing masculinity.

He jerked spasmodically and groaned. Then, unable to stand any more, he pulled her up to him. She lay against him for a moment, the contact with his hard male body causing her to tremble with raw desire. Pushing herself up on her hands, she watched him through slitted lids, aching to make the union complete.

She stared down into his proudly arrogant face, stamped with the pride of his heritage. Then she lowered her mouth eagerly, her lips touching his in a tantalizing kiss, her hands searching out his hard muscles, reveling in the satiny feel of his naked flesh.

Finally she could stand it no longer. Placing his throbbing manhood at the center of her femininity, she surged against him, feeling the penetration immediately.

"Oh, God!" she whispered in a shaky voice. "It feels so good."

Her words seemed to send him out of control. He plunged wildly, surging deep within her body. Once inside, he was still for a moment, and she moved desperately above him, urging him on.

She scattered fervent kisses across his face and neck, tasting the salty beads of perspiration that had gathered on his face.

As though he could hold back no longer, he began to move inside her and she was swept into a tumultuous storm of sensual radiance. The fury of it grew and grew, sending her wild with desire. Her heart pounded loudly in her ears and she failed to hear the sound that made him stop and listen.

"What is that?" he asked harshly.

The sounds came again. A whimpering, testing sound. Forrest. He was waking.

"It's the baby," she said, raising up on her elbows and lifting herself away from him as her motherly instincts took over.

"Baby?"

"Yes. Forrest."

"Yours?"

"Of course," she said, vaguely, her eyes on the door, her ears tuned to the baby's cry. "I must go to him."

"God!" He rolled to one side of the bed, shoving her away from him in the same movement. "Couldn't you wait?" He stood up and yanked at his trousers.

"Wait?" She stared at him perplexed.

"Yes, goddammit, did you have to—"

The whimpering suddenly became a wail, no longer testing, but fully indignant now. Forrest wasn't used to being ignored.

"I'll explain everything," she gasped, dragging on her dressing gown and hurrying to the door. "Just wait a few minutes." With that, Rebecca turned from the room.

It didn't take long to quiet Forrest, simply a matter of feeding and diapering. She waited until he was asleep again, then hurriedly returned to her bedroom.

It was empty.

# Chapter Nineteen

Rebecca stood beside an elaborate tea table, balancing a delicate cup and saucer in her hand, wondering silently how she had allowed herself to be talked into attending this elegant affair.

Mostly, it had been to soothe Aunt Bess since the older woman, concerned over Rebecca's loss of appetite and peakedness, had been threatening to send for the doctor.

So, Rebecca was here, at Cynthia Wallace's tea, escorted by Jake, who was now across the room embroiled in a political discussion.

It had been three days since she had seen Lone Wolf, and she had spent most of that time worrying about him, wondering if he was all right. She had found it hard to sleep at night and now it was catching up with her. She felt totally drained and hoped Jake would soon be ready to leave.

The voices were unusually loud as she circled the room, or maybe it just seemed that way for she had been nursing a headache all day, and now the blood throbbed in her temples, pounding in rhythm with a thousand war drums. The black felt hat with the blue ostrich feather that was perched atop the curls carefully arranged at the back of her head felt exceedingly heavy for some reason. Her corset felt restricting, and she wondered why fashion dictated that women should wear such a thing.

As she wandered among the expensively clad men and women, she knew she was dressed equally expensively, in a tailored suit of blue silk with a black velvet collar which only added to the heat. She could hear the French gray accordion-pleated underskirt rustling against her feet as she walked.

She smiled politely at the elite members of society, longing to be free from the milling crowd, free to feel the wind on her face, the sun on her head. She longed for the freedom of her doeskin dress, and her moccasins.

But most of all, she longed for Lone Wolf. Where was he? Why hadn't he come for her? What if he came while she was gone? She should have stayed home and waited instead of allowing Bess to talk her into accompanying Jake to this crush of people.

Rebecca pushed the thought from her mind, worrying would do no good. Her gaze swept the crowded room, lingering for a moment on Jake in conversation with several business men. He looked, as usual, very handsome in his stylish clothes. The brown, cloth sack coat and nankeen trousers that he wore were the latest in fashion, and the black silk cravat worn around his neck set off the white linen shirt and red velvet waistcoat. Rebecca knew he was much sought after by the females of Pittsburgh society and their maternal counterparts.

"Mrs. Morgan?" a masculine voice inquired at her elbow, and she turned to see a tall, distinguished-looking, middle-aged man with gray hair and equally gray eyes.

"Yes," she said. Although she should be accustomed to the name she had chosen to give credence to her supposedly widowed state, it still had an unfamiliar ring to it.

"We haven't been formally introduced, Mrs. Morgan," he said. "And I apologize for approaching you this way. If you would like me to fetch our hostess to perform the necessaries, then of course I shall do so."

Put that way, it seemed unreasonable for her to insist on it. After all, he didn't look like someone who would approach a young lady of breeding in a flirtatious manner.

"No, that won't be necessary, Mr. —" she trailed off inquiringly.

"Martin." He bowed low over her extended hand. "Amos Martin of the *Pittsburgh Clarion*. At your service, Mrs. Morgan."

"The *Pittsburgh Clarion*?" she inquired, her blue eyes showing her puzzlement. She recognized the name of the local newspaper, but somehow Amos Martin didn't fit her idea of a reporter.

"The *Pittsburgh Clarion* is a newspaper, Mrs. Morgan," he explained kindly, not in the least put out. He was used to explaining the *Clarion* to the weaker sex. "The *Clarion*'s purpose is to keep the public informed on what is happening around the world."

Rebecca's lips twitched. She couldn't really blame him for thinking she knew nothing of newspapers for most women of this day and age were sheltered from

348

the harsher elements of the world by their menfolks, and knew nothing beyond their own small world of fashion, babies, and how to keep their men happy.

"I know this is rather rude of me to approach you like this," he continued. "But I've been told by a reliable source that you spent some time with your brother out in New Mexico Territory. And I'm sure our readers would welcome any firsthand knowledge you would have on the situation between the settlers and the Indians out there."

Rebecca paled. "I'm afraid I have little knowledge of what goes on between the white population and the Indians," she said in a stilted voice. "I was only there for a short period of time. Five months, in fact."

"Yes, I quite understand," he said. "And your brother would naturally have kept you well protected, but it's been reported the Indians ride right into town and I thought you might have had occasion to see Geronimo." His gray eyes studied her curiously, as though he sensed her uneasiness.

She knew she had reacted to his questioning badly. She would have to tread carefully if she didn't want this newshound on her trail. She had been told that, once a reporter scented a story, nothing could stop him until he had exposed every detail to the public eye. She was determined that no breath of scandal should touch her son, so she stretched her lips into a semblance of a smile.

"No," she said and was glad her voice gave no indication of her inner turmoil. "I'm afraid I had no occasion to meet Geronimo."

"From what I've heard of him, you're probably better off," he said, smiling at her. "From all accounts, he's a fierce savage. My source said Geronimo lives on the reservation under government sanction by day, and sneaks off at night to raid and pillage the countryside."

"Mr. Martin," she said, unwilling to be drawn into a conversation about the Indians, but unable to let such a misconception pass her by. "I'm told, on good authority, that the Apaches are treated abominably on those reservations. I imagine Geronimo may feel the need of leaving the reservation to provide food for his band. Surely, he can't be blamed for that."

"But the government provides them with food. That provision was included in the peace treaty."

"I'm very well aware of that, Mr. Martin." Her eyes were direct as she continued. "A committee should be sent to investigate the reservation agents, for, despite the words of the peace treaty, the Indians receive so little food that they are near to starving to death."

"I must apologize to you, Mrs. Morgan," he said gravely. As her startled eyes met his, he added. "I'm afraid I'm guilty of taking you for just another faint-hearted female, when you are obviously a learned woman who genuinely cares for her fellow man. I would like to speak to you longer about this, if I may," he said gravely. "If what you say is true, and I feel you are well aware of the facts, then perhaps the government should take a closer look at the situation. Under the circumstances you have outlined, it will be hard to keep an all-out war from breaking out. I have just returned from Washington, and it seems to be the general view there that it is only a matter of time before Geronimo will give in. They are even likening his situation to Quanah Parker's." At her puzzled look he explained.

"At one time, Quanah Parker was a powerful enemy of the whites. When he was still on the warpath, no one in the state of Texas was safe from the Comanches, but, since he signed the peace treaty, you couldn't ask for a more exemplary citizen."

"His name sounds familiar, but I can't seem to place it," she said, her forehead wrinkling in thought.

"Quanah is the son of Cynthia Ann Parker and Peta Nocona. Have you heard her story?"

Rebecca shook her head.

"Well, Cynthia Ann was abducted from her home at Parker's Fort in central Texas by the Comanches back in eighteen thirty-six when she was just nine years old. She married Peta Nocona when she was just a teenager, and bore him three children. Quanah was the oldest, and there was another son." His brow furrowed as he searched his memory. "Oh, yes, now I remember. The second son was called Pecos. The youngest child was a little girl who her mother called Prairie Flower. Well, as I said before, Quanah was the one who proved to be the troublemaker."

"What happened to Cynthia Ann?" she asked. "Is she still with the Comanches?"

"No," he said slowly. "Cynthia Ann Parker died about thirteen years ago. She died in captivity, but I'm afraid it was the so-called 'civilized' whites who held her captive."

"I'm afraid I don't understand," she said, sensing an underlying sadness in his voice. "Was she imprisoned for some reason?"

"She certainly seemed to view it that way," he said. "I had occasion to meet and speak with her just a year before her death. And she had such an air of hopelessness about her that it was hard to bear."

"Did the Comanches mistreat her?"

"No. To the contrary. She loved her Comanche husband and wished for nothing more than to return to him. In fact, she tried to escape several times but was always caught and returned to her well-meaning relatives."

"How did she die?" Rebecca asked.

"She starved herself to death."

"How dreadful!"

"Yes. I'm sure she felt there was nothing left to live for after the death of her daughter, Prairie Flower. She just gave up and refused to eat."

His eyes were astute as they studied her pale face. "It's certainly no story that a well-bred gentleman should be telling a young lady. Especially at such a fancy tea party. But then," he added, "I never really could lay claim to being much of a gentleman. I apologize sincerely for any distress my conversation may have caused you though."

"No. Please don't apologize," she said quickly. "After all, I did ask you to tell me about her. Perhaps you would call on me at my Aunt Bess's home one day. I've got a few views on the subject of the Apaches that I would like to air." She knew her aunt would be scandalized at the invitation, but here was an opportunity to let the public know what was going on out west between the white settlers and the Indians.

"I would like that," he said formally. "And I assure you, Mrs. Morgan, although I am a newspaperman, you can speak freely to me, and your name will never be mentioned in any way."

Her brow arched. "I'm afraid I have misled you, Mr.

Martin. I really have no intimate knowledge of the subject, but I will admit, I heard talk while I lived with my brother. And I firmly believe there are many areas where the cavalry's treatment of the Apaches would bear investigation. Maybe if the whites honored the terms of the peace treaties, then they would find Geronimo, and others like him, easier to deal with."

"What you say could be true, and I would like to speak further with you on the subject for you seem to know about what has been going on out there. I'm not entirely convinced that Geronimo can be handled as easily as Quanah Parker though. It's reported that the Apaches are the most vicious of the Indians, even to their own people. I've heard it said they even slice the nose off a wife suspected of being unfaithful."

She shivered, her color draining away as a feeling of foreboding came over her at his words.

"Oh, say. I do apologize," he said, his gray eyes suddenly concerned. "That was very uncivilized of me to speak in that way. I'm afraid I tend to forget such information is too delicate for the ears of a young female. Since my wife died ten years ago, I have been too much in the company of men to remember how such words affect the more fragile sex."

"No. Please don't apologize," she said quickly. "It wasn't what you said. It's just that the air in here has suddenly become very stifling."

"Would you like to walk outside in the gardens?" he asked solicitously.

"No, thank you. I came with a friend. He should be about ready to leave." She looked around the room, instantly spotting Jake still deep in conversation. As if sensing her eyes on him, he looked up, said something to his companions, then came across to join her.

"I'm sorry about that, Becky," he apologized. "I didn't intend to leave you alone so long, but I've been trying to catch Councilman Williams for weeks now."

"Don't worry about it, Jake," she said, tossing him a casual smile. "I assure you, I'm not the least bit put out. And Mr. Martin, here, has kept me adequately entertained."

"Good afternoon, Amos," Jake said, his sleepy brown gaze moving to take in the newspaperman. "I didn't expect to see you here."

"I really didn't expect to be here myself, but Mary is my goddaughter, and I have a hard time refusing her anything."

Rebecca took a sip of tea, immediately wrinkling her nose in revulsion. Her tea had grown cold as she and the newspaperman had talked.

"Let me fetch you a fresh cup," Jake said, having caught her reaction to the cold tea.

"There's no need," she said. "I've had quite enough."

"Are you sure?" he asked.

"Yes."

Rebecca happened to glance at Amos Martin and something in his eyes caused her to look at Jake again. He was looking at her in a way that bothered her. It was a possessive look. That was the only way she could describe it. She had refused to see it before and now she felt saddened by it for she knew he was coming to care far too much for her. She could never return his affection, for she was in love with Lone Wolf.

She should never have accepted that first invitation of his, but she had been selfish, needing his casual friendship desperately. She wondered if he would feel the same way about her if he knew of her months in captivity, and the truth about her baby's father. Somehow, she felt it would make no difference to his feelings for her and she warmed to him, casting him a sweet smile which he misinterpreted. She could easily tell by the sudden flaring of hope in his eyes.

A stir near the door distracted her attention from Jake, and her glance moved across the room to see what had caused such excitement. Her blue eyes widened in shock, her breath caught in her throat, and her heart began to beat frantically in her chest. Her gaze raced over the man's face, and her hopes soared.

"Lone Wolf?" she whispered, her voice cracking as she took an involuntary step forward, then stopped, her brows drawing together in a puzzled frown.

Her Apache husband was dressed in the height of fashion in a black frock coat, white linen shirt, and a black silk cravat tied at the neck. She allowed her gaze to move over the black pants tucked into the black boots he was wearing. They hugged his lean legs, drawing her eyes to the muscular length of them.

She felt a stab of jealousy at the way Lilybelle, the blond beauty from Savannah, was clinging to his arm. The girl was dressed in a gown of rose silk, with a petticoat of silver lace peeking out from beneath when she walked. Milk-white shoulders rose above the low-cut bodice, giving her a dainty fragility that appealed to the masculine sex, and her cheeks were faintly flushed at the attention she was receiving.

She didn't realize how intensely she had concentrated on him until suddenly, as though drawn by her stare, he turned his head, and flicked a glance in her direction. As their eyes locked, she flinched at the savage look in his gray eyes. Her disturbed pulses beat wildly in her veins, and her eyes widened.

"What's the matter?" Jake asked, following her hypnotized gaze.

Embarrassed at being caught staring at a man in such a way, even if he was her husband, she quickly averted her eyes, a blush coloring her face becomingly.

"Well, well," Jake drawled. "Just look what blew into town. I thought maybe he had left for good."

She threw a puzzled look at him. "Do you know him?"

"Why yes," he said, turning an astute glance on her flushed face. "That's Grant Mallory."

"Grant Mallory?" She turned to stare at Jake. "You know him?"

"Yes," he laughed grimly at the question. "It may have been a while since I saw him last, but after all the run-ins we've had over various political matters, I'd know him anywhere." His sleepy brown eyes studied her flushed face intently. "Have you met him, Becky?"

She hesitated. Something was wrong here. How did Jake come to meet Lone Wolf? And why did he call him Grant Mallory? Would Lone Wolf acknowledge her? And what was even more important, why hadn't he returned for her? If she admitted she had met him, wouldn't Jake's next question be, where? If anyone were to learn he was an Indian, his life would be in danger, for there was still a warrant out for his arrest.

Suddenly, as the reality of what she was seeing penetrated her brain, she felt as though a knife had been plunged through her heart. She didn't know why he had been living with the Indians, but Lone Wolf was a white man.

And he had deceived her.

"I — I guess I haven't met him," she said, lowering her eyes to hide her turmoil. "For a moment there, he looked like someone I used to know." Suddenly, she couldn't take any more of the noise and confusion. Putting a hand on his arm, she gazed up at him, her blue eyes appealing. "Jake, I suddenly have the most horrendous headache. Would you mind if we leave?"

"Of course not!" he said, his voice concerned. You'll excuse us, Amos?"

"Certainly," the older man said, his eyes on Rebecca's white face. "I'll bid you both good-bye now." With a smile, he left them, moving on to a group of men nearby and was swiftly deep in conversation with them.

"If you like, I'll fetch your shawl, and make our excuses to our hostess, Becky," Jake said. At her nod of acquiescence, he added. "Just wait right here until I return."

She watched Jake thread his way through the crowd, stopping occasionally to speak to someone, then, unable to help herself, she turned her gaze to the man who had his head cocked, listening to the words of the blonde at his side — the man Jake had identified as Grant Mallory.

Grant lifted his head, his eyes scouring the room until they came to rest on her. For an eternity they stared at each other. A terrible pain lodged in her heart, and her eyes misted over. He took a step forward, then stopped suddenly, turning his attention to Lilybelle, who was speaking rapidly to him. She laughed at something he said, and a hard lump formed in Rebecca's throat.

She had to get away from here! She looked around frantically, searching the room for Jake but he was nowhere in sight.

A hand touched her arm, and she stopped breathing.

## Chapter Twenty

With her heart thumping loudly in her ears, Rebecca slowly turned around, heaving a sigh of relief when she recognized Jake.

"Is anything wrong?" he asked, his brown eyes narrowed alertly as they searched her pale features. He wrapped a steadying arm around her shoulders, tightening his grip as he felt her betraying tremble.

She threw him a weak smile of reassurance. "I'm all right, Jake. I just felt faint for a moment." Despite her efforts at control, her voice was decidedly shaky. "Do you think you could get me out of here before I disgrace myself?"

"Of course," he said. "We'll leave immediately."

She had known she could count on him. Hadn't he proved his friendship over and over again throughout the years? Unlike Lone Wolf, she never had cause to doubt Jake's loyalty. Together, they made their way across the overly crowded room.

"Leaving already?"

A shiver raced up her spine as she recognized the harsh voice instantly. She felt reluctant to face the speaker and her heart thudded rapidly as she slowly turned around, raising her wide, blue eyes gradually until they fell on the face of the man who blocked the doorway.

For a moment their eyes locked. She stared at him, mesmerized, unable to look away from his cold gray eyes. Blood rushed to her temples and tension filled the air.

"Yes. We are," Jake said gruffly. His sleepy eyes surveyed the other man with something akin to dislike. "I'm afraid Becky has a headache."

For a moment Lone Wolf's eyes left Rebecca, falling on Jake. His gray eyes began to blaze as they fell on Jake's arm around her shoulders, and she felt alarmed at the fury she felt emanating from him.

"I want to speak to you alone, Rebecca," he commanded.

Color darkened her face and she bristled at his arrogance. "I'm afraid that's quite impossible," she said crisply. "As you can see, we were just on the point of leaving." Her eyes met his, blue ice meeting gray steel. "If you'll excuse us—"

"No. I'm afraid I must insist on a moment of your time." Lone Wolf's voice was smooth as velvet, his eyes, banked-down fires.

"As I said, we have no time," she said shortly.

She was beginning to feel desperate. Pain ate away at her, crumbling her defenses. She must get away from here.

How could Lone Wolf—no, Grant Mallory—do this to her? He was deliberately trying to embarrass her in front of her friends, confronting her this way. He was intentionally taunting her.

"Jake," she said, turning to him. "Are you ready?"

"Yes," Jake said crisply. She could feel the tenseness of his body beneath the arm still wrapped around her shoulders. He glared fiercely at Grant, his attitude decidedly threatening. "If you'll step aside, we'll be going."

"Rebecca won't leave unless she leaves with me," Grant said, still blocking the doorway.

Jake stiffened. "Whatever your problem is," he said softly, menacingly, "you won't solve it this way. If you don't get out of the doorway, I swear I'll remove you bodily."

"You can try," Grant stated, still unmoving, fixing Jake with an unblinking stare. His mouth was stretched into a tight, hard line, and his fists were clenched tightly at his sides.

"Move out of the way, Becky," Jake commanded, releasing her, his eyes burning with anger.

"Stop it, Jake," Rebecca said in a shaky voice. "Can't you see he wants a fight?" She turned cold eyes on Grant. "Would you please let us pass, Mr. — Mallory. You're causing a scene."

She saw his lean body tense, his muscles rippled beneath his coat, and his hands clenched into fists. His eyes were like coals of fire as he stared back at her, refusing to budge.

"You're not leaving so early, are you, Becky?" The plaintive voice came from her back, and she turned, heaving a sigh of relief as she recognized Cassie.

"Yes, I'm afraid we have to go, Cassie," she said, taking the woman's arm in a firm grip. "I've been wanting to talk to you about that huge magnolia tree in your garden. Why don't you walk with us to the carriage? Did you get it around here? I don't think I've ever seen one before."

Cassie smiled with pleasure. "I guess you're one of the few who haven't heard the story of my magnolia tree," she said, her eyes flashing with amusement. She cast a smile at Grant, said, "Excuse us, Grant," and turned back to Rebecca.

Rebecca held her breath, then let it out slowly, as Grant allowed himself to be moved aside. He threw a dark look at Rebecca, then his gaze met Jake's, promising retribution at a later date. As Rebecca moved outside, escorted by Cassie, she noticed Jake had lingered. His eyes were locked tight on Grant, and she reached for his arm, pulling him swiftly with her.

Cassie was chattering away and Rebecca heard not a word she said. She just nodded when it seemed appropriate and that seemed to satisfy the little woman.

Jake waited until the story of Cassie and John's romance had been retold, then politely bid Cassie good afternoon. Holding himself stiffly, he helped Rebecca into the carriage, waiting until they were well away from the Wallace mansion before he spoke in a hard, angry voice. "What did you do that for? I could have handled him."

She didn't even pretend not to understand. "There was no need to cause an even bigger scene. Everyone was watching us. Do you think I want to have everyone gossiping about us? Besides, it would have ruined Mary's tea party."

"That would have been preferable to having him think I'm afraid of him." His brown eyes were pained as they held hers. "You didn't mention that you knew him."

362

"It didn't seem important."

"Not important?" His eyes were watchful. "He didn't seem to feel that way. I would even go so far as to say it was damned important to him."

She could think of no answer to that.

He was silent for a moment, and she gave a relieved sigh. Perhaps he would let it rest. She relaxed against the seat.

"What's between you and Grant?" he suddenly demanded.

That jerked her upright. Suddenly, her nerves could stand no more. She glared furiously at him. "None of your business!" she snapped.

He flinched, obviously taken aback. His brown eyes were hurt. "You're right, of course. It's none of my business. I do apologize."

She felt a deep regret for hurting him. "I'm sorry, Jake," she apologized. "But I really don't want to discuss Grant Mallory."

He nodded, his face grim, then turned to gaze out the window. His voice was slightly muffled when he spoke. "I seem to have been taking a lot for granted, haven't I?"

"Jake, you'll always be my oldest and dearest friend," she said, putting a hand on his arm and squeezing it gently. "If it hadn't been for you, life would have been lonely during my growing-up years. But friendship is all I'll ever be able to give you. I hoped you understood that."

"You're in love with him, aren't you?" His voice was curiously flat, emotionless.

"Yes," she said, knowing there was no use in lying to him. Jake had always had the ability to see right

363

through her.

He squeezed her hand gently, then, with a heavy sigh, leaned back in his seat, remaining silent until the carriage pulled up in front of her aunt's house.

Without a word, he helped her from the carriage and walked her to the front door. "Becky," he said, his eyes roaming hungrily over her wan features. "I'll probably not be seeing you for a while. I've let the work pile up at the office, and there's a big case coming up soon. And—dammit! I need some time to think."

"I'll miss you," she said softly, her blue eyes on his. She hesitated, wondering if she dared say more. "Jake, if I could have fallen in love with anyone, it would have been you. You're very dear to me, you know that, don't you?"

"I know," he smiled wryly. "And if you'll give me a little time, then I'm sure I'll be able to cope with the idea of your caring for someone else—even Grant Mallory. But right now—" He turned to leave, then stopped. "Does he love you, Becky?"

"I don't think so."

Sudden hope flared in his sleepy brown eyes, then just as quickly died. "But that really won't make any difference to your feelings for me, will it?"

"No." She had to be honest with him. She owed him that much. "I'm sorry, Jake."

He nodded. Then, forcing a smile, he gave a jaunty wave of his hand and strode down the walk.

Feeling completely weighed down with guilt, she entered the house, called to her aunt to let her know she was home, and climbed the stairway to the upper floor.

She went straight to Forrest's room and entered the

nursery quietly. The baby was sitting on the floor, toys scattered around him, and his nanny was sitting in a rocker, gazing out the window into the bright sunny afternoon with what one could only feel was a longing to participate.

"Why don't you go for a walk, and get some fresh air, Nanny?" she asked. "I'll stay with Forrest for a while."

Nanny's blue eyes lit up, a wide smile spread over her freckled face. " 'Twould be fair nice, mum. The sunshine feels so warm from here, it would tempt even the angels." She rose from the rocker quickly before her mistress could change her mind. "The laddie's already had his tea, mum. I'm sure he'll not be needing anything before I return."

"If he does, then I'm perfectly able to get it for him," Rebecca said, smiling at the red-haired girl to take the sting from the words. She did appreciate the girl's feelings, but she resented having someone else look after her baby all the time.

He belonged to her.

She wondered if it was natural to feel so possessive over one's child. She hadn't noticed any of the other mothers acting quite so possessive. But then, it wasn't fashionable among the well-to-do to allow their children much time. A daily ritual of an evening visit for a few minutes seemed to be all most of them could spare. But, she remembered with longing her own mother caring for her, helping her into her nightclothes, listening to her prayers, and tucking her into bed with a kiss. Her memories had dimmed with the passing of time, but they were there. Was she so wrong to want the same for her child?

She played with Forrest until Nanny returned, then

kissed the baby's coal-black head, smiled gently at him, and left the nursery. Going straight to her room, she crossed to the window and pulled the draperies back to stare outside. She had kept her emotions at bay thus far by blanking things from her mind. Now she could no longer do that.

She couldn't shake the feeling of betrayal that had been with her since she discovered that Lone Wolf was Grant Mallory, a white man. All this time she had pictured him in danger — hunted by his white counterparts — and he had been safely installed in a house just across town.

Suddenly she stiffened.

He could have come to see her anytime he wanted. There was nothing, no one, to stop him from going wherever he pleased.

A white man. And he had used her.

He had known all along — all during the time he held her captive — exactly what she would face when she returned to her people. And yet he had not cared. He had returned her to her brother — a tarnished woman — to face the prejudices and enmity of the white people. All this time she had actually believed he had overcome insurmountable odds, traveled across thousands of dangerous miles, compelled by an all-consuming desire to find her, when actually he hadn't come to Pittsburgh for her at all.

He lived here.

Her mind still found it hard to accept. Nevertheless, it was true. Bitter tears welled up in her eyes, threatening to overflow at any moment. She blinked rapidly, swallowing hard.

As she stared down on the wide lawn below, she

remembered the way he had blocked the doorway, his eyes blazing angrily at her, and a smile that didn't quite reach her eyes played across her face.

Yes. He had been decidedly annoyed. In fact, she would be safe in saying he was quite angry, and Lone Wolf—Grant Mallory, that was—did not handle anger well. She had many occasions to remember when he had proved it.

She had defeated him too easily. She knew well that he would not accept defeat. Her eyes glittered and her mouth thinned tightly. He would come tonight.

But he damned well wouldn't get in.

She leaned out the window, her eyes on the big oak tree growing beside her window. She had never even wondered before how he had managed to enter her room. She had just accepted that he was there.

Well now she knew. He had climbed the old oak tree. One of the limbs, stretching out from the thick trunk, was twisted and gnarled, reaching to within a foot of her window. The limb was strong enough to take his weight.

Pulling her head back in, she examined the window closely. Since it was on the second floor, it had no lock.

But if she could manage to wedge a board between the top and bottom panes, that would put a stop to opening the window.

She reached out and pulled the window down with a snap. James always made sure the windows on the first floor were secured, and this was the only window he could reach so there would be no need in worrying about the others. She left her bedroom, intent on searching for something to use as a wedge.

Later that evening she dressed in a stiff, tan, silk

faille gown with fine flame-colored piping. Although she didn't feel like eating, she knew her absence at the table would cause comment, and, besides, she wanted some answers to her questions.

Elizabeth waited until they had been served, then asked if she enjoyed the tea at Mary's.

"Yes, it was very nice," Rebecca replied. "She had quite a crowd there. Jake commented that she must have invited the whole town."

"Very likely. Mary does love parties. Did Grant Mallory attend?"

"Yes, as a matter of fact he did." Rebecca gave an inward sigh of relief. She had wanted to question her aunt about the man who filled her thoughts but hadn't known how to raise the subject. She was silent for a moment trying to think of a way to begin her questioning so her aunt wouldn't be suspicious.

"Did you have occasion to meet him?"

The question startled her. "Yes, Aunt, I did. And I must say, his manners leave a lot to be desired."

"Oh?" Elizabeth's blue eyes flashed with amusement. "Did you think so? I've always found him very mannerly. Perhaps he was just feeling hemmed in. Grant has never liked socializing. In fact, I'm quite surprised to hear he was in attendance."

"You said he had been away for a while. Do you know where he was?"

"No. I think someone said he was in Europe, but I couldn't say just where. He was always close-mouthed about his personal affairs, even as a boy. I think it's so sad to see a situation like his."

"What do you mean?" Her puzzled eyes studied her aunt.

"Well," her aunt hesitated. "I don't like to gossip, but I suspect you're the only one who doesn't know. Yes, I'm sure you should be told, especially since he called this afternoon to see you."

"He called to see me this afternoon?" Her pulse leaped wildly as her fork clattered against her plate.

"Yes."

"Why wasn't I told?"

"It was while you were with the baby, and I knew you wouldn't want to leave him while Nanny was gone. I suggested he come another—"

"I don't want to see that man!" Rebecca burst out, half-rising from her chair as though she suspected he was hiding under the table.

"Then you don't have to see him, dear," her aunt said mildly. "Now do sit down and finish your dinner."

Rebecca obeyed, knowing she was only drawing attention to herself, but it was a moment before she could still her wildly beating heart. Finally, something her aunt had said surfaced in her mind. Picking up her fork and casually spearing a piece of meat, she lifted it to her mouth and chewed, her eyes on the white linen tablecloth. Then she swallowed and looked at her aunt.

"You intimated there was something unusual about him, Aunt, but you didn't say what," she said in a casual tone of voice.

"About who?" Elizabeth asked, startled. Obviously, her mind had been wandering.

"Grant Mallory," Rebecca said tightly, trying to curb her impatience.

"Oh, yes." Her aunt laid the fork down on the side of her plate and cast a worried look at Rebecca. "Like I said, I wouldn't speak of it if he hadn't called, asking for you. But I'm sure Robert would want me to tell you about it. I know your father would if he were still living."

"Tell me what, Aunt Bess?" Rebecca asked, keeping a tight rein on her temper.

"Why, about Grant's being a half-breed Apache Indian, dear," Elizabeth said.

"A half-breed," Rebecca whispered, her face paling.

"Yes. His mother was an Apache Indian as I understand it. His father, John Mallory, left the family home for the gold fields of California when he was only twenty. That was back in the forties during the big gold rush. He was one of the lucky ones who struck it rich. After his mine played out, he decided to do some traveling. He came home a few years later a wealthy man." Her eyes lit with amusement. "He was a fine figure of a man and, with all the wealth he'd accumulated, he could take his pick from the ladies." She smiled in memory. "I was just a girl at the time of course, only thirteen or fourteen, but my heart was captivated as well." She sighed. "But I was much too young to even be considered. Martha White was the lucky one." Her eyes danced. "I'll never forget their wedding. I wore a pink satin dress over five crinoline petticoats, with the largest hoops imaginable beneath them." She sighed. "Yes, it was a beautiful wedding. It was so sad it ended the way it did."

"In what way?" She had to keep her aunt talking for she felt a great need to know it all.

"Well, Martha proved to be barren. And John did want an heir. They had been married for eight years when John left Pittsburgh for several months. When he returned, he had Grant with him." Her smile was sadly

370

rueful. "He was a wild, savage little boy, even at nine years old. Anyone could see at a glance he was John's son, even if he hadn't chosen to publicly acknowledge him. It couldn't have been easy for him, uprooted from his family, taken by a father he'd never seen. And of course, everything was so different here. He had a hard time adjusting to civilization. And I'm afraid Martha didn't help. She resented him from the beginning. But then, can she really be blamed? Grant tried to run away several times, but he was always caught and returned to John. Finally, Grant and his father struck an agreement. Grant would stay with John to be educated during the winter if he would be allowed to return to his people in the summer."

"I've never heard his stepmother mentioned before. Is she still living?"

"No. I'm afraid not. Grant had only been with them for a few years when she committed suicide."

"Suicide!"

"Yes. I don't really think she meant to die. I think she was only trying to scare John enough to make him send Grant back to the Apaches. But she miscalculated and took too much opium—with tragic results. That's when Anne came to live with John. Her husband was killed in a mining accident shortly after they married so she was grateful for the home John offered her." Her expression grew pensive. "Anne was the closest thing to a mother Grant had."

Rebecca's heart ached for the little boy Grant had been. It must have been hard enough for him without having to feel he was responsible for the death of his stepmother as well.

And that explained his anger when she called him a

371

bastard. If she had only known — but how could she? Children could be so cruel, and he must have heard it many times during his growing-up years.

She sighed, fighting the urge to go to him. That still did not excuse him for what he had done to her, but she was afraid. Knowing these things about him might make it hard for her to refuse him entrance when he came, but refuse him she must. If she only had herself to think of, it wouldn't matter, but did he really expect her son to go through what he had? He had married her in the eyes of the Apaches, but in the eyes of the white men, she was nothing but his mistress.

No. She refused to allow this to happen. She had more pride than that. But did she? Would she really be able to refuse to let him in if he should come? If only she didn't sleep so light. If she — Suddenly her eyes lit up as an idea took shape in her mind.

"Aunt Bess," she said hesitantly. "I've had the most awful headache lately."

"Oh, dear," Elizabeth said. "Maybe we should have sent for the doctor after all."

"No," Rebecca said quickly. "I wouldn't even have mentioned it, but I have had a hard time sleeping lately, and I wonder if I could just take a bit of your sleeping medicine this one time."

"Well — I guess it would be all right." Elizabeth said. "And you have been looking peaked. You could certainly use a good night's rest. But be sure to use it sparingly, dear. Just one dropper should be plenty."

"Thank you, Aunt Bess," Rebecca said, pushing back her chair and rising from the table. "I believe I'll retire now. And Aunt Bess." She hesitated a moment only. "If Mr. Mallory should call around to see me again, please tell him I'm not accepting calls."

"Oh dear," Elizabeth said. "You don't mean to be rude to Grant just because of his Indian blood, do you, Becky? He can't help that at all, you know."

"I see nothing at all wrong with his blood, Aunt Bess. He is descended from a proud race of people and there is no shame in that."

"Then why?"

"Because he is rude. He can certainly help that."

"If he was rude to you dear, then perhaps he came to apologize," was her aunt's mild reply. "In which case, you should certainly give him the chance to redeem himself."

"I don't want to see him, Aunt!"

"All right, Becky." Elizabeth held up a staying hand. "Then you shan't see him."

"Thank you, Aunt Bess."

As she left the room looking for the laudanum, she knew her aunt's worried look followed her.

## Chapter Twenty-One

The vast, ebony sky was peppered with starlight, periodically obliterated by the gushing burst of flames from one of Pittsburgh's outlying furnaces, but Grant, waiting quietly in the shadows, hidden by the thick shrubs in the garden, remained untouched by the beauty of the night. A warm breeze lifted a lock of dark hair, blowing it across his face, and he pushed it away impatiently, his cold, gray eyes fixed intently on Rebecca's window.

An hour had passed since she had drawn the draperies and the darkened window suggested she had retired for the night. His body was motionless, and the only sound heard throughout the garden was the chirruping of the crickets in the bushes.

Although his face was expressionless, his mind was in turmoil. Pain kept eating away at him while he turned the question over and over in his mind.

Was the baby his?

He cursed himself over and over again. He was a fool, and she had every right to be angry with him. He had been so crazy with jealousy when he saw her in the garden with Jake, he had left without giving her a chance to explain. His fear of losing her was so great he had automatically jumped to the conclusion she had betrayed him, and the baby was fathered by another man.

But what if he had drawn the wrong conclusions? What if the baby was his?

If such were the case, would she ever forgive him for doubting her? His heart plunged as he remembered the way he had acted at the party. He had wanted to kill Jake.

God! If this was love, this constant ache in his gut and mind, then he could damn well do without it. How he had ever allowed himself to fall in love with her, especially after what had happened to his mother was beyond his comprehension.

He remembered well his mother's permanently sad eyes looking with such longing towards the distant horizon—waiting, always waiting, for someone who never came.

John Mallory, his aristocratic father, had been greedy, refusing to leave the luxuries of the white civilization for the dangers and freedom of the red man, even though professing to love his Apache wife. If he had not married a white woman who was barren, he would probably never have returned for his son.

The harsh grating of a window closing caught and held his attention.

He tensed.

The butler was locking up for the night.

Quietly, he waited, seeming nothing more than an insubstantial shadow among the many other shadows throughout the garden.

Soon, it would be time. Just a few moments and he would see her. He would not allow himself to think about what he would do if the child were not his. His Apache brothers would—but no—he stifled the thought before it was born. He could never deliberately harm Rebecca.

He waited a moment longer, listening to the silence. It was time.

Moving to the base of the big, oak tree, he grabbed the lowest branch, making his way to the twisted and gnarled limb that reached out to her window. He stopped, his brows pulled together in a thunderous scowl.

The window was closed.

His lips twisted in a grim smile. She wanted him to know she was angry with him. But did she really think a closed window would keep an Apache from his wife?

Reaching out, he closed his long fingers over the lower window frame and pushed.

It didn't budge.

His gray eyes narrowed, and his eyes held a hard glint. He pushed harder. It didn't move.

*What the hell?*

Had she locked the damned window? If so, she was being ridiculous. Did she really expect to keep him out that way?

Doubling up his fist, he prepared to smash through the pane of glass, then paused. The sound might attract the rest of the household.

He had enough problems without being jailed for burglary. He would have to ask her permission to enter. The last three nights had been hell, and he refused to leave here without an answer to his questions.

He forced his grim face to relax into a semblance of a smile, knowing from past experiences she didn't react well to his anger. Then, making a fist, he rapped gently on the window.

Silence.

A flame began to burn deep within; his lips tightened into a thin line. He shouldn't have to sit in the darkness on a tree limb, rapping for entrance to his wife's bedchamber.

He took a long, slow breath, calming himself. He knocked again, a little harder this time, and the window made a clattering sound. There was no way she could fail to hear.

Again there was silence.

His gray eyes began to burn with his mounting anger, a muscle twitching in his jaw. Did the little fool think she could avoid him indefinitely? She had known he would come or she would not have locked the window against him. That alone should tell him something. She obviously did not want to answer his questions because the child was not his.

She had betrayed him!

Well, she would not get away with it! She was his wife, and, if she thought because they were not wed in the white man's church it wasn't binding, she would find she was mistaken.

She could even bring her brat with her if she wanted to, but she *would* return to him.

He had been a fool to take her home. As it turned out, he had been of little help to his people. He should have stuck to his original plan and kept her with him at the cliff dwellings until she was expecting his child.

Grimly, he unbuttoned his shirt, wrapped it around

his fist to muffle the sound, and smashed the window. The breaking glass sounded abnormally loud to his ears, and he waited, motionless, listening.

Nothing stirred.

Hardly daring to breathe, he inserted his arm and unlocked the window. It grated harshly as he pushed it up and entered, expecting to be confronted by her fury at any moment, but only silence greeted him.

Puzzled, his gaze searched the moonlit room, narrowing sharply as it fell on the figure lying so quiet and still in the four-poster bed. How could she have slept through the sound of the glass breaking? Was she just pretending to be asleep?

His eyes burned with rage as he leaned over the bed. His gray eyes lingered for a moment on her brown curls lying tousled against the white pillow. She was the picture of innocence, but he knew better. His hands slid around her smooth, white throat. His thumbs rested on her windpipe but there was no change in her breathing. It was as though she were totally unaware of his presence.

His hands moved to her shoulders, grasping them roughly. He lifted her slightly, shaking her hard.

Her head lolled to the side; she was limp to his touch.

Suddenly, fear stabbed through him, his pulse raced madly.

Cupping his hands around her face, he looked closely at her. A light breeze stirred the drapes, allowing a shaft of moonlight to fall across her features. Her face was pale and the area around her eyes looked bruised. Afraid of what he would find, he lowered his face next to her lips and her steady breathing made im relax visibly.

"Rebecca," he whispered huskily, swallowing around a lump in his throat. "Wake up."

She slept on.

Frustrated, he stood up, banging his elbow against something on the nightstand; something that fell to the floor with a loud clatter. Swearing softly, he picked the object up and carried it to the window where the full moon cast its pale glow.

Laudanum! His eyes flew to the figure lying so prone on the bed. His brows drew together, his eyes anxious. *What if she had taken too much?*

Sighing, knowing he would be unable to leave for fear she would stop breathing, he picked up a chair, moved it to her bedside, and sat down.

All through the lonely night he kept his vigil beside the bed, his eyes never leaving the still figure. His ears were tuned to her quiet breathing. Just before dawn, he gave a long, drawn-out sigh, rose from the chair, and left the room by way of the window. A few moments later, he returned and laid something on the nightstand beside her bed. Then, leaning over, he touched his lips lightly to hers, then left the room as silently as he had come.

Rebecca opened sleep-drugged eyes and stared blearily at the patterns on the ceiling. She groaned softly, closing her eyes again. Her tongue felt thick in her mouth, like a wad of cotton, refusing her even enough moisture to wet her dry lips.

Carefully opening one eye, she reached for the water jug beside the bed. Couldn't reach it. Edged a little closer to the bedside table and, leaning on one elbow, grabbed the handle. Gripping the pitcher tightly, she poured water into the waiting glass, then set the jug back down. She drank eagerly, returning the empty glass to the nightstand. Suddenly her one eye opened wide and the other popped open.

Resting on the table beside the water pitcher was a single red rose. Her breath caught, her pulse began to race wildly as she picked it up, bringing it to her lips.

Her gaze moved to the window, and her breath caught. The locked window hadn't stopped him. Her glance fell on the broken glass on the floor, evidence of his visit. Yes, he had been here. She sat up and scooted off the bed. She had to clean the glass up before anyone noticed it. She picked up a trash basket and searched for something to use as a scoop. Questions filled her mind as she searched. Why did Grant leave the flower? What did the rose mean? Her blue eyes softened as hope blossomed in her breast.

The opening of the door startled her.

"So you're finally awake, mum," Nanny said, entering the room. " 'Twas that worried, I was. The—" She stopped abruptly, her eyes widening as they fell on the broken window. "What happened?"

"I tripped on my gown and fell against the window," Rebecca prevaricated quickly.

"Oh, mum," Nanny sympathized. "Are you hurt?"

"No." Rebecca said. "What did you want?"

"Want?" Nanny said, puzzled at Rebecca's abruptness.

"You came to see me, Nanny," she said coolly.

"It's the wee little laddie, mum. He's fretful this morning, and I'm thinkin' he needs to spend a bit of

380

time with his mum."

"Forrest is sickening?" Rebecca's maternal instincts surfaced immediately. She dropped the trash basket and reached for her dressing gown.

Nanny shook her head, sending red curls flying every which way. " 'Tis my way of thinkin' he's not sickenin', mum. Surely 'tis only the wee laddie's teethin' time, so don't be worryin' yourself overmuch about him."

"I'll go to him right away," Rebecca said, pulling the wrapper over the white lawn nightgown, and hurrying to the door. She looked back at the nanny. "Would you have someone see to the window, Nanny?" she said, then hurried swiftly to the nursery, where she gathered the fretful baby into her arms. His gray eyes lit up as he recognized her, his mouth widening into a smile, highlighting the two gleaming ivory teeth and the reddened gums. She cuddled him to her breast, caressing his silky black hair that was so like his father's.

Her eyes filled with sadness. Life was so unfair. Her baby needed a father.

If only Lone Wolf had loved her. She had no doubt he would want his son badly enough to take her as well. But could she settle for that? Supposing he grew tired of her and left her. He would not leave the baby behind. She could not risk losing her son. He must never know Forrest was his baby.

She stayed with Forrest during his feeding, then bathed, dried, and powdered the soft, satiny skin before dressing him in diapers and rompers. By the time she had finished, his eyelids had grown heavy. She smiled tenderly, kissing his soft baby cheek and left him with Nanny.

When she entered her room, her gaze went straight to the window. Someone had cleaned up the shattered glass while she was gone. Her eyes drifted to the nightstand, falling on the red rose. Someone, probably Nanny, had put it in a vase on the nightstand.

Her lips tightened into a thin line, her blue eyes glinting as she stalked across the room, picked up the vase, carried it to the opened window, and flung the contents out into the garden.

Her eyes stormy, she grabbed her brush off the dresser, pulling it unmercifully through her tangled brown hair. Then, leaving her hair curling wildly about her shoulders, she dressed herself in a blue gown and went in search of her aunt. She found her in the dining room.

"You're late this morning, dear," Elizabeth said, lifting a delicate teacup to her mouth and sipping. She looked elegant as usual in a gown of the same rich color as her hair.

"Yes, Aunt," Rebecca replied. Her stomach turned over at the sight of all the food laid out but, refusing to give in to it, she helped herself to bacon and egg from the silver dishes on the sideboard. As if needing to prove she had complete control over her body, she added two biscuits, then seated herself across from her aunt.

Elizabeth looked at the plate heaped with food in front of her niece. "Well, I'm glad to see you're not off your food," she commented dryly.

Rebecca pasted a smile on her face, carefully averting her eyes from her aunt's. She speared a forkful of egg and lifted it in her mouth, making a great show of chewing the lumpy mess before forcing it down her tight throat.

"You look a little pale dear," Elizabeth said, leaning forward in her chair and eyeing her niece anxiously. "Are you unwell this morning?"

"No. I'm all right, Aunt Bess." Rebecca flicked a quick glance at her aunt before returning her attention to the food.

"Good," her aunt said, leaning back in her seat and relaxing. "Oh, by the way, we had an early caller this morning."

Rebecca's heart fluttered wildly, and she took a calming breath, almost certain what was coming. She remained silent, seemingly intent on her breakfast.

"Are you the least bit interested?" Elizabeth asked, casting a reproachful look at her niece.

"Of course," Rebecca said stiffly. "Who—who was it?"

"It was Grant Mallory, dear," Elizabeth replied, her blue eyes studying Rebecca thoughtfully.

Rebecca swallowed convulsively. She picked up a biscuit, broke off a thimble-sized bite, and put it to her mouth, trying to appear unconcerned.

"You know, dear," Elizabeth continued, "Grant is really a very nice man. He asked to see you, and when I tried to explain—" She stopped, hopefully. When Rebecca remained silent, Elizabeth's lips tightened. "Really, Rebecca, I don't know what's got into you lately. I was so embarrassed to have to tell him you wouldn't see him . . ." her voice trailed off. "I don't suppose you've changed your mind?"

Rebecca lifted her head and gave her aunt a cool stare. "No, I haven't. And I'm wondering if there is any point to this conversation," she said, barely keeping her voice calm.

"Yes, there is, Rebecca!" Elizabeth snapped. And to Rebecca's astonishment, the little woman drew herself up straight, her eyes flashing at her niece. "What I'm trying to say is, when I told him you wouldn't see him, he didn't just fade away discreetly. Grant is a very determined man. One who doesn't give up easily. He demanded immediately to know your reason for refusing to receive him. When I explained it was because of his rudeness to you, he apologized profusely to me and asked for a chance to proffer his apology to you."

"I won't see him!" Rebecca snapped, fear rising wildly in her, causing her to act imprudently. Her aunt could be easily led, but Rebecca had never been able to push her.

"And I say you will, miss!" Elizabeth said sharply, her temper sparked by Rebecca's attitude. "This is still my house, and I refuse to let you allow prejudice to get in the way of good manners."

"Prejudice? I'm not prejudiced!" Rebecca's voice rose in confusion. "Why should you think I'm prejudiced?"

"Yes, prejudiced! Grant's had to deal with a lot of people looking down on him because he's half-Apache, but I didn't raise you up that way. Just because the man has the misfortune to have mixed blood doesn't give you the right to treat him unkindly in my house!"

Rebecca laid her fork down beside the plate, knowing she could not force another bite down her tight throat. "If you only knew how wrong you are, Aunt Bess," she said quietly. "You're right, you did raise me better than that. His Indian blood is not the reason I won't see him."

"Then explain yourself," Elizabeth persisted, continuing to eye her niece doubtfully. "If it's not prejudice, then make me understand."

"I can't."

Suddenly, Elizabeth's face showed consternation. "Becky—" She reached over, gripping Rebecca's wrist, forcing her to look at her. "He didn't—treat you—" Elizabeth paused, swallowing convulsively. Her voice had lowered to barely above a whisper. "—in a way unbecoming a gentleman, did he?"

For a moment the temptation was great to say he had. After all, it was true. But she found herself unable to place such blame on him to her aunt. "No, Aunt," Rebecca said. "I just don't happen to like him. He—he was unbearably rude to me."

Elizabeth searched her niece's face. Finally she sighed. "I wouldn't be so insistent about this, Rebecca, but, if you continue in your refusal to see him, it's likely to be construed as prejudice."

"I've just said it's not."

Elizabeth frowned. "Nevertheless, I must insist that you give him a chance to apologize."

"I'm sorry, I can't see him, even to please you, Aunt Bess." Rebecca stood up, her chair grating as she pushed it away from the table. "Tell him whatever you want if he calls again." With these words, she left the morning room.

Several hours later, Rebecca sat in the chair in her bedroom, knitting a sweater for Forrest. A knock sounded on her door. "Come in," she said, looking up to see the butler.

His usually placid expression was disturbed, his face slightly reddened. In fact, upon closer inspection, he looked quite flustered. "Mr. Mallory has come to call

385

on you, madam," he announced.

She looked at him sharply. She had already informed James she was not receiving visitors, and under normal circumstances that would have been enough. Was this Elizabeth's way of bending her to her will? Well, if it was, then it had failed. "Please extend my apologies to Mr. Mallory and tell him I'm not receiving callers at this time, James," she said evenly.

"Yes, madam," James said, the flush leaving his face and his lips twitching slightly at the corners. There was a curious self-righteousness in his rigid stance as he left the room.

She returned to her knitting, but her thoughts followed the butler down the stairs to where Grant waited. He wouldn't like her refusal to see him. Her eyes flashed angrily, and her needles clicked together as her fingers worked furiously.

When the knock sounded on the door, her pulses leaped wildly, but she forced herself to be calm, knowing instinctively he wouldn't force himself past the butler.

James entered at her bidding. He was sweating profusely, mopping at his forehead with a linen handkerchief. When he put the square of linen away, she could see the lines of strain in his face. "I'm sorry to keep disturbing you, madam," he said hoarsely, "but the gentleman insists. He said I was to convey the message that he would not leave until you see him."

She felt sorry for James. He was acting totally out of character. Grant must be giving him a lot of trouble, but she couldn't let that sway her decision. "Then offer Mr. Mallory a chair, James, and pour him a stiff drink, because he has a long wait ahead of him. It is not my intention to leave my room at all today."

Fresh beads of sweat broke out on the man's forehead at her words, and his Adam's apple bobbed up and down. He swallowed convulsively, looked pained, then squared his shoulders. "Yes, madam," James said, his voice hoarse. "I will convey the message to Mr. Mallory."

Rebecca watched him leave, her eyes lingering on the closed door. It wasn't too late to change her mind. He was just downstairs — a few steps away. She could . . .

No. She wouldn't give in.

Picking up her knitting, she bent her head over it, carefully keeping her mind a blank. As her needles clicked together, she refused to allow herself to think about Grant waiting downstairs. She was afraid, if she did, her desires would overcome her good sense, and she would run to him, begging him to take her with him, in whatever capacity he chose.

An hour later, there was another rap on the door, and James entered. His face was its usual composed self. "The gentleman has left, madam," he said, and his voice registered his satisfaction. "I just thought you would like to know."

"Thank you, James," she said quietly, feeling curiously forsaken. Now that Grant was no longer in the house, an overpowering sense of loneliness washed over her. Her eyes filled up and a tear traced a path down her cheek. Angrily, she wiped it away with the back of her hand.

"Is there anything I can do, Miss Becky?"

She started at the softly spoken words, unaware that James had lingered in the room. His eyes were sympathetic as he waited for her answer. "That's — that's all, James," she said, her voice quivering in spite of herself.

A few moments later the door closed quietly.

Grant's eyes resembled chips of ice as he closed the wrought-iron gate with a snap. Gravel crunched beneath his feet as he strode stiffly away from the big house.

Rebecca hadn't even shown him enough courtesy to tell him herself but had relayed the message by that damn, self-righteous butler of her aunt's! Well, he refused to be humiliated further. Damned if he would come crawling back again, begging like some damned cur, hoping for some spark of kindness from her. For all he cared, she could stay up in her ivory tower. His lips curled bitterly. Maybe ivory tower wasn't exactly the word. She was a bit tarnished for that, with at least two lovers, and God knew how many more to her credit.

A horse-drawn carriage rolled by, sending a cloud of dust boiling up, coating him with gray dirt and ash. He brushed at his clothes, feeling a sudden longing for the clean mountain air, the seclusion of the forest — the city of the ancient ones — Rebecca.

He looked back at the house, his cold, gray eyes moving over the large, oak tree shading the wide lawn. The same oak tree whose branches were so convenient to Rebecca's window.

He stopped.

His eyes held on the tree, his brows drawn together in a frown. According to the butler, she was in her room. Suppose he were to climb the tree and confront her? Could he make her listen?

*No.*

*That's all past. There's the child to consider now.* He felt a pain deep within. Why hadn't she waited for him? It could have been his child.

But it was too late, and, after all, if he had to lose out, Jake, at least, was a fairly decent sort. But dammit, it was hard to let her go. He still wanted her. Even knowing she had been unfaithful, he still wanted her. And what the hell was wrong with Jake anyway? It didn't make sense. If Jake wanted her, then why the hell didn't he marry her? Could it be possible she still felt bound to him?

Suddenly the answer to why they weren't married seemed vitally important to him. He had to know. He turned around, his footsteps carrying him in the direction of the Logan mansion.

# Chapter Twenty-Two

He strode up the avenue, his expression as dark as the cloud that hung eternally over Pittsburgh. There was no need for him to check the house numbers located on each gatepost for he knew the Logan mansion well, having had occasion to be inside it many times in years past.

As he reached a pair of wrought-iron gateposts he stopped, opened the gate, and followed the gravel path to the large, brick house. The green grass had been raked free of leaves that fell from the large oak and elm trees that shaded the wide lawn. Square flower beds boasted an abundance of stiff cannas, lilies, and red sage.

Grant climbed the wide front steps, pulled the wrought-iron knob, which rang loudly inside the house, and waited. Nothing happened. He reached for the knob, pulled it, heard the ringing noise repeated and waited.

Growing impatient, he lifted the knob again, but before he could ring, the door was thrown open abruptly. A stout little woman, dressed in gray calico the same color as her hair, peered out at him.

"Whatcha be wantin'?" she inquired.

"I came to speak to Logan," he said.

"He be sleepin'," the woman said abruptly, pushing a loose hairpin into the bun perched on top of her head.

"Then wake him up," Grant said, having no intention of being put off again. Rebecca's refusal to see him still rankled, and he had no intention of accepting the same from Jake. He meant to see him, even if he had to take the house apart, brick by brick.

"I couldn't be doin' that," the woman said sternly, putting reddened hands on her heavy hips and eyeing him with baleful eyes. "The master wouldn't take kindly to bein' woken this mornin'."

"And I won't take kindly to being refused, I'm afraid," he said, pushing past the woman.

"Here now," she said, hurrying after him, slamming the door behind her. "You can't be comin' in here this way."

"I'm afraid I am in," he said softly. "Now, where will I find him?"

"I'll tell him you're here," she grumbled, glaring at him. "But he won't take kindly to bein' woken."

"Yes, you've already said that, madam. I'll wait for him in the library," he said, stepping into the room and closing the door behind him.

The library was large and airy, designed solely for comfort, with overstuffed leather furniture. A deep-piled Turkish carpet covered the floor. Bookshelves filled with books lined three walls from floor to ceiling. Jake was obviously an avid reader. Grant moved to the

391

nearest bookshelf, recognizing works by Edgar Allan Poe, Nathaniel Hawthorne, and both the Brownings. He was still reading the titles when Jake arrived.

"Oh, it's you," he said. He came into the room and shut the door behind him. "What's all this, anyway?" Jake demanded, eyeing him with distaste. He tied the belt on his green, striped silk morning robe and raked his fingers through his unruly hair. Moving to the nearest chair, he sank down on it as though his legs would no longer support him.

"Oh, God! I feel awful," he said, closing his eyes and leaning his head against the backrest.

Only silence greeted his complaint, and he opened one bloodshot eye to glare at Grant.

"What do you mean by coming around here at this time of the morning stirring up my help?"

"I came to find out why you don't marry her?"

"What?" Jake frowned, then groaned as though the action had caused him more pain. "Sorry, old boy," he said. "I'm afraid I imbibed a little too freely last night. You'll have to repeat the question."

Grant stared at him, finding no sympathy for the man. How could Rebecca possibly love this man? "I said, why don't you marry her?"

"Who?" Jake lifted his head and groaned again. "I think I need a drink." He pushed himself up, moved on shaky legs to a nearby cabinet and extracted a bottle of scotch and a glass. "You want some?" he asked, unconcerned with the niceties. He poured a stiff measure in the glass.

"At ten in the morning?" Grant eyed him with

disgust.

"At whatever time I get out of bed after a night like last night." Jake groaned again, draining the glass of scotch in one gulp. Then, wiping a hand across his face, he sprawled in the nearest chair. "Now what was the question again?"

"I asked you why you haven't married Rebecca?" Grant gritted through clenched teeth.

Jake narrowed his reddened eyes, his expression wary as he watched the other man intently. "I'm surprised at you, Grant. Why should you be so concerned about my intentions toward Rebecca?" he asked. "After the way you acted yesterday, I feel I should be the one to ask questions."

They were interrupted by a tap on the library door. It was immediately flung open and the woman who had let him into the house stood on the threshold. Her face was rigid with disapproval as she entered, carrying a silver tray containing coffeepot, cups, creamer, and sugar. With her every move declaring her outrage, she crossed the room and set the tray and its contents, none too gently, on a small table near Jake's chair, then with a loud sniff, spun on her heel and marched from the room.

Grant waited until the door closed behind her, then snapped. "I didn't come here to be lectured, Jake. All I need from you is an answer to my question."

"Give me one good reason why I should give you one," Jake said, a grin appearing on his face.

Grant's hands clenched tightly, his knuckles showing white as Jake's grin widened. The other man seemed to find the situation highly amusing, and Grant was having trouble controlling his temper.

"What you're asking is damned personal, in case you haven't realized it, old boy. And frankly, I see no reason to answer your question, especially since you've gone and upset Mrs. Gruber." Jake's brown eyes became accusing, his expression mournful. "I hired her because of her cooking ability. At her best, she could rival the great chefs of Europe. But when she's upset — well, there's the rub. When Mrs. Gruber is upset, then her expertise just seems to completely disappear."

Grant felt rage boiling up within him. He had demeaned himself by coming here to make Jake explain his relationship with Rebecca, and the man sat there gabbling on about his housekeeper. His hands clenched into fists, and he jammed them hurriedly into his pockets. He walked stiffly to the window, stared out over the wide lawn. He felt like grabbing Jake and beating the hell out of him, but that would gain him nothing. He fought for control and turned back to face Jake.

"I didn't come here to listen to a lecture on your housekeeper's cooking skills, Jake," he snapped. "It doesn't matter to me whether she can cook or not. I realize we're on different sides of the political fence, but that has nothing to do with this. It's a personal matter and it's damned important."

"To whom?" Jake asked, leaning forward to gaze alertly at Grant.

"To me."

Jake lifted an eyebrow. "Why should I be interested

in helping you?" he inquired casually. "After all, as you said, we're on different sides of the political fence and there's never been any love lost between us. On top of that, you've been spoiling for a fight since I ran into you yesterday." His eyes flared with temper that quickly died as he pressed his fingers to his temples. "God!" he groaned, closing his eyes. "That hurts."

Grant stared at him, his face expressionless, refusing to allow pity for the other man's obvious pain.

After a moment, Jake opened his eyes, glaring balefully at Grant. "You still here?" he asked. "I wish you'd leave and torment some other poor soul for a while. I'd think you would be satisfied since it's your fault I have this miserable headache in the first place."

"How do you figure that?"

"I don't think I'll tell you that," Jake said, seeming to gain a peculiar enjoyment from Grant's frustration. "I have a mind to keep the reason to myself. Just take it from me, you're to blame. Anyway, feeling the way I do, I'm not all that inclined to satisfy your curiosity about something that should concern only Becky and myself."

Grant felt cold rage flow through him. He didn't like the way Jake constantly used the shortened version of Rebecca's name so casually. Of course, if he was Rebecca's lover as Grant suspected, then he was on intimate terms with her. A knife-sharp pain stabbed through him at the thought.

"I demand to know if you're Rebecca's lover!" he said harshly.

Jake's sleepy brown eyes widened in surprise. He

recovered quickly and laughed. "Well, you can just go to hell, old boy."

Grant strode to the chair, gripped the front of Jake's dressing gown in his hands and yanked him to his feet, garnering some satisfaction as the other man winced from the sudden movement.

"You bloody idiot," he grated harshly. "I'd like nothing better than to beat you to a pulp. Don't give me an excuse to do it."

Jake grimaced, his eyes pained. "Right now, you could probably do it," he said wryly. "I'm afraid I'm not in any kind of shape to put up much resistance at the moment." He studied Grant's savage expression. "But somehow, I don't think you'll get much satisfaction out of beating a man with a tremendous hangover . . . if you'd care to postpone it until tomorrow, I could give you a run for your money."

"You'd be surprised," Grant said, giving the other man a hard shake.

Jake turned a sickly green. "You'd better not repeat that action, old boy, unless you want me to toss my oats all over your coat."

Grant uttered an oath and shoved him back down into the chair. He stood glowering at him for a moment watching Jake pour a stiff drink and down it hurriedly. Jake gave a sigh of relief and sank back against the chair, some of the color returning to his face.

"At least tell me if you love her."

"Yes." The word was spoken without hesitation.

Grant stared at him. If he loved her then why weren't they married? Could it be Jake was ashamed of

396

her because of what she had been through? Pain knifed through him at the thought.

"I have to know. Are you ashamed of her because of what happened out west?"

"What the hell? Ashamed of her? Are you crazy?" Suddenly Jake's brown eyes grew watchful. "You said 'because of what happened to her out west.' What, exactly, do you mean by that?"

"Don't you know?"

"Hell! If I knew, would I be asking you? I haven't heard of anything that hap—" He stopped. "Surely you aren't referring to her husband?"

"Yes." Then he did know.

"How did you know about her husband?"

Grant's eyes became hooded. No. Jake didn't know about Rebecca's abduction and subsequent marriage to an Apache. His brows furrowed.

"What, exactly, do you know about Rebecca's husband, Jake?"

"Only what everyone else does." Jake gave a heavy sigh and ran a hand across his eyes. He threw a wary look at Grant. "While you're making up your mind whether or not you want to beat me up, do you think I could have a cup of that coffee Mrs. Gruber left?" He glared accusingly at Grant. "Although I suppose it's probably gone stone cold by now."

Grant's lips tightened. He moved to the window, gazing unseeingly outside. If everyone else already knew this "secret" about Rebecca's husband, why was Jake being so damned close-mouthed? He paced back across the room, his eyes on Jake as he poured coffee into a cup, added sugar, then stirred.

Jake threw a weary look at him. "I wish you would quit pacing," he said. "You're going to wear a hole in the damned carpet. Why don't you come sit down and have some coffee with me? Perhaps we can pacify Mrs. Gruber if we drink it all."

"Jake, would you quit stalling and tell me what I want to know?"

"If it'll get rid of you," Jake groaned, taking a swallow from the delicate china cup and leaning his head on the back of the chair. He closed his eyes again and said, "I don't even remember what it was you wanted to know."

Damn! Did he have to start all over again?

Sighing wearily, he bent over the table, helping himself to coffee, then he poured a stiff measure of scotch in the cup. Sitting down, he took a swallow, grimacing with distaste. Jake was right. The coffee was only lukewarm. He looked up to find Jake grinning maliciously at him.

"I see you've lost your distaste for early morning scotch."

Despite himself, Grant's lips lifted in a wry smile. "I guess I feel like you look," he commented.

Jake's grin widened. "You might've poured some of that stuff in my cup too," he complained.

"As soon as you've told me what I want to know."

Jake glared at him, took a sip of the cold coffee, and grimaced. "Hell! I can't drink this stuff. Yank on that bell rope, old man, and get Mrs. Gruber in here." He sighed. "She's not going to like being summoned again, but I can't drink this stuff."

Grant found the heavy bell rope dangling by the door and pulled it.

After Mrs. Gruber had brought fresh coffee, Jake cleared his throat. "How did you come out in Washington?" he asked.

"About as usual," Grant said coolly. "The majority feels the only way of handling the trouble between the whites and the Indians is by force. They refuse to believe they are the cause of most of the Indian uprisings by their refusal to make the cavalry abide by the peace treaties. Most of them know what's going on out there but prefer to close their eyes, rather than face up to it."

"Perhaps if they didn't have a prior knowledge of your parentage, your opinion would carry more weight," Jake said. "I think the biggest dissenters — men like General Carruthers for instance — use your Apache blood against you, claiming it's the only reason you speak out in the Apaches' behalf."

"Do you believe that?"

"Hell, no!" Jake exclaimed. "There was even a time I thought you might be right and considered joining forces with you."

Grant was surprised. "What changed your mind?"

Jake frowned. "I'm not really sure. I think it was about the time you left . . . last time. Yes. That was it. You left for Europe and Carruthers came along and began telling his version of the problem out west. It differed greatly from your version." His brow furrowed. "Somehow, I've always been a little suspicious of his accounts of the problems."

399

"How so?"

"Well, the man is too theatrical—too . . . I guess 'phony' is the word I'm looking for. Something about him doesn't ring true."

"If you'd be willing to listen for a few minutes, I'd like to tell you what's been happening out there," Grant said, unable to pass up the opportunity that had presented itself. Jake could be a powerful ally in Washington, and he owed it to his People to put his personal feelings aside long enough to put Jake in the picture.

They talked for an hour, Jake inserting questions occasionally and, when Grant had finished what he had to say, the pot of coffee stood empty.

"It's quite apparent Washington needs to send a congressional investigative delegation out to the reservation," Jake said. "But whether or not we can convince them to do it, is another thing. Every time they get ready to act, a report comes in similar to what happened to Becky's husband and they shelve the matter."

"And what happened to Rebecca's husband?" Grant asked, feeling they had run full circle.

"She went west to stay with her brother and married a cavalry man. They hadn't been married but a few months when he was killed by the Indians."

"Killed by the Indians?" Grant's lips tightened.

"He had gone out with a small patrol, intending to capture one of the outlaw bands that had been raiding in the area. They were ambushed by Geronimo and his men. When the fighting was done, the entire patrol had been wiped out. Just like Custer. The Apaches

400

killed them all—slaughtered—every man of them. And as if that weren't enough, they carried the outrage even farther. Scalping them—dismembering the corpses. The cavalry had to gather up the pieces in order to bury them," he stated grimly, his voice harsh.

As Grant listened to Jake, his expression had undergone several changes. Surprise at what he was hearing. Then disbelief, until finally, his expression was as cold as his wintry gray eyes.

How could she have spread such a lie, he wondered, his lips tightening into a thin line. Did she have to make up such a gruesome tale, knowing how badly it would reflect on the Apaches? Wouldn't it have been enough to just say he was dead? Had she manufactured the story because she felt hatred for his people and wanted revenge, or had she just found it a convenient way to explain her predicament? He could certainly see the merits of inventing such a tale, because anyone with any sensibility in him at all would never dream of questioning her for details.

"What I'm wondering," Jake said softly, startling him into awareness, "is where do you fit in Becky's life? I'd have sworn she didn't even know you."

"Then you'd have been wrong," Grant said.

"Obviously," Jake agreed drily, his eyes never leaving Grant. "But it beats me how it came about. After all, you've been in Europe for the past five years, haven't you?"

"What's that got to do with it?" Grant asked, evading the question.

"Well, until she left two years ago, Becky had never

401

been out of Pittsburgh since she came here as a child."

"What of it?" Grant asked arrogantly.

"So where did you meet?" Jake asked, his face expressionless. "Becky didn't know you when she left two years ago. You went straight to Congress when you came home from a five-year stay in Europe . . ." He let his voice trail off, waited, then when no answer was forthcoming, spoke again. "When did you meet her?"

Grant's eyes became hooded, hiding his expression from Jake. Five years ago when he had decided to rejoin his Indian family, he had spread the word around that he was going on an extended tour of Europe to explain his absence, and leave the door open to both worlds. The Mallory name and wealth had proved enough to sway a few members of Congress more than once, and he intended to use every means at his disposal to help his People.

"Where I met Rebecca really doesn't matter," he said, rising abruptly. It seemed like a good time to make his exit. Jake had made a remarkable recovery from his hangover, and Grant didn't feel like pushing his luck. Jake was bound to ask questions he didn't want to answer. "Thanks for the coffee," he said. "I'd like to speak to you again on the Indian situation." He hesitated. "I don't suppose you would go with me to Washington next month? They've agreed to grant me a congressional hearing. Another voice, especially yours, could add a lot of weight."

"I'll think about it," Jake said thoughtfully. "If there is even the remotest possibility it would help end this

402

senseless slaughter, then I might consider it."

"Why not come to the San Carlos reservation and see for yourself."

"When are you going?"

"I hadn't thought. How about next week?"

"I think it could be arranged," Jake said easily. His sleepy eyes were hooded. "You can get away that soon?"

"I've nothing to keep me here," Grant said bitterly.

"Well, let me know for sure. If you decide to make the trip, I have a colleague who would go with us." At Grant's look of inquiry he said, "Sam Rayburn."

"He's a good man," Grant said. "If he would do that, it would add another powerful voice at the congressional hearing." He gazed steadily at Jake. "It's a very good idea. And nothing could stop me from making the trip."

"Nothing?" Jake inquired softly.

Grant knew Jake was subtly inquiring about his relationship with Rebecca, but he refused to acknowledge it. He still didn't understand exactly what was going on between her and the other man, but his feelings had made an abrupt change. He was no longer willing to allow the other man a chance with her. Not even for the sake of the baby. She was *his* wife, and dammit! she would *remain* his. But if there was a chance he could help his people, then his personal feelings would have to be set aside for the moment.

He met Jake's steady gaze. "I'll be ready."

"I'll talk to Sam. And we'll decide on the day. Just once more thing, Grant." Grant's body stiffened. "Next time you come — will you try to keep from upsetting my housekeeper? She has a way of taking her resentment out on my meals."

"Yes. Well, please offer her my apologies," Grant said, turning to leave. Although he hadn't accomplished what he came for, perhaps it hadn't been a complete waste of time. Jake Logan was reputed to be a fair man, and, if he could gain his political support, then he had a better chance of helping his people at the congressional hearing next month.

Jake walked to the front door with him, opened it and waited until Grant had stepped outside. With a nod of his head, Grant left him, descending the wide front steps.

"Grant."

The words were so soft, he nearly didn't hear them. He stopped, turned back to find Jake watching him with an indescribable expression.

"She doesn't love me," he said. Then, he closed the heavy door to the mansion.

# Chapter Twenty-Three

Rebecca strolled beside Robert as he pushed the baby walker down the graveled walkway that circled through the park. The air was hot and heavy, too heavy for comfort in the confining corset and heavy brocade gown she wore.

At least Forrest was enjoying himself. The baby's eyes were wide and alert as they darted here and there, taking in everything as they moved forward. The bright colors — especially the red flowers — seemed to captivate him, as did the other children who stopped to stare at him with unconcealed curiosity.

"Hot, isn't it?"

"Yes," she said, her lips lifting in a wry smile as she turned to look at her brother. "But it's not unusual for this time of year. You're just used to a drier climate."

"Yes." He took a white square of linen from his coat and wiped the perspiration from his face, then stuck it back in his pocket. "It's easy to see why father chose to make his home out west."

His words turned her thoughts to New Mexico — and Grant. She grew pensive. Robert had arrived unexpectedly late yesterday afternoon and had immediately commented on the fact that she looked tired.

He was right.

". . . Mrs. Henderson told Juanita all about it," Robert rambled, not noticing his sister's inattention. "She said . . ."

Rebecca couldn't remember when she'd been so weary but, unlike Robert, she didn't think a walk through the park was going to help her. She hadn't seen Grant for three days now: three days of misery while she cursed herself for refusing to see him. Perhaps she had been wrong in her suspicions. She should have at least given him a chance to offer an explanation — any kind of explanation would have done. Her eyes were sore from lack of rest and seemed to be filled with grains of sand. Her head ached, and she knew she was emotionally exhausted.

". . . and Major Canton has been replaced by . . ."

A burst of high-pitched laughter sounded in the distance, and Rebecca winced. They were nearing the children's playground.

". . . I didn't go to the wedding but Mary Beth made sure I heard all the de . . . Becky, are you listening to me?"

"What? Oh yes," Rebecca said. "Of course I am. What did you say?"

"I was telling you about Melanie and Lieutenant Young's wedding."

"Lieutenant Young and Melanie?" She was startled. "They're married?"

"Yes." Robert studied her intently under lowered brows. "Aunt Bess said you haven't been sleeping well lately." He guided the walker around a large stone in the middle of the graveled path.

"Look at Forrest, Robert," she said, deliberately turning his attention to his nephew. "He's trying to pick one of these red cannas. You wouldn't expect a baby his age to notice so much."

"Oh, he's a bright youngster," Robert agreed. Then he grinned. "But so is his uncle." He stared down at the top of Forrest's head. "I should have come sooner though. I hadn't expected him to be quite so big."

"He is six months old, you know. And he's not just big. He's busy. He runs Nanny ragged half the time."

Robert frowned. "That's the reason I hired her. He'd have been too much for you to handle alone." His look touched penetratingly on the dark shadows smudged around her blue eyes, on her mouth drooping at the corners. "Which brings us back to the question of why you aren't sleeping better."

She groaned inwardly. She had hoped to put him off, but foolishly had only reminded him of it. She dared not let him know that, far from being dead, Forrest's father had turned up in Pittsburgh. Magnificently alive. She knew Robert wouldn't take the news lightly. If he didn't try to punish Grant himself, then he certainly would turn him in to the local authorities. If she revealed Grant's identity, she could endanger his life. And no matter how bitter she was, she still loved him deeply.

"We have to discuss this sometime, Rebecca," Robert said sternly. "Something's happening here. I don't know what it is, but I intend to get to the bottom of it."

"Nothing's happening," she denied, her pulsebeat quickening. "You're just letting Aunt Bess's fears get to you." Forrest had twisted in the walker in his eagerness to reach the bright colors and she bent to straighten him, using the excuse to escape her brother's questions.

It did no good.

"It's not just Aunt Bess, Becky. I might have believed that if I hadn't seen the shape you're in myself. Good God, girl! You look as though you haven't slept for months, and your nerves are shattered as well. And what's this nonsense about Grant Mallory? Aunt Bess said he insulted you." His eyes were turbulent. "I think I should pay a call on him."

"No, don't do that, Robert." She cast him a panic-stricken look. "It didn't really amount to much."

"Not amount to much? Then why have you taken this stand? She said you were rude to the man." His eyes were penetrating as he studied her flushed face. "It's not like you to act that way, so I'm assuming you had a good reason."

Suddenly one of the wheels on Forrest's pushcart stalled and he bent to remove the piece of gravel lodged between the wheel and the axle.

Rebecca sighed with relief, glad that he had been sidetracked. When he straightened up, she forestalled further questions. "When were Melanie and Lieutenant Young married, Robert?"

"Last month."

"Did you attend the wedding?"

He smiled curiously. "That's what I was just explaining, Becky. Geronimo's been raiding our herds and we lost quite a few head. I let most of the hands go to the wedding. You know how they look forward to any kind of shindig. Anyway, I didn't dare leave the ranch unguarded. Damned Apaches, anyway."

He cast her a quick look. "Does it bother you to hear

me talk about the Indians, Becky?"

"Of course not," she said. "Why should it?"

"Well—after what happened to you—" He broke off, his face darkening with anger. "Sorry I brought it up," he said gruffly. He was thoughtful for a moment. "Becky. About Grant Mallory. I really think you should let the man apologize. Despite his parentage—" He darted a glance at her. "I suppose you do know he's a half-breed Apache?" At her nod, he continued. "As I was saying, despite his parentage, he has a great deal of influence here and in Washington as well. I would hate like the devil to make an enemy of him." He hastened to add, "Naturally, if your honor needed defending, I wouldn't hesitate for a minute. But since that doesn't seem to be the case . . ."

She shook her head as he seemed to be waiting for some kind of reassurance from her.

"Good. Because he would make a powerful enemy, and we don't need that." His face was thoughtful as he studied his sister's bent head. "I hear he's just returned from Washington. I'm not in the least bit surprised, since he's always lobbying for the rights of Indians. As if an Indian should have any rights," he grumbled. "We've set aside the reservations for them, but they're a savage bunch and refuse to stay there. Seems like the more land you allow them, the more they want. You can't really blame Grant Mallory for trying to help them though. After all, his mother was Apache. I guess he'd just naturally feel sympathy for them."

"Yes, I suppose he would," she mumbled, feeling as though she had been kicked in the stomach. Grant in Washington, lobbying for Indian rights? But then, why not? Come to think of it, he wasn't a man who would leave any stone unturned in his efforts to help his people.

"So you see why you must stop acting so stubborn," Robert said, making her wonder if she had missed part of his conversation. This time she *had* been listening.

At her look of confusion, he said. "Weren't you paying attention, Becky? I said, you have to accept the man's apology."

"All right, Robert," she said, prudently giving in. She realized now how badly she had handled the situation. By trying to stay away from Grant, she had only called attention to herself. If she didn't agree to see him, Robert wasn't going to let up. He would just keep hammering away at her until he wore her down. On the other hand, if she agreed, stipulating Robert must be present, she could hear Grant out, pretend to accept his apology — for that was the excuse he gave — then dismiss him. That should satisfy Aunt Bess and Robert both.

"Good girl," he said, smiling at her with approval. "I knew you'd be sensible about it. I'll ask Mallory to stop by." He stopped and plucked a yellow daisy from the grass and tucked it behind her ear. "How about a smile?" he said.

Although her heart wasn't in it, Rebecca made the effort and it seemed to satisfy him.

The gravel path lined with tall shrubs of lilacs and sumacs curved ahead, blocking their view of anyone approaching from the other direction.

"Well, speak of the devil!" Robert said, his words just loud enough for her to hear.

Her head jerked up, something in his voice warning her. Her pulse quickened, her breath catching abruptly. As Grant, with Lilybelle clinging tightly to his arm, walked into sight, Rebecca felt the thrust of emotion that this man—who called himself by the names of Lone Wolf and Grant Mallory—was always able to arouse in her. But a new emotion had been added as well. One that she hated to give a name to, even silently in her mind.

Jealousy.

The blond beauty looked ravishing in a gown of green silk, with a jaunty hat decorated with green ostrich feathers and tilted over one eye.

Rebecca grasped Robert's arm, moving closer to him, seeking protection from the sudden fury that surged in Grant's eyes as they fell on her clinging to her brother's arm.

"So," Grant drawled. "The little mouse finally decided to come out of hiding." His gray eyes raked over her figure insolently.

Robert frowned, his gaze moving over Rebecca's flushed face, then back to Grant's furious glare. His body stiffened with resentment. "I can appreciate you're probably feeling shabbily treated," he said stiffly. "However, my sister has reconsidered, and she's ready to accept your apology."

"Your sister?" Grant relaxed slightly. "You're Robert Shaw?"

"Yes," Robert said, offering his hand. "I don't believe we've ever met, but I've had occasion to hear you speak in Washington."

"What did you think of my speech?"

"Let's just say I didn't agree with you. You haven't spent any time with the Indians since you were a boy, and I'm sure you'd find them different now that you're

411

grown. I suggest you go out west and live the nomadic life of the tribes. After a little bit of that you might be ready to agree they're better off on a reservation. I'm not blaming you for your position though. It's easy to see why you'd want to help them."

"Yes, I imagine it is," Grant said. Rebecca knew by the sudden set of his mouth that he hadn't missed Robert's subtle reference to his parentage.

Changing the subject abruptly, Grant turned to the blonde by his side. Lilybelle jerked her gaze away from her intent study of Robert and simpered up at Grant, then again at Robert when she was introduced.

"Charmed, I'm sure," she drawled softly, lifting her hand toward Robert and lowering her thick lashes demurely.

Robert clasped her fingers in his, raising them toward his lowering mouth. He appeared fascinated by the blonde.

"Now that my apology's been accepted, I'd like to speak with Rebecca," Grant said, taking her upper arm in a firm grip. "Would you see Miss Lessard home, Shaw?"

Desperation flared in Rebecca's eyes as Grant began to drag her away. Evidently, remembering his brotherly duties, Robert said abruptly, "Hold on, Mallory." He took his sister's other arm. "I can't allow Becky to go off alone."

"She won't be alone," Grant said grimly. His eyes darkened, becoming the dark gray of slabs of Pittsburgh steel as his fingers tightened around Rebecca's arm. "After all," he said, his tone of voice modulating into that of someone patiently stating an obvious fact. "I'll be with her."

Robert stiffened. "Even so," he said, sternly. "I can't allow her to go with you." His eyes warred between puzzlement and anger. "She's accepted your apology, Mallory, that'll have to do."

Grant's eyes sparked. His voice was soft, but deadly. "She's coming with me."

"Are you wanting to fight?" Robert growled, his temper barely held in check, his mouth tightening grimly. "Because I'm not letting her go with you."

"Robert," Rebecca said. "Please—"

"*You* won't allow it!" Grant snapped, interrupting her savagely. "You have no right to prevent it!"

Robert's expression underwent several changes. Surprises, confusion, consternation, and finally overwhelming anger. "I'm her brother. No one has a better right." He glared at Grant's hand on Rebecca's arm. "Now take your hands off her!"

"I'll argue some other time with you about who has what rights over Rebecca. For now, I'm taking her with me."

A harsh laugh rang out. Then, Lilybelle, tired of being ignored, took Robert's arm in a firm grip, drawing his attention. "What's all this fuss about?" she asked, making an effort to soften her voice. "If Grant is going to insist on taking your sister with him, why don't we jsut let him?" Her eyes flirted outrageously with him. "It would give us a chance to get to know each other better. Besides, we're attracting a crowd here."

Robert scowled darkly. His narrowed gaze fell on Lilybelle, then moved to the two men and three women who had stopped, attracted by the argument. He dropped Rebecca's arm, and his fists clenched tightly.

413

He gritted his teeth, his eyes sweeping back to Grant, passing over Forrest, then snapping back to the baby, sitting quietly in the pushcart taking everything in with his wide gray eyes.

Robert's eyes returned to Grant. "You're spoiling for a fight, Mallory. But it'll have to wait until there's no innocent babe looking on. You name the place. I'll be glad to oblige."

Grant's lips curled in distaste at the mention of the baby. Then, unwillingly, he glanced for the first time at the dark-haired child sitting so patiently in the stroller. Immediately, his eyes sharpened to alertness, and a curious stillness came over him. He took in the smooth coppery skin, the jet-black hair curling wildly over the baby's head, and the gray eyes staring innocently at him.

Rebecca held her breath, waiting.

Grant's gaze met hers and held, seeking an answer. She lifted her chin, returning his look steadily. She had nothing to hide. He stood stunned, as though she had confirmed his suspicion. Then, gray eyes blazed, burning into her face accusingly.

She made a protective movement toward Forrest, but, before she could reach the child, Grant's expression softened and he knelt beside the stroller. He poked an investigative finger at one chubby, miniature hand. Forrest grabbed the finger instantly in his surprisingly strong grip and hung on. His mouth opened in an enchanting smile, displaying his two ivory teeth. The child, a miniature of his father, gurgled with delight, trying to pull the large finger to his mouth.

Rebecca's eyes filled as she saw Grant kneeling with such tenderness beside his son, and a pain squeezed

414

her chest. It was quite obvious to anyone who cared to see that the two were father and son.

Casting a swift look at Robert, her heart sank. He had a look of confusion on his face, as though he were in possession of some knowledge but refused to admit it, even to himself.

Suddenly, he turned toward her, catching her unawares. Her cheeks flushed, and his eyes flared.

"You bastard!" Robert snarled, grabbing Grant's arm and pulling him upright, away from the baby. "It was you all the time!" His fist came up, and he struck out at Grant.

Rebecca cried out. "No, Robert. Don't!"

Throwing up his arm, Grant blocked the blow and shoved Robert back.

Bellowing with rage, Robert flew at him again. Grant side-stepped, hitting out with his fist. Robert staggered back, blood streaming from one nostril. He wiped the blood on his sleeve and shook his head, then closed in again.

"No! Stop it!" Rebecca cried, grabbing her brother's arm and clinging. He tried to shake her loose, but she hung on, like a barnacle or a determined limpet. She had to stop them before one of them was hurt.

"Stand back, Becky," Robert roared. "He deserves a beating for what he did to you, and I'm damn sure going to see he gets it." Jerking his arm free, he shoved her roughly away from him.

She staggered, losing her balance for a moment, and Grant caught her firmly against his large frame, steadying her.

"You all right?" he asked.

"Let her go, you damned savage!" Robert snarled,

rushing at him again. "Take your hands off my sister!"

"Get back, Rebecca," Grant snapped, pushing her aside, every bit as roughly as Robert had. "The fool's insane."

As Robert lunged forward, Grant side-stepped. But not enough. Robert caught him at such an angle that the furious momentum propelled them both to the gravel path, with Robert on top.

Robert drove a long, slogging blow to Grant's face, slamming the back of his head hard against the gravel.

Grant grunted and dug his chin against his chest so that any further punches would knuckle harmlessly against his skull. Then he pitched his weight to roll them on their sides.

The shrill scream of a woman's voice sounded in Rebecca's ears, but she paid no attention. Her mesmerized gaze refused to leave the two men she loved most in the world. They were both bruised, and blood was streaming from both men's nostrils, but still they fought.

Then, Grant's fist lashed out, catching Robert in the throat, and Robert collapsed, wheezing for air.

Grant began to climb slowly to his feet, but Robert rolled catlike up onto his feet, driven by fury, refusing to stop even though he had taken as much as he had given. He sprang at Grant, connecting with a slug on the side of his opponent's face. Grant's fist returned the blow and sent Robert sprawling again.

An anguished wailing demanded Rebecca's attention and she turned, startled. She had almost forgotten the baby, and the struggling men were getting too close to him. She made a dash for Forrest's pushcart, snatched the child into her arms, and scooted back, away from the brawling men. Holding Forrest against her shoulder, she patted him soothingly, her tears matching his as she tried to comfort him.

"I say," came a masculine voice from behind her. "Someone really ought to stop them."

Rebecca spun around, startled. A crowd had gathered. The murmur of agreement suggested others were of the same mind, but no one came forth to volunteer.

Forrest began to cry in earnest, and Rebecca's anxiety knew no bounds. Were they going to kill each other before they stopped? Helpless tears spilled over, sliding down her pale cheeks.

Finally, she could take it no longer. The baby's distressed wails and the thudding and grunts of the men as they knocked each other about were too much. She could do no more.

Her life was crumbling all about her with no hope for the future in sight. She turned to leave and found herself confronted by a furious Lilybelle.

"One of them is going to be killed, and it's all your fault," the blonde said spitefully.

Rebecca flinched.

"I had nothing to do with it!" she said. She wasn't going to let this alleycat see her weakness. "Anyone with eyes in their head could see I tried to stop them!"

"Maybe you should have tried harder!" Lilybelle sneered. Her voice was spiteful. "Anyone would have to be blind not to see Grant is the father of your child. And I'm a long way from being blind."

"I haven't tried to deny it," Rebecca snapped. "But I fail to see where it's any of your business."

"You don't mind everyone knowing you were Grant's mistress?" Lilybelle asked in surprise. "What hap-

417

pened? Couldn't you take the rejection when he tired of you and threw you out?"

"You don't know what you're talking about!"

"Oh, don't I?" You know, of course, that Grant is a half-breed Apache Indian. So what do you think that makes your son?"

"It makes my son fortunate. Part of a noble breed." She made to move off, then stopped. There was one last thing that needed to be said. "I only wish he could be as proud of the other three-quarters of his heritage."

Rebecca looked at Grant and Robert, rolling and fighting on the ground. Then, her eyes swept over the avidly watching crowd—and Lilybelle. Numbly, she clutched the wailing baby to her breast and walked away, her shoulders held tautly straight. She didn't even care that now all of Pittsburgh would know the truth. It wouldn't take long; news of the fight and its cause would spread rapidly, both upstairs and down.

But damn them all for their bigotry! She had nothing to be ashamed of. Nor did Forrest. And if they couldn't build a life here without scorn, she would take him somewhere where they could.

*But where?* The only place she wanted to take him was back where they both belonged. With his father. With the Apaches.

A pain burst in her chest and spread its aching fingers outward in sharp little bursts.

That was the one place they couldn't go. The one place they were least wanted.


Rebecca leaned her head against the back of the rocker and closed her weary eyes. Forrest, finally allowing himself to be comforted, had fallen asleep, leaving her free to seek the silence of her room. But Aunt Bess had been waiting, eager to know what had happened. Rebecca, unable to speak without falling completely apart, had remained mute to her questioning until finally Elizabeth had left her alone.

Rebecca's eyes moved to the window, but she remained seated, rocking herself back and forth, her fingers clutching the double mug in her lap. She forced herself to remain calm. Whatever was going to happen, already had. She could help no one by breaking up.

Again she wept, bitter tears spilling down her face, going unchecked as she rocked. Misery welled from deep inside, stabbing through her: hopeless, lonely misery.

Suddenly the door burst open and Robert entered. Obviously he had not bothered to wash before coming to her. His face was bloodied, one eye swollen and his brown hair stood out wildly on his head. He took one look at her, sitting quietly rocking, her face splotched with tears, and came to a halting stop.

"Becky . . . ?" he asked hesitantly. "Are you all right?"

She looked at him but remained silent.

He cleared his throat, averting his eyes from her obvious pain, and raked a hand through his tousled brown hair. "Why didn't you tell me he was here?" he asked.

"Because I knew what would happen," she whispered huskily.

His lips tightened. "I can see now why you couldn't sleep."

She said nothing.

419

He walked to the window, staring outside grimly. When he spoke his voice was savage. "This isn't the end of it. I intend to file charges of abduction and rape against him."

"You have no proof."

"No proof! Your word should be enough. If it isn't, then the baby is all the proof I need."

"I'll deny the charges."

"Becky, why would you do that?" He stared at her in frustration. "Dammit! Anyone can see the baby is his! There would be no use in denying it."

"I'll swear I was willing. The authorities wouldn't dare interfere."

"Becky!" His voice was shocked. He pulled her from the rocker, his hands tight on her arms. "He abducted you!" he hissed, giving her a hard shake. "How could you even consider letting him get away with it? Don't you understand? The man has ruined your life!"

"Maybe I don't see it that way, Robert," she said, pushing at him. When he continued to hold her, she glared at him. "Take your hands off me, Robert."

He flushed, dropping her arms.

"I've told you over and over again it wasn't Lone Wolf who took me. It was Black Bear!"

He snorted. "Maybe so. But *this* Indian even used a fake name!"

"Neither of his names are fake. One is just civilized . . ." The words hovered in the air scornfully. "The other's Apache."

"Apache!" He scoffed contemptuously.

Finally, as if he had reached the end of his patience, Robert said. "Becky, after what the Apaches did to Mother . . . how can you possibly defend the man?"

Rebecca waited until she had his full attention. "Because I love him, Robert." When she spoke, her words were calm, certain, convincing.

"Oh, Becky," Robert slumped onto the edge of the bed. "I don't think I know you anymore. I feel as though the Apaches kept my sister and sent back someone else, someone who only resembles Rebecca Shaw. I'm trying to understand, really I am, but it's damned hard."

"I know," she said. "I even appreciate what you're going through." She smiled wearily. "One of these days though, you'll fall in love, and you'll know how I feel. Until then, you'll just have to believe me." She stood up and crossed to the window, pulling the draperies aside and gazing down on the wide lawn below. Her fingers tightened on the fabric. She couldn't stand it any longer — she had to know.

"Is Grant all right?" she asked.

"Hell, yes! He looks better than I do," Robert growled. "He knows how to fight, I'll give him that." He levered himself up and began to pace, his hands dug into his pockets.

"Where is he?"

"I suppose he must have gone home. He needed to clean up a bit. Like me," he admitted wryly. Then his eyes narrowed. "What are you going to do?"

"The only thing I can. I'm going to beg. Do whatever's necessary to convince him to take me back." Her laugh held no amusement. "Maybe he'll even do it now that he knows about the baby."

"He didn't know before?"

"Obviously not. And I guess it complicates things that I didn't actually tell him. At first, there never seemed to be enough time. Later, I thought he realized." Though she didn't say it aloud, she knew she had one thing more than the baby in her favor. Grant—Lone Wolf—still desired her. And if that's all she could have, then it would have to do.

"Oh, Becky." Sadly, Robert pulled her into his arms. "I'm afraid I've failed you miserably."

"No, you haven't." She pushed herself gently away. "You've been the best of brothers. Never forget that."

The time had come for her to choose her destiny. She could no longer straddle both worlds. And if she had to part with one of the men she loved, that man wouldn't be her Apache husband. God willing, her fate lay with him.

And with his people.

She smiled, her desire apparent in the brave angle of her chin. "Will you make sure Aunt Bess doesn't worry? I'll be back later for Forrest."

She walked out, turning her back on the bemused acceptance creeping across Robert's face.

# Chapter Twenty-Four

Rebecca paused before the front door of an intimidating Victorian mansion. Grant's house, immense in size, was situated in a part of town where his neighbors bore names like Carnegie and Mellon.

She slid her palms down the front of her navy-blue skirt in a vain attempt to dry them. Then she tugged at her matching princess-style jacket. Not just her future hung in the balance here. The man her son would be rested on the outcome of the next few moments.

She dampened her lips, realigned the small, already straight, navy hat that tilted jauntily over one eye, leaving aquiver the blue ostrich feathers decorating it.

Despite her brave appearance her stomach was tied in a square knot and her knees wobbled. She drew in a breath of courage and banged the door clapper.

Then she waited. Each second stretched out like an eternity, a rubbery thread of time elongating past endurance. In a moment, she thought, it would break, and the world would again move at the proper speed.

But it didn't. Seconds piled into minutes. Where was he? He had to be here.

As if the sheer intensity of her will could make him be somewhere he wasn't, she grasped the knocker again and dropped it with a loud clang.

The door swung open on the questioning gaze of a solidly built middle-aged man. Disappointment bit sharply into Rebecca. And a little bit of cowardice. In fact, she almost quailed at the icy superiority in the man's eyes.

But she hadn't come this far to back down now. She collected her own ounce of arrogance. "Mr. Mallory, please."

She could have sworn his chilly stare slid down his haughty nose and icicled off the end. "Who shall I say is calling?"

"Rebecca."

His brow lifted inquiringly.

"Just Rebecca?"

"He'll know."

She was a bit surprised when the manservant allowed her to enter. She had half expected him to leave her standing outside. He ushered her to a parlor and informed her he would inquire if Mr. Mallory was receiving visitors.

"He'd better be," Rebecca muttered grimly when she was alone. But she wouldn't put it past him to refuse to see her. Hadn't she done it to him? She sank down on the sofa, her fingernails digging into her palms, but found herself too restless to sit still.

Rising, she moved to the open French doors. The pungent fragrance of honeysuckle filled her nostrils. Any other time she would have been soothed by the sweet perfume. But not today.

What if he refused to listen to her? She knew he still desired her, but perhaps for him, desire wouldn't be nough. It had a habit of coming to an end. Unlike ove, it didn't last.

She had one trump card though. She had Forrest, nd Grant wanted his son. And she wanted Grant adly enough to use any means at her disposal.

Hearing footsteps, she swung around as Grant valked into the room. Silently, she examined his face. It vas scraped and bruised, but he didn't look as bad as Robert. Black riding breeches molded his thighs, atching and holding her gaze.

He wore black Hessian boots, and a white muslin hirt made his bronzed skin look even darker. His hick, black hair was rumpled as though he had pushed iis fingers through it more than once.

"Where's my son?" he asked, his voice grating aarshly against her ears. His gray eyes were icy as they licked over her. His lip curled as he took in her ashionable apparel, as if he guessed the care she had aken with her appearance.

"I left him with my aunt." She clasped her hands behind her to hide their trembling.

Every nerve in her body registered his nearness, rying out for his touch.

For a moment, he seemed to be fascinated by her mouth. Then his eyes skittered away, and he moved vith casual ease to a rosewood occasional table, picking up a gilded statue to run his thumb caressingly over it. With his back to her, his voice seemed distant when he poke. "Is he all right?" The strong emotion that was :vident in his stiff back intensified the harshness of his vords.

"Yes."

He clenched the hand hanging by his side, opened

it, then clenched it again.

"He was asleep when I left," Rebecca murmured.

How could he be so matter-of-fact, she wondered in desperation as she took in the unyielding quality of his stance. My God! The man had been doing everything in his power to see her the past few days. Now she was here. Did he have nothing to say to her? Had he decided it no longer mattered?

Silent seconds drew out interminably, seconds in which neither of them spoke. Then, just when she knew she could stand the suspense no longer, he turned to face her. "He's a handsome little fellow," he said.

"I know."

Again there was an uncomfortable silence, and they stared at each other, their gazes locked together. She knew she should say something but she didn't know what. She hadn't realized it would be so hard to talk to him.

"He looks like you," she blurted, her eyes unconsciously appealing.

"Yes. How—how old is he?"

"Six months."

He sighed deeply. "Did you know when you left me?"

She objected to his choice of words, because surely it had been he who had left her. Nevertheless, she wouldn't quibble. "I suspected, but I wasn't sure."

"Yet you just walked away without a word?" His voice was clipped, frozen, but his gray eyes burned furiously. "I want my son," he snapped.

"No!" Her refusal was sharp, angry. Her heartbeat thrummed wildly in her ears. "He's mine! If you try to take him, I'll fight you every step of the way. The only way you can have him is to take me as well," she said npassively. "There's not a court in this land would give im to you. It's either both of us or neither."

Something undefinable flickered across his face, and is gray eyes held a strangely satisfied gleam. He ocused on her desperation. "As you wish," he said, urning away again and jamming his hands into his ockets. "I'll have the banns posted right away."

"The banns?" Her eyes widened, as hope sprang trong to her breast.

"Naturally. You'll be my wife in this world as well as hat of the Apaches. I'll not let my son be a bastard in ny society."

"Of course." She lowered her eyes and her spirits took downward plunge. For a moment there, she had ctually thought he wanted her. "Whatever you say, rant." Woodenly, she walked to the door. It was more han time to leave.

"Rebecca, come here." His head was drawn back, his ray eyes proudly alert, missing none of the dismay tched on her face.

Her hands clenched tightly on the doorknob, her nuckles white. Her heart leaped wildly. She pivoted, er eyes narrowing suspiciously.

"I said, come here," he repeated, pointing to a spot in ront of him.

He was obviously bent on stripping her of every bit f her pride. Her lips tightened, and her blue eyes lashed angrily, but she moved toward him. If he vanted her complete surrender, then that's what he vould get. But she could salvage a little of her pride if he pretended she was coming to him for the baby's ake. He had no way of knowing it was a lie.

She stopped in front of him. Temper, born of pride,

tilted her head back to let him feel the full force of he
anger.

"Now ask me to take you back," he gritted, his eye
gleaming with wicked satisfaction. "Tell me you lov
me, and make me believe it."

Oh God! He wanted blood!

She stared at him, gathering together every shred o
her self-control.

She loved him so completely it was like a pai
constantly eating away at her. She had been only half
alive when she thought him dead. It only took hi
touch to spark the fires of her love. But now, he wa
asking for more than complete surrender; he wa
intent on destroying her.

She tried to protest, but not a word came from he
throat. She swallowed hard, her eyes on the sensuou
lines of his mouth, then placed a trembling hand on th
side of his face, feeling the muscles twitch beneath he
palm. She raised herself up on tiptoes and lightly
touched his mouth with hers.

"I . . . love you, Grant," she whispered huskily
"Would . . . would you please take me back?" His body
was tense and he seemed to be fighting something
inside himself. A quivering shudder, an arrow o
desire, raced through her. Relinquishing her pride, she
put her arms around his neck, pulling his mouth dow
to her trembling lips.

He yanked her to him, his kiss savage. "God
Rebecca," he groaned finally against her lips.

Then he dropped his mouth to hers again. Dropped
his mouth and raised his arms. He struggled for a
moment with the pins in her hat, finally plucking it
from her head, still loosely pinned. It dragged at her

428

hair, jerking one strand free, but she ignored the discomfort, even welcomed it. Then it was fully off, and he tossed it onto a chair and combed his fingers through her hair until it lay in a silky brown cloud about her shoulders and back.

"God. How I've wanted to do that," he said. His eyes were dark, slumbrous with desire as his mouth closed on hers in brutal possession, denying her even the smallest breath. He seemed unaware of his strength, ravaging her with the hunger of a starving man.

She quivered beneath his touch, wanting him desperately. There were so many things to settle between them—so many questions that needed to be answered—but they would have to wait. Opening her lips, she offered the sweet moistness within, withholding nothing. They could talk later. Right now, she needed him.

Her arms, seeming to possess a will of their own, tightened around him. She could feel the muscles tense in his back, the male strength of him pressing against her. God. How she loved this man. And if he would only allow it, she would follow him to the ends of the earth.

His fingers found the buttons of her jacket, fumbled with the fastenings, and she drew back slightly, allowing him to undress her.

He loosened the last button and pulled the jacket off, tossing it aside. Then he stared down at the sheer cambric fabric that outlined her breasts thrusting against her chemise. With agonizingly slow movements, he bared her breasts, his fingers brushing softly against the tautened peaks.

"You're beautiful," he whispered, lowering his head

and closing his mouth over one nipple.

She uttered a small moan. It had been so long. Her knees threatened to buckle beneath her.

The faintly starchy, faintly musky scent of his body was overpowering to her senses, and, just when she thought she could take no more, he straightened, taking her lips again, crushing her breasts against his chest. She could feel the thudding of his heart pounding erratically against his chest, hammering in unison with hers, and she knew he was as excited with passion as she was. She felt blinded by the fury of their emotions, lost to everything but desire.

Her lips throbbed from his bruising kiss. *Yes*, she exulted silently. He swept her into his arms, carrying her to the couch and laying her down.

Before she could gather her scattered wits, he had stripped away the rest of her clothing, tossing it carelessly aside, exposing the rest of her satiny smooth flesh to his glittering gray eyes.

She gazed at him, her mind whirling, her body trembling as she waited for him to undress and join her.

Then, unable to wait any longer, her hands went to his belt buckle. Her fingers were trembling so much they fumbled badly. Finally, she managed to unclasp it and began to work on the buttons of his fly. She needed him desperately.

He sat down and pulled off his boots. They hit the floor with a thud. His shirt was thrown aside.

As she watched him with eyes darkened passionately, she suddenly remembered where they were—and the manservant. Anxiously, she levered herself up on both elbows, glancing suspiciously at the door. "Grant," she whispered. "What about—him?"

"Who?" he asked, stopping in the act of discarding his breeches.

"Him!" she hissed, her eyes darting from Grant to the door. "Your manservant. Suppose he comes in." She blushed scarlet, expecting the door to open at any moment.

"He wouldn't dare," he grated.

Then he joined her on the couch, stretching out beside her, his breathing heavy, his gray eyes hungry with passion.

"No," she said, turning her head. "Not here! Not now! He might come in!"

"Yes, here," he said, holding her tightly, kissing the end of her nose. "And, yes, now." He kissed her eyelids closed, feeling the shiver of excitement that she was unable to control. "And . . ." He took the hand that had been pushing at him, and kissed the tip of one finger. "He won't . . ." He kissed another fingertip. ". . . come in, because . . ." He kissed two more fingertips. ". . . I sent him away."

"You sent him away?" she breathed, her eyes beginning to shine. "When?"

"As soon as I knew you were here." His gaze was steady as it held hers.

"But you didn't know then why I came."

"I didn't give a damn why you came." His lips trailed across her face, deliberately tantalizing her, torturing her already sensitized nerves.

Her pulses beat erratically, her limbs shivered, as his mouth found the sensitive skin of her neck. He nipped greedily at the rapidly beating pulse of her throat, turning her into a mass of raw, quivering feeling.

"How — how long will he be gone?" she asked, feeling as though she could stand no more. She was already vibrating like a tightly strung violin string.

He sighed, raising his head and looking at her with pained eyes. "He won't be back today at all. Is there anything else you want to know?"

She shook her head. "No," she breathed softly, slipping her arms around his neck. "Nothing at all." She pulled his head down and took his lips in a long, satisfying, sense-drugging kiss.

His mouth feasted on her lips as his hands moved down, caressing her breasts, her hips, leaving a fiery path where they traveled that seeped into her very bones. His mouth lifted and moved lower until it reached the tender curve of her breast and closed over one tautened nipple.

His manhood was hard against her body, throbbing, teasing at her and she groaned, a wild tremor shooting through her as she felt the moist, sucking sensation of his mouth on her breast. Shock waves of pleasure rushed through her, increasing with each passing moment, causing an aching need to grow within her.

She threw her head back, arching wildly beneath him, crying out her need. Her hair was damp with perspiration, curling in tendrils around her face and neck. Her fingers threaded through his thick black hair, and she pressed against him desperately, yearning to know physical release.

Suddenly, in one swift, fluid movement, he raised himself up. His strength pulsated against her thigh, brushing against her sensitive, feminine core.

She raised her hips, urging him on, raining fervent kisses along his neck. Her nostrils were filled with the

432

clean, male scent of him, and she thought she would go mad if he didn't take her soon.

His hands teased her buttocks, raising her up, widening her thighs. But still, he held himself back, waiting, his eyes watchful, wary, as they held hers.

Finally, she could stand it no more. "Please, Lone Wolf," she begged, her blue eyes pleading as she gazed into his. "Don't torment me. Take me now."

As if that was what he was waiting for, he entered her, sliding between her flushed thighs, burrowing deeper and deeper. Rebecca uttered soft moaning sounds as he filled her with his strength. She had no thought beyond that moment—that feeling—as he began to move in the age-old ritual of desire. He gripped her tightly, plunging with frenzied movements, increasing his pace as he went, until that last blinding thrust when her body tightened and her back arched and she screamed wildly, an earthquaking shudder passing through her in a climax so volatile she thought she must be dying.

As she lay facing him, relaxing in the aftermath of their intense coming together, she felt at peace with her world. Although she had felt married to him all along, she was glad they would soon be married in a church. Even if he didn't love her now, with time, he might. And she had been given that time. Her blue eyes were filled with stars as they met his and she smiled.

Her smile wavered, then died.

His face was still, his gaze watchful, waiting.

"Lone Wolf . . . what's wrong?" she asked. Her breath caught as uncertainty flickered in her blue eyes. Her pulses began to hammer violently.

A shadow seemed to cross his face. "Will you ever be

able to forgive me?" he asked huskily, his voice pained.

She stared at him, wondering if she had heard right. "Forgive you?" she whispered. "What for?"

"For the way I've treated you."

She couldn't speak. Her throat was dry, her body trembling. Was she crazy? And did she detect a tremor in his voice?

"What does Jake mean to you?" he grated, staring fixedly at her. "I have to know."

"Why?"

He clenched his teeth, his nostrils flaring with fury. "Don't continue this torture, Rebecca."

She sat motionless, wondering if he could hear her pounding heart. "Why is it torture, Lone Wolf?" she asked huskily. "Why should you care what Jake means to me?"

"Because I love you, dammit!" he snarled, his face dark with bitterness. "Because you bewitched me from the first moment. And because I can't stand the thought of another man touching you." His breathing was audible, and a red flush washed up his face.

She looked at him with hope and fear and wariness. Her face was flushed, her eyes abnormally bright, her smile wavering. "Do you?" she asked softly. "Do you really love me?"

"Yes, damn you! I love you!" His arms tightened about her. "I couldn't bear it if you left me."

"I won't leave you," she said softly. Her eyes filled with moisture. "Don't you really know how much I love you?"

There was a sharp intake of breath at her words. One hand lifted her chin, allowing him to gaze deeply into her eyes, searching for the truth. "I'd give anything if I could believe you," he whispered.

She trembled wildly. "Must I convince you?"

"Would you be willing to try?"

"Yes."

He reached for her, and she buried her face in the curve of his neck. It was a beautiful world they shared. Both worlds.


Rebecca lay in the big, four-poster bed in Grant's bedroom later that evening. She had sent word to Robert and Aunt Bess not to expect her until morning. She tilted her head and gazed up into her husband's face.

"I still can't believe you love me," Rebecca said. "It all seems like a dream."

"If it's a dream, then I never want to wake up," he whispered huskily, kissing her ear.

"You said I bewitched you from the beginning, but when did you start loving me?"

"I've loved you from the first moment I saw you," he said. "You were lying on the ground, blistered from the sun. Your gown was torn to the waist and you had blood on your face but I thought you were the most beautiful creature I had ever seen."

She drew away from him. "And you still took me home?" she whispered, her voice harsh with remembered pain. "If you loved me, how could you just ride away from me?"

"I had to do it, Little Blue Eyes. I knew you wouldn't be safe with me." He sighed heavily, smoothing back her silky hair. "Nothing has changed either. I still cannot take you with me when I go."

"You can't take me?" Her eyes sparked as they held his. "What, exactly, do you mean to do with me then?"

"You'll stay here in Pittsburgh of course. I'll come whenever I can to—"

"Visit us," she finished sweetly, raising up on one elbow. She glared furiously at him. "No!"

"No?" He raised one dark eyebrow.

"No!" she snapped. "Wherever you go, we go too."

"Be reasonable, Rebecca," he said, pulling her tense body back into his arms. "And relax."

"I am being reasonable," she said coolly, resisting him. "And I can't relax. You have no right to expect that of me. I need a husband, and Forrest needs a father. What's more, you have no right to deny our son the chance to grow up among his People." Her blue eyes were cold as they held his. "And I'll tell you another thing, Grant Mallory. If you even attempt to leave without us—we'll follow you."

He drew her resisting body tight against him. "You would really do that? You would leave the life of luxury you have out here and choose the Apache way of life?"

"I have chosen it. My husband and son are Apache. Therefore, I am Apache."

"Do you fully understand the danger that could lie that way? The winters are cold and long, game is scarce—"

"Whatever lies ahead, I have a right to share it with you."

"I can hardly believe what you're saying," he said, kissing her eyelids. "I've missed you so much. This past year has seemed an eternity."

"Lone Wolf," she said softly, hesitantly. "One thing bothers me."

436

"Then tell me what it is, Little Blue Eyes. I want no more misunderstandings between the two of us."

"Well. If you missed me so much, why didn't you come straight to Pittsburgh when you were well enough to travel? Why did you go to Washington before coming here?"

"I wanted to come here first, please believe that," he said softly, kissing the end of her nose. "But when I learned you had left the west, I thought you had run away from me. I didn't really intend to let you know I was in Pittsburgh. Then I saw you at that party and couldn't stay away."

"You weren't going to see me?" Her voice was hurt.

"I said, I wasn't going to let you see me. There's a difference."

"I'm so glad you changed your mind."

"Not half as glad as I am. Although I must admit, I had a bad time for a while."

She snuggled closer. "I wish you had come here first."

"I'm afraid Congress won't wait for my convenience," he said dryly. "They were in session and there's so much trouble out west. I knew it was only going to get worse until, possibly, a full-scale war broke out, involving all the Indian nations. I felt if I could make it to Congress for the scheduled convening, then possibly they would grant me a hearing."

"Did they?"

"Yes. It's next month." He sighed. "That brings me back to something else. Jake Logan and Sam Rayburn are going with me to that hearing, but first, we're going to the San Carlos reservation. Two voices such as theirs, added to mine, will lend a lot of strength to what we have to tell them."

"You said Jake's going with you?" Her eyes were thoughtful. She raised herself on one elbow and looked at him. "Grant," she said. "I've just had an idea. Do you remember Mary's tea?"

He nodded. "How could I forget it?" he asked dryly.

She smiled. "Yes. Well, I met a man there—"

"Oh, no!"

"What's the matter?"

"I thought Jake was my only competition." He grunted sharply as she jabbed him with her elbow.

"It's not like that," she said. "Just listen to me. This man I was telling you about—well, he works for the Pittsburgh *Clarion*, and he's very interested in what's happening out west with the Indians. I think he might come to San Carlos too."

"If you're right, then we might be able to enlist the help of one of the largest newspapers around." His eyes were thoughtful.

"Do you think that would help?"

"It certainly couldn't hurt anything."

"Grant," she said pensively. "How did you get Jake interested? When you met at Mary's tea, you two looked ready to tear each other's throats out."

"That's what love does to you," he said wryly. "It takes two grown, civilized men and—"

"Civilized? Are you referring to yourself?" Her eyebrows lifted delicately.

"Yes, civilized!" he growled. He frowned at her. "And don't interrupt your Apache husband, woman."

She giggled but remained silent.

He looked at her approvingly. "You'll learn." Then frowning, he asked. "Now where was I?"

"Telling me what love could do to two civilized—"

she prompted, cuddling up against him.

"Oh, yes. Well, as I was saying. Love takes two grown men and makes—" He broke off. "Will you stop all that wiggling around? I can't even think straight." He eyed her sternly. "Do you want to know about Jake or not?"

"Not really," she said, smiling invitingly up at him.

He groaned. "Come here," he said, his lips covering hers with satisfying swiftness.


Rebecca was to be wed in her mother's wedding gown, a fragile creation made of ivory silk satin, cut in a long princess style. Thousands of hand-sewn seed pearls adorned the bodice and the long, flowing sleeves.

Once she was dressed, Rebecca was enchanted by her own image, staring at herself in the cheval mirror, hardly daring to believe it was her, and this was really happening.

"Stand still, Rebecca, while I attach this veil," Elizabeth said.

Rebecca obeyed, barely moving while her aunt attached the five-yard-long, Irish lace veil to the golden brown curls arranged on the top of her head.

"Well, I think you're finally ready," Bess said, standing back to view her niece with moist eyes. "I'm glad you and Grant were willing to give in to an old woman's dreams and be married at home, Becky."

"Pish-tosh," Rebecca said. "You're no old woman." She hugged her aunt.

Elizabeth wiped a tear away and smiled. "I believe I hear your music," she said.

"Thank you, for everything, Aunt Bess," Rebecca whispered, her eyes filling with tears. "I'm going to miss you."

"Nonsense!" Elizabeth said. "You'll only just be living across town. We'll see each other every day."

"I guess so," Rebecca said, not wanting to spoil the night by telling Elizabeth they would be leaving for the San Carlos reservation in a few days. There would be time enough later to tell her. Tonight, she wanted no shadow intruding. "Well, come on," she said, drawing a deep breath. "They're waiting for us."

"Becky, are you sure about this?" Elizabeth's eyes were concerned. "Have you really thought about what marrying Grant really means? Because if you haven't, it's not too late to call it off. I never understood what the hurry was to begin with. One minute you're refusing to see Grant, and the next, I discover you're going to marry him."

"No. I'm not having second thoughts," Rebecca assured her.

"You do love him enough? You realize you'll become a social outcast by marrying a half-Apache?"

"I love him more than life itself. And I'm proud to be his wife."

Elizabeth seemed to recognize the truth of her words and hugged her swiftly. "Well, then. What are we waiting for? They've already gone through the wedding march several times. He'll be thinking you've changed your mind." She grasped the doorknob and opened the door.

From the parlor came strains of the wedding march.

"Are you ready?" Robert asked, stepping from an alcove in the hall and placing her hand on his arm.

"Yes. I'm ready," she said, her eyes smiling into his.

"Becky," he said, his blue eyes intent as he searched her face. "Are you sure?"

A lump formed in her throat as she held his gaze and she couldn't speak. She wanted Robert's blessings but realized all she could hope for at least was his acceptance. Perhaps, she thought, in time she could have the other. She lifted her chin and nodded her head.

"I'm sure," she said.

He expelled his breath. Then, as the wedding march began to play over again, they walked slowly down the stairs. The wooden railings on the staircase had been covered with ferns and honeysuckle. At regular intervals, clusters of honeysuckle and yellow roses were intertwined. Below them the guests craned their necks, each hoping to get the first glimpse of the bride.

As they reached the bottom of the stairs, she saw him for the first time. He was standing beneath a canopy before the altar twined around with greenery and yellow roses.

A thousand butterflies fluttered in her stomach, and she clutched Robert's sleeve as though it were a lifeline. Was she crazy? She hadn't seen Grant since he told her he would make the arrangements last week. He had said he would be kept busy planning the trip to the San Carlos reservation.

Her steps faltered, and Robert turned a questioning look on her. She kept her eyes on Grant, and, as she drew nearer, her gaze locked with his and her doubts disappeared.

He was magnificently handsome in his dark-gray suit and brocade vest. With his white shirt emphasizing the bronze tone of his skin, his bearing proudly erect, thoughts of another wedding ceremony she had shared with him filled her mind. She remembered how the firelight had slithered across his silken black hair as he stood beside her in his fringed and decorated buckskin. And now, they were being married again.

As she reached the altar, Grant took her hand and she could see in his eyes that he, too, was remembering.

Her eyes were filled with Grant, and she was hardly aware of Robert leaving her side. With hands tightly clasped, she and Grant made their vows, and then she was lifting her face to receive his kiss. It was long and passionate.

When he lifted his head, he whispered, "Now we are doubly bound, Little Blue Eyes. All men will recognize that you are mine. In this world as well as the world of the Apache. Our marriage will be twice as strong now."

# *Epilogue*

The sun went down in the western sky in a burst of orange and gold as Rebecca and Lone Wolf topped the rise and pulled up their mounts. Spread out below them was Chief Tall Feathers' village.

Rebecca breathed in the pure, pine-scented air and turned to Lone Wolf with a smile. "It's good to be in the mountains again," she said softly.

"Are you tired?" he asked.

"A little, but I don't mind. I'm just glad to be going home."

Home. The word rang between them. She knew he was pleased she had used it, but it hadn't been just for his benefit. She *did* feel a sense of homecoming.

She looked at Forrest, sleeping peacefully in his cradleboard, which she had suspended from the pommel of the saddle. He had been a good baby, never whimpering or fussing on the long ride to the village. He would make a good Apache son.

Lone Wolf's eyes traveled over her appreciatively, taking in the soft doeskin dress and the moccasins that she had managed to keep and take with her. She had braided her brown hair into one, long braid that flowed down her back.

He smiled softly at her. He had found his wife was a very determined woman. She had insisted on accompanying the men to the San Carlos reservation and then on to Washington. She had felt it wouldn't hurt their cause any to have it known a white woman was also concerned about the quality of life the Indians on the reservation were receiving.

Yes. He had made a good choice when he picked her for his wife. His eyes swept over the baby, then back to Rebecca waiting patiently beside him. He reached out and took her hand.

"Come, Rebecca. Our people wait below."

Now you can get more of **HEARTFIRE**
right at home and $ave.

Preview
Four Brand New
ZEBRA
*Heartfire*
Romance Novels...

## *FREE for 10 days.*

## No Obligation
## and No Strings Attached!

*Enjoy all of the passion and fiery romance as
you soar back through history, right in the
comfort of your own home.*

Now that you have read a Zebra **HEARTFIRE**
Romance novel, we're sure you'll agree that
**HEARTFIRE** sets new standards of excellence
for historical romantic fiction. Each Zebra
**HEARTFIRE** novel is the ultimate blend of intimate romance and grand adventure and each
takes place in the kinds of historical settings you
want most...the American Revolution, the Old
West, Civil War and more.

# <u>FREE</u> Preview Each Month and $ave

Zebra has made arrangements for you to preview 4 brand new HEARTFIRE novels each month...FREE for 10 days. You'll get them as soon as they are published. If you are not delighted with any of them, just return them with no questions asked. But if you decide these are everything we said they are, you'll pay just $3.25 each—a total of $13.00 (a $15.00 value). **That's a $2.00 saving each month off the regular price.** Plus there is NO shipping or handling charge. These are delivered right to your door absolutely free! There is no obligation and there is no minimum number of books to buy.

---

## *TO GET YOUR FIRST MONTH'S PREVIEW...*
## *Mail the Coupon Below!*

## MORE SEARING ROMANCE
### by Elaine Barbieri